The Lonely War

2010 Rainbow Awards
1st Place Best Overall Gay Fiction Award
1st Place Best Characters
1st Best Setting
1st Best Gay Historical

"… I was so overcome with emotion during the last few chapters that I could barely see to read through my tears. I highly recommend this read, and I urge you to buy the book."

—Top2Bottom Reviews

"A brilliant work that will linger in your heart and soul."

—Edward C. Patterson

"…a complicated, interesting, gripping examination of humanity in the face of war."

—Boys in Our Books

"I found it a truthful telling of one man's life and a faithful account of the war in Asia. I also found a love story that will stay with me long after the last page has been read. I fell in love with all these brave men and I wish them well wherever they might land."

—Speak Its Name *Five Star Read*

"This story made turning off my Kindle at night one of the biggest challenges of my day for several days…."

—Gay/Lesbian Fiction Book Reviews

THE LONELY WAR

Alan Chin

DSP PUBLICATIONS

Published by
DSP PUBLICATIONS

5032 Capital Circle SW, Suite 2, PMB# 279, Tallahassee, FL 32305-7886 USA
http://www.dsppublications.com/

The Lonely War
© 2015 Alan Chin.

Cover Art
© 2012 Catt Ford.
Cover content is for illustrative purposes only and any person depicted on the cover is a model.

ISBN: 978-1-63216-797-2
Digital ISBN: 978-1-63216-798-9
Library of Congress Control Number: 2014953993
Third Edition May 2015
Second edition published by Dreamspinner Press, April 2012.
First edition published by Zumaya Publications, November 2009.

Printed in the United States of America
∞
This paper meets the requirements of
ANSI/NISO Z39.48-1992 (Permanence of Paper).

Sincere thanks to Stephen Gregoire, Doug Slayton, Kyle Childress, and Casey Conroy for their valuable input and their attempt to keep me honest in the telling. I am also deeply indebted to my husband, Herman Chin, without whom I would still be floundering around page 67 and wondering how three years of my life had flittered by unnoticed.

Part I
The Pilgrim

It has been said that "Common souls pay with what they do, nobler souls with that which they are." And why? Because a profound nature awakens in us by their actions and words, by their very looks and manners…

—Ralph Waldo Emerson, *Essays*

Chapter One

March 20, 1941—0800 hours

IN THE spring of 1941, the Japanese army surged across the border from China to extend their bloody campaign to all of Southeast Asia. As war crept south, the French, English, and American foreigners scattered throughout Indochina hastened to Saigon, where they boarded ocean liners bound for their homelands. Meanwhile, the Japanese army massed at the outskirts of Saigon, poised for another victorious assault. The city held its breath as the invaders prepared for the onslaught.

Andrew Waters pursued his father across a bustling wharf, still wearing his boarding-school uniform and clutching a bamboo flute.

The ship that loomed before him was a floating city, mammoth, with numerous passenger decks topped by two massive exhaust stacks muddying the sky. It had berthed at the port of Saigon—an inland port on a tributary of the Mekong—for a full week. Now, Andrew saw the crew scurrying to get underway.

The wharf trembled slightly. Andrew heard the rat-tat-tat of gunfire over the sirens blaring from the center of the city.

Andrew's father sported a tussore silk suit of superlative cut and a Panama hat tilted so that the brim hid his right eye. His tall figure marched purposefully toward the black-and-white behemoth, and his normally long gait lengthened with a noticeable desperation.

Andrew, who was nearly eighteen, paused while panting from an acute nervy rush. He searched the sky for planes. They were still beyond his field of vision, but the drone of bombers echoed through the cloud cover. The rumble of explosions grew loud and the air carried the faint stench of sulfur.

He hurried on, jostling through a mélange of beings: Caucasians dressed in fine Western clothes (like his father), rich Chinese in their silks, merchants in long-sleeved jackets, coolies wearing only tattered shorts. Voices around him were shouting while the harsh twang of a military band playing "Auld Lang Syne" vaulted above that unbridled fusion of humanity.

Behind Andrew trotted an aged wisp of a monk who wore the traditional orange robes and held a string of wooden prayer beads. Each bead was the size of a marble and had the chalky gray coloring of Mekong silt. The monk's thumb deliberately ticked past each bead, one after another, like a timer counting down the seconds. Behind the monk came the porters carrying four steamer trunks.

At the gangway, his father told Andrew to make his good-bye, and he sprinted up the ramp with the porters in tow.

Surrounded by a press of bodies, the youth reverently embraced the monk. The old man's arms wrapped around Andrew and drew him nearer. The monk's breath tickled his neck, which helped to dissolve his anxieties.

Using the native tongue of South China, he whispered, "Master, I'll come home as soon as I can."

The monk's face contracted, as if Andrew had posed a difficult question. "Andrew, war and time will whisk away everything that you love. This is our farewell."

The youth wiped away a tear that broke free from his almond-shaped eyes and slid down his amber-colored cheek. "Master, I will remember everything you have taught me."

"You will forget my lessons, Andrew. Such is the nature of youth. But remember this: you are American by birth, so they will surely draft you. On the battlefield, resist the hate that is born from fear. Nurture only love in your heart. To love all beings is Buddha-like and transcends us from the world of pain, for love is the highest manifestation of life. To experience love's full bounty is life's only purpose, so tread the moral path before you and sacrifice yourself to love. All else is folly, a dream of the ego."

"Master, I do not understand about sacrificing myself to love."

The old monk's eyes opened wide and his lips spread into a grin. "Meditate on what I have said. Understanding will come when you are ready."

The monk methodically bundled his string of beads into a ball, roughly the size and shape of a monkey's skull, and forced them into Andrew's left pant pocket. "Keep these beads to remind yourself of our time together."

The pressure against Andrew's thigh felt awkward. As the monk pulled way, Andrew became distracted, thinking of how fortunate this man was to be wise and compassionate in the midst of the impending carnage. Andrew realized that it took impeccable courage to maintain one's morality during perilous times, courage that he himself did not possess. He had always assumed that he would live a quiet, studious, and spiritual life under this old monk's guardianship and eventually become the old man who stood before him. But that image, of course, had been shattered when war turned the world on its head. Now all Andrew could think about was getting on that ship and sailing to safety, if such a thing existed.

The ship's whistle cut the air, long and terrible, and loud enough to be heard throughout the city. The monk pressed his hands together in front of his forehead and bowed, silently, with finality.

Another blast from the ship's whistle sent the youth running up the gangway, leaving the earthy world of South China behind. He joined his father on the first-class deck. Entombed in steel—underfoot, heavy riveted plates of metal curved into walls—Andrew jammed together with the other passengers at the railing, peering down at the apprehensive faces. Their body heat added to the stifling temperature. Sweat dribbled down his neck. He had to gasp to get enough air.

Lines fell away; the gangway was hauled aboard. Tugs pushed the ship into the middle of the channel and withdrew, leaving the ship to the whim of the current.

Andrew stared straight down at the seemingly dense, opaque surface of the river. It reflected the cloudy sky, making the water seem gray rather than its usual brown, with yellowish streaks of oil running with the current. To Andrew, the flat, moving surface seemed strangely alive, carrying him along, muscling him downstream, as if it was some overwhelming force whose motives he could only guess at.

On the dock, Asian women held their infants over their heads for a last look. Handkerchiefs waved. The band played on.

Andrew saw the first planes against the darkening sky, droning above the city. Explosions grew even louder. From his perch on the first-class deck, he saw sections of the city erupting. He turned northeast, toward his boarding school. Flames. That entire section of the city was engulfed in fire, as if Hell had opened its mouth to swallow it whole.

"Clifford," he whispered.

A searing stab of regret lodged in his chest. He had been forced to abandon the object of his adolescent love, and he imagined himself dashing through the chaotic streets to reach the boarding school. There was still time, he thought. They could disappear into the forest. They could live on, together. He wanted to perform that fatal act of love, but he wondered if he could muster the courage to defy his father.

Reluctantly (at least it felt that way to him), he climbed the railing to dive overboard, because he realized that the love he shared with Clifford wasn't a trifling adolescent crush at all, but rather a deep and consuming love—a love that had somehow lost itself in the joys of youth, like water in dry sand, and was only now understood.

His father pulled him back, forcing him to stay and suffer what felt like an unquenchable loss. Locked in his father's embrace, he entered a narrow canyon of desolation, knowing that the days and hours and minutes ahead would be heartbreaking and that he might not be strong enough to endure it.

The ship's siren sounded three blasts for its farewell salute. The engines throbbed and propellers chewed the river. The noise swelled to a din like the ending of the world.

The passengers on deck could no longer hide their sorrow. Everyone wept, not only those people parting but the onlookers as well; even the dockhands and porters shed tears.

The ship launched itself downstream under its own power as the military band played "The Star-Spangled Banner."

To Andrew, the orange-robed figure crushed within the throng on the dock seemed at odds with the fires raging across the city. He now fully understood the monk's words—that war would steal everything he loved. A way of life, their way of life, had perished. Pain flooded his whole being, like a baby prematurely ripped from its protective womb.

He pulled away from his father and staggered further along the deck to cry without letting his father see. He positioned himself at the rail, one arm folded around a steel support beam and his face pressed against the hot metal.

People on the wharf seemed to hesitate, then regretfully turned and scurried away. He watched the smudge of orange, scarcely visible and standing at the edge of the pier, utterly still, quiescent, until the harbor faded from view and the land disappeared as well, slowly swallowed beneath the curve of the earth.

Chapter Two

April 18, 1942—0700 hours

FOUR sailors toiled under the deadweight of their seabags—marching two up, two back—with their heads bowed to avoid the equatorial sun's glare. They trailed the executive officer of their newly assigned ship, who led them away from the orderly grid of gravel roads and Quonset huts that made up the Viti Levu Naval Repair Facility, toward the harbor where several warships rested at anchor. Each sailor had his seabag slung over his right shoulder and carried a folded cot under his left arm.

The full brunt of the sun hammered Seaman Andrew Waters. Sweat turned his dungaree uniform a dark shade of blue, and the muggy air made his breathing feel like ingesting lukewarm seawater.

To take his mind off the heat, Andrew studied the confident gait of Lieutenant Nathan Mitchell. The exec's khaki uniform was freshly pressed; its only blemish was a small sweat stain under each armpit. A green canvas belt hugged his waist, and from it hung a canteen over his left hip and a holster over his right. The holster partially concealed a Browning .45 automatic.

Mitchell was lean for his six-foot-one height. Andrew thought his bronzed skin and fawn-colored hair made him appear too young for his rank of lieutenant. Andrew guessed the officer's age to be about ten years older than himself—twenty-eight or nine—and at that moment, Mitchell whistled a happy tune on this excruciatingly hot morning.

By the time they passed the Port Director's office, sweat streamed off Andrew's forehead, and he felt his remaining strength drain from his legs, making it nearly impossible to carry his burden. *I've failed again,* he thought. Time after time he had struggled to pull his weight with his shipmates, but his slim frame was not built to endure physical hardship. At home he used his sharp intelligence to prove his worth, but the US Navy only valued brute strength and moronic obedience from its seamen. In this theater of fighting men, he was a failure.

He would have loved to drop his seabag and sail home to the boarding school to bury himself in literature, music, and mathematics. But that was not an option. So he swallowed hard, making a last-ditch effort to keep up with the others.

He managed a dozen more steps along the dock before he saw, through sweat-blurred vision, Seaman Grady Washington begin to stagger like a drunkard and stumble backward. Andrew dropped his gear and jumped to break Grady's fall, grabbing the young Negro from behind. The deadweight of his unconscious shipmate drove them both to the dock.

Sprawled under Washington, crushed against the wooden planks, it seemed as though a strong man had pinned him, holding him prisoner. It felt like a personal affront.

Andrew yelled to Lieutenant Mitchell, who still held a tune on his lips.

Mitchell turned to stare at the fallen sailors. He pointed to one of the other men and said with an authoritative voice, "Hudson, help Waters carry that man to the shade."

Petty Officer Third Class Joe Hudson, a swarthy sailor dressed in frayed dungarees, lowered his gear to the dock. He grabbed Grady under both armpits and muscled the sailor to the shade beside the Port Director's office. The lieutenant followed as he unhooked the canteen from his webbed belt. He told Andrew to hold Grady's head up while he knelt and poured water over the comatose sailor's nappy head.

Grady coughed, his eyelids fluttered.

With the officer kneeling only two feet way, for the first time Andrew was able to furtively study the lieutenant's face. His heartbeat quickened. The man's cheeks were attractively sunburnt and supported a straight nose and powerful eyebrows. Andrew detected a keen intelligence simmering behind those eyes, which were clear and discerning and the color of pale jade. Their intensity startled Andrew. He inhaled sharply, catching a whiff of the officer's scent. Beneath the pleasant odor of talcum powder, he discovered the aroma of sweat-moistened skin.

Andrew tried to look away, but he couldn't help but follow the path of a bead of sweat sliding from under the officer's hat, making its way along the reddish cheek and strong jaw, where it clung to that beautifully sun-kissed skin. Andrew felt himself drawn to the officer like the moon draws water.

Grady's eyelids popped open and his eyes rolled around in their sockets like loose marbles. His lips trembled with unrealized words, as if he might possibly have a speech disorder.

Mitchell pressed the canteen to the black sailor's lips, trickled water into the pink cavity, and poured more water over his head.

"You fainted from the heat, sailor," Mitchell said. "Happens all the time."

"You'd think a jungle bunny would be used to the heat," Hudson quipped while mopping his shaved head with a purple handkerchief, "being from Africa and all."

Andrew glanced up, scrutinizing Petty Officer Hudson and Seaman John Stokes, who stood in the shade, casually watching the scene. Stokes was a Nebraska farm boy with strawberry-colored hair and a Milky Way of freckles scattered across his face. He carried himself with an ungainly youthfulness, as if he was still growing into his body. His pillbox hat was bleached an absolute white and tilted so far forward that it hid his eyebrows.

"Button that mouth, Hudson," Mitchell barked. "We don't tolerate racial slurs on the *Pilgrim.*"

"Sir," Hudson replied, "does that include half Japs, too? I thought we was here to kill Japs."

"One more insulting remark and you're on report. Is that clear, sailor?"

"Aye, sir. Crystal."

It's starting already, Andrew thought. *Okay, survival rule number one: never show fear. Rule number two: deflect opposing force by pulling your adversary off balance.*

Andrew eased Grady's head onto the dock and stood to face Hudson. He swallowed. Hudson was built like a heavyweight prizefighter. His face revealed the bent bulb of a nose that had been crushed and remolded, a dished cheekbone, and scars over both eyes. His body looked distorted and menacing, and his swagger was common among the "old salts" who had a hard need to prove they were the stud bulls of the herds.

Andrew held him with an unflinching stare. "It's time you learned the difference between Japanese and Chinese," he said with a slight French accent. "For the record, I'm half Chinese, half American."

"Chinks and Japs is all the same," Hudson snarled. "They all smell yellow to me."

"The Chinese are our allies," Andrew said. "They've fought the Japanese on and off for over eight hundred years. Japan has been kicking America's butt for only, what, five months?"

Hudson sneered. "In the old Navy, we didn't put up with smart-mouth chinks and namby-pamby niggers. In the old navy you could trust the man next to you with your life. But those days is gone, and for a buffalo-head nickel I'd get the hell out this new Navy."

"That's it, Hudson," Mitchell said. "You're on report."

"Only a nickel?" Andrew dipped two fingers into the pocket of his dungaree pants and extracted a quarter. "Here's two bits. Tell the discharge officer to keep the change." He flung the coin at Hudson. It tumbled through the air, hitting the petty officer in the chest, dead center.

Hudson clenched a ham-like fist. "Sass me again, you yellow monkey, and I'll kick you bowlegged!"

"Can the bickering, right now." Lieutenant Mitchell stepped between them. "On my ship, we get along, do our jobs, and if anyone makes waves, I jump on them with both my size-twelve's kicking. Another word out of either of you and it will cost you your next five liberties. Understood?"

"Yes, sir," they sang out.

"Hudson and Stokes, wait at the whaleboat. Waters, help me get Washington on his feet."

Andrew knew he could safely confront Hudson with the lieutenant on hand, but even so, relief swept through his center like an ocean wave. This, he knew, was the first barrage of an ongoing battle, and once aboard ship, Mitchell wouldn't be conveniently on the spot to protect him.

Hudson and Stokes retrieved their gear and marched down the pier. Andrew pulled Grady to a sitting position.

Mitchell handed Grady his canteen. "Clear your head before you try to stand, sailor."

Grady clambered to his feet and handed the officer his canteen. "Thank you, suh," he drawled. "I reckon I'm fine now."

Andrew and Grady hoisted their gear and followed the lieutenant to the whaleboat nestled at the pier's head. Andrew admired the boat's functionally beautiful lines, with its broad beam and both ends sporting a sharp bow. The Navy still used these boats because they inspired confidence in a heavy sea and landing through rough surf.

Hudson sat on a thwart near the bow with Stokes behind him. Three oarsmen manned each side; a coxswain stood at the tiller. All seven dungaree-clad crewmen glared at Andrew and Grady as they passed their seabags to an oarsman. A facade of disbelief turning to anger spread over each face.

"What'd I tell you?" Hudson sneered.

The redheaded coxswain spit over the gunwale.

Grady climbed into the boat while Andrew gazed at the redhead standing at the tiller. The man's lips seemed too small for his mouth, stretched over teeth that were somewhat pointed and bared to the gums, like a rabid dog. Andrew's absentminded scrutiny of the stranger proved dangerous, because he suddenly realized that the redhead was staring back at him so aggressively that his intention was clearly to make an issue of the matter.

"Look alive, Waters," the lieutenant said.

Andrew dropped beside the lieutenant with his right shoulder pressed to Mitchell's left, their knees touching. They pushed off and were borne along by rowers. The boat seemed to fly over the blue-green plane. Andrew noticed the clocklike cadence of the oars, the rowers' labored breathing, and the faint scent of the lieutenant's sweat-moistened skin, still hovering under the pleasant aroma of talcum powder.

They passed a line of predators at anchor—destroyers, a cruiser, a submarine—all swarming with deckhands and welders and riveters, most of whom were stripped to the waist and covered with grime.

Andrew stared out over the bay. The morning was like true summer, with the sea smooth and bright under the sun and a slight breeze off the water to soften the heat's edge. He glanced at the horizon. A line of dark cumulus clouds galloped toward them from the southeast.

Mitchell shifted beside him. His eyes followed the young sailor's gaze. "You see it?"

Andrew no longer contemplated the oncoming squall. He felt the lieutenant next to him, heard the man's clear voice fuse with the sound of his own shallow breathing. His pulse thumped at his temples as he turned to gaze into those jade-green eyes. His mind floundered for a heartbeat before he said, "Should hit around sundown, sir."

Mitchell nodded.

Andrew's eyes widened as they approached his new ship, and his spirits sank. She lay low in the water, the USS *Pilgrim*, Destroyer #119. Her twenty thousand tons of steel was shaped like a knife—her forecastle rose high above the water from bow to bridge like a sturdy handle and fell sharply away to a low main deck that ran from conning tower to stern like a thin blade. Four smokestacks sprouted from her superstructure, their gaunt columns smudged the sky with black smoke. Andrew counted two bulky gun turrets with five-inch guns perched on her forecastle, a half dozen torpedo launchers along her amidships, and two stern-mounted depth-charge racks. *She's an awesome mass of destructive power wrapped in gray steel.*

A deeply spiritual young man, Andrew was about to board a ship whose sole purpose was to destroy human life. He felt his testicles draw close to his body as the *Pilgrim* grew large before him. He silently told himself that even on this death machine, he must stay true to his pacifist principles.

The whaleboat came to rest alongside a limp chain ladder hanging from the *Pilgrim*'s quarterdeck. Mitchell scurried aboard, saluted the colors, and turned to supervise the gear being hoisted over the railing. A gaggle of sailors flocked to the afterdeck, all leaning over the railing cables to get a glimpse of the new men. A few catcalls cut the morning air, but most of the men simply glared down at Andrew.

He stood in the whaleboat with his legs spread for balance, his head rising above and falling below the level of the *Pilgrim*'s main deck. He hesitated, studying the torpedo launchers along the amidships, before climbing the ladder with the awkwardness of a landsman. Here, then, was a final moment of perception before his surrender: the deadly gray hulk, the crew's defiant stares, the dark line of clouds advancing on him, and Mitchell's jade-colored eyes beckoning him aboard.

He stepped on deck by a deliberate act of will (it felt deliberate, although he was too numb to form thoughts), surrendering to his fate.

For a moment, still, nothing seemed different. It felt like another failure, as if he could still jump overboard, swim to shore, and all would be set right. But a brutish sailor wearing oily dungarees charged along the narrow deck, deliberately slamming into him with a beefy shoulder. Andrew stumbled over a tangled nest of air hoses, landing hard on his butt. The sailor snarled, "Stay the fuck out of my way, Jap-boy!"

Andrew's stomach folded in on itself as he realized this crew was roughly the same as the one on his last ship. He could feel their apprehension. He knew that he, and even Grady for that matter, would never be accepted. They were already marked as outsiders and that's where they'd stay.

He inspected each face that leered at him, one by one, without directly staring at them. No one seemed dangerously hostile, which lowered his anxiety a notch, but at the same time he knew there would always be the truculent stares and off-color remarks. Every hour of every day would be a trial, as it was on his last ship, the *Indianapolis*. With the realization of what was in store, his spirits sank to a new low, settling near the murky rock bottom of his soul.

He pulled himself to his feet and studied his surroundings. Chaos—hoses snaked between piles of machine parts, power tools, oily rags, and scraps of rusted steel. Shirtless men with grease-stained bodies chipped at rust while welders used acetylene torches to mend bulkhead seams. The repeating thunderclap of metal striking metal reverberated belowdecks.

He stepped over a pile of debris to stand next to his seabag. A brass plaque on the bulkhead informed him that this ship was named after Chester H. Pilgrim, a battleship commander who had died in the North Atlantic during the First World War.

Chief Henry Swiftcreek Ogden marched up and scrutinized the four newcomers. His stout body had an imposing posture. Two scars cut across his cheek. Cobweb-like lines etched his iodine-colored face from hairline to Adam's apple, covering everything except his stony eyes. He made a sound, more of a grunt than a word, but it carried a truculent undertone that conveyed an unmistakable disapproval.

Andrew glanced at Mitchell, searching for some kind of protection.

As crewmen rigged the hoist to haul the whaleboat aboard, Mitchell told Ogden, "Chief, issue these new men bunks and assign them to watches. I'll interview them before lunch."

"Aye, aye, sir. You men grab your shit and follow me."

The chief glared at Grady and Andrew. He gestured with his head toward the bow and sauntered to the crew's quarters under the forecastle deck. The men hoisted their gear and followed.

While Andrew balanced his seabag on his shoulder, he sneaked another glimpse at Mitchell. A shy grin lifted the ends of Andrew's mouth. He felt a shimmer of adoration for the man without knowing precisely why. As he turned to follow his shipmates, the grin retreated and, reminding himself of survival rule number one, his body moved with a deliberate swagger.

Chapter Three

April 18, 1942—1000 hours

WHILE overseeing the stowing of the whaleboat, Mitchell heard a bellow reverberate from the forecastle that sounded vaguely like a wounded buffalo.

Chief Ogden popped through the open hatchway with his eyes blazing and his jaw locked, which happened, Mitchell knew, whenever he was faced with a situation that was not standard Navy protocol. A twenty-six-year chief, Ogden had served his entire career on destroyers. He was also a full-blood Shoshone. He was not the chief of his ancestral tribe but, because he was a chief petty officer, everyone aboard mockingly called him "Chief" or even "Big Chief."

Mitchell stared at the whaleboat gliding over the rail. He held a mild disdain for Ogden's propensity to exaggerate harmless issues into insurmountable obstacles. He hoped to avoid whatever problem had surfaced, so he let a long moment pass before he glanced back and felt himself nailed by the chief's sanguinary gaze.

"What's up, Chief?"

"Lieutenant, you gotta see this."

The chief led Mitchell into the crew's quarters, a dozen compartments under the forecastle deck that were arranged in honeycomb-like rows and connected by narrow passageways. Each compartment had bunks stacked five high on three bulkheads, and a double row of lockers covered the fourth wall.

As Mitchell entered the compartment, he sang out, "As you were," before anyone could come to attention. The compartment reeked of sweat and moldy clothing and something else, something Mitchell felt more than smelled: hostility. The entire compartment seethed with testosterone-laced resentment. Several crewmen stood in a loose half circle, staring at Andrew Waters, who knelt on the deck with his back against his locker.

Light from a porthole, muted and steel-tinted, silvered the contents of Andrew's seabag, which were spread over the deck: a teak statue of the Buddha seated in meditation, three orange robes, a stack of yellow silk undergarments, strings of prayer beads, an iron bell, a three-foot-long bamboo flute that was as thick and smooth as a King snake, and a stack of books, long and narrow, the likes of which Mitchell had never seen before.

Ogden rested his fists on his hips, scowling. "Where the hell is your Navy-issue gear and what the fuck is this shit?" He kicked the stack of undergarments across the deck.

"I can explain, sir," Andrew said, gazing up at Mitchell. "There wasn't room in my seabag for everything, so I left some things behind. I planned on buying more uniforms from the ship's store."

"What are these books?" Mitchell asked, after studying the religious articles for a time.

"Buddhist scriptures, sir."

Mitchell felt the crew's hostility level jump a dozen notches. He knelt at the edge of the pile, a few feet from Andrew. From that distance he could smell Andrew, an odor reminiscent of fresh-baked bread. The scent shielded him from the sour odor of the forecastle.

Mitchell stared at Andrew's face. He flinched at the intensity of those eyes that gazed deeply into his own. The sunlight pouring through the porthole caused tiny golden flecks to sparkle within Andrew's black pupils, giving off a soft, nearly imperceptible light. He inspected the face surrounding those eyes. A yellow stain clouded the flesh under the left eye, obviously from a blow a week ago. The right cheek had purple discoloration from more recent blows, and one side of his lower lip was raw and puffy, looking as if he had been smacked hard only a minute before Mitchell entered the compartment.

Mitchell was surprised that he had only now noticed this bruising. The face had a pleasing quality, delicate and finely boned. *But,* the officer thought, *this kid had been on the losing end of plenty of fights recently.*

Mitchell noted that Andrew appeared relaxed, as if he had expected this confrontation and it was playing out exactly as he had planned. Andrew's self-control seemed all the more amazing given the crew's tense confusion.

The halo of calmness surrounding Andrew touched something within Mitchell. It seemed to bear his own signature in some way, reminding him of himself, or a part of himself he had forgotten. He couldn't help liking the look of this kid with a beaten face and mysterious eyes.

He felt some stimulus form between them, a connection that was neither friendship nor sexual, but had attributes of both. He tried to analyze this feeling, wondering if this wasn't a moment full of significance, in the hope that some meaning of his life, some epiphany, some poetry, would come to him, but it was beyond his understanding. He simply chalked it up to his old tendency of being drawn to wounded things, like the hawk with a broken wing he'd once mended, and his three-legged dog, Smoke, who had lost his front leg in a bear trap.

Looking down so as not to stare, Mitchell caressed the uneven binding of a scripture book while admiring the rough, handmade paper. He reached further, to a stack of Western-bound books, and noted the titles—Shakespeare's *Tragedies*, *Moby Dick*, *The Iliad*, Plato's *Symposium*, *The Analects of Confucius*, and Yeats's complete works. Again he felt that nameless force ripple between them.

"You read more than scriptures." Mitchell lifted the volume of Yeats's poems, opened the cover to the index page, and scanned the table of contents. "I haven't read Yeats since college." He recognized several poem titles. "I'll have to confiscate this evidence for a few days," he said with a smirk, "and I'll need to sequester these other books from time to time in order to make a proper judgment."

Andrew looked up at the other sailors before focusing on Mitchell again. "I care not what the sailors say: all those dreadful thunder-stones, all that storm that blot out the day can but show that heaven yawns."

Mitchell glanced up, staring into those dark eyes, now so bright. His lips parted but he couldn't speak, not quite believing he was hearing a sailor quoting Yeats.

Andrew whispered, "I bring you with reverent hands the books of my numberless dreams."

Mitchell remembered that line from one of his most cherished Yeats poems. He shook his head. All he had ever heard spewing from the crew were strings of four-letter words, some less vulgar than others. He smiled and winked at Andrew, who offered a shy grin. That grin seemed oddly complicated, disarming, and now his entire face, like his eyes, shimmered with life. It was hard, nearly impossible, to associate this young man with all the other rough and odious sailors aboard.

Mitchell stood. "Chief, this man has every right to practice his religion," he said. "No harm done."

Each bystander's mouth dropped, except Hudson's, because he gnashed his teeth.

The chief wagged his head. "This man needs dungarees and dress whites. We can't have him running around naked. If he threw away his old uniforms, that's destroying government property." Ogden spit the charge with such force that the men around him retreated a step.

Mitchell kept his cool by mentally listing the important tasks he could be doing if the chief wasn't such a drama hound. He turned to Andrew. "The *Pilgrim* is too small to carry clothing in the ship's store. We carry ninety-eight sailors, five officers, and precious little storage room." He glanced sideways at Ogden. "Chief, take him ashore and have the PX issue him a full complement of gear. We'll withhold his pay until every last pair of skivvies is paid for in full."

Mitchell winked at Andrew again. "And make sure they issue him a Bluejacket's Manual so he can read about the proper care of government property."

"Aye, aye, sir!" Ogden's smile showed a full set of pearly teeth. Hudson visibly gloated.

Mitchell asked if there were any other issues, and the chief shook his head no.

"Suh, I was wonderin'." Grady Washington stepped forward. "Why was we issued cots if we have these bunks?"

Laughter erupted from the men. Mitchell explained. "Sailor, this steel bucket soaks up the sun's heat all day, and by lights-out these quarters are a hundred and ten degrees of hot, holy hell. In fair weather, the men use cots to sleep on deck. You'll be thankful for that cot by midnight."

Mitchell pointed to Andrew's pile on the deck. "Chief, see that this is squared away."

"Aye, aye, sir!"

ANDREW knew that, for any other crewmember, loss of pay meant deprivation of barrooms, brothels, and restaurants on their nights of liberty. The punishment inflicted on him would be devastating to any one of them, but the only things that made an impression on him were those secret winks that Mitchell had shared with him, and, of course, the officer's unexpected kindness. For the first time since joining the Navy, Andrew had been studied and found acceptable.

Watching the lieutenant's fingers stroke the book covers made Andrew feel as if his own face were being caressed. The words "has every right" and "no harm done" rang throughout his consciousness and made his head tingle. And Mitchell was taking something of Andrew's that was so ingrained and loved by Andrew that it felt as if the officer were taking a sliver of his soul.

Andrew held himself utterly still, feeling the warmth radiating inside his chest. He had only truly loved two people in his life—Master Jung-Wei, the old monk who had run the boarding school in Saigon, and Clifford Baldrich, his boyhood companion—but he felt something like love blossoming again. *If this is indeed love*, he thought, *it has happened unexpectedly, like a flash of lightning from a bright, blue sky.* And for the first time, his love was intensified by the repeating note of sexual longing running through the joyful composition playing in his heart.

He resisted it, telling himself that it was impossible, that regardless of Mitchell's understated sexiness and the man's kindness, he couldn't possibly love this man he had seen for the first time only an hour ago. But there was no denying the warmth in his chest. What else could it possibly be? What other feeling could crush him so utterly, so beautifully?

He was smitten, and as he surrendered to it, his entire being transformed: loneliness, fear, loss, all vanished, soaring off into a void. He pictured himself, face nuzzled against that sunburnt cheek, kissing the neck that smelled of sweat and talcum, the officer's torso pressed against his belly, grinding.

These images made it clear he could no longer ignore or deny his homosexuality. Accepting his nature brought no shame or regret. He simply embraced his warm adoration for Mitchell that, for the moment at least, had chased away his overwhelming isolation.

DURING the time spent ashore at the PX and later on a tour of the ship with the other new men, Andrew hardly heard a word Chief Ogden said. He floated in a cloud of Lieutenant Mitchell.

Ogden guided them through officers' country, which was the superstructure between the forecastle and the quarterdeck that included the communications shack, the navigation bridge, the fire control station, and the officers' living quarters. While walking through the navigation bridge, the others stared down onto the forecastle deck, eyeing the two five-inch gun turrets with their twenty-foot barrels pointing out to sea, but Andrew saw only Mitchell, who leaned over the chart table, scribbling on a notepad.

Andrew inched toward the officer, close enough to once again catch a whiff of sweat-moistened skin lingering under the pleasant odor of talcum powder. His head spun from a rush of emotion jolting up his spine. He wanted more than anything to caress that sunburnt cheek. His hand drifted toward Mitchell, but he stopped himself and quickly turned to face the others.

Andrew realized that for him to feel complete, he must somehow make the officer return his love. He was aware, of course, that he couldn't seduce Mitchell, and that the officer would never feel the sexual longing that he felt. But he had experienced an intense connection when they were staring, eye to eye, in the forecastle, and he was confident that Mitchell had felt it too. He vowed to somehow make this officer care for him. *That will be enough,* he thought. He would allow himself to love this man entirely, if only the officer returned some measure of affection.

He was playing with fire, he knew. Buddhist teachings state that the flame of human suffering always begins with the spark of desire; his desire for Mitchell would eventually build into a blaze of anguish. But he was willing to accept that future pain so he could momentarily enjoy this delicious rush of love and longing.

The main problem with his quest, he realized, was the difficulty in creating an intimate friendship with an officer. The Navy maintains a barrier between the ranks of commissioned officers and enlisted men that is more formidable than tempered steel. To the enlisted man, officers are the unquestionable authority aboard ship and must be obeyed even to the death. In order to keep personal feelings from affecting the officer while giving a difficult order to a crewmember, or a crewmember's personal feelings from getting in the way of following such an order, strict limits were placed on exchanges between ranks in order to keep those personal feeling from developing in the first place. Exchanges between officers and enlisted men were limited to the business and functioning of the ship. Personal banter of any kind was taboo. This device operated constantly, on ship or ashore, in battle and out.

An immediate sense of danger clung to Andrew as he schemed how to vault over the gulf that separated enlisted men from the officers, like Icarus preparing to leap off a cliff wearing wax wings.

Chapter Four

April 18, 1942—1100 hours

MITCHELL found Hudson lounging on the port depth-charge rack, smoking a stubby cigar. He beckoned the petty officer with a nod of his head. Hudson tossed his cigar over the side and trailed the lieutenant to the galley, where they grabbed mugs of coffee. They strolled through a passageway to the wardroom and sat facing one another at the officers' dining table.

Mitchell opened Hudson's file as he sipped his coffee. It was traditional Navy coffee, brewed unduly strong, with a pinch of salt. He felt his face tense up as the bitterness made his eyes pool with water. "This bilge will dissolve your fillings."

"Ain't nothin' like raw Navy joe, sir." Hudson smirked and gulped a mouthful. His cheeks bulged and he nearly spit it out, but he swallowed and locked his jaw against the taste. "I hear the mess situation is real bad, sir. It's causing an ugly morale problem."

Right on target, Mitchell thought. *We've got a cook who can't read a recipe and no one else will strike for cook because the crew derides anyone who works in the galley. And with only one cook, I can't even give old Cocoa a night of liberty because he has to stay aboard to prepare meals for the watch. I'd sell my mother for a competent cook.* He took a hopeful look at Hudson but dismissed the thought. Hudson was obviously too proud.

Mitchell had approached every ship's executive officer at each port, begging to trade a boatswain's mate, or helmsman, or even a machinist's mate in exchange for a cook. No takers. Most simply laughed and shook their heads. A few gave him a sympathetic pat on the shoulder and suggested another ship he might try.

Mitchell pulled a pack of Lucky Strikes and a book of matches from his shirt pocket. He offered Hudson a cigarette and lit one himself.

"Before we get sidetracked onto the ship's problems," Mitchell said, waving out the match and dropping it into an ashtray, "let's talk about you. You've been in the Navy twelve years and you're only a petty officer third class. Why is that?" The lieutenant skimmed through the file while smoke curled above his head.

"Bad luck, sir. I made first class twice. I do my job and try to uphold the Navy code, but then along comes the code and kicks me on my ass." Hudson shook his head, making a show of seeming bewildered. "I'm okay with my rank, sir. What's important is that I do my job and that I get some liberty every now and then. I mean, I love the Navy—the shipboard life, traveling to exotic ports, riding the tail of a storm on the open sea. There ain't nothing like it, sir."

"Says here you were busted four times, each one for fighting, and you hospitalized an MP who tried to break up a brawl that you started. Seems you're quite the wild man whenever you drink. But here's a letter of commendation for your actions aboard the *California* at Pearl."

"Just doing my duty, sir. Them swabbies was plain stupid to get caught belowdecks, and someone had to help them."

Mitchell closed the file and held Hudson's eye.

"We've got a green crew. The average age is only twenty, and most of them enlisted after December seventh. We desperately need men with your experience to set an example. That means doing your job, keeping your mouth shut, and helping the officers harmonize this crew into a cohesive fighting unit. The only thing you've shown so far is name-calling and instigating trouble. That stops now!"

Hudson's gaze fell to the tabletop, with him showing no sign that the message had sunk in.

"You called Waters a half Jap and would have prompted a fight if I hadn't been there. That behavior is unacceptable. You will show Waters the same respect that you show the others."

"Sir, I was respectful. I called him a half Jap, even though there ain't no such thing. Just like there ain't no such thing as a half nigger. You is or you ain't, and that boy is yellow to the bone."

"I suppose you hate Chief Ogden for being an Indian?"

"At least his grand-pappy was born on American soil instead of some stink-hole in Asia or Africa."

"Waters and Washington are every bit as American as you and I, and they are as important to the operation of this ship as you are. You will treat them with respect, and that's an order."

"But, sir—"

"Shut up! You're here to listen." Mitchell stared him down without flinching, letting a silent half minute pass. "Keep your nose clean and I'll put some stripes on your arm, but if you don't, I'll run your ass into the brig for the duration. Then we'll see what the Marines at Camp Pendleton can do with you."

Hudson cocked his head to one side to study the lieutenant, obviously trying to gauge whether or not the man would stand behind his threat.

"If we weren't at war, you'd already be rotting in a cell. We're your last chance to turn things around. Now get the hell out of here and report to Chief Ogden for a job assignment in the engine room, and tell him to send me Seaman Stokes."

Mitchell read Stokes's service record until the sailor ambled into the room and sat at the table. He noted that Stokes had a strong physique without seeming athletic. The same color of red hair that covered his head also covered his arms and the back of his hands. He was twenty years old and had a friendly, likeable demeanor, and he looked at Mitchell without displaying any degree of challenge or evasion. A skilled helmsman, his low-key personality would fit in seamlessly. *No problem here,* Mitchell thought. He read another page and felt a surge of excitement hit him like an electric jolt.

"Says here you had cooking experience in civilian life."

"Not really, sir. I worked a sheep ranch up around Steamboat Springs. Whenever we sheared the sheep, I helped out cookin' because we had so many extra hands. That only lasted a few weeks every year, and I only grilled mutton and baked beans and such. It wasn't real cookin'."

"Your fitness report indicates you're a competent helmsman, but we desperately need a cook. How about it?"

Stokes gathered his dignity around him like a blanket and said, "No, thank you, sir." His tone made it clear that no amount of persuasion would change his mind.

"I could order you to strike for cook," Mitchell said, using a taste more authority in his voice.

"Sir, it is my understanding that men who've had a venereal disease can't work in the galley."

"True, but your medical record is spotless. According to this, you're clean as a whistle."

"Yes, sir. But the first liberty I get, I'll go ashore and chase down every two-bit whore in town. I'll come back with syphilis, the clap, crabs, chancres, and even leprosy if that's what it takes to keep me out of the galley."

"Alright, sailor. You've made your point."

Following Stokes's interview, Andrew entered the room and sat, looking sharp in his new dungaree pants and denim shirt. An easy smile creased his lips and his eyes shone. Mitchell felt genuine warmth in Andrew's smile.

"You're quite an enigma," Mitchell said. "Nineteen years old, have a French accent, are Chinese-American, and I'm guessing you're a Buddhist monk on active duty aboard a warship. Help me fit all these pieces together."

Andrew's smile widened. "It's simple, sir. My father works for Standard Oil, who does business throughout Asia. He was based in Saigon, where he met my mother. I was born a short time later. I was six when she died, and Father put me in a boarding school run by Buddhist monks. I also attended a French high school for my formal education, which was where I learned to speak English with a French accent. There was one monk, Master Jung-Wei, who encouraged me to walk the spiritual path. I was planning to do that, but in forty-one the Japanese began their offensive into Indochina. My father was called back to America and he took me with him."

"You're a monk?"

"Never took the vows. I don't really consider myself a Buddhist. I follow the Dharma, but I'm simply a man trying to live a moral life, which means I'm sober, celibate, never lie or cheat, and I bring no harm to any creature."

"Admirable, but considering we are at war, how can you work aboard a warship and not harm others?"

"Sir, I joined the Navy because that was my father's wish, and we Asians have no choice but to obey our family elders. He said I have a duty to his country even though I don't consider myself an American. I know a little about Chinese medicine, so I had hoped to train as a medic. I requested a transfer to the medical corps, but it all fell apart and I ended up a regular seaman."

"If you don't consider yourself an American, what are you, Chinese?"

"No, sir. I consider myself a human being—nothing more and nothing less."

Startled by the sincerity in Andrew's voice, Mitchell sat speechless, having no idea how to respond to such a comment. Finally he said, "We don't need another medic. Says here you worked in the ship's laundry on the *Indy*."

"Yes, sir. I hated it. They assumed an Asian would be good at laundry. Goes to show there's no shortage of bigotry in the Navy. Please don't put me doing laundry."

"What other skills do you have?"

"I'm fluent in French and Chinese, as well as English. I also speak a little Japanese."

"We don't need an interpreter either."

"I'm an excellent cook. During school breaks my master took me to his monastery, where everyone took turns working in the kitchen. My master was an impeccable chef, a true artist. He taught me many secrets." Andrew leaned against his seatback. "Is there something wrong, sir? Let me assure you I can cook French, Chinese, and Japanese dishes."

"You're willing to strike for cook?"

"Yes, sir. I only ask that I be allowed to cook, rather than be only a coolie pot-scrubber."

"I'll be damned!" Mitchell said, followed by a bark of laughter. "Waters, you've answered my prayers." Mitchell realized that he was showing too much emotion and checked himself.

In the silence that followed, both men smiled warmly at each other. Again, Mitchell felt caught up in Andrew's gravitational pull. A satisfying connection formed in his chest, as if a puzzle piece had fallen into place that bridged other pieces.

"I won't touch a weapon, sir," Andrew said. "What a man takes into his hands, he takes into his heart, and I will not allow killing to enter my heart. Same for lying, drinking spirits, and whoring. I refuse to corrupt myself. Don't misunderstand, sir. I'm not a religious fanatic, simply a human being raised by men who value spiritual awakening above all else."

"Simply? I doubt there is anything simple about you. I'll respect your pacifist feelings for now, but I'm confused. Your record from the *Indianapolis* shows that you were put on report nine times in the last month alone, each time for fighting."

"Sir, I'm a pacifist but I'm not a coward, and I'm not so enlightened that I always turn the other cheek. You saw what happened with Hudson. Men find me an easy mark. I was continually harassed on the *Indy*."

"Looks like you're a rather intriguing problem."

"With all due respect, sir, I know exactly who I am and what I am, and I'm quite comfortable with that. If the crew doesn't accept me, that is their problem, and ultimately your problem."

Mitchell had never commanded anyone this young with so much poise and confidence. This kid was a fresh surprise, but Mitchell sniffed a whiff of trouble in the air. *Perhaps working in the galley, separated from the others, is a great idea.*

"Have Chief Ogden introduce you to Cocoa, our cook. You'll work under his supervision."

They sat in silence, and Mitchell watched a line of red rise from Andrew's collar. Something was happening, and Mitchell puzzled at what it could be. He felt as if there was more to discuss, but didn't know what. There was a kind of hidden movement in Andrew's eyes, a rising and falling intensity.

He offered Andrew a reserved grin, which Andrew returned. Then came the moment when Mitchell could no longer stare, so he dismissed Andrew. As thrilled as Mitchell was to finally have another cook, he felt a slight disappointment as Andrew left the cabin.

The interview with Grady was quick and routine. Raised in Joplin, Missouri, he was soft-spoken and his movements were as studied as a Broadway actor's. His high cheeks and curved eyelashes made his face rather handsome. His skin was the color of creamed coffee, but it was not shiny like some Negroes; it had the softened look of crushed velvet.

Grady requested an assignment to man a deck gun, obviously wanting to prove himself in battle. Mitchell explained that since Grady had been trained as a steward's mate, and that was what the ship needed, Grady would pull double duty as the captain's steward and the wardroom attendant until a replacement came along. What Mitchell didn't tell him was that, although the Navy had recently begun to enlist Negroes as regular seamen with equal pay and status, Mitchell had not heard of any colored man being given a job other than steward or cook's helper (dishwasher). Mitchell had no problem assigning him to other duties, including manning the guns, but he was painfully aware that others would have serious objections to it, most notably the captain.

Grady was visibly disappointed, and Mitchell felt sorry for him, but at the same time, his spirits soared in anticipation of telling the captain about the new cook.

Chapter Five

April 18, 1942—1200 hours

AFTER inspecting the engine repairs in the ship's oven-like bowels, Mitchell climbed the engine room ladder and strolled to the quarterdeck for lunch. He carried a clipboard and jotted notes as he walked.

Officers usually took their meals in the wardroom, but while in port, a table was set up under the quarterdeck awning so the officers could eat in cooler conditions.

Lieutenant Horace Tedder, the medical officer, and Ensign Otis Moyer, the chaplain, relaxed in wicker chairs around the table, sipping coffee from brown mugs. As Mitchell came close to the table, he overheard Tedder telling Moyer about his morning activities.

"After reveille," Tedder explained, "the skipper and I inspected the mess hall and crew's quarters, then came sick call. I'll tell you, the ingenuity of these goldbrickers astounds me. They must have a medical book stashed somewhere aboard, because nobody could invent such elaborate ailments. This morning, Smitty gave such a detailed description of his stomachache I knew it was a phony. I told him I needed to perform an emergency appendectomy using only a local anesthetic. I'll bet he doesn't even know what an appendectomy is, but he jumped up and ran out of sick bay so fast you'da thought his pants were on fire." Tedder joined Moyer in a belly laugh.

Mitchell knew something was up when he heard Tedder laugh. Having grown up in Seattle where the temperatures are cool, Tedder was always miserable in the tropics, so to see even a smile on his face was shocking. His silver hair was oiled and neatly parted, but his uniform looked like he had slept in it. He was a civilian dressed in officer garb. If it weren't for the war, he would be sitting in his office in a two gas-station town, sneaking shots of whiskey between seeing elderly ladies complaining of back pains.

"Okay, Doc, I'll bite. What's up?" Mitchell asked.

Tedder sipped his coffee and glanced at the burly, dark-haired chaplain. Both men grinned.

"It seems we have a new cook," Moyer said.

"Seaman Waters. Did you meet him?" Mitchell grabbed the coffeepot and poured himself a mug.

"No, we just now found out about it," Moyer replied.

"How's that?" Mitchell asked.

"You'll see."

Mitchell wondered what game these two were playing as he put the pot down and sat on the edge of a wicker chair. As he sipped his coffee, his eyebrows lifted high on his forehead.

"Goddamn, this is great. Do I detect a hint of chicory?"

"Affirmative," Moyer beamed. "Our slumming days are over, thank the Lord."

Mitchell noticed Captain Ben Bitton rambling onto the quarterdeck from the forward conning tower, looking stern, unflappable, and fit for his fifty-two years. Beneath his salt-and-pepper hair and hiding behind his tortoiseshell glasses were his piercing hazel eyes, which revealed his self-assured temperament. His khaki uniform was crisply pressed and his shoes buffed, communicating respect for his position and underlining his attention to detail.

Before they could all rise, Bitton said, "As you were, gentlemen."

Silence descended over the table, and Mitchell bent his head over the clipboard on his knee, updating the repair paperwork. Bitton poured himself a mug of coffee before relaxing into a chair. Moyer and Tedder watched the captain's face while seeming not to notice him at all. The captain sipped his coffee and grinned. Never one to go overboard, his grin, however, was very telling. He drank the rest of his coffee in silence and filled another mug while Moyer and Tedder exchanged gleeful smiles.

Grady emerged from the passageway leading to the galley. He carried a silver tray, which he put on the officer's table. Dominating the tray was a frosted pitcher of lemonade and four equally frosted glasses. In that crush of sweltering heat, the officers stared open-mouthed at the visible corona of coldness surrounding the tray.

"My God," the captain said. "He even chilled the glasses. What the hell's gotten into Cocoa—first, delicious coffee, and now this?"

"There's good news and bad," Mitchell said. "One of the new seamen is striking for cook. This is obviously not Cocoa's doing."

"Don't tell me the bad news. I want to enjoy this." Bitton took his spectacles off and slid them into his breast pocket. His hazel eyes blinked several times, as if testing the vision before him. He grabbed the pitcher handle and ceremoniously poured himself a generous portion. He sipped the frigid ambrosia, smacked his lips, and took three long gulps.

Mitchell watched a remarkable change come over the captain. His shoulders visibly lowered as his whole body relaxed. Like a snake uncoiling, the muscles in his face released the tension that had been a permanent fixture.

"God has answered my prayers," he said. "This new cook will raise morale in no time. Glorious, utterly glorious. Why, the coffee alone will lift everybody's spirits."

Moyer took the pitcher and refilled the captain's glass before pouring three others. The officers gulped the frigid tartness while making low moaning noises.

Setting his empty glass on the table, Mitchell wondered how much he should tell the captain about Andrew. He knew that within the captain's spartan cabin there were only two items on the shelf above the bunk: a Bible and a bundle of letters bound with a rubber band. The captain read his Bible for an hour every night. The letters were all from his wife, and he selectively read them before sleep took him. The captain was a staunch Methodist, and Mitchell felt apprehensive about what his reaction would be when he learned that Andrew practiced the same religion as the enemy.

"Nathan, how do we stand on repairs?" Bitton asked.

"Great, Skipper. The depot gang is nearly finished and our men are working damned hard helping them."

"Excellent. Did you hear any more scuttlebutt ashore about Bataan?" the captain asked.

"Yes, sir. The rumors we heard are true: the Nips cut our boys to ribbons. Some forces fled to Corregidor and they're holding out for reinforcements, but thousands were taken prisoner and there's no knowing how many died."

"Poor bastards," the captain said, shaking his head. "Starved, devastated by malaria, made to fight, and in the end, killed or taken prisoner."

Mitchell nodded, "They had a poem that was written up by a war correspondent named Frank Hewlett:

We're the battling bastards of Bataan,
No mama, no papa, no Uncle Sam,

No aunts, no uncles, no cousins, no nieces,
No pills, no planes or artillery pieces,
And nobody gives a damn."
A leaden silence settled over the officers.

Finally, Tedder said, "I don't understand how a nation of bucktoothed flower arrangers who run around in bath robes and sandals could defeat MacArthur's troops. Our boys are better trained, better equipped, and they dress like men."

"Obviously, those are erroneous generalizations," Mitchell said. "They're a tough bunch."

"What about MacArthur, did he make it to Corregidor?" Moyer asked.

Mitchell grinned. "Corregidor? Hell, they smuggled him clean out of the Philippines. He's in Australia, building an invasion force to retake Bataan. An interviewer asked him about his escape and he said: *It was close, but that's the way it is in war. You win or lose, live or die—and the difference is just an eyelash."*

"An eyelash, my God," Bitton said. "Hell of a man. I'd give anything to lead men into action. I'd love to see if I've got his kind of mettle." Bitton lifted his head and his voice trembled. "All these fierce battles are raging, and here we sit in the war's backwaters, escorting supply ships, carrying mail, towing targets, and every other menial fleet duty. Well, it's not very heroic now, is it?"

They all lowered their eyes.

"Sooner or later," Bitton continued, "we'll have the chance to prove ourselves, and we better damn well be ready when it comes."

Grady sauntered onto the quarterdeck carrying another tray, which he set next to the pitcher of lemonade. There were four plates on the tray, and each officer leaned forward to see what more surprises were in store for lunch.

On each plate sat the same kind of greasy canned-meat sandwich on day-old bread that they had endured for the last two months. Beside the sandwiches were mounds of mustard-yellow potato salad and dill pickle slivers.

One by one the eager smiles fell into frowns.

Tedder cleared his throat and said, "Maybe I'm simple, but I don't see anything heroic about MacArthur's dashing to safety with his tail between his legs."

The captain shook his head. "He has the most brilliant military mind of our time. It'd be devastating if he were captured. As it is, I'll bet there are some yellow bastards who have red faces now for letting him slip through their fingers."

Tedder pulled a plate toward him, grabbed a sandwich, and held it under his nose. Before he chomped down, he said, "I can't help feeling sorry for those men left holding the bag." He ripped off a mouthful of sandwich and chewed savagely.

Cocoa emerged from the galley, with Andrew close on his heels. Cocoa's stocky waist supported a grease-stained apron that draped below his knees. His T-shirt was stretched tight over his protruding belly and had a large, yellow stain under each armpit. His face, round with a waddle of fat hanging under his chin, was normally pale, but at that moment it glowed a scalded red. They both came to attention beside the officer's table.

"Request permission to speak, sir," Cocoa said, with his chin pulled absurdly high.

"What is it, Cocoa?" Mitchell asked.

"Sir, it's this new man, Seaman Waters. Much as I need the help, sir, he just won't do."

Mitchell exhaled sharply. "And why is that, Cocoa?"

"Well, sir, for one thing, I put him in charge of beverages and the first thing he does is make nine urns of coffee, one after the other. When he gets one made, he pours it out and starts over, like he's loony. Them urns is twenty gallons each. Then I find that he's used up all my lemons. And there's the crew, sir. I mean, I don't mind having a half Jap for a kitchen coolie, but the crew is saying they won't eat no raw fish heads and rice. They think he's a plant sent here to poison them. They refuse to eat anything he touches."

"I take it this is the bad news?" Bitton asked.

Mitchell nodded, and all four officers turned to stare at Andrew.

Mitchell asked, "Why did you make an urn of coffee and pour it out?"

"I've never brewed coffee in an urn, sir. The way Mister Cocoa showed me made the foulest-tasting sludge, so I experimented with how much coffee to water mixture would taste best. I remembered that chicory cuts the bitterness, so I tried that too. I'm sorry about the lemons. I thought the officers would prefer something cold rather than hot coffee. And about the fish heads?" Andrew grinned. "Mister Cocoa is fixing something for dinner he calls chitterlings. It's a stretch for me to believe that the crew would eat a hog's ass but not a fish's head, but maybe that's my upbringing."

Each officer tried and failed to suppress a smile. Mitchell said, "I'll gather the crew and have a heart-to-heart with them about being more accepting."

"Beggin' your pardon, sir," Cocoa said. "You can talk from now until the time I get religion and the men ain't going to accept him. They got an ugly resentment that's running bone-deep."

Mitchell glanced at Andrew. "I'm afraid the crew's refusal to eat your cooking leaves us in a bind. I'll have to restrict you to kitchen cleanup."

Cocoa's sudden smile showed a full set of dingy teeth.

"Sir," Andrew said, "I believe it was Voltaire who said: *We should be tolerant of everything but intolerance.*"

All the officers were clearly stupefied, having never before heard an enlisted man quote a philosopher.

Andrew swallowed hard. "I have a suggestion, sir. Let me cook for the officers. If you accept me, perhaps the crew will follow in time. I can cook French, Chinese, Siamese, and Japanese cuisine. And if it's for only five officers, I can make every meal special."

Mitchell studied his hands on the table, considering Andrew's proposal.

Andrew's voice became raw. "He doesn't even wash his hands after using the head. I do."

Tedder swallowed loudly and dropped his sandwich back onto his plate.

Mitchell shook his head, but before he could say anything, Captain Bitton interrupted.

"A splendid idea. We'll put him in charge of the officer's mess on a trial basis. But I won't have Japanese food served aboard this ship—anything but Japanese."

Mitchell was stunned. Personnel issues were the executive officer's responsibility, and Bitton never interfered with letting his subordinates manage their own affairs. It was unheard of for him to step in and overrule a junior officer in front of a crewmember.

"One more thing, sir," Andrew said. "To cook Asian food, which is what I do best, I'll need supplies from the Chinese merchants on the island."

The captain nodded. "Cocoa, requisition whatever he needs. You men are dismissed."

Cocoa and Andrew disappeared down the passageway as Bitton laced his fingers together, cracking his knuckles. He leaned toward Mitchell.

"Nathan, you should have seen that coming. Now the crew is affected. You're obviously too wrapped up with repairs to pay due attention to personnel issues. Let this be a wake-up call for us all. We are a fighting ship at war, gentlemen. If the crew is defective, the ship is defective." Bitton paused before adding, "If there are weaknesses aboard this ship, we have to weed them out and correct them. Our lives depend on us honing these men into a cohesive fighting machine."

Mitchell felt the pressure of his palms on his clipboard. A stray nerve kept pulsing in his neck, reaching up to spread across his skull. He wanted to defend himself, but he could only manage to nod in agreement.

"What about the other new men," Bitton asked, "any problems there?"

"They dumped a troublemaker on us named Hudson, machinist-mate with a chip on his shoulder. He needs a kick in the pants and I intend to give it to him the next time he steps out of line. The other two should fit in fine."

"Any other surprises with this Chinaman?"

"Well, Skipper, he's half Chinese and was raised by monks in Indochina. He speaks several languages, including Japanese, and he's a Buddhist."

The captain's eyebrows rose and he sat silent for half a minute before turning to Chaplain Moyer. "Well, Otis, looks like you've got your work cut out for you with this kid."

Chapter Six

April 18, 1942—1300 hours

FROM the navigation bridge, Mitchell watched Andrew hail a passing fishing boat and slip them a note. Twenty minutes later, a withered Chinese man in a dugout canoe glided alongside and haggled with Andrew for the better part of an hour. A short time later, a dozen native canoes pulled alongside. Baskets, sacks, bamboo cages, and sweaty earthen jars were lifted over the railing to cursing sailors, who carried them to the storage lockers: live ducks, chickens, sea turtles, lobsters; a hog carcass the color of old wax; sacks of rice; bushels of mangos and pineapples and guavas and papayas; bottles of soy sauce; baskets of fresh gingerroot and lemon grass and bean sprouts.

Mitchell shook his head, wondering who the hell was going to eat all those supplies. He glanced over at Ensign Fisher to make a funny comment, but the ensign seemed a million miles away.

Fisher had an aristocratic face that radiated a facade of superiority even when he was lost in thought. He leaned against the bridge railing with a pair of binoculars dangling from his neck and struck a pose that reminded Mitchell of Gary Cooper in the movie they'd shown on the quarterdeck a week before.

Fisher had studied law at Yale for a career in politics, and Mitchell suspected that Fisher joined the Navy solely to swing the veteran votes his way when he ran for Congress. He liked Fisher and would have loved to give the ensign the benefit of a doubt, but he had the niggling suspicion that all of Fisher's motives were self-serving.

Mitchell turned to the captain. "Chowtime, sir. Shall we see if this new kid is worth the two tons of provisions we brought aboard?"

The three officers left Chief Baker in charge of the bridge and descended three levels to the wardroom. They found Tedder and Moyer perched at the table, sipping iced tea. A silver platter of appetizers—shrimp dumplings with a soy-based dipping sauce and steamed pork buns—alongside a frosty pitcher of unsweetened tea sat in the center of the table, which was dressed with a snowy-white linen tablecloth.

As the officers took their seats, Tedder beamed. "We were about to start without you. Sweet Jesus, these things smell good."

"Otis, will you say grace?" the captain asked as he removed his tortoiseshell spectacles and slipped them into this breast pocket.

Bowing their heads, Moyer began, "We thank you, Lord, for the blessings we are about to receive. May your gift strengthen our bodies to perform your will against our enemy."

"Amen," they all sang out, not letting him ramble on as he usually did.

Beside each silverware setting rested a pair of wooden chopsticks. Mitchell lifted his pair and adjusted them in his right hand. He raised a dumpling, dipped it into the dark sauce, popped it into his mouth, and chewed. The others held their breaths, waiting for his verdict.

A wave of savory elation flowed from his tongue to his brain. He quickly counted the number of dumplings and divided by five. *That only leaves me three dumplings and one bun*, he thought. *I need to have a talk with Andy about proper quantities.*

Mitchell finally swallowed. "Fantastic." He awkwardly lifted a pork bun with the chopsticks, took a quick bite, and moaned.

Bitton grabbed a fork, saying, "I don't care how good they are, I'm not using those damned sticks."

The room went silent for the two minutes it took the officers to polish off the appetizers. Only Mitchell used chopsticks. They all leaned into their seatbacks, smiling at the empty tray while waiting for the captain to comment. He remained quiet, so they mimicked his silence.

Grady sauntered into the cabin, wearing a virginal white steward's coat, buttoned all the way to the collar. He whisked the tray away.

"Nathan, did we complete all the repairs?" Bitton asked.

Mitchell nodded. "She's now as seaworthy as we can make her, skipper."

Grady hurried through the hatchway, balancing a tray crammed with bowls, a soup tureen, and a breadbasket. The fragrance of turtle soup suffused the cabin. Each man leaned forward to stare as Grady placed the tray on the serving table, filled five bowls, and served each officer. He set a basket of warm baguettes in the center of the table and exited the cabin.

"Excellent," the captain said. "Now that the old girl is fit, we can spend time at sea doing battle drills."

Mitchell lifted his spoon and dug in. Thick and meaty, the soup's richness permeated his mouth and warmed his stomach. The baguettes were crusty on the outside and soft and fragrant on the inside. A hush settled over the table as he sampled a spoonful.

He lifted his head. "I do believe this is the tastiest soup I've ever eaten. It's remarkable."

Heads nodded.

Ten minutes later, Grady served the main course of roasted duck in a red curry sauce resting beside sautéed vegetables, with a side dish of stir-fried noodles topped with chunks of fresh lobster, cooked sweet and gingery.

Each man gawked at his plate while Grady slipped from the cabin.

"Nathan," Bitton said, "I think it's safe to say we should give our Mr. Waters a promotion to seaman first class and make him the permanent officers' mess cook."

"Amen," Moyer said, grabbing his fork and digging into his noodles.

Above the whir of the electric fan over the vent hole, the only sounds were silver scraping china and the occasional slurp from Ensign Moyer. The absence of conversation lasted for the several minutes it took the officers to devour their food.

The curry ignited a delicious fire in Mitchell's mouth and broke a sweat across his forehead, but he couldn't stop eating the blistering dish as fast as decorum allowed.

Bitton swallowed the last bit of succulent duck and wiped his forehead with a napkin. He turned to Moyer. "Otis, what's the latest poop from the crew?"

Mitchell knew that Moyer held a fascination with what continually happened in enlisted country. He once explained that he saw the officers as the ship's brain and the enlisted men as the nervous system—officers made decisions and issued orders, enlisted men carried those orders to the affected part of the ship and made things happen. He was tenaciously interested in the crew's behavior and studied them as if he were comparing different specimens of insects under a magnifying glass. To Moyer, the sailors were not so much individual men who drank and fought and complained and held opinions, but rather, collectively formed that mysterious component that was the *Pilgrim*'s soul. He loved hearing gossip concerning the crew and always had some interesting story to tell. It was unclear where he got his information, whether in the confessional or from spies who informed on their shipmates, because he never revealed his sources.

Grady entered the room, and the officers fell silent while he removed the plates and brought in dessert. He placed a plate with a wedge of Bavarian cream pie and two scoops of coconut ice cream in front of each officer. The pie had slivers of toasted almonds on top and trembled next to the ice cream. He also set a cheese plate, with flakes of sharp cheddar and warm baguette slices, in the center of the table, and served each officer a cup of green tea before leaving the cabin.

The captain shook his head. "Gentlemen, we've hit pay dirt." Laughter filled the room as he nodded at Moyer. "Well, Otis. You were about to say?"

Moyer swallowed a mouthful of pie. "Well, Skipper, as you can imagine, these new men have caused quite a stir among the crew. They don't like fraternizing with Waters or Washington. They call them 'The Dirty W's.' The good news is that these new men are bringing the crew together, bound by a common hatred."

Mitchell felt heat gathering about his scalp and knew it was not caused by the curry.

Bitton frowned. "And the bad news?"

"The crew has organized a betting pool. They're betting on which W gets thrown overboard first."

Mitchell slammed his fist on the table hard enough to rattle the china. "God dammit! I won't stand for this." His voice quivered and he could feel the veins bulge in his neck. "Spread the word that if anything happens to either of those boys, I'll rip this crew a new asshole. If these boys so much as stub a toe, this crew won't see liberty for the duration of this war. I'll put them all on bread and water!"

The captain's face flushed and his voice rose above Mitchell's. "I couldn't agree more. A gift from God drops in our laps—a real chef, a man who takes pride in his work—not to mention Washington, who is a perfectly capable steward. I'm not losing either of these boys because of ignorant bigotry. I pity the poor son of a bitch that tries to harm these boys. By God, I do." He stared into each officer's face, as if to insure they understood the seriousness of his threat. The silence became deafening.

Grady stepped into the room again, balancing a tray on which he carried a bottle of Jack Daniels, a bowl of ice cubes, and five tumblers. He placed the tray next to the cheese plate before stacking the dirty dishes. The subordinate officers stared at the captain as tension sizzled in the air.

"Where the hell did he find that?" Bitton muttered, his voice returning to normal. "Washington, tell Seaman Waters to report to me immediately."

"Yes, suh."

Two minutes later, Andrew hurried into the room and came to attention.

"Seaman Waters," Bitton said. "Dinner was superb, except for one thing."

"Yes, sir, I know. I should have served a variety of cheeses with dessert, but I couldn't find any. If we moor at a French-Polynesian island, I'll find some Brie, Camembert, and perhaps a fine bleu."

Bitton was visibly flabbergasted, and Mitchell had to suppress a smile.

Bitton recovered himself. "I'm talking about the whiskey. Transporting liquor aboard a United States warship is a criminal offense. I'm responsible for everything that happens aboard the *Pilgrim*. We can both be court-martialed."

"Sir, I didn't know. I'll throw it overboard." Andrew leaned forward to grab the bottle.

"No!" the captain barked, freezing Andrew in midreach. "Now that it's here, it's Navy property, and we have an obligation to use it wisely."

The junior officers visibly relaxed. Tedder slid his tongue over his lower lip.

"I appreciate a stiff drink after dinner as much as any man," Bitton said. "But only at anchor and only when the engines are shut down. Is that clear?"

"Yes, sir."

"Where did you find a bottle of fine whiskey? God knows it's worth its weight in gold."

"Sir, there's a thriving black market on the island. I traded fourteen cases of Hershey bars for one case of whiskey, and I got two cases of burgundy wine in exchange for ten cases of cigarettes. I would have served wine with dinner, but I couldn't find where they stowed it. Would the captain care for wine with dinner at sea, or is that restricted to being served at anchor as well?"

A full minute passed before Bitton, visibly stunned, mumbled, "Restrict the serving of all alcohol to in-port dinners. There's one other issue. I must say that if you were trying to make a good first impression, you overshot the mark by a nautical mile. Based on your performance tonight, Lieutenant Mitchell and I agree that you are, as of now, promoted to Seaman First Class and the permanent officers' mess cook. Normally the XO would inform you of a promotion, but I wanted to be the first to congratulate you. Well done, sailor."

"Thank you, sir."

"That is all, Waters. Keep up the excellent work."

Bitton pulled a pipe and tobacco pouch from his hip pocket. While he filled the pipe bowl, Mitchell withdrew a pack of Lucky Strikes from his breast pocket, took one, and threw the pack on the table for the others. Moyer measured two fingers of whiskey and two ice cubes into each tumbler while the men lit up. Each man paid careful attention to smoking and sipping his tea, but each man kept at least one eye on the whiskey.

Bitton finally grabbed his glass and knocked back his whiskey. The junior officers, except for Mitchell, joined him.

Mitchell paused another moment, savoring the anticipation, letting saliva gather in his mouth. He lifted his glass, and his nostrils flared as he inhaled the fragrant whiskey. He finally downed it in one long, sweet swallow. A lovely burn ignited his throat and he felt it settle in his full stomach. When a pleasant buzz hit his head, he immediately craved another, and he saw from the way his fellow officers stared at the bottle that he was not alone. His mind turned to Andrew, and his level of respect ratcheted up several notches. Once again, he felt that connection ripple through his center.

"Hell of a temptation, hey, gentlemen?" the captain said, waving out his match and tossing it into the ashtray. Sweet-smelling smoke stained the air. "I don't think that's putting it too strongly." He slid his spectacles from his pocket and placed them on his face. "Much as I'd love to have another drink and see what other surprises jump out of the woodwork, I think we've left Chief Baker in command of the bridge long enough, so I'll take my tea and join him."

The officers rose. Mitchell stubbed out his cigarette and followed the captain, while the others sat again to finish their tea.

Chapter Seven

April 18, 1942—1800 hours

ANDREW rambled into the galley in time to see Grady and Cocoa polishing off the last of the pie.

"Buddha-boy," Cocoa said through a mouthful of cream filling, "that's the finest meal I ever ate aboard ship." Cocoa consumed another spoonful. "What I can't figure is why you ain't eatin' any of this. You fix a banquet, and sit there eatin' steamed rice and vegetables. You got some kind of weird stomach problem?" He winked at Grady.

"I eat what I like," Andrew said, as he stacked dirty dishes in the sink.

Grady said, "Never ate chow like this. All I ever had back home was pork belly, greens, grits, and good ol' cornbread. But this spicy stuff taste's real good, like Creole cookin'. Say, Andy, I'll help you clean up."

Andrew was afraid Grady would stain his pristine steward's coat. "Thanks, Grady. Appreciate the offer, but I've got it covered."

"Hey, you and me need to help each other out. It's us two against all these crackers. They're waitin' for the chance to take us down. I overheard the officers say that the crew's got them a bettin' pool. They bet on anythin', like when we get our next liberty or how soon we'll see action. I heard they're bettin' on which one of us get thrown overboard first."

"Oh yeah?" Andrew said with a smirk. "What kind of odds am I getting?"

"Man, you don't want to know. You make up your own mind, but as for me, I don't care how hot the forecastle gets, I ain't sleepin' on deck. Even that cracker Cocoa's smiling sweetly and actin' all buddy-buddy, but don't go trustin' him. I heard him put a bet down on you, sho' 'nough."

Andrew glanced over at Cocoa.

"Believe only this," Grady continued, "all we got here is each other. You watch my back and I'll be watchin' yours, and maybe we'll get through this alive."

Andrew envisioned it happening. It would transpire during the twelve-to-four watch, that loneliest and darkest hole of the long night. It would start with the muffled thud of a splintering skull, and, already dead, he would plunge over the side and into the sea's cold embrace. His body would drift close to the ship until the stern's vortex sucked him into the whirling propeller blades. The vision crystallized in his mind, and the smirk faded from his lips.

Andrew scrutinized Cocoa with an accusing stare. "You bet on me?"

"You're not going to believe this...." Cocoa stopped himself.

Andrew shook his head.

"Shit," Cocoa said, "and I thought we was gonna be pals." Cocoa couldn't even finish the last of his pie. He tossed it into the garbage bin, plate and all, and stomped out. Grady nodded his head, as if that proved his point perfectly. He stalked out himself, leaving Andrew to clean the galley alone.

Andrew's spirits fell as he surveyed his new domain. The room felt heavy with greasy odors. Too many meals cooked in too small a space had compressed into a thin film of yellow grease that covered every surface and stained everything the same lifeless color.

Andrew trudged to the sink and turned on the tap. Steam congested the already sweltering room. The soap he added had a disinfectant stench. He held his breath while stacking a tower of metal trays in the soapy water and launched himself into the physical act of meticulously washing each tray, mug, dish, and utensil. His mind emptied until his head was a mute cavern. It became simply movement, a ballet written in C minor—C for cleaning and minor for the effect it had on his spirits.

The hiss of the PA system startled Andrew as it resonated throughout the ship, followed by the shrill cry of the boatswain's pipe. "Now hear this. Now hear this," began the announcement. Captain Bitton's voice magnified the humid air. "Men, it is my pleasure to pass on some good news that came over the harbor circuit."

Andrew halted in midtask with his ear cocked toward the nearest speaker, attached to the bulkhead.

"Yesterday at eight hundred hours, our time," the captain said, "General James Doolittle led an air strike aimed at the very heart of the enemy. The carrier *Hornet* launched twenty-eight B-25 bombers, six hundred miles off the Japanese mainland. They dropped their payloads on Tokyo to successfully achieve our first bombing raid over Japan. There is no word on the extent of the damage or the number of casualties. That is all."

Jubilant seamen raised a deafening roar below decks, but Andrew sank deeper into depression. *Blowing people to bits is nothing to cheer about,* he thought. *How many new widows were made today, how many mothers lost their sons, how many branches were severed from family trees?*

There was nothing else to do but stow the clean dishes, but his depression still weighed heavy on his heart, so he scoured the pots and mixing machines and counters and walls. An hour later, Andrew surveyed his domain again. *A job well done*, he thought.

Satisfaction lifted his mood as he hauled himself to the deserted crew's quarters. Lights-out was still hours away, so the men were lounging in the mess hall. Andrew looked forward to the pure silence to go with his solitude. He thought a cold shower would revive his exhausted body and he unbuttoned his shirt with unsteady fingers.

He opened his locker and there on the top shelf sat his Buddha statue. But in the dim light, he saw that someone had taken a knife and hacked the face off the wooden deity.

Andrew's fingers caressed the statue's wounds. The faceless Buddha sat as serenely as ever, unconcerned about the violation, but Andrew felt heat burning his temples. The statue itself meant little, but someone sneaking behind his back, too gutless to confront him to his face, infuriated him. He felt no compulsion for revenge, but he wanted to know who the culprit was. He considered long and hard about how to identify the coward, until an idea clicked in his head.

He rebuttoned his shirt and pulled Jah-Jai, his flute, from the locker. Holding the instrument with both hands, he ran his fingers over the smooth finish.

Jah-Jai was made of thick bamboo. Beautifully subtle veins weaved through the wood, and each hole was worn smooth from years of use. It had been a gift from Master Jung-Wei, who had hand carved the instrument and taught Andrew how to call forth its voice.

Andrew sauntered into the oven-like mess hall. The compartment reeked of a mixture of fried potatoes, burnt chicken fat, and human sweat. He wandered through the rows of tables with his flute held chest high as he studied the remaining empty seats with a troubled scowl, trying to find the safest spot available.

He saw Grady sitting in the far corner with his head bent over a sheet of yellow paper, writing a letter. Andrew rambled toward him and swung into the next seat over. He glanced at Grady, as if noticing him for the first time. Grady offered him a relieved grin.

Cocoa played bridge at the next table with Stokes, Kelso, and Nash. Hudson was perched on a table in the center of a group of spellbound crewmen, chewing on a half-burned cigar and recounting what it was like at Pearl on that fateful day. Although he described the horrors of battle, he used tones that might be used to depict something thrilling, as if he were bragging about an alluring sexual conquest. His chest swelled, stretching his T-shirt tight across his pectorals. Each movement of his hands and each facial expression broadcasted his arrogance, even as his words tried to assume modesty.

Sailors gathered around Hudson like baby chicks huddled around their mother with open mouths. Even the old salts listened as they read novels, sewed, or played cards. Only Andrew ignored him. Only Andrew did not bow to his pride.

Andrew brought Jah-Jai to his lips and notes rippled across the smoke-filled room with a cheerful refrain.

Andrew's snub visibly diminished Hudson's dignity. Hudson raised his voice to drown out the flute's melody, but Andrew continued to play, seemingly unaware of him. Hudson paused to stare. He gestured in Andrew's direction with his stubby cigar held between two fingers. "Hey, rookie. Can that chink music."

The room hushed. Every head swiveled toward Andrew. Hudson pulled out his Ronson, relit his cigar, and exhaled an authoritative puff of smoke in Andrew's direction.

Andrew reminded himself of survival rule number one as he lowered Jah-Jai. "I'd hardly consider Mozart a chink. However, I can play Handel if you'd prefer. Is he racially acceptable to everyone?"

Mozart affected Andrew deeply. His spirits soared from the music and he realized that he was not being as cautious as he should be. He swallowed hard, noting a metal taste in his mouth.

Hudson's face flared purple. "I'll get a handle on your fucking balls if you keep playing that shit!" The bluster in his voice showed he meant what he said.

Laughter erupted around Andrew. Scornful laughter—what a penetrating thing it was. Giddy and gay and joyful, yet it touched a hidden nerve ever so masterfully. Only Andrew and Grady remained silent.

"Speaking of balls," Andrew said, loud enough for all to hear. "Whoever defaced my statue, I understand that you're angry, but try growing enough spine to confront me to my face."

"Don't strain your milk over it, rookie," Hudson said. "It's only a piece of wood."

Hudson's matter-of-fact tone proved that he knew what had taken place, but Andrew was sure that he didn't do it himself. Andrew's lips tightened into a frown as he wondered if the whole crew knew about the violation. He had assumed it was the act of a single person, but now he was not so sure. *Are they all in on it?*

"Say, Andy," Grady said, "can you play any jazz on that thing?"

Andrew realized that Grady was trying to divert his attention away from the scorn. He patted Grady on the shoulder and gave him a grateful nod. "I was raised in a French school. The French love good jazz even more than good wine."

"Can you play 'Swinging Shepherd Blues'?"

Andrew raised the flute and blew while Grady sang in a low smoky voice, as if they were in a neighborhood speakeasy surrounded by friends. *"In a mountain pass there is a patch of grass where the swingin' shepherd plays his tune…."* Grady was hardly a professional singer, Andrew thought, but his voice gave a soulful feeling to the music. Fingers snapped and toes tapped the deck. *"His sheep never stray, dancin' all day till they see the pale and yellow moon…."*

Stokes threw his cards on the table and jumped up. He seductively swayed his hips as his feet carried him around the room. All the sailors smiled as he passed their table—all, that is, except Hudson.

Kelso struck a feminine pose, batting his eyelashes and poofing up his hair like a brash schoolgirl. Wolf whistles soared as Stokes danced over and took Kelso in his arms. As they twirled around the room, onlookers cheered each difficult move and whistled at every lewd gesture.

"Wail on, shepherd, let it echo through the hills…."

As Andrew played, he kept an eye on every man in the room. Kelso and Stokes performed their lewd boogie, others returned to their card games and writing letters. Hudson, having lost his audience, frowned.

Andrew noticed Smitty, the redheaded coxswain who had stared him down in the whaleboat. He skulked toward the hatch with his head bent, and disappeared through it.

Andrew had only been aboard a day, but that was enough time to notice that most of the enlisted crew had a talent for expressing obscenities. Smitty, however, managed to squeeze the word "fuck" into every sentence. If he felt particularly good or particularly frustrated, he used the word three or four times per sentence. That didn't make him guilty, but Andrew now had a particular feeling about him.

Andrew and Grady performed three more tunes before calling it quits. The men groaned, wanting more.

"If you play like that," Stokes said, slapping Andrew on the shoulder, "you must have some Louisiana bayou blood in you somewhere."

"Yeah," Hudson said, and spat on the deck. "He ain't your regular kind of chink."

A muffled, pinging noise sounded overhead, making everyone look up. A collective sigh propagated through the hall. The squall that had crawled toward the ship all day had finally overtaken them and engulfed the ship with rain.

The men, one after another, piled through the hatchway and ran to their lockers. Andrew was last to leave. He climbed through the hatch and stepped into the cooler temperatures brought on by the squall. Heavy raindrops stuck his face.

Rain. The clean scent of it reached into Andrew's lungs and lifted his heart. *Yes,* he thought, *even this steel hell has an element as pure as rain.* He tilted his face up and opened his mouth, gathering a mouthful of freshness.

The wind drove sheets of water against the ship, rainfall so heavy that Andrew couldn't see the shoreline or the other ships at anchor. Even in that protected bay, the *Pilgrim* rocked like a native woman's hips as she meandered along the beach. Outside the reef, on the open sea, white, foamy jets leaped into the air.

Turning forward, Andrew saw most of the crew grouped together on the quarterdeck, bathing naked in the wild rain. Waves broke across the deck, hurling seawater over their ankles as the ship pitched side to side. They scrubbed themselves from scalp to toes while leaning into the wind-driven rain.

They all had deeply tanned faces and arms, but their bodies glowed a pale white; all except Hudson, who had an apelike pelt covering his chest, back, shoulders and legs.

Andrew smiled boyishly at the sight of eighty naked men drenched in lather and rain. He ran to his locker, ripped off his clothes, and grabbed his cake of Lifebuoy soap. On deck, the rain buffeted his amber skin with force. He felt reluctant to join the others, but he saw Grady on the fringe of the bathers and rushed to stand beside him.

A joyous excitement animated the party, as if the men were all happily drunk. Swept up in the energy, Andrew surprised himself by laughing out loud.

He turned away from the crowd to let Grady scrub his back, and there, above him, stood Mitchell under the bridge awning. Their eyes locked through the slashing rain. Mitchell leaned over the bulwarks, raindrops soaking his head.

Andrew felt a strong urge to cover his nakedness. The feeling grew until he finally turned around, but he still felt the officer's gaze on his backside. He waited a minute before turning to see Mitchell still staring at him. Only when several bathers moved between him and Mitchell, swallowing Andrew in the crowd, did Mitchell walk inside the wheelhouse, where he was protected from the storm.

The setting sun momentarily broke below the cloud cover and the light caused the raindrops to gleam silver. Andrew inhaled sharply and held his breath. The men seemed to dance in liquid light. The sight of the crew being pelted with silver droplets caused him to exhale slowly.

As the squall passed, Andrew darted to his locker, toweled off, pulled on clean skivvies, and stared up at his bunk. They were stacked five high and his was the top one. Only eighteen inches of space separated the mattress and overhead, allowing him roughly the same space as a coffin.

To maneuver into his slot, he had to fling his body seven feet in the air, up and sideways at the same time. He missed by six inches with his first two leaps, but managed to land on fresh-laundered sheets his third.

He rolled onto his back and stared at the overhead, twelve inches above his nose. A woman's genial brown eyes gazed at him. Taped to the overhead was a picture of a Vargas pinup girl ripped from an issue of *Argosy* magazine. He grinned as he studied her wavy hairdo and shapely legs. He carefully peeled the picture from the overhead, folded it in half, in half again, and let it drop to the deck, knowing that a crewmember would find and treasure it.

Andrew listened for the sound of rain battering the ship, but the storm had passed and he only heard the crew, setting up cots along the main deck. The murmur of their conversations echoed through the night air. Careless bursts of laughter peppered with obscenities soared above the steady rumble of voices.

Because the men slept on deck, he and Grady had the compartment to themselves. He was not sleepy. He simply wanted to lie in his allotted space and relish the sensation of being perfectly clean. A breeze drifted through the open portholes and he focused on the sensation of air moving over his skin.

His mind wandered through the day's events and he envisioned that smile on Lieutenant Mitchell's face. He smiled back at the image. Mitchell winked at him and he winked too. The image leaned closer and Andrew lifted his hand to caress that sunburnt cheek. He fantasized the officer leaning closer to kiss him. He could almost feel those lips touching his, and he laughed at himself.

He indulged in this reverie for another half minute before letting the image evaporate. *It is enough,* he thought. *On this killing machine, it is enough to lie on crisp sheets and caress the memory of Mitchell, enough to anticipate the next time I'll see him.*

His mind gravitated into nothingness and he floated in a comfortable dimension of no thoughts, no fears, no hopes, and no disappointments. A half hour later, he drifted into sleep.

When the dream came, he was a boy again, reliving a memory. He and his schoolmates followed Master Jung-Wei through a rainforest. The boys wore the traditional saffron robes and shaved heads of acolytes. Master Jung-Wei was thin and bald, and his ivory-colored eyebrows were perched high on his wrinkled face.

Clifford Baldrich marched at the end of the line. He was Andrew's only friend and the only pure European in the school. His father was a diplomat with the British consulate in Saigon. Clifford was pale, and his angelic face swept below his silky brush of blond eyebrows.

They hiked along a path that led to a clearing on a mountain slope. Andrew saw their destination below: nestled beside a lake at the base of the mountain sat the Bai Hur Sze Temple, where he would spend the summer months between school terms. The clutch of red-roofed buildings looked like an illusion floating between the azure lake and the fiery mountains of Siam. Gliding above the lake were hundreds of the cranes that made the monastery famous.

When Long-Jin, the oldest acolyte, spotted the cranes, he began his favorite game of poking fun at Clifford. He teased Clifford that his hair was the same color as a crane's feathers. Laughter burst from the other boys as Long-Jin scrunched up his elongated face, set between two enormous ears, and imitated a birdcall.

"Fly here, bird-boy," Long-Jin shouted. "Stretch your neck and fly to the treetops, bird-boy."

Clifford's face reddened and he tried to respond, but he was too flustered. All he could do was stutter the first syllable of his defense, which sent the boys into fits of hysteria.

Andrew stepped between the two boys and gave Long-Jin a cold stare. "You taunt Clifford because you're jealous of his beauty." Long-Jin's face drooped as Andrew added, "Although it's true that your looks are ordinary, you shouldn't feel ashamed of your snout-like nose and elephant ears."

"A half caste's opinion is like farting in the wind," Long-Jin snarled. "It stinks for a moment and blows away, leaving nothing."

Andrew continued, unfazed. "I would gladly have a bird's white feathers and graceful body."

"Andrew." Master Jung-Wei's penetrating voice turned every head. "I shall call you, Lingtse," the master told Andrew. "Ling meaning spirit and Tse meaning stone. For I can see that you are destined to become one of the Pebble People."

Andrew had never heard of the Pebble People, but he nodded as if he knew them well. His pride swelled as the other boys exchanged questioning glances, but his curiosity refused to stay silent, and he finally asked, "Master, who are the Pebble People?"

A smile broke across the monk's face. "Throw a pebble into a still pond and what happens? Ripples. Waves move across the surface in all directions. You are a person who, when placed in any situation, will cause waves and bring change to everything."

"Master, you name me after a tiny pebble?"

"You hold the essence of the Pebble People. That is your nature. Whether you are small and make ripples or huge as a mountain and make a tsunami depends on how you live your life."

The monk bent and randomly selected a stone lying beside the path. He popped it into his mouth to wet it and spat it onto the palm of his hand. "See what happens when the pebble gets thrown into a pond."

They all leaned forward and stared. Glistening with saliva, the stone looked polished. Andrew saw that the small gray mass was intricately marbled with fine blue lines and had golden specks imbedded throughout that sparkled in the sunlight.

"Keep watching," the monk said.

The sun's rays dried the pebble, transforming it into an ordinary gray stone.

"Is that good?" Andrew asked.

"What is good and what is bad I cannot say. We all have Chi, and when we focus our Chi, it reveals our nature. We can bend our Chi to achieve any purpose. Lingtse, you must be careful how you use your Chi because it has such a disruptive quality."

Andrew wondered if this was a gift or a curse. He glanced at Clifford and decided he would prefer being a lovely crane gliding above a lake rather than a dusty stone lying along a path. He spread his arms, pretending that they were limber wings, and ran along the path with his arms rhythmically gliding up and down. Right on his heels, Clifford mimicked Andrew's arm movements while laughing with wild delight.

In his sleep, Andrew smiled. The dream faded, and once again he floated in emptiness.

Chapter Eight

April 18, 1942—2330 hours

NIGHT descended with only the glimmer of stars to disturb the inky sky, and with night came the long and lonely watches. Andrew drifted in a light slumber. He had no sooner submerged into deep unconsciousness than he felt a tug on his shoulder.

"Eleven-thirty, sailor. You've got the twelve-to-four bridge watch."

Andrew rolled over.

Another tug. "On your feet, sailor. And wake up the XO on your way to the bridge."

Andrew yawned, smiled. He jumped to the deck, tottering about on unsteady legs while he climbed into his dungarees. He hurried to the galley and made coffee for the relief watch.

Stokes and eight others gathered around the urn, all looking as tired and jagged as Andrew felt. Over coffee, they traded glances but not words. Andrew ignored their truculent stares. He filled another mug and weaved through the corridor heading toward officer's country, drawing aside the curtain that served as a door to Mitchell's quarters.

Red light from the passageway infiltrated the cabin. Andrew saw that the room was an iron cube seven feet long and slightly wider. Against one bulkhead rested a narrow desk piled high with naval publications, files tucked in manila envelopes, and a stack of freshly laundered khakis. Above the desk and running the length of the room was a metal shelf supporting a platoon of books standing at attention. Andrew brought his face to within inches of the book spines so he could read the authors; Joyce, Eliot, Proust, and Shakespeare were all he could make out in the weak light.

Nestled against the other bulkhead and crouching low to the deck was the bunk that cradled the sleeping lieutenant. Mitchell lay on his side, with no blanket. He wore skivvies with his name stenciled above the curve of his butt, and also a T-shirt that stretched across his chest, showing the imprint of his pecs and his bullet-shaped nipples. Mitchell looked rumpled and peaceful, angelic.

Andrew touched Mitchell's arm, gently shaking the officer until his eyes opened. He stretched languorously, like an old house cat, and yawned while slipping a hand up under his T-shirt to stroke his midriff. The sight of that triangle of pale waist with the soft trail of hair flowing down from his bellybutton doubled Andrew's heart rate.

"Time for your watch, sir," Andrew said, his voice scarcely more than a whisper. "I've brought some coffee." He stood frozen as the officer sat up.

Mitchell's face was streaked with two red lines caused by creases on his pillowcase, and his disheveled hair stood out at rakish angles. He seemed more human now than in sleep.

"Thanks, Andy," he said, taking the mug. He sipped and swung his legs over the side of the bunk. He set the mug on the desk and grabbed his trousers. "That'll be all, Andy."

"Yes, sir." Andrew was surprised that, in the privacy of the lieutenant's quarters, Mitchell had called him by his nickname. Only Clifford had called him that. Even his father called him Andrew.

ANDREW glided through the corridor leading to the bridge, following Mitchell, Stokes, and Ogden. The bridge, like the entire inside of the ship, was illuminated with dim red light rather than white to keep from being seen by enemy planes and ships.

Ogden positioned himself next to the captain's chair. Stokes took his post at the port railing, lifting his binoculars to scan the dark water for any sign of another ship, and Andrew did the same on the starboard side. Mitchell relieved Ensign Fisher, who reported the current status: all quiet. That done, Mitchell ambled to the operations desk and wrote an entry into the Rough Logbook.

"How about that Doolittle?" Fisher said. "Bet that put the fear of God into those yellow bastards."

Mitchell bestowed an arid smile on Fisher before scanning the darkness beyond the bow. He said, "I would love to have seen Hirohito's face while the bombs were falling. That SOB must have shit his drawers, thinking he might be next."

Fisher slapped Mitchell's shoulder as he headed for the hatch. "You have the bridge, Mr. Mitchell." He smiled. "And yes, it would be great to see that murdering bastard get what he deserves."

Hearing the officers' comments, Andrew felt the hot knife of indignation slide into his gut. He tilted his binoculars upward to scan the starlit sky. Through the firmament and beyond the myriad of familiar shapes—the Hunter, the Bear, the Pleiades—and even beyond the dim specks from the most distant stars, he surveyed the darkest regions of the unknown. His mind emptied and he felt himself become the unknown until a voice echoed in his head.

"Begging your pardon, sir," the voice said, sounding vaguely like his own. "My father had business dealings with the Japanese government for twenty years and he knew quite a bit about the Emperor. He said that Hirohito is a pure man, free of all vanity and pride, and he is only concerned with the well-being of the Japanese people."

Andrew knew he'd trampled on military etiquette, but his indignation had forced him to speak.

Mitchell stared at Andrew.

Stokes's fingers tightened on the railing in front of him and he held his breath. An immediate sense of danger gripped the air. Andrew had vaulted over that gulf that separated enlisted men from officers, and he hung suspended over that chasm, Icarus-like, soaring too close to the sun. Stokes let out his breath, unable to hold it any longer.

"You're suggesting that the Japanese supreme leader is an honorable man? Pure?" Mitchell said. "He slaughtered a million Chinese and bombed Pearl Harbor! The man's a fanatic, no better than Hitler."

Andrew stepped closer to Mitchell, drawn by the timbre of the man's voice. He knew Mitchell should have reprimanded him for expressing a personal opinion, so Mitchell must have been intrigued by his statement. That bolstered his courage and allowed him to continue.

"Sir, the Japanese people regard Hirohito as a god, a deity. He does not rule Japan, he reigns over it, which means he abstains from politics. From everything that I've heard, he loves and guides his people with compassion, much like the Buddha. I believe that the resolution for war came from the military-controlled government, not Hirohito."

"You're telling me he's not a warmonger? My God, he comes from a feudal background. They're all warmongers, all the leaders of Japan."

"Sir, Hirohito's grandfather, Emperor Meiji, once wrote:

All the seas, everywhere,

Are brothers one to another.

Why then do the winds and waves of strife

Rage so violently through the world?"

Mitchell shook his head. "Regardless, what they did at Pearl was cowardly and monstrous."

"Sir, in 1924, Japan was strapped with overpopulation and an extreme depression. They used territorial expansion into Manchuria as a solution, transforming a bandit-infested wilderness area twice the size of California into a prosperous nation. That solved unemployment, overpopulation, and produced raw materials for the homeland. But of course, war always goes beyond politics, because once begun, war becomes self-serving. Victory compelled the military to go further. They dreamed of creating one great Asian nation, a brotherhood of all Asian people. That meant driving out the French, English, Dutch, and Americans. But typical of most military leaders, they saw coercion as the only means to their glorious end."

"Sounds like you approve."

"I approve of Asia freeing itself of Western domination, but not of Japanese methods. My mother's family lived in Nanking. When the Japanese invaded the city, the atrocities lasted a month. A third of the city was gutted with fire. Twenty thousand soldiers were marched from the city and massacred, twenty thousand! As many women and girls were raped and mutilated. Over three hundred thousand civilians were slaughtered. My family was wiped out." Andrew paused. "No, Lieutenant, I don't approve at all."

"If that happened to my family, I'd want to kill as many Japs as possible."

"You mean to say, you'd kill as a justified means of revenge? Sir, what makes you different from them?"

Mitchell's nostrils flared and his eyes smoldered. "There's a vast difference. I'm a patriot! I'm defending my country."

"In my view, that is exactly what the Japanese are doing: defending their nation. In '37, they invaded China, and in '41, Roosevelt put an embargo on Japan, cutting off all supplies, including oil. Roosevelt used the embargo to strangle Japan into being weak and defenseless. Japan was forced to choose between being a third-rate country begging for Western crumbs or going to war and becoming a superpower. America is like the hunter who traps a tiger in a cage and stands in the open doorway. You cry self-defense when the tiger lunges for freedom and you have to kill it to save your own skin. If you're placing blame, don't overlook Roosevelt."

"Japan was wrong to attack China."

"Why was it right for the whites to invade the continent of America and slaughter the native Indians, but wrong for the Japanese to do the same in China?"

In the darkness behind them, Ogden audibly sucked in his breath.

"You make it sound like the war is all the result of racial issues," Mitchell said.

"I don't see any other way to view it. Why should there be a Monroe Doctrine in America and an open-door policy in Asia? Why was it perfectly acceptable for England and Holland to occupy India, Hong Kong, Singapore, and the East Indies, but a crime for Japan to follow their example? After stealing land from Indians through trickery and massacre, why should America be so outraged when Japan did the same in China?"

"They had no claim on China and no right to attack us."

"That reminds me of a line in *Henry V*," Andrew said. "'And God forbid, my wise and learned Lord, that you should fashion, wrest, or bow your reading, with opening titles miscreate, whose right suits are not in native colors with the truth; for God doth know, how many now in health shall drop their blood, in approbation of what your reverence shall incite us to.'"

"My God, you quote whole passages of Shakespeare?"

Andrew continued, "'Therefore take heed how you impawn our person, how you awaken the sleeping sword of war.'"

Mitchell smiled and added, "'We charge you in the name of God take heed; For never two such kingdoms did contend without much fall of blood, whose guiltless drops are every one a woe.'"

Ogden became visibly agitated. He cleared his throat in an effort to make Andrew realize that he was way out of line, but it was Mitchell who heard the chief's snarl.

Mitchell stared at Andrew with a confused expression, as if wholly aware of how much he had enjoyed their exchange and equally aware of how wrong it was to get sucked into a personal conversation.

Andrew sensed the officer's abrupt mood change. He raised his binoculars and scanned the darkness off the starboard bow. He'd gone too far, carried away by his feelings of love. He knew that, to continue their debate, the lieutenant must be the one to rekindle it. He waited, praying that Mitchell would renew the conversation. He gazed into the night while his wool watch cap caused his head to itch madly, or could it have been the anticipation of the officer's next statement?

Thirty silent minutes crawled by. Mitchell kept glancing at Andrew and the tension on his face seemed to build as the minutes crept by. Mitchell finally cleared his throat. "Why are you standing a lookout watch? Cooks are exempt from watches."

"Sir, you confiscated my salary to pay for my new uniforms. Skeeter Banks is paying me a dollar a night to stand his midnight-to-four. I have to get up at eleven-thirty and three-thirty to make coffee for the watches, so I figured I might as well stay up and earn some money."

Once the silence was broken, Mitchell seemed to relax.

"Sometime when we're not on watch, you'll have to tell me how you can justify the attack on Pearl. No declaration of war, no warning, nothing."

Andrew could hardly believe the offer. Three hundred lifetimes had passed in that thirty-minute silence. Convinced that their interchange was over for good, his heart had retreated into its shell. Now he strained to hide his joy.

"The answer is simple, sir. I can explain anytime you would care to hear."

"Simple? How's that?"

"America has ten times the resources that Japan has. Ten times the oil, the manpower, the raw materials, and the military might. Ten times! You have to ask yourself why a nation would wage war against such overwhelming odds. Simply, America is consumed with the war in Europe. Japan felt that if they could knock out the Pacific fleet with one blow, that would buy them two years to secure their position as ruler of the Western Pacific."

Mitchell nodded while the discussion, phoenixlike, launched itself again. They debated war and motives until the top of the hour, when Mitchell made a log entry. For the next hour, they discussed how a country had an identity, and how a country's psyche was an aggregate of the egos of the people who form that country's population. The last hour of their watch was consumed with discussing why men strived for power, so much so that they risked life and honor for it.

Mitchell talked more than he had since stepping aboard the *Pilgrim*; he said so himself, with an air of surprise.

Stokes and Ogden stood at their posts, listening to the give and take in a debate between two intellectual equals. They occasionally exchanged questioning glances, as if trying to stitch together the threads of logic. The lieutenant had a reputation among the crew for having a head on his shoulders, being a man who could express his opinions, but Andrew held his own with the officer.

At 0345 hours, the captain scaled the ladder to relieve Mitchell.

Andrew rushed to the galley to make fresh coffee for the relief watch. After, there were a few precious hours of sack time left, so Andrew headed for his bunk. In the empty forecastle, he pulled off his clothes, stepped into a clean pair of skivvies, and hurled himself onto his bunk.

The temperature in the forecastle had cooled to near comfortable, and he settled himself on his back with hands clasped under his head. He felt dog-tired but he was too excited to sleep. He relived portions of his conversation with Mitchell in his head, hearing the tones in the officer's voice and seeing the vivid expressions on the man's face. It was thrilling to match wits with him, like holding his own against a superior chess player. He felt a flash of loving unity with that rich mind.

His memory turned to what he had seen before the watch: Mitchell asleep, naked save for his T-shirt and underwear, the beautifully peaceful face, the muscular lines of his chest, and the curve of his hips pressed against those bleached skivvies.

Andrew resisted his impulse to masturbate, but the vision turned to more concrete sexual images. He heard the officer's slow exhalation, sounding like a soft moan. Andrew's breathing deepened. He wrapped the memory of Mitchell around him like a velvety cocoon and lured his intellect into nothingness—no thoughts about conversations, no visions of sunburnt skin, no scent of sweet breath.

He drifted in tranquility, which lasted only a moment before sleep took him.

Chapter Nine

April 20, 1942—0500 hours

THE ship vibrated like a tuning fork, a low-wave oscillation that traveled through the superstructure and up Mitchell's legs. His skeleton carried the pulsation to every cell in his body. The excitement of getting underway supplanted his calm demeanor. For him, going to sea on any ship was always exhilarating, and always a little sad.

From the bridge, he watched the deck crew unmoor the ship with clocklike precision. With the swing of the tide, the bow pointed toward open sea. Propellers slashed the water. The ship hesitated, her twenty-thousand-ton bulk resisting the clout of her engines, and she inched forward under her own power. Her movement was imperceptible at first, but built in strength and speed until the bow wave grew to a three-foot arc and two man-made combers funneled away from her sides.

She steamed into open water before the sun rose, swaying and creaking as she sliced through waves at 15.7 knots—which was SOA, or standard Speed of Advance—toward the line in the east where water met the sky. While underway, the *Pilgrim* operated in a battle-ready status called "Condition Able," where the men stood watch four hours on, four hours off. It was a grueling schedule that left the men insufficient time for sleep and induced a zombielike state.

Bitton cleared his throat. "Full speed ahead, Nathan. Orders came a half hour ago directing us to Papeete. Let's put the spurs to her. We'll do battle-readiness drills on the way. Run a standard zigzag pattern until oh-nine-hundred tomorrow."

While Mitchell knew zigzagging was a defensive maneuver, to make the ship harder to hit with torpedoes by making it an erratically moving target, he had always believed that the practice had negligible value and used more time and fuel. It was, however, required by Navy regulations, so he didn't argue.

Andrew popped onto the bridge with a coffeepot and a tray of mugs, saying that breakfast was ready at the officers' leisure. Mitchell gratefully poured himself a mug and thought of Andrew long after his departure. Their debate had made the watch pass in a flash, and now Andrew had had the thoughtfulness to deliver coffee. Feeling the hot liquid warm his insides, Mitchell finished his mug and left the captain in command of the bridge while he hurried to the wardroom.

Tedder and Fisher sat at the table, finishing their breakfast. A pitcher of orange juice, freshly squeezed and pulpy, sat beside a platter of sliced pineapple, mango, and papaya. There was also a plate of fragrant cinnamon rolls and a basket of warm baguettes.

Mitchell scanned the crowded table as he took off his cap. "Wow! Look at all this chow."

Fisher winked at the medical officer.

As Mitchell settled himself at the table, Grady breezed through the hatch with a coffeepot in hand. He poured Mitchell a cup and drawled, "Suh, would you like the banana pancakes, poached eggs on toast with hollandaise, or the tomato, shrimp, and spinach omelet?"

Mitchell's mouth fell open while the other officers traded gleeful laughter.

"No powdered eggs, burnt toast, and crispy Spam?" Mitchell asked.

"I can ask the chef, suh, if that's what you want."

"No. Please inform the chef that I'll have the poached eggs."

"An excellent choice," Tedder said. "Although the omelet was ambrosial. I couldn't decide, so I had both. And save room for the cinnamon rolls. They're a sliver of paradise."

"Keep that up and you'll end up looking like Cocoa."

Grady cackled as he exited the wardroom.

Mitchell served himself some fruit and a baguette. He eyed the cinnamon rolls, but decided to save those for last. The coffee tasted delicious, and he finished off his cup and poured another.

Grady burst into the wardroom, out of breath and eyes bulging as large as goose eggs.

"Suh, come quick. They's fightin' in the mess hall."

Mitchell held a golden slice of mango below his nose. He popped it into his mouth and rose to his feet, falling in behind Grady as he ran down the passageway.

The trouble had started when Andrew carried a tray of cinnamon rolls behind Cocoa, who was serving up flapjacks on the chow line, and placed them on the next serving station. There were three dozen rolls on the tray; the frosting glistened and the spicy cinnamon aroma wafted on the air.

As Andrew walked to the galley, Hudson, who was waiting in line for his breakfast, yelled at Andrew that nobody was going to eat his chink cooking. His voice ricocheted off the bulkheads and into the consciousness of every sailor in the room. All the men traded questioning glances, as if wondering if they should follow Hudson's lead or follow their noses.

Stokes sat at a table chewing rubbery flapjacks. He jumped up, marched to the front of the chow line and helped himself to four cinnamon rolls. Everybody glared as he returned to his seat and devoured a roll. He took his time sucking the gooey frosting from his fingers before starting on another roll.

Skeeter Banks stepped out of line and bypassed the flapjacks altogether. He loaded his tray with six rolls. An instant later, eighty sailors lunged for the remaining rolls. Men cursed, shirts were ripped, and fists hurtled through the air like hail.

Mitchell stationed himself at the hatchway, red-faced and both hands on his hips, watching a whirlwind of flying trays and overturned chairs and biting, gouging, fist-pounding men. In the eye of the storm, Ogden stood with his feet planted wide and his arms stretched out. His voice thundered as he tried to break up the men.

Cocoa saw the lieutenant and bellowed, "Attention on deck!" His voice recoiled off the walls and the fight unraveled. Exhausted men struggled to their feet and came to attention while mopping blood from their faces and checking for loose teeth.

"Chief," Mitchell snarled, "who started this fight?" He struggled to keep his voice even, but the way he hissed the question through his clenched jaw made his anger more than apparent.

Ogden scratched his chin. "Sir, Seaman Waters started it. Yes, sir, he's to blame."

Mitchell's eyebrows lifted high on his head. He scanned the room but didn't see Andrew. "Waters, front and center."

Andrew rushed into the hall and stood next to Cocoa behind the chow-line serving stations.

"I'm here, sir."

Mitchell glanced over his shoulder at Andrew. He turned to Ogden. "Chief, explain to me how Waters is responsible, seeing as how he was in the galley when the fight took place."

"Well, sir, he laid out a tray of cinnamon rolls, but the little bastard only made enough to tease us. The men started fighting to see who would get a roll."

Silence. Mitchell glared at Ogden, not quite believing the absurdity of the situation. He finally turned to look at Andrew.

"Sir, I didn't make more because I didn't think they would eat my cooking. At least that's what everyone said until the fists started flying."

Mitchell noted the concern etched on Andrew's face.

"I'll be happy to cook more next time."

More strained silence as Mitchell's anger drained away. "Waters, from now on you will ensure there is plenty to go around or I'll haul your butt before the captain. Is that clear, sailor?" He barked the question, but at the same time, he winked one eye.

"Aye, sir. Understood loud and clear."

Mitchell had his back to all the men in the room except Cocoa and Waters, so Cocoa was the only other person who saw the nonverbal exchange.

Thirty minutes later Mitchell stood on the bridge describing the incident to the captain.

Bitton frowned.

"They've accepted him," Mitchell said. "Once things settle down, they'll be happy as clams eating his cooking. It's exactly what we wanted."

Bitton shook his head. "The officers are his first priority, Nathan. I don't want the quality of our meals dropping because he spends time cooking for a hundred men."

Mitchell grinned. "I'll see to it, sir."

"This is no laughing matter, Nathan. We've struck gold here, and I don't want it tarnishing." Bitton scowled as he pulled his pipe and tobacco pouch from his hip pocket and filled his bowl. "Damn that Waters," he said. The ends of his lips lifted into a smirk as he brought the pipe stem to his mouth and struck a match over the bowl. He exhaled a cloud of sweet-smelling smoke and said, "Damn that Waters," again for good measure.

FOR the next two days the crew drilled from breakfast until dinner— general quarters, weapons firing, collision, fire, abandon ship, even surprise drills in the middle of the night. The crew's performance improved until each action was accomplished with smartness and speed. Captain Bitton timed each drill as he chewed on the stem of his pipe, which seemed to sputter as many sparks from the bowl as it did tendrils of gray smoke. By the third day, even he allowed himself a slight nod after each performance.

Mitchell often dropped by the galley between drills, saying, "As you were. Just need a drink." His visits became so frequent that Cocoa and Grady stopped gaping at each other with raised eyebrows.

Andrew came to expect Mitchell during the lulls and always had cold lemonade, iced tea, or a special snack waiting. Mitchell chatted easily with Andrew, his body relaxed and his smile genuine. They talked about the dinner menu, progress of the drills, or supplies needed at the next port.

On the midnight-to-four watch, there was no longer any pretense of protocol. They debated politics, philosophy, and literature. They discussed topics as equals and as friends. Ogden and Stokes simply manned their posts and listened while the two friends exchanged viewpoints.

What Ogden and Stokes gleaned from the conversations always made interesting scuttlebutt for the rest of the crew. The men regarded Mitchell as an intellectual, and now they judged Andrew to be that same rare breed of animal. They were proud that one of their own could go toe-to-toe with the brains running the ship, but at the same time, there was an uneasiness about the personal relationship developing between officer and enlisted. It was a serious breach of the naval code, and that meant trouble was brewing.

An hour before dawn on their fourth night at sea, the *Pilgrim* steamed through the Sea of the Moon off Tahiti's western coast and plowed into Papeete Bay at seventeen knots. On that windless morning, the *Pilgrim* crossed the bay, came about, and tied up to the fueling dock north of town. The engines shut down and a hush fell over the ship even before the deck crew could secure all lines.

The sun peeked over the horizon. Effulgent light bathed Papeete's bustling marketplace and lively wharf area as the town came to life. Mitchell stood beside Andrew at the quarterdeck railing, absorbed in the spectacle of the world changing colors before their eyes.

Andrew finally said, "I better get it in gear if you want your breakfast." He brushed past the officer and disappeared through the open hatch.

Watching him go, Mitchell noted the way the sunlight tumbled off his lean body and, suddenly feeling hungry, he checked his watch to see how long he had to wait for his breakfast. He strolled to the wardroom and joined the other officers gathered around the dining table. To his surprise, Bitton handed him a tumbler of neat whiskey.

Bitton earned a sharp glance from Mitchell, which he ignored, while lifting his glass high. "We live in a time of absolutes, gentlemen. At the end of the day, it's all about whether our ship, our crew, and we are still alive to tell about it."

Mitchell noted, from the level of liquid in the bottle and the boozy smile on Tedder's face, that this was not their first round of drinks that morning. All five officers hoisted their tumblers and everyone but Mitchell swallowed their whiskey. Mitchell only brought his glass to his mouth and wet his lips, in order to not to offend the captain. He placed his glass on the table.

Bitton held out the bottle. "One more? Should make breakfast that much sweeter."

Everyone but Moyer and Mitchell held out an empty glass. Moyer flashed a sheepish grin, "Not for me. I've got services this morning."

On Sunday mornings the crew split into shifts for breakfast and church services. First the Protestants enjoyed an early breakfast while the Catholics attended Mass on the fantail. Even though Moyer was Episcopalian, he chanted in Latin, gave the sacraments, and even heard confessions after Mass from anyone who needed to get something off his chest. Because he was not Roman Catholic, he had no official authority from the Church in Rome to perform these services, but in wartime one had to make do, and giving the boys a semblance of Mass was better than nothing. After Mass, the Catholics piled into the mess hall and the Protestants assembled on the fantail for a sermon on how a virtuous sailor should apply himself during shore leave. They finished by bowing their heads in prayer and singing a few well-known hymns: "The Old Rugged Cross" and "Onward Christian Soldier."

Bitton attended the Protestant service, but the other officers never attended either. Mitchell stood the morning OOD watch, and Fisher and Tedder had no religious interests.

Bitton joined Mitchell on the bridge before the second service. They peered thirty feet below at the forecastle deck as Andrew strolled to a clearing forward of the gun turrets and behind the anchor chains.

Andrew wore orange saffron robes covering yellow silk undergarments. The inner robe was secured around his waist like a sarong to cover his lower body. The upper robe hung on his left shoulder, looped around his back under his right armpit, and swept across his chest and over his left shoulder. It hid most of his upper body but left his slender neck and right shoulder bare. Prayer beads hung from his left hand and his feet were clad in leather sandals.

Andrew faced the sun and struck a pose with his feet eighteen inches apart and arms held chest high. As oblique sunrays spread an ethereal glow around him, he began to move.

Bitton's face flushed. "What in holy hell is going on?"

"He calls it tai chi," Mitchell said. "I gave him permission. He told me that, and I quote: 'the unstained purity of the eternal present is maintained consciously by moving from one pose to another with all one's concentration.'"

"What the hell does that mean?"

Mitchell chuckled. "I think he's trying to attain a state of detachment through motion. That's why all his movements are so precise and simple—no gesture is hurried."

Andrew glided without the slightest expression on his face. He spun, bent, and dipped this way and that as if in a trance. All the while his hands gracefully traced patterns on a canvas of air.

It must take incredible strength to perform those moves so slowly, Mitchell thought. *He makes it look effortless, like a silk scarf floating on the wind.*

"Never thought I'd see such a thing on a warship," Bitton muttered.

"Neither did I," Mitchell replied, entranced by the beauty of the shifting cloth.

Bitton shook his head. "Have the padre pound some sense into him."

"Ben, there's nothing wrong with him practicing his religion."

"You're forgetting your duty," the captain barked. "This crew needs to integrate into one team, and that means one point of view. This boy is way off base with this religious ballet stuff. I want him schooled in the ways of the Lord, the true Lord."

Mitchell's mind swirled with one argument after another that he thought might sway the captain, but he knew that Bitton's mind was snapped shut, like a bear trap, as long as he watched Andrew perform.

Andrew eventually became a statue, balanced in every respect and quiescent as stone. He held that pose for five minutes before sinking to the deck. He folded his legs into a lotus position, lifted Jah-Jai from beneath his robes, brought the flute to his lips, and played a concerto in a minor key.

Mitchell was hunched over the chart table when he heard a sudden burst of Mozart. The sound drew him to the windows that overlooked the bow, and onto the port bridge wing to hear better. He felt the melody vibrating from his head to the base of his spine as he stood gazing down on Andrew, lost in the sonority of that beautiful morning. The music seemed to ripple through Mitchell's body in airy gushes. His pulse raced and beads of sweat coated his upper lip. It was the sexiest thing he had ever witnessed.

Mitchell watched Andrew until the sailor rose and glided down the forecastle. After Andrew slipped out of sight, the officer surprised himself by joining the remainder of the services on the fantail. He stood behind the last row, on the fringe of the believers.

Moyer read from the book of Luke, gripping his Bible and speaking with a trembling voice as he told of the love between Jesus and his disciple, John. How, at the Last Supper, John laid his head on Jesus's breast.

Mitchell listened to the intimate tones of Moyer's voice while trying to picture the loving scene. He imagined the Savior's hand holding out the bread that represents his body, and he focused on the smooth skin spread over delicately formed bones. Moyer mentioned Calvary, and Mitchell's vision shifted to the Savior's nakedness lying against the rough wood, awaiting the press of the nails.

A sheen of sweat spread over Mitchell's forehead. His midsection tightened as the vision expanded and he imagined his own cheek pressed against the taut skin of the Savior's breast. He stared up into the Savior's eyes and was jolted back to reality as he realized that his vision had Andrew's almond-shaped eyes and amber-colored skin.

"Let us pray," Moyer said.

Mitchell did not bow his head with the others. He was afraid to close his eyes, afraid that the vision would return. He gazed at the sky over Moyer's head as if he were looking for a sign from the Holy Spirit.

Moyer's voice swelled as he recited the closing prayer. The expression on his face looked as if a vision of heaven had penetrated his eyes.

Mitchell left the service in a daze. He stumbled down the steel deck on his way to the wardroom to retrieve his glass of neat whiskey.

CHAPTER TEN

April 23, 1942—1000 hours

A JEEP from naval headquarters drove onto the dock and parked alongside the quarterdeck. The driver pulled two weather-stained mail sacks from the jeep and hoisted them aboard. Seaman Cord cried, "Mail Ho!" His call echoed along the deck and was repeated by other voices throughout the ship.

Cord heaved the sacks to the port side of the quarterdeck, opened one, and grabbed a fist-full of moldy letters. He stood on a torpedo launcher to elevate himself above the sailors gathering around, yelling the name on a letter. When the owner shouted a quick "Here," Cord tossed the envelope in the direction of the voice while reading the name on the next letter.

Hudson sauntered to the crew's quarters. He switched off the overhead lamps and sluggishly climbed into his bunk like a weasel crawling into its hole. He laid his head on his sweat-stained pillow, dragging his right arm over his face to cover his eyes with the inside of his elbow. He lay stock-still, as if trying to ignore Cord's voice calling out names.

Andrew breezed into the forecastle still wearing his orange robes and a dreamy smile. He flipped on the overhead lamps on his way to his locker and peeled off his upper robe.

"Turn the lamp off when you leave," Hudson said with a throaty snarl.

Andrew whirled around, somewhat surprised. "Sorry, didn't know anybody was in here. Guess we haven't been aboard long enough to have mail routed to us. Maybe by the next delivery."

"I never get mail," Hudson snapped. "No family, no sweetheart, no one to write to, and no one to get a letter from. All my family is here on this ship. It's all I got."

Andrew felt overwhelmed that Hudson of all people would make such a personal confession to him. He faced his locker and stripped out of his inner robe and yellow undergarments, carefully folding and storing the fine material. He climbed into his work dungarees and switched off the lamps. As he stepped through the hatch, he leaned his head back inside the compartment.

"I never get mail either. I have family, my father, but he got used to ignoring me when he traveled on business. Guess it's a hard habit to break." Andrew paused, groping for something to add, but he came up empty. He closed the hatch, leaving Hudson alone in the dark.

GRADY strolled into the wardroom carrying a handful of letters and a package.

"Mister Mitchell, Suh, you gots a letter and a box."

"Anything for me?" Ensign Fisher asked.

"Yes, Suh. Five letters, and one don't have no stamp."

Fisher smiled as he took his letters. The one on top had only his name written on the envelope. He held the envelope under his nose.

"Yes, Suh. It smells real pretty. Like this girl I know'd back home."

"Perhaps you'd like to read it to me as well," Fisher said.

Grady flashed his white teeth. "If that's what you want, Suh. I can read. I been educated."

"That will do, Washington," the captain said, snatching his two letters.

Mitchell stuffed his letter in his breast pocket and studied his battered, oblong package. He recognized the swirling handwriting, ripped the brown paper, and opened the box. It held a note, a Bible, and a book of poems by e.e. cummings. The note read:

Darling,

Here's the poetry you asked for. I was lucky to find it in a used bookstore on Third Street, marked down to $0.75. I've included the Bible that Reverend Thorn gave me last Sunday. I know you don't believe, but please read a little each day. You may find comfort in it, as I surely do.

I found a wedding dress in the catalog last week that I think you will like. It's not too expensive but it is lovely. I want you to be proud of me. I know you can't tell me where you are, but please give me some indication of when I will see you again.

Until then, all my love,

Your Kate

Mitchell heard paper tearing. He glanced up to see Fisher ripping a letter in half without opening it. The ensign checked the return address on another letter and ripped that one too. Mitchell watched while he ripped four letters in half, and finally opened the last one, the one without a stamp.

"Let me guess," Mitchell said. "The ones you didn't read are no doubt from the last batch of ladies you left standing at the pier as we sailed from Pearl. But what about the one you opened? No stamp means it's some charming little thing waiting for you here in Papeete. Someone connected with the Navy, because she was able to drop that letter in the mail pouch without sending it through the post."

Fisher nodded, grinning.

"How do you do it?" Mitchell asked. "How do you get so many women to fall for you? No offense, but you're no Clark Gable, and I've seen you in the head with your morning woody, which is not terribly impressive. So what is it?"

Fisher's grin spread into a smile. "I love women—short or tall, fat or slim, brunette or blonde, slant-eyed or round, single or married—it makes no difference. I love every woman I meet because I have the ability to see past her skin and social situation to the jewel of her spirit. Of course it helps to come from a wealthy family that schooled me in country-club charm."

Mitchell scoffed. "So who's the little bird waiting in port?"

Fisher held the letter under his nose. "Admiral Gleason's wife. Seems the admiral is out on maneuvers, so she's asked me to tea. It must be lonely out here for an officer's wife."

Mitchell let out a low-pitched whistle.

"Nathan," the captain said. "Pass that Bible over to our young Romeo here. He needs some examples on moral behavior. Let me remind you that your conduct ashore reflects on this ship. Dabbling in the admiral's business will have serious consequences."

Not wanting to get caught in a moral debate with Bitton, Mitchell excused himself and hurried to his cabin. He pulled the letter from his pocket, ripped open the envelope and unfolded the scented paper.

Dearest,

I'm going mad in this backwater town. People have noticed that I'm with child and everybody has turned vicious. Even your mother believes that I became pregnant in order to snare you.

Living near your parents while we wait for your return is in many ways a comfort, but these townspeople are so hateful. I've got to go someplace where people are more educated. I'm moving to San Francisco so that I can be there when you return.

You're kind and gentle, and I'm truly happy when I'm with you, but if you don't love me, if you feel trapped by our situation, then please tell me. I won't marry a man who doesn't love me. The baby and I will somehow find our way without you.

I'll send you my new address when I'm settled. I love you more than any woman has a right to. I hope you feel the same love for our baby and me. We will be waiting for your speedy return in San Francisco.

A thousand times I love you,

Your Kate

Do I love her? he asked himself. He had met her in Washington, DC while working as an aid with Naval Intelligence. She had come to the ranch to meet his folks during his last leave.

He could envision her clearly on that winter morning. She rode an old, soft-eyed gelding named Dollar. Mitchell rode his own horse, a six-year-old Appaloosa stallion named Caesar, who kept dancing around while flagging his long tail, not content to meander at Dollar's pace. Caesar would toss his head like haughty royalty and prance ahead until Mitchell reined him in. Even Smoke, who followed from a respectful distance with his nose to the ground, seemed impatient.

Whenever Dollar managed a brief trot, Kate would cling to the saddle horn and squeal with a mixture of fear and delight.

He felt sure she didn't enjoy the ride, but there was two inches of snow carpeting the pasture and the view of the mountains was magnificent. The crisp air had a hint of sweetness. The mountains were covered with pine, and down in the meadows the aspens were bare, like white roots growing toward the sky. That landscape had touched his heart with its clattering streams and glistening pastures; it swallowed him whole with its fathomless, uncomplicated open space. It was grand to be alive and able to share the grasslands with someone on such a morning.

They came across tracks stitched across a meadow that led into a steep canyon. Smoke began to follow the tracks, but Mitchell's whistle brought him back.

"What made those tracks?" she asked. "A deer?"

With an effort to hold a straight face, he told her, "Naw, not a deer, and it's too big for a coyote. Must be a mountain lion."

She looked up the canyon where the tracks led. "Mountain lion! Nathan Mitchell, you take me back to the house this instant. Do you hear me?"

He couldn't hold it any longer. A burst of laughter flew from his throat as he bent forward over Caesar's neck. The horse took several side steps, adjusting to the shift in weight.

Her cheeks burned red, angry red. She turned old Dollar in the direction they had come and gave his ribs a good kick. Dollar took a couple of quick steps and began to amble toward the barn. She didn't say another word the long ride home.

In the barn, she lay on a pile of hay while he pulled the saddles and blankets off the horses and brushed both animals down. The barn was warm with the rich smell of horse and hay and manure. He pulled a hoof pick from his pocket and methodically cleaned the dirt from Dollar's hooves. He did the same to Caesar.

She beckoned to him with her hands and he lay beside her. The horses, standing in their stalls, watched with their ears pricked forward, sensing a change in mood.

"You think it's funny to tease a city girl. I think you're mean, but I forgive you." She kissed him, not a girlish peck but a sensual kiss that opened his mouth and allowed her tongue to explore. They made love for the first time.

"Do I love her?" He repeated the question. *It doesn't matter*, he thought. *She's having my baby.*

He crumpled the sheets of paper into a tight ball, tossed it onto his desk, and hurried topside to inspect the liberty party.

Chapter Seven

April 24, 1942—0700 hours

THE captain mustered the liberty party, which was all but a skeleton watch, on the quarterdeck. Using a fatherly tone, he said, "Now look here, men. I know you're anxious for liberty and all you can think about is getting drunk and laid, which has got you all so excited you're about to burst. It may help you restrain yourselves from temptation ashore if you release some of that sexual tension before you leave the ship. Remember, the Navy does not condone the practice of masturbation, no matter how excited you are. But while you're in the shower getting cleaned up for liberty, feel free to scrub your dicks as long and hard and fast as you like."

Laughter spilled over the ranks.

"That's a tradition in the Navy," the captain added. "That's why on warships, whenever it rains, every man aboard gets a hard-on."

More nervous laughter—even the captain let go with a belly laugh. Mitchell and Fisher stared at each other with raised eyebrows, having never seen him so jovial.

AS THE Officer of the Deck, it was Mitchell's responsibility to inspect the liberty party before allowing them ashore. Anyone who failed inspection had to stay aboard. As the liberty party prepared for inspection, Mitchell ambled through the crew's quarters to hurry along the stragglers. A buzz of excitement traveled through the crew like electricity through a lightning rod. The fatigue of the last four days' voyage had vanished. The men were high on the promise of cold beer and soft, sweet-smelling women.

Mitchell saw Smitty checking himself in the mirror for what must have been the twentieth time. His aura of aftershave was substantial. He took his hat off, combed his grease-laden hair again, and replaced his hat, tilting it forward on his head. "You devil," he said. "You're going to get you some tonight, lover-boy."

"Put it in gear, Casanova," Mitchell said. "Time to move out."

Mitchell noted that Cocoa stood by his locker, only half-dressed. He had had his dress uniforms tailor-made to fit him like a glove before they left San Francisco, but that was thirty pounds ago. Mitchell watched Cocoa puff, swear, and suck in his gut while straining to shimmy into his cotton jumper. Once dressed, he bulged from the ill-fitting uniform at every opening, stretching every seam. Mitchell shook his head and ambled on deck to inspect the liberty party.

The men sparkled in their dress white jumpers and pillbox hats rolled over at the sides, but the reek of cologne made Mitchell's eyes water. He crawled along the ranks to allow Cocoa enough time to finish dressing and sneak into the last row. He checked the sharp creases of each man's trousers, razor-cut hairlines, and buffed shoes.

Mitchell came to a full stop in front of Cocoa, who resembled a cream-filled donut being squeezed so tight that the filling oozed out. He considered keeping the cook aboard until he could change into a suitable uniform, but he was not sure Cocoa had a dress uniform that still fit, and he knew all too well how long it had been since Cocoa's last liberty. Mitchell glanced up at the bridge wing to ensure the captain was not looking and dismissed the liberty party. With a loud cheer, the men raced down the gangway.

Mitchell joined Moyer and Tedder on the quarterdeck, easing himself into a wicker chair and pulling a pack of Lucky Strikes from his breast pocket. He cocked his head as music floated from the nearest loudspeaker. The duty radioman pumped Benny Goodman over the PA system. Mitchell couldn't help tapping his foot to the swinging beat.

Bitton strolled up, settling into a chair. He pointed the stem of his pipe in the direction of the liberty party galloping down the dock. "Those men are racing as fast as they can into one hellacious binge."

"Might not be a bad idea to have a hair of the dog they're chasing," Tedder said.

At that moment, Andrew walked through the hatch carrying a tray crowned with a bottle of Jack Daniels, a bowl of ice, and four tumblers. A smile spread over each officer's face as they anticipated the sweet feeling of being tipsy before lunch.

AFTER lunch, while Andrew scrubbed dishes, Grady rambled into the galley from officer's country. "Chaplain Moyer wants to see you in the wardroom."

Andrew dried his hands and hustled forward, coming to attention before Moyer.

The room was stuffy even with the vent fans blowing full out.

"Sit down," Moyer said, swiping at the sweat meandering down the side of his face. He showed a nervous smile as Andrew sat in the chair across from him.

"I want to talk to you about a couple of issues. First, I wanted to say how sorry I am that someone defaced your statue."

"How did you know?"

"Nothing happens aboard this ship that I don't hear about." Moyer smiled again, still noticeably uncomfortable. "Any idea who did it?"

"It doesn't matter who, but it seems there are some things aboard you don't know."

"You got me there." His smile faded. He stared at his hands, which were fiddling with a paperclip. He swallowed. "There's a rumor that you're developing a close friendship with Lieutenant Mitchell."

"We talk from time to time."

"The men are calling you his puppy dog. Aboard ship that could only mean one thing. Look, when I studied to become a member of the clergy, I witnessed many examples of intimacy between men. Although I don't approve of it, I understand what loneliness does to a man."

"What are you saying?"

"I'm trying to say —" The words lodged in his throat. He fell silent, still staring at the paperclip in his hands. "Be careful. You could damage his career if things go too far."

Andrew dropped his eyes, staring at the green-felt tabletop. Heat rose to his head even though he knew he had done nothing wrong.

"I understand that Buddhists don't believe in God," Moyer said. "That's too bad. In times of confusing emotions, we Christians find comfort in asking for God's help. It makes our trials easier to bear."

"Tell me something, sir. Is your life really any easier because of your belief in a god?"

Moyer stared into Andrew's eyes for the first time. He hesitated, struggling for an answer, as if he were trying to determine if he could trust Andrew with a secret he wanted to get off his chest. He moistened the corner of his mouth with his tongue. "That's none of your business, okay?"

"I'm sorry, sir," Andrew said, holding up a hand. "I only wanted to understand. I didn't—"

"Personally speaking," Moyer cut him off. "No. In fact, the opposite is true. My belief in the Divine keeps me living in a state of hell. It's especially hard for me during these trying times because I feel that God has turned his back on me. I've spent my life trying to ease the suffering of others, but I've never gotten even a glimpse at a sign that he acknowledges my efforts, or even my existence."

Andrew nodded. Minuscule particles charged the humid air. Andrew watched them dance through the space between him and the officer. Moyer leaned across the table.

Andrew froze, somewhat startled by the ensign's gesture. He felt a buzz at his temples where his pulse seemed to throb stronger than normal. He had an overpowering urge to place his palm on Moyer's forehead and push him against his seatback.

"There's a woman at home, Sara Walker," Moyer said, "who helps people living on the poor side of the tracks. She has a close relationship with God. It is obvious from her willingness to suffer so many hardships to help others, yet, she is forever cheerful and always sees the good in everybody. But she has never once worshipped our Lord in church or even bowed her head in prayer." He inhaled a deep breath. "I asked her why she never attended church. She told me that after the death of her child, she spent what she called 'a night of nothingness.' After that, she lost faith with all traditional beliefs and developed a personal relationship with God."

"And you envy her?"

The ensign nodded. "She is with him always, while I have been abandoned. You know, people assume that the holiest people, the saints, exist in continual divine ecstasy, but that's simply not so. Many saints have been keenly aware of God's absence. There's even a name for it. It's called the Phenomenon of Darkness. Don't confuse this affliction with loss of faith. It's more like an empty feeling of unknowing. With me, this emptiness is so great that nothing touches my soul. I want God with every fiber of my being, yet, between us there is an appalling separation. At times I feel a terrible loss, that God doesn't want me. At other times there is a worse feeling, that he doesn't exist at all." Moyer cocked his head. "In your religion, do you ever have such doubts?"

"For Buddhists, God is not some separate being existing some place far away called heaven. We see the universe as one living force, made up of all the trillions upon trillions of life forms, of which you and I are a part. If you want to call this life force 'God,' I have no issue with that. That means, of course, that we are all God, that collectively we create God, like the cells of our body combine to create us."

Moyer swallowed and nodded.

"Anytime I wish to view God, I see all the various forms of life around me all melding together. If I wish to understand God, I look within my own heart, because I, too, am a manifestation of this life force. For a Buddhist, to understand one's self is to understand the whole of God."

Andrew paused, because Moyer was simply staring at him in a daze. Andrew reached across the table and gave Moyer's hand a gentle squeeze. "This Christian idea that God is separate from all other life seems very sad. I understand why you have these feelings of abandonment and doubt."

Moyer bowed his head, as if to hide the emotions boiling up from his heart.

Andrew lowered his voice to a mere whisper. "My master told me that we all have demons, fears inside our heads. These fears cause anger, hatred, greed, and envy. They in turn cause all our pain and sorrow. Overcoming these demons is the most important task a man can undertake."

Moyer raised his head and smiled sadly. "I understand. Thank you. By the way, I give services every Sunday morning on the fantail. Will you come and hear God's word?"

"No, thank you, sir. You've told me everything I need to know about your God."

ANDREW decided to take a leisurely SSS (shit, shower, and shave) while the ship was deserted and before starting dinner. He plodded to his locker and stripped to his skivvies, grabbing his cake of soap, shaving cream, razor, and a terrycloth towel.

Assuming that he would have the head to himself, he was disappointed when he heard a shower spraying full force and a drain sucking water. He inched closer with timid steps, checking to see who was there. To his surprise, Grady stood under a showerhead, his member standing full and thick, and Grady was fisting it with a look of delirium on his face.

Andrew wanted to back away, but he couldn't take his eyes off his naked friend. His gaze wandered over the smooth, dark body until it found that patch of black brush above the swollen member and those hanging balls. The sheer size of that dick was inspiring—alarmingly big, its head a lovely plum color.

Andrew's own sex stirred and his pulse beat like a jackhammer. He turned and crept to the line of sinks before someone caught him with tented skivvies while ogling his sexy friend.

Staring into the stainless steel mirror, he gripped the sink with both hands and forced himself into thinking about the dinner menu—corn chowder, stir-fried vegetables with shrimp, steamed rice, some kind of pudding—until his member softened and his pulse relaxed. He turned on the faucet, tested the water temperature, and lathered his face. He took his razor and scraped away the foam from under his nose. He had no hair on his face, but he liked to go through the ritual anyway.

The hissing shower stopped and he heard Grady drying himself. Silence. The sound of the razor scraping skin seemed loud in his ears.

Suddenly, he saw Grady's face next to his own in the mirror. Arms wrapped around Andrew's waist and hugged him from behind. He gasped, feeling hot breath on his neck. His body jerked forward and back. The feel of Grady's bare skin was instantly galvanizing.

"Baby, if God ever made beautiful, he done made it with you," Grady crooned. His fingers followed the contours of Andrew's bare chest and he gently squeezed Andrew's BB-sized nipple. Grady's other hand slid into the loose fly of Andrew's skivvies and took hold of Andrew's growing shaft. His touch felt like melting wax on Andrew's tender skin.

Andrew panicked.

"Relax Andy-boy. Juss relax and lemme make you feel good."

With his heart thumping, Andrew gripped the sink with both hands to steady himself. He involuntarily leaned into Grady's nakedness, feeling himself melt into that sumptuous skin. Grady's erection poked at his backside through his thin cotton skivvies, worming its way between his legs.

Andrew's mind froze, partly from the excitement but mostly from fear of being caught. He managed a hoarse whisper, "Please don't." His voice sounded tentative, vulnerable. He couldn't stand the sound of it.

Grady gently kneaded Andrew's genitals. "I see the way you look at Mitchell. Everybody's talkin' about how you been eyein' him and what it means."

Grady began rocking his hips with tantalizing slowness, his erection berthed between Andrew's legs. Andrew's entire body quivered, his cock poked straight up through his fly. Every spot that Grady's satiny skin touched ignited in fiery sensations.

"Someone will see us." Andrew was desperate, pleading.

"Everybody's gone ashore or standing watch. It's just you and me, pretty boy." Grady's fingers stroked Andrew's torso. He hooked both thumbs into the waistband of Andrew's skivvies and peeled them down until they dropped to the deck. Now Andrew felt Grady's hot flesh sliding between the silken cleavage of his naked thighs. Grady's hand playfully teased Andrew's cock and his lips caressed Andrew's neck.

Andrew's knees weakened as he imagined that it was Mitchell driving him into delirium. He arched his head, resting it on Grady's shoulder, moaning as he surrendered to the delicious rush of pleasure.

Grady's hips ground against Andrew's backside more needfully. Fingers gently pulled Andrew's chin sideways until Grady's lips brushed against Andrew's. They kissed, working their passion toward a delicious pinnacle. Andrew could taste him, like warm blood or hot metal, and now that he had tasted him, it was not enough. He wanted more, needed it even though he knew it would ruin him.

Grady's tongue explored and conquered Andrew's mouth while his hips bucked.

Andrew's breath came in gasps. His body contracted. He felt a sensation starting in his testicles that burst upward. He moaned into Grady's open mouth. They were nailed together, naked, shivering. Grady's hand cupped Andrew's hairless balls as a stream of thick semen spattered the stainless steel mirror above the sink. Andrew jerked violently and Grady rode him like a bronco, their mouths locked in a continuous kiss.

"What the hell is going on?"

Mitchell stood at the hatchway, his uniform starched and crisp, his hands fisted on his hips. Veins bulged out of his neck with the same fiery color as his face. "I want you men in uniform and standing in my office in five minutes."

Andrew was paralyzed, stricken, not yet fully comprehending this abrupt change in circumstances.

"Is that clear?" the lieutenant barked.

"Aye, aye, sir!" they said in breathless tandem.

THEY stood at attention beside Mitchell's desk.

"I talked with Chaplain Moyer at lunch today," Mitchell told Andrew. "He said the poop is, you're a homosexual. Apparently, everybody is trying to figure out if it's true, and what I saw is pretty convincing evidence."

"I don't know if it's true or not, sir."

"How can you not know? Do you like girls or men?"

"Sir, I've had no experience with girls. Raised in a boy's school, a monastery, and now the Navy, I've always been surrounded by boys, never girls. I've lived a celibate life. But in my boarding school, there was an English boy, Clifford. We were inseparable. We never had sex, but I can tell you dead-on that I love him. We slept in the same dorm room, and after the monks extinguished the lamps, he would slip into bed with me and we cuddled together. No sex, only sleeping in each other's arms."

Andrew paused. There was no trace of embarrassment in his confession. "When we were older, he showed me how to masturbate and we did that all the time, though never to each other. You see, Lieutenant, waking up with Clifford, feeling his body, and smelling his boyish scent was the most loving experience of my life. Sometimes he's all I think about, my time with him. I often think that he and I were all that ever mattered. So if loving another boy makes me a homosexual, then I guess I am."

Mitchell pictured the two lads curled together in adolescent love. A taste of envy softened his anger. "Did you ever want to have sex with Clifford?"

"If he had asked me, I'd have done it in a heartbeat. I'd do anything for him, but it never crossed our minds."

Mitchell nodded; his eyes encouraged Andrew to say more.

"I don't want to be a homosexual, but I have to admit, I found it thrilling when Grady was stroking me. And when he kissed me, an explosion went off inside my chest and I couldn't breathe. I was so scared and excited and confused, but it wasn't like being with Clifford. Clifford was tender and loving. Grady made a volcano erupt inside of me." He paused, as if searching for something to add. "Now you know as much as I do, sir."

Mitchell turned to Grady. "What do you have to say for yourself, sailor?"

"Suh, I don't know what came over me. I knows Andy is a little fruity because of the way he looks at you with those needful eyes. And being stuck on board while everybody's ashore poundin' pussy, I thought I could slip it to him, shoot my load, and no harm done."

A thunderbolt struck Mitchell. Grady's suggestion that Andrew was sexually interested in him made him realize that the energy hovering between him and Andrew was some form of sexual intimacy. Mitchell stayed obdurately silent, remembering their conversations, those cherished moments on the midnight-to-four watches and the friendly conversations in the galley. He finally turned to Andrew, but he couldn't look in the sailor in the eyes.

"I'll file a report that states Washington seduced you and that you wanted no part in it. You'll both sign it. It means prison time and a dishonorable discharge for Washington, but he should have thought of that beforehand."

Andrew shook his head. "You'll ruin his life. He deserves another chance."

Mitchell momentarily reconsidered his decision, but said, "You like Shakespeare, don't you, Andy, *Henry V*? Isn't there a line that says: 'Sir, you show great mercy if you give him life, after the taste of much correction'?"

"Yes, sir, but Henry replies, 'Alas, your too much love and care of me are heavy orisons 'gainst this poor wretch! If little faults, proceeding on distemper, shall not be wink'd at, how shall we stretch our eye when capital crimes, chew'd, swallow'd and digested, appear before us?'"

"Nevertheless, I've made up my mind."

"If you bust Grady, sir, you'll have to bust me too. As soon as he touched me, I wanted him as much as he wanted me, maybe more so."

"Don't be stupid. This means brig time at Pendleton."

"I could have stopped it, but didn't. I am every bit as guilty."

Mitchell felt a new level of respect creep into his steeling gaze. He knew his duty, knew exactly what must be done, but a switch turned in his head and he made an uncomfortable decision.

"We'll play it your way. I won't report what I've seen, but I'm transferring Washington off this ship at the earliest opportunity. It will take a week to process the paperwork. Meantime, I'll be watching both of you like a hawk. Is that clear?"

"Sir, perhaps you should transfer me instead," Andrew suggested.

"Negative!" Mitchell felt a stab of panic in his chest. "You're too valuable to this ship."

After dismissing the sailors, Mitchell sat at his desk, staring at a stack of communications that he should have been filing. He felt defeated and confused and haunted by the certainty that he had done the wrong thing, but the mere thought of Andrew doing brig time, that beautifully unique spirit locked in a dark cell, sent shivers up his spine.

Chapter Twelve

April 24, 1942—1400 hours

ON THE southern outskirts of town, a secluded stretch of yellow beach scorched under the tropical sun. Cocoa settled himself on the sand under a curving palm tree. He pulled off his shoes and socks and leaned against the tree trunk, enjoying the breeze on his face, the sun on his toes.

From here he could see the town and the gray warships in the harbor: a cruiser, two destroyers, four troop transports and one dilapidated tanker. He reached into the paper sack next to him and pulled out an icy can of beer. He grabbed the opener hanging with his dog tags on the chain around his neck and punched two triangular holes in the top of the can. Foam oozed over his fingers. He drew the can to his lips and knocked his head back. The beer, purchased twenty minutes earlier, was still cold enough to make his chest hurt. He drained the can, let go with a drawn-out burp, and tossed the empty onto the sand.

He grabbed another can, punched two more holes. Sipping this beer, he savored the bitter flavor. As the first beer settled in his empty stomach, he felt the buzz hit his head, that keenly gratifying feeling of being borderline drunk in the early afternoon. A pint bottle of whiskey hid in the paper bag, getting cold beside the other beers, but he was saving that for later.

He leaned against the tree, listening to the surf caressing the sand, a steady rhythm that lulled his mind into a fog of slow sensations. Under the sound of surf was that beautiful perception of silence—no growling ship's boilers, no knocking engines, no foul-mouthed sailors bitching about pulling K.P., and no smart-ass comments about the food. Nothing here but a beer, a beach, and some whiskey to look forward to. It was all he wanted. He needed it like he needed another breath to fill his lungs.

He relaxed, loosening that stone that was lodged in his chest. The one that now felt as small as a spit wad, but sometimes felt as large as a ship's anchor.

He drained the beer, tossed the can alongside the other empty, and reached into the paper bag. He smiled as his fingers glided over the pint bottle. Changing his mind, he latched on to another cold can, teasing himself with anticipation. He popped two triangular holes in the can again and sipped, knowing he had a lovely day in front of him. He didn't want to get too drunk and end up sleeping his time away. *Better to go slow and enjoy this freedom of being nobody, being nothing more than a drunken sand crab on the beach, not having to act the part of the sailor, or the cook, or the man, or any other damn thing.*

He knew that he acted differently toward each person on the ship, that his demeanor changed when talking with Mitchell as opposed to Hudson, or Grady, or the skipper. Each man engaged a subtly different set of responses. He once thought that the sum of all those different responses made up the man, but lately he had begun to think that the man, Cocoa, was that blurry indefinable mass hovering behind all those facades.

He laughed for the sheer pleasure of hearing himself. Yes, he thought, he'd be that gray mass for a few precious hours. Later, he knew, hunger would drive him into town for a cheap dinner and a good woman. Or maybe, he thought, it's the other way around. He smiled to himself and sipped more beer. Right then it was enough to feel the sun on his toes and cold beer running down his throat, and he intended to enjoy every second of that simplicity.

ANDREW was plucking a chicken when Mitchell trooped into the galley.

"Seaman Waters, we received a priority action dispatch," Mitchell said. "Orders from CincPac—Commander in Chief, Pacific Fleet. The skipper wants to sail as soon as we can gather the liberty party aboard. You will accompany me ashore to help round them up."

Seaman Waters? What happen to Andy? Andrew knew then that their friendship would never be the same.

On their way to the gangplank, Bitton intercepted Mitchell on the quarterdeck. The captain took him by the arm and drew him away from Andrew, but not quite out of hearing distance. Andrew overheard everything.

"The orders are direct from Admiral Nimitz," Bitton said, holding up the flimsy sheet of carbon-blurred dispatch. "We sail to Bora Bora, pick up a detachment of marines, and make flank speed into the hot zone to an island called Guadalcanal. We drop the marines on the beach and hightail it back here. I want to sail in two hours."

"Might be tough to round up everyone, but we'll do our best, sir."

"I'm counting on you, Nathan. Whoever we can't find gets left ashore until we return."

Andrew realized that Mitchell had selected him to help gather the liberty party out of fear of leaving Grady and him on the ship together without supervision.

They marched down the rue Pomare on their way to the center of town. Embarrassed by Mitchell's lack of trust, Andrew felt compelled to say something, but he had already said all there was to say about the washroom incident. He waited for Mitchell to open the conversation. Mitchell, however, walked with his jaw locked tight, as if he were afraid to open his mouth lest something dangerous fly out.

A nameless, irascible obstacle lodged between them, separating each from the relationship they had so carefully constructed. Andrew suspected that their friendship had abruptly ended primarily because Mitchell was now aware of that intimate presence that hovered between them, and he was afraid—terrified of his own feelings. He wondered if Mitchell was perceptive enough to realize it too, but he would not broach the topic.

They spoke only in the line of duty. Mitchell gave an order, "Check that bar across the street while I check this one."

Andrew returned an illusively contemptuous, "Aye, aye, sir."

They worked their way toward the center of town, checking every bar, brothel, hotel, and restaurant. On the rue de Paul Gauguin they ran into Stokes strolling arm in arm with a pretty girl.

Stokes introduced his companion, Miss Chew-Gin Lee, and explained that her mother was a native islander and her father was a Chinese merchant who owned a local grocery store. He said that her name was Chinese for "autumn pearl" but that she was prettier than any pearl he'd ever seen.

Chew-Gin blushed a lovely shade of pink while keeping her eyes focused on the ground. She demurely leaned into his solid mass, as if dreamily leaning against a shade tree on a summer afternoon.

Andrew noted her finely embroidered dress and her impeccable manners. Chew-Gin was clearly no prostitute. It was equally clear that Stokes was smitten by the way he gazed into her face. Stokes, like himself, had fallen deeply in love within a matter of hours. Andrew wondered if this was natural or if the pressures of war somehow created these desperate feelings in the blink of an eye.

As Mitchell ordered Stokes to report aboard, said that the *Pilgrim* was shoving off, a fearful expression ripped across his features. He pulled her closer, unable to respond. He finally blurted out, "But, sir, we've only had an afternoon together."

"I can't help that, sailor," Mitchell replied. "On your way to the ship, stop at the Royal Papeete Hotel. You'll find Ensign Fisher there. If he's not in the restaurant or the bar, ask at the front desk to see if he's checked into a room. Tell him that leave is canceled. Got that?"

"Aye, aye, sir."

"And Stokes," Mitchell's voice dropped as he said, somewhat humorously, "I'm sure she's a wonderful girl, but don't even think of going AWOL on me. We'll be back here inside of a week and she'll be in your arms again."

"Aye, sir."

COCOA shuffled along the outlying streets off the rue Jeanne d'Arc. The street was lined with palm trees and nipa shacks. He searched for a run-down barroom or shabby whorehouse where he could linger at a table, nurse a whiskey and beer chasers through the evening, and perhaps enjoy some chitchat with an island girl.

The first bar he passed was Quinn's, a typical waterfront establishment. But it was already half full and getting rowdy. *No,* he thought, *won't do.* He found a semi-open-air dance hall attached to a Chinese restaurant where, for a reasonable price, they served a plate of chow mein and fried bananas along with a glass of beer.

He stood at the doorway, scanning the patrons and smelling the musky blend of perfume, native tobacco, and frying oil. He recognized only one sailor, an old acquaintance whose name had slipped his mind. Cocoa waved cordially as he crossed the room and sat at the corner table.

After eating his fill, he sipped his beer and watched a sailor dance with a bargirl to some lively music from an Edison phonograph. In addition to the dance girls, there were a dozen prostitutes congregated at one end of the unpolished wooden bar. Cocoa watched a sailor walk up to one of them to ask how much. The girl motioned for him to bend down to her level, and when he did, she whispered her price in his ear. The sailor nodded. She giggled and they disappeared out the back doorway where a lane lined with nipa huts disappeared into the dusk.

Half a dozen sailors from the *Pilgrim* crowded through the door, and Hudson was among them. Cocoa considered moving on, but he liked the feel of the place and the music suited him. He watched Hudson grab the first girl he passed and haul her to the dance floor. The big man moved across the floor like some loose-jointed animal, sliding his feet in extravagant patterns. His left hand held the girl against his loins while his right hand roamed over her backside. She tried to break free of his groping hand but he held her tight, laughing as he spun her around. He laughed the kind of arrogant guffaw that made other men want to slug his face; they seldom did, however.

The men from the *Pilgrim* took over two tables at the edge of the dance floor, ordering pitchers of beer and a bottle of island hooch. They talked in exaggerated voices as they surveyed the room, as if expecting some show of admiration from the others. But everyone ignored their bravado.

After a time, Hudson joined the group and added his voice to the flaunting banter. By the time the drinks came, they seemed vaguely indignant to the perceived snub, which dampened their mood and visibly angered Hudson. He downed a shot of fiery hooch, chased it with a full glass of beer, and poured himself another round.

Cocoa's attention alighted on a woman with slim legs and silky hair that cascaded over her hybrid-brown shoulders. Her body was covered with a cloth wrap that was the same color as the pink orchid she had tucked into her hair. She was a dancer, the one Hudson had dragged onto the floor.

Cocoa shoved his empty plate aside and ordered a whiskey from the hostess, but he changed his mind. "Honey," he yelled after her, "make that a Rum Collins. One that will grow hair on my chest."

He lit an Owl cigar and smoked it neatly, connoisseur-like, rolling the cigar this way and that while he sipped his drink. He felt contempt for Hudson, who always chewed the ends of his cigars. Cocoa nodded at the dance girl with the pink flower in her hair. She smiled and sauntered to his table. He saw why she made a point of not smiling before then. With her mouth closed, she was rather pretty.

"You buy me whiskey?" she said in broken English.

"Sure thing, Kitten. Sit right down." Cocoa signaled the hostess for another round.

At the other tables, Smitty gulped his beer and slammed his mug on the tabletop. "This fuckin' place is dead. Let's find a joint with live music and prettier girls."

"These whores look fine to me," Skeeter Banks said, scanning the room. "Say, isn't that Cocoa horning in on Hudson's girl?"

Hudson turned to stare at the corner table. His eyes narrowed as the girl sitting with Cocoa glanced at him with a patronizing grin. She shimmied closer to Cocoa, took hold of his arm, and snuggled up to him.

"Say, Hudson," Smitty said, "that fuckin' bitch is playing you for a sucker."

Skeeter laughed. "She dumped you for that smelly ol' cook. What gives with that?"

Hudson swallowed a double shot of hooch. He stood and crossed the room with three quick steps, grabbed the girl's arm, and yanked her to her feet.

"This bitch is mine." Hudson glared at Cocoa. "You got anything to say?"

Nausea gripped Cocoa's gut as he looked into Hudson's whiskey-eyed face. He paused for an instant to make sure that his voice would sound smooth and without any trace of fear.

"Take her. Plenty more where she came from."

Hudson snorted contemptuously. Cocoa could only stare as Hudson dragged the girl to his table. He sat on his chair and pulled the girl onto his lap, wrapping his arms around her to keep her there. She struggled to free herself, but he had her arms pinned to her side and she only managed to squirm on his lap, a movement that brought a lewd smile to the big man's face.

"That's right honey, you keep rubbin' that spot with your hot little fanny."

She leaned into Hudson to bite his shoulder, but he slapped her face, hard, stunning her. The room went silent except for the Andrew Sisters crooning on the phonograph. All eyes watched as Hudson grabbed her jaw and turned her head to look into his eyes. "You little spitfire, you're gonna sit right here while I finish my beer, then you and me are going out back and you're gonna straddle the best cock in the

Navy." He glanced around the table as if to assure himself that no one would challenge his boast.

At that moment, Mitchell and Andrew ambled though the front door and scanned the room. Mitchell said with an authoritative voice, "You men from the *Pilgrim*, liberty is canceled. Fall-in on the street."

Hudson's lip lifted, baring his upper teeth in a gesture that was somewhere between a sneer and a snarl. "I ain't going nowhere until I've had me some of this little bitch right here." He brutally pinched the woman's breast, and she shrieked.

"All right, Hudson, that will do. Unhand that woman and fall-in."

Cocoa watched the two men glaring eye to eye. He waited for Hudson to drop his gaze and bow to the prestige of authority standing before him.

The room went still. The Andrew Sisters' song came to an end and the phonograph repeated a harsh scratching noise.

After a dozen interminable seconds of watching the hostility seething behind the big man's face, Cocoa understood that Mitchell had made a serious blunder. He was enmeshed in an explosive situation, because Hudson was visibly grappling with the realization that the officer was ever so casually taking away his prize. *With his customary arrogance,* Cocoa thought, *Mitchell had stripped away Hudson's dignity in front of his shipmates, which was a dangerous mistake.*

Hudson leaped to his feet, dropping the woman and kicking his chair across the dance floor. His eyes zeroed in on the lieutenant's face as he crossed the room with an animal-like trot. His right hand balled into a fist, cocked and ready to knock Mitchell into next week. He lunged, drove his fist forward while his eyes never left his target. But before he connected with Mitchell's wide-open mouth and bugged-out eyes, Andrew tackled the big man at the knees and they both fell sideways, sprawling on the gritty floorboards.

Hudson's legs unflexed and, with the speed of a cat, he jumped to his feet, upsetting a table and spraying mugs of beer in all directions. Men scrambled to get out of his way. Mitchell recovered himself and called Hudson to attention, but the big man ignored him. He grabbed Andrew by his black neckerchief, pulled Andrew's face up to fist level, and smashed Andrew once, twice, a third time. He let go of the necktie and Andrew tumbled backward with the fourth devastating blow. Hudson took a quick half step and savagely kicked Andrew's gut.

As the big man stepped back to deliver another kick, Mitchell tackled him, knocking them both to the floor.

Hudson hit the floorboards and rolled like a log crashing down a hillside. A crowd of spectators circled the three men. Andrew lay unconscious while Mitchell held his head up, trying to revive him. A deep cut over Andrew's left eye bled profusely down his face. Mitchell's fingers probed the mangled jaw, skull, and neck for broken bones.

Hudson staggered to his feet and paced to and fro, waiting for either Andrew or Mitchell to rise off the floor so he could continue the drubbing.

Cocoa found the whole episode indigestible. He knew Andrew had thrown himself in the line of fire because Andrew had feelings for the officer. He'd seen the way Andrew looked at Mitchell. He didn't approve of those feelings, but he thought Andrew had done an honorable thing. And even though Cocoa agreed with the unwritten Navy code that a strong man has every right to beat the pulp out of a weaker one, given enough provocation, there was something in the ferocity of Hudson's attack that went beyond the code, something sinister, as if Hudson's hatred of Andrew had somehow caused the whole incident to happen in the first place.

Cocoa mumbled to himself, "Bastard's got it in for the boy, hated Andy from day one. Somebody should stuff his weenie in a bun and chow down." Cocoa swallowed the last bit of rum with two gulps and slammed the glass on the table. He lumbered to his feet and belched. "What the fuck," he said. "God hates a coward."

He could see Hudson was unsteady from too much booze. It might be enough of an advantage. He squared his shoulders and moved from one foot to the other, testing his movement. He felt fine. He hadn't had enough rum to slow him down, but he wished he had on his regular, loose-fitting uniform. He felt too restricted in his liberty dress whites. Cocoa walked over to Mitchell, who was bent over Andrew. Blood from the cut over Andrew's eye had drenched the front of his white jumper.

Cocoa rubbed his hands on his pant legs to wipe the sweat off before he faced Hudson. "You're pretty hot stuff with a boy, asshole. What have you got when they come a little bigger?"

Hudson's face colored to a vibrant shade of purple, but he smiled as he bent his knees and leaned forward, lowering his center of gravity.

"You're beggin' for it, you crummy son-of-a-bitch, and I'm the man to give it to you."

Everyone surrounded Hudson and the cook. The two men moved in a circle, facing one another with fists held high. Someone in the crowd yelled, "Fight!" The cry was echoed on the street. Locals and sailors crowded into the bar while men along the walls stood on tables and chairs to see.

Before the first blow was struck, however, Chief Ogden jostled through the crowd with his arms raised over his head. Everyone assumed he would break things up, but it only took Cocoa an instant to realize that Ogden intended to referee the fight. At that moment, Cocoa cut the air with his right fist and connected with Hudson's jaw, knocking his head back six inches.

Hudson reeled backward, shook his head, and charged forward. They exchanged blows. Whenever Hudson moved in close, Ogden stepped in to pry them apart.

Cocoa was grateful for the chief, for in the clinches Hudson could do more damage with his heavy body blows. But with regulation boxing, Cocoa used his superior footwork to sidestep those blows and move in with skillful jabs to Hudson's face.

The crowd roared encouragement to both men, but the majority were clearly pulling for Cocoa.

After a dozen swings and misses and as many lunges, which Cocoa sidestepped, Cocoa saw that the big man was already tiring. It took more energy to swing and miss than to connect, and Cocoa figured if he could keep sidestepping those powerful swipes he would soon have the upper hand. He jabbed and hooked effectively, intently executing his plan.

Hudson did connect every now and then. Cocoa took several staggering blows to the face and gut. He tasted the blood oozing through his mouth, but his vision stayed clear and he moved better than Hudson, whose swings were wild and dangerous. It was obvious that Hudson went for a knockout blow with every punch.

Hudson swayed to and fro between swings. He blinked his eyes constantly, as if trying to clear his vision.

Sensing an advantage, Cocoa stepped up his offensive, aggressively taking it to the big man with clockwork precision. Every blow landed on Hudson's face, opening up several deep cuts.

Blood oozed into Hudson's eyes. He swung blindly.

The cook fought carefully, passing up one chance after another to deliver a knockout punch. He was not ready to let the big man off the hook. He intended to cut Hudson's face to ribbons before ending the fight, so that Hudson would think twice before ever tangling with him again. Hudson would remember this fight every time he looked in a mirror.

Cocoa felt good physically, and the pain in his jaw was not too bad. He still moved well and his only concern was that Hudson would connect with one of his powerful swings and knock him out cold, or worse, knock him down where Hudson could finish him off with kicks to the gut. He was taking a risk by prolonging the fight, but he kept at it, cutting Hudson's face with one good jab after another until he had lashed both the big man's eyes shut and opened up several more gashes on his cheeks. Cocoa landed so many blows that his hands cramped from the pain.

The crowd grew impatient. Someone yelled, "Take him out, Cocoa. Drop him like a turd."

The front of Hudson's dress jumper had turned solid red. He made animal noises, sniffing at the blood blocking his nostrils. He lunged this way and that, obviously desperate to land one good blow before his strength gave out. Through his blindness, his big right fist finally connected with something solid. As it did, his feet slipped out from under him and he fell flat on his butt. The room went silent. Something clicked off in Hudson's mind, and he slumped forward, spent.

BEHIND the ring of men, Mitchell had brought Andrew to consciousness and helped him to his feet. Andrew scrutinized the scene and grabbed Mitchell by the shirt, begging from bloody lips for Mitchell to stop the fight.

Mitchell cut through the ring of spectators and stepped between the combatants with his arms raised, bellowing, "You men stop fighting this instant!"

Cocoa lowered his fist.

Hudson, however, must have been beyond hearing or seeing anything. He swung an iron fist that connected with the side of the lieutenant's face, knocking the officer off his feet and into the crowd of onlookers. That was when Hudson slipped on a pool of his own blood and went down like a sack of spuds.

Andrew stooped over Mitchell, slapping the officer's face until he regained consciousness. When his eyes finally popped open, Cocoa grabbed him by the shoulders and lifted him off the floor. "Better get you both to the ship and put some raw steaks on your faces before the swelling starts."

Andrew and Mitchell gazed at each other's broken and bruising faces, and through their pain, they both grinned.

The sky had darkened. Palm trees bent before the wind and rain began to fall. The downpour pummeled them all the way to the ship.

An hour after the men were aboard, the *Pilgrim* steamed out of Papeete harbor, gray as the night with her portholes and deck lights darkened.

Chapter Thirteen

April 25, 1942—0500 hours

THE *Pilgrim* drove northeast at twenty-two knots through a swirling sea, heading straight for Bora Bora. The crew grew edgy. Mitchell overheard the men calling their hurried departure "a major piece of grab-ass," which could only spell trouble.

In the rain-drenched dawn, she maneuvered into Povai Bay, berthed alongside the fuel depot, and began taking on fuel. Mitchell waited under the quarterdeck awning, watching an Army troop truck thunder onto the wharf and stop beside the ship. The canvas flaps in the rear opened and a detachment of armed marines scrambled out. They hoisted crates of communication gear on their shoulders and marched aboard.

Mitchell greeted the squad leader, Lieutenant Bernie Hurlburt, who stood at medium height but seemed shorter in his damp fatigues. Thick, black eyebrows framed his piercing brown eyes. His face was square and flat, as if during childhood someone had smashed his nose with an iron skillet. Hurlburt commanded a dozen men—one sergeant, one corporal, ten privates—all trained in guerilla warfare. He saluted Mitchell and they clasped hands.

Both men had firm handshakes. They glared eye to eye, measuring each other's mettle.

"Chief Ogden," Mitchell said, "show these men to their quarters and stow this gear." He turned to Hurlburt. "Lieutenant, please join the ship's officers in the wardroom for a briefing as soon as your men are squared away. By the way, I have a man doing brig time. I'll expect your men to provide a security guard while you're aboard. The chief will show you to the brig."

Thirty minutes later, with the ship headed out to sea, Hurlburt joined the *Pilgrim*'s officers around the green felt table. They sipped coffee and munched on sugar donuts while waiting for the captain.

Hurlburt had fastidiously dry-shaved, changed uniforms, and rebuffed his combat boots. His face, however, was as green as his fatigues, no doubt caused by the ship rolling though ten-foot swells.

"Say, this coffee's delicious," Hurlburt said.

"Wait until you get a load of breakfast," Moyer said. "You'll think you're in your mama's kitchen. That is, if you still have an appetite by then. You look a bit green."

"I'm not used to my stomach sloshing up and down like a yo-yo."

"No doubt you're accustomed to riding in heavy transports," Mitchell said. "These tin cans get tossed around in a rough sea. Right now is not so bad, but we're heading right up the ass of a bad storm. You and your men may find the going pretty tough."

Before Hurlburt could respond, Captain Bitton entered the wardroom and stalked to the head of the table. He cleared his throat. "Gentlemen, the Joint Forces have been kicked around the Pacific for five months, and the brass is finally fed up enough to launch an assault. A joint operation, dubbed Operation Watchtower, is being planned by Admiral Nimitz at Pearl and MacArthur in Melbourne. The first targets for invasion are the Solomons, followed by New Guinea and New Britain. The operation is still in the planning stage and it will be months before we land troops, but the *Pilgrim* is now taking part in a top-secret intelligence-gathering operation targeting an island the Japs call Gadarukanaru; we Americans call it Guadalcanal. The *Pilgrim* will drop Hurlburt and his squad on the island to gather and report information on troop strength, enemy ship movement, and any progress the Japs make on building an airstrip. This mission will be known as Operation Green Stealth."

Hurlburt stood to address the officers. "Gentlemen, Guadalcanal is Japan's southernmost outpost. It lies ten degrees below the equator. Ninety miles long and thirty miles wide, it has an eight-thousand-foot-high mountain range that cuts up its middle like a backbone. The only possible spot for military operations is a narrow strip along the northern coast. It has a deep-water port and is one of the few islands in the Solomon chain with enough level ground for an airstrip that can accommodate heavy bombers. Before the Japs came, there were only a few Catholic missions for the natives. Now we figure it stations over two thousand Japs. This island is key for securing the entire area. Once again the Navy gets to taxi the marines into the hot zone, and we thank the Navy for their part. Fortunately for you boys, it's an in-and-out operation. You drop us on the beach and hightail it to safety. My men will setup a mobile base and stay hidden until our troops charge ashore. We are strictly an observe-and-report operation. If we're lucky, the Japs will never know we're there."

Mitchell had a queer feeling that something was wrong. He was not sure if it was Hurlburt's arrogance that didn't sit well or something about the mission. He gave the captain a pensive look and asked if a submarine would be better suited for the drop-off, being that secrecy was such a critical element.

"Right on target, Nathan. The *Tigerfish* was slotted for the job, but we lost contact with her four days ago. Besides, we can get in and out three times as fast as any sub, not to mention that God is looking out for us; He's created a typhoon over the Cook Islands that's heading due west. It's the perfect shield. No other ships will sail within two hundred miles of that storm. I plan to ride that baby's coattails right into the slot."

"Sir," Fisher said, "that's an arduous haul even in a normal sea, but riding the back of a typhoon? Is she up to the task?"

Bitton nodded. "The risk is high, but it could save thousands of lives. The invasion is too critical to go in without knowing what we're up against, and the sooner we know, the better." Bitton's gaze bore into each face, one at a time, as if he were assuring himself that everyone understood the mission's significance. "We'll cruise at maximum speed under radio silence, lights out, and we won't waste time zigzagging. There shouldn't be anyone close to the storm anyway. We'll hit the island in the darkest part of night. I want the whaleboats painted black so no one spots them taking the lieutenant's party ashore."

"Do I understand you correctly, Lieutenant," Tedder said, "that you intend to live for two or more months undercover? Can you carry enough supplies for that long a stay?"

"We're trained to live off the land. I'd like to take food, but we'll have our hands full moving the radio equipment from camp to camp."

"What will you eat?" Fisher asked.

"Bananas, papayas, crocodiles, lizards, fish, snakes, insects."

"Well, Lieutenant," Tedder said, "let me know what medical supplies you need. God willing, we'll have enough to spare."

COMPARING the stability of the *Pilgrim* to his last ship, the *Indianapolis*, a cruiser four times the *Pilgrim*'s size, Andrew had noted in his first days aboard that the destroyer's rolls and plunges were more severe. But even with that exaggerated movement, he had kept his sea legs, a fact that gave him a twinge of satisfaction. But after two days of chasing a typhoon, enduring fifteen-foot swells that created gut-heaving dips and vaults, he realized that his pride was premature.

The ship groaned over every wave. The wind screeched at a pitch that hurt his ears. Andrew, like everyone else, had not slept for two days because the ship rode like a bucking bronco, with a paroxysm of twists, lunges, and plunges—the whole menu. He had to constantly concentrate on keeping his stomach calm and his feet on the deck. The black, puffy crescents under his bloodshot eyes were only partly due to the fight with Hudson. Most of the swelling had subsided, but bruises still curled under both cheeks and his lips were a raw, raspberry color. The pain had diminished into a dull ache, but he was so exhausted from lack of sleep that his head was numb and he had difficulty forming thoughts.

Cooking was nearly impossible. Andrew stood at the stove, grilling a shallot pancake coated with sesame seeds, which he held down on the grill with a spatula to keep it from hopping around like a jumping bean. It was a slow process, because he could cook only one pancake at a time.

The ship lunged and, once again, Andrew's butt hit the deck with a thump. He rolled sideways, tumbled under the sinks, braced one arm through the plumbing, and lifted himself to his knees. As the ship rolled again, he tasted bile against the back of his throat. He swallowed hard, managing to control it, but he leaned over an empty bucket in case.

Cocoa stood across the galley with one hand clutching the overhead pipes, swaying with the ship. His face glowed reddish purple and his left eye was swollen to a slit, making it appear locked into a permanent wink.

Andrew yelled, "Two days of this—how long will it last?"

"How long will what last?" Cocoa said as a grin spread his puffed-up lips. Cocoa was in his element. For two days it had been his turn to show Andrew how to cook—that is, how to prepare food as the galley careened up, down, and sideways. Cocoa instructed without a trace of arrogance, and between the fight with Hudson and the cooking lessons, they had formed a definite, albeit fragile, camaraderie.

"So tell me," Cocoa said. "What gives with you and Mister Mitchell? He ain't been down to see you since Papeete. You two have a lovers' spat?"

"He's got better things to do than watch this room spin around."

"True, but that never stopped him before Papeete. I figured you two were sweethearts, the way he hung around here, and you with those puppy-dog eyes for him. Now he doesn't give you the time of day. Could it be that you're not as special now that your face ain't so pretty?" Cocoa chuckled to himself, clearly enjoying a good tease.

Grady stumbled through the hatchway to get the appetizers for the officer's lunch. As the smell of shallot pancakes hit his nose, he held his stomach and vomited, barely missing Cocoa as he splattered the deck. Fortunately for him, he didn't splash any on his pristine white coat.

"Not again," Cocoa yelled. "Get your black ass on deck for some air. I'll clean this up." Cocoa grabbed the mop and dropped it into a sink. He turned on the hot water and tossed in a dash of soap. "Never thought I'd end up nursemaidin' a—" He looked at Andrew with an apology etched across his face. He turned off the water, wrung out the mop, and swabbed the deck.

Andrew decided to make a Caesar salad and, for dessert, vanilla ice cream with a crushed cherry sauce. He gathered the ingredients, shredded the greens, cracked the eggs over a bowl, and added a splash of oil, mustard, and a tin of anchovies. He located a wheel of Parmesan in the pantry and sliced off a wedge, then grated a snowy mound of cheese. The ship lunged and he fell again. He crawled to his feet, poured the rest of the ingredients into a bowl, and whisked with practiced flicks of his wrist. Now he focused on the cherry sauce. After taking a carton of canned cherries, he crushed them, added syrup, a dash of brown sugar, and stirred it all together.

Once the sauces were done, he pulled a slab of beef from the walk-in refrigerator and proceeded to slice off thick, red steaks, concentrating on the knife as if it were a precision instrument. He grilled them only enough to warm the center, added a dab of horseradish, and placed them on plates already filled with salad.

He studied the menu: shallot pancake appetizers, rare prime on a bed of Caesar salad, ice cream with crushed cherry dessert, and cheese with yellow pears to go with coffee. It was not as much as he wanted, but it was the best he could do while riding a roller coaster.

Grady stumbled through the hatchway to take the officers' dinner to the wardroom. Stokes was right on his heels.

"Are you ready?" Stokes asked Andrew. He zeroed in on the bowls of cherry-covered ice cream sitting on the counter while moistening his lower lip with his tongue.

Andrew dropped a spoon into a bowl and pushed it toward him. "Knock yourself out. I made plenty."

"Jesus, thanks."

Andrew stuffed a knapsack with food—everything on the officer's menu, including a container of ice cream. He walked to the pantry and positioned his body so that Cocoa could not see what he was up to. He pulled a whiskey bottle from behind two large jars, filled a flask, and tucked the flask in his hip pocket. He hid the whiskey again and, returning to the galley, donned a pea coat and watch cap.

He turned to Stokes, who had a layer of cream around his lips. "Take the thermos and I'll take this." Andrew slung the knapsack over his shoulder.

They trudged down the center passageway, cut through the mess hall, and stepped onto the deck outside, clutching at the hatchway stanchions. The wind slanted rain horizontally across the deck. It whipped Andrew's pant legs and drove drops of water into his face with stinging force. They inched along the deck, groping for handholds.

The bow plunged into a trough and disappeared into the next wave, spouting streams of water as it rose again. Water funneled down the deck. A moment later a wall of black water rose over the port side fifteen feet higher than Andrew's head. When it seemed the wall was about to fall on them, the ship lurched upward, balanced on top of the wave, and plunged. Another wall rose on the starboard side. Watching the *Pilgrim*'s hull twist over every wave, Andrew wondered how much stress the twenty-five-year-old vessel could tolerate. If she foundered, he knew, there was no hope of a rescue ship reaching them.

Andrew felt himself panting from an intense, nervy rush as he crawled toward the fantail with Stokes dogging him. He used both hands to grab hold of different parts of the ship as they struggled by the torpedo launchers. Out of nowhere, a wave collapsed upon them, rocketing them along the deck. Andrew kept from being swept overboard by locking an arm though the port depth-charge rack. Stokes saved himself by latching on to Andrew's legs.

They scrambled to their feet and ran before another wave could catch them. Stokes threw open the hatch leading into the airless cell that was used for the brig. Andrew peered down into the faintly luminous compartment. An armed marine sat in front of the cell, which surprised Andrew until he remembered that whenever marines were stationed aboard a Navy ship, they always took responsibility for guarding prisoners.

They descended the ladder and the marine stood while loosely holding his M1 rifle.

"We've brought dinner for the prisoner," Stokes said.

"I need to check that bag. This prisoner gets only bread and water."

"Give me a break, corporal," Andrew said. "I can't bake bread in this storm."

"Orders are orders."

Andrew set his knapsack on the deck but didn't lift the cover. He pulled the flask from his hip pocket and unscrewed the lid. The pungent aroma of whiskey filtered through the air. Andrew winked at the corporal. "Medicine," he said, in a drawn-out way, and told the guard that he intended to pour about half of the whiskey into the coffee and give the corporal the other half for safekeeping. Andrew suggested that the corporal cop a smoke break in the chow hall while they fed the prisoner.

The corporal nodded as Stokes unscrewed the thermos lid and Andrew added a healthy dose of whiskey. He handed the flask to the corporal, who disappeared up the ladder and out the hatch.

Behind a wall of bars, Hudson sat cross-legged on the deck. He was seminaked and his shaved head leaned forward, as if bent in prayer. Bruises shaded everything from chin to scalp, his eyes were swollen, and pus oozed out of the eyelids like tears. His lips were easily twice their normal size and his left ear was so swollen it resembled a cauliflower.

"Hey, sailor, chowtime," Stokes said.

Andrew knelt on the deck and pulled two containers from the knapsack.

Hudson lifted his head and tried to focus through the slits of his puffy eyelids. "Thought you were gyrenes come to nursemaid me." He strained to stand, and with bandaged hands grabbed hold of the bars to steady himself. "Say, is that ice cream? Sweet Jesus, pass that here, quick. I'm a starved man."

Andrew stuck a spoon into the ice cream and passed it through a hole in the bars. Hudson lunged for it and wolfed it down, smearing gobs of cherry-colored cream around his lips as he shoveled it in. Through a mouthful he said, "Say, rookie, show me your face."

Andrew moved closer and Hudson inspected the purple bruises and swollen left cheek.

"Lord, I did some damage, but nothin' that won't heal proper. Rookie, you should know better than to come between two men in a fist fight."

"Had to. It was the only way to save you."

"Save me? You was saving me? Ha! Listen rookie, I don't blame you. I mean, everybody knows you have a crush on him. And to tell you the truth, he is the whitest son of a bitch that ever wore a gold braid, but don't try to bullshit old Hud into believing you was helpin' me."

"If he hadn't tackled you," Stokes said, "you'd be doing ten to twenty in Sing Sing instead of three days bread and water. No doubt in anybody's mind whose ass he saved back there, even if you're too stupid to figure it out."

Hudson fell silent, chewing as he glared at Andrew.

"Never figured it that way. Guess I owe you."

"Look, Hudson, let's put it behind us." Andrew said.

"Call me Hud. You earned the right. And I still owe you."

Hudson polished off the ice cream and they passed him the plate of steak and the thermos of coffee. He took a whiff of the coffee and his broken lips spread into a smile. He drank two deep gulps and glared at Stokes though his puffy eyelids.

"So where the hell were you when we was tearing the town apart?"

"With a girl. The girl I aim to marry."

"She sure is pretty," Andrew told Stokes. "With a girl like that, a fella can't live in the White House, but you can sure be happy raising babies in Papeete."

"Marry," Hudson scoffed. "She must be a great piece of ass if you're thinking of getting hitched. Take it from me, don't buy the cow when you're already up to your ass in milk."

"She's not like that," Stokes said with a shy grin. "She's a virgin and she'll stay that way until our wedding night. Her father owns a grocery store. She was working the counter and I saw her through the window. Man, her smile lights up the moon. Andy, is there anything special I need to know about marrying an Asian girl?"

"How would I know? I was raised in a boy's school. I've never been with a girl."

"Hold on there," Hudson said. "Forget about this virgin bullshit. I've been with women in every port. Take it from me, boys. Any woman between the age of sixteen and sixty, married or single, will spread her legs when the right man comes along."

Stokes and Andrew gaped at each other, while Stokes's face colored a precise shade of red.

"I don't give a damn who she thinks she is," Hudson said, "she'll do it with a dozen different men in the same year if a dozen right men happen to come along. With most of them broads, you get a shot of whiskey in 'um, and any swinging dick's the right man. Yes sir, they're all whores underneath those fancy clothes and pretty manners. I don't know how many nice girls have given me a dose of the clap, but if you line them up end to end, it would sound like a fucking standing ovation."

Hudson stuffed a slice of steak into his mouth and chewed while waiting for a response. Both Andrew and Stokes dropped their gaze to hide their embarrassment. Hudson's chewing slowed to a standstill under their unresponsiveness. He swallowed, choking on his crumbling prestige.

"Hud," Andrew said, "have you ever been with a woman that you didn't meet in a barroom or a whorehouse? I mean, one that you didn't pay for?"

"That's got nothin' to do with anything. We all pay one way or another. I keep things simple by taking women who operate on a cash-only basis."

"So, you've never had a woman who felt love for you?" Andrew tilted his head to one side. A wave of sadness rushed through him.

"Don't you feel sorry for me, God damn you. I chose this life and no man has the right to look down his nose at me. You don't even know what the fuck you're talking about. You're the virgin in this conversation, so keep your stinking yap shut."

It occurred to Andrew that Hudson was searching for something every time he went after a woman, but he couldn't find it because he was looking in the wrong places.

"I hope someday you find what you're looking for," Andrew said.

"Rookie, thanks for the chow and thanks for saving my ass from Sing Sing, but take your pity somewheres else. I don't need that shit thrown in my face, so fuck off." Hudson turned his back and waited for them to leave, head bowed and silent.

Andrew glanced at Stokes, who shrugged his shoulders. Andrew began to apologize, but Stokes touched his shoulder, shaking his head, and nodded at the exit hatch.

They gathered the empty dishes and returned topside. Out on the rolling deck, there was no sign of the corporal. They checked the mess hall and carefully searched the fantail, with no result. They fought through the howling wind to the aft-crew's quarters, where the marines were berthed, and found Lieutenant Hurlburt lounging on his bunk. Andrew asked the officer if the corporal was down there. Hurlburt replied negative, so Andrew was forced to tell him about the smoke break and the possibility of the corporal being washed overboard.

Hurlburt leaped to his feet and ran up the ladder. The crew made a full search of the ship before they reversed course and spent four hours hunting the dark water for the missing marine, without success.

ANDREW marched into the wardroom and snapped to attention before Bitton, Mitchell, and Hurlburt, who were seated at the green felt table.

"Seaman Waters," Bitton said. "You're here because our mission is now in jeopardy. You see, the marine we lost was the only one in Lieutenant Hurlburt's squad who could speak and read Japanese. The lieutenant feels that, to do an adequate job, he needs someone with enough command of the Japanese language that they can read any document that might fall into their hands. You are the only other person aboard who may have that knowledge. Can you give us an idea of how well you speak the language?"

"Sir, I read Japanese better than I speak it, because they use many of the same characters as the Chinese. I should be able to make out what a document says, although it won't be easy."

"Excellent," Bitton said. "The other consideration is your lack of training in jungle warfare. I'll let Lieutenant Hurlburt be the judge of whether you would be an asset or a hindrance to his mission." Bitton glanced at Hurlburt, passing the conversation to him while Mitchell chain-lit a Lucky Strike.

"While you were in Indochina," Hurlburt said, "did you spend time in the wild country?"

"I had a number of experiences in the forest."

"How much time did you spend there?" Hurlburt asked.

Andrew struggled with the question. "Time is a measurement that doesn't apply in the wild country, as you call it. Time only applies to civilized things, sir."

Hurlburt nodded.

"I don't understand," Bitton said.

"Sir, I once stood on a ridge looking into a ravine where a springbuck was feeding. As I watched the buck, I noticed a tiger stalking it. I couldn't actually see the cat, it blended with the foliage and it crept so slowly, but I could feel its presence. Believe me, it was terrifying and beautiful at the same time. After an eternity, the tiger crouched into position, ready to pounce. The buck lifted its head and cocked its ears. At that moment, when the springbuck recognized the tiger, the entire universe stopped. I mean, it literally halted. No wind, no sound, no movement, no me, and certainly no time. In that place, that still universe, I didn't exist. I was reduced to simply witnessing the interplay between the cat and the buck. I have no idea how long that lasted. It could have been a century for all I know. It certainly felt like it."

Andrew paused for a moment, looking from one face to another. "The cat and the buck both sprang. In the instant that it took my mind to comprehend that the cat had lunged, it was over. Before my mind could engage, the buck had already gotten away and I was left trying to understand what had happened in that eternity that lasted a thousandth of a second. What I'm trying to explain is that, in the wild, simple things can span ages and complex relationships begin and end in the blink of an eye. Time has no relevance. It is a measurement that exists only in the human mind." Andrew took a deep breath, exhaled, and added, "So how much experience have I had in the forest? Enough. In daylight and at night, enough."

Bitton cleared his throat and said, "Waters, because of the danger involved in this mission coupled with your lack of training, I won't order you to go. If we decide that you would be an asset to this mission, you will have to volunteer. Are you willing?"

Andrew stared at Mitchell, pausing to consider. "Confucius said: To shirk your duty when you see it before you shows want of moral courage. I was the cause of the corporal's death. It seems it's my karma to replace him."

Mitchell closed his eyes, his chin dropped.

Bitton nodded. "That is all, Waters. We'll inform you of our decision as soon as we make it."

As Andrew exited the room, Hurlburt said, "I'll take a chance on this kid. He knows what he's talking about and he doesn't try to bullshit you into believing he knows more than he does."

"No." Mitchell's voice rang raw. "As exec, I'm responsible for the crew, and I won't go along with this. Andy's had no training in jungle warfare."

"Andy? You're on a first-name basis with this boy?" Bitton asked. "Let's not forget we are at war, and when the need arises, we are asked to do the impossible. Waters could mean the difference between success and failure, and that translates into lives saved at invasion time."

"But sir—"

"I'm overruling you this time, Nathan. Much as I hate losing the best damned cook in the Navy."

"Sounds to me," Hurlburt said to Mitchell, "like you're letting personal feelings cloud your sense of duty. If that's true, you need to sort out your priorities."

Mitchell leaned close to Hurlburt. His eyes narrowed. "You bring him back with so much as a stubbed toe, Lieutenant, and I'll track you down and crawl right up your ass with personal. You read me, mister?"

Chapter Fourteen

April 27, 1942—2000 hours

THE *Pilgrim* took a brutal thrashing as it drove through a cross-swelling sea, rolling over the top of white-ridged waves and plunging into cavernous troughs. Anything not tied down vaulted across the deck. Two inches of water streamed through the passageways, and pumps worked at full capacity to keep the old lady afloat. Men staggered about like drunkards, ate cold food, and couldn't sleep in bunks that galloped like elevators gone haywire.

The crew's consciousness acclimated to the pounding in the same way people acclimatized to the heat of the desert. But even so, the men stayed on edge. They didn't like their situation. Within the cramped quarters of the forecastle, they were jumpy and easily moved to quarreling, which led to open fighting.

Secured to his bunk with makeshift straps that he had fashioned from ropes, Andrew closed his eyes and tried to force his mind into sleep. Exhaustion finally lulled him into unconsciousness.

When the dream came, he saw himself alongside Clifford at the Bai Hur Sze Temple, exploring the compound. This revered historical and religious shrine had been constructed in the Ming Dynasty, sometime before the fifteenth century. Andrew had never seen anything that rivaled the temple's beauty. The carved stone buildings were surrounded by immaculate gardens, which were equally magnificent in design and simplicity. Beyond the gardens and amidst the golden sun rays in the morning sky soared the famous cranes.

"Le-Le-Le-Let's catch one," Clifford whispered, gazing at the birds wheeling above. Clifford's beauty was only marred by one flaw: he stuttered. He had difficulty uttering the first sound of any sentence. Once the threshold of the sentence was breached, the rest of the words flowed smoothly through his lips. But that first syllable became embroiled in his mouth, caught in a precarious struggle, like a delicate bird trying to extricate itself from a net.

Andrew nodded, and the boys ran into the rushes skirting the water. Only a few yards from the shoreline, a majestic crane waded beyond a stand of willows, lifting and placing its feet with precision. They dropped to their hands and knees. Andrew took the lead, snaking through stalks of willows. The bird froze, intent on a fish below the surface. They slowly rose to a crouched position, Andrew nodded, and they sprang forward with arms outstretched and fingers grasping.

The crane flashed its slender wings and disappeared, while the boys splashed into the lake empty-handed.

The shock of frigid water felt exhilarating, and laughter spilled from their lips. They hauled themselves to their feet and realized their robes were now soaked and befouled with mud. They sloshed to shore and removed their robes, spread them along the bank to dry. They lay side by side on the bank to let the sun warm their bodies.

"Will you become a monk?" Andrew asked.

"Na-na-na-no. I-I-I-I'm going to fly airplanes across the sky. Ha-ha-how about you?"

Andrew thought for a moment. "If I were a monk, I could study the scriptures and play my flute all day long. But I want to be a mountain climber. I'm going to scale Everest."

"Lingtse and White Crane, up to no good it seems. How did your robes become soiled?" Master Jung-Wei had walked up without a sound and now stood above them, his shadow falling over their pale bodies.

Andrew dropped his eyes. "Master, we fell into the lake trying to catch a crane."

"It is not desirable to possess a crane," Master Jung-Wei said with a sagacious nod. "That brings unhappiness to the bird and unnecessary responsibility to the boy. If you wish to have a crane, be a crane."

Clifford's laughter sparkled. "Ha-ha-ha-how can a boy be a crane?"

"The essence of the bird is within you. You carry the same fundamental nature of every living creature. Within you are the saint and the murderer, the crane and the swine, the butterfly and the serpent. All these possibilities lie within your being." He paused, as if to let silence underscore his words. "You must choose which you will be and walk that path one step at a time."

Andrew sat up, crossed his legs, and arched his back. His eyes narrowed in fierce concentration as he spread his arms like wings and imagined himself floating on currents of air high above the lake. Silence engulfed him. His only sensation was the cool morning breeze on his skin. There on the ground by the lake, for Andrew Waters, the universe seemed to fold in on itself. It came to him in a flash of knowing, all the master's lessons. He truly was a perfect, unlimited life force, bound only by his own thoughts. A shock of joy shivered through him as he felt the weightlessness of flight, lifting… lifting… and for an instant, he was a glorious crane.

Andrew was shaken out of his dream.

"Look alive, sailor, you've got the watch."

It was his last midnight-to-four watch before reaching the island, and his last chance for reconciliation with Mitchell. He untied his restraining ropes and immediately became airborne. He hit the steel deck with a thud and tumbled into the line of lockers. Dressing was a wild affair, like pulling on clothes while riding a rodeo bull, but Andrew crawled into his uniform, life vest, and watch cap in only a few jarring minutes. He sloshed through the corridors to the galley, where he made an urn of coffee. When the coffee was brewed, he poured a mug, placed a saucer over the top, and stumbled through the ship to Mitchell's cabin.

Andrew scratched on Mitchell's curtain door, but there was no answer. He drew the curtain aside and stepped into the cabin. The room was as orderly as always. Books were jammed on the shelf. A wooden hanger held a uniform to a wall hook, neat, pressed, and ready to cover the lieutenant's body. It swayed out from the wall with each roll of the ship and swung back flush, like a clock's pendulum measuring time.

Ropes held Mitchell to his mattress. Andrew took a moment to admire the sleeping form before shaking the officer's shoulder.

Mitchell was slow to wake because he had taken phenobarbital in order to sleep. He finally opened his eyes and stared up. He lifted his left arm and glanced at his wristwatch.

"I brought some coffee, sir. Do you need help getting those ropes off?"

"I can do it," Mitchell said with a drug-blurred voice.

Mitchell unstrapped himself. He wore only his skivvies, and two angry red welts lashed across his skin where the ropes had held him, one across his chest, the other across his legs. Mitchell rolled out of bed and took the coffee. He gazed into Andrew's bruised face, as if searching for something to say, but there was only the awkward hush that towered between them like a stone wall.

Mitchell sipped his coffee. "Thanks, Andy. I'll be with you in a minute," he croaked. He opened his mouth to say more, but before he could, Andrew ducked behind the curtain door.

Andrew heard a muffled, "Shit," on the other side of the curtain.

Five minutes later, Andrew followed the lieutenant onto the red-lit bridge.

"Barometer's holding steady at 29.32," Fisher said. "The wind is at force seven." He stood with his elbow hooked through the side of the captain's chair. "Storm's one hundred and twenty-five miles due west. We're riding her ass pretty tight."

Andrew relieved the watch at the port side of the wheelhouse. A northeasterly wind whined through the guy wires and heeled the *Pilgrim* over each time she rolled to starboard. Horizontal lines of rain blew across the bow and drummed into the pilothouse windows. Andrew peered into the blackness, but it was impossible to see anything but the white spray flying over the bow.

Mitchell relieved Fisher, made a log entry, and checked the latest movement of the storm on the charts. After verifying that everything was as it should be, he staggered to the window and stood two feet from Andrew, staring out to sea.

Andrew's mind groped for words of reconciliation, but he couldn't think of how to restore the rapport they had once shared. The one relationship they still had was the rigid naval code. It was a fine thread binding them.

They stood for thirty silent minutes. Mitchell checked the barometer, made a log entry, returned to Andrew's side, all perfectly quiescent.

Ogden's eyebrows rose as he clasped the engine room telegraph with both hands. He leaned toward Stokes. "Hell's bells, what's up with those two?"

Stokes had his legs spread wide for balance. His hands gripped the wheel and his eyes were glued to the gyrocompass. "Beats me. They haven't said a word since Papeete. The lieutenant is probably still sore about the fight."

A mountainous wave broke over the bridge and buffeted the ship far over to starboard. Andrew tumbled to his hands and knees while the others tossed about, clutching for handholds.

"Hard left rudder," Mitchell yelled. "Chief, have Baker ballast all empty tanks."

"About Goddamn time," Ogden said to Stokes. He grabbed at the phone and buzzed the fire room. "Chief, flood your empty tanks, on the double."

Sweat beaded on Mitchell's upper lip. As he helped Andrew to his feet, he seemed to grope for something to say, but Andrew beat him to it.

"Will she founder, sir? Are we going to make it?"

"All our hatches are sealed and our engines are pumping out over thirty thousand horse power. As long as our screws keep turning, we'll be fine. This is not as dangerous as going ashore with the marines. That's what you should be worried about."

"Yes, sir, I know. I get sick to my stomach every time I think about it."

"You can change your mind. You're more valuable aboard the *Pilgrim*."

"I can't be responsible for any more deaths. Next time it could be you."

"I can't lose you, don't you see?" Mitchell hissed, loud enough for only Andrew to hear.

"No, I don't see. What are you saying?"

"I'm saying—" His words trailed off. He couldn't voice what was on his tongue, not even to himself.

Sensing that Mitchell still cared for him, Andrew's anxiety fell away. A sensation of exhilaration swelled up in him, from being in a dangerous situation and suddenly feeling unafraid.

Kelso stumbled into the pilothouse. "Another storm warning, sir." He lunged for the captain's chair with one hand and held out a radio message to Mitchell with the other.

Mitchell read the message. He staggered to the chart table, picked up the dividers and a pencil, and made some calculations. He jotted another entry into the ship's log before joining Andrew once again.

"Hundred twenty-five miles due west. We should be clear of it sometime late tomorrow."

"I look forward to seeing the sun again," Andrew said. "Funny what we take for granted."

Mitchell draped his right arm over Andrew's shoulder. "I've taken you for granted," he whispered. "Now that I'm losing you, I realize how special you are to this ship, and to me."

A wave of dizziness hit Andrew and his knees weakened as he felt their friendship germinating again. For the first time in four days, he felt happy.

Chapter Fifteen

April 28, 1942—0200 hours

ON THE fourth night out from Bora Bora, Andrew's exhaustion catapulted him into a deep and dreamless sleep that did much to restore his strength. At 0200 hours, Lt. Hurlburt tugged on his shoulder, telling him it was time to gear up. Andrew stirred and, opening his eyes, had the most peculiar sensation; his bunk gently rocked back and forth. The compartment rode comparatively smoothly, and the only sound was the rumble of the engines.

He untied the ropes holding him to the mattress, bounded out of bed, and pulled on his borrowed marine outfit—green T-shirt and skivvies, fatigues, combat boots. But before pulling on his over-gear, he removed the shoestrings from his Navy boondockers and tied them together, then he tied the shoestrings to both ends of his flute and slung it across his back, carrying it under his green jacket like a hunting bow.

His loose-fitting clothes felt awkward. He took a moment to reconsider his decision, and chased the thought away with a shake of his head. He climbed into a life vest, cinched the straps tight, and covered his head with a metal helmet. The helmet, like his borrowed fatigues, was too big—the front edge dropped down over his eyes. He had to tilt his head back in order to see straight ahead.

On deck, he saw the sea running slightly rough with long ground swells. The sky pressed low with a blanket of gray clouds. He felt a peculiar quality in the blackness that surrounded him.

Now that the storm had passed, most of the men slept topside on cots spread across the deck. Chief Baker ambled among them, shaking the crew to consciousness.

Andrew joined the marines for a breakfast of eggs laid over rare beefsteak, fried potatoes, and mountains of crispy toast. Andrew had no taste for red meat, but he chowed down, knowing that this would be his last real meal for months. He ate his fill, sopped up the egg yolks with a piece of toast, and washed it down with strong coffee.

Hurlburt entered the chow hall. "I want everyone to leave their brain buckets behind. I don't want anyone jeopardizing this mission with a clank of a chin strap or your helmet thudding against a tree branch."

Andrew was only too happy to shed his helmet. He wished he could shed the whole assignment and stay with Mitchell, but that was no longer an option.

At 0300 hours, they filed out of the mess hall and geared-up. The marines lined up on the quarterdeck for debarkation while Baker supervised the lowering of the black whaleboat. The marines were dressed in fatigues with heavy packs strapped to their backs and rifles slung over shoulders. They waited silently.

Mitchell ambled up to Andrew, who stood at the end of the line.

"Well, sir, I guess this is it," Andrew said.

"Wish you'd change your mind."

Andrew gave a nervous grin. "'In peace there's nothing so becomes a man as modest stillness and humility: But when the blast of war blows in our ears, then imitate the actions of a tiger: stiffen the sinews, summon up the blood, disguise fair nature with hard-favor's rage.'"

At that moment, he really didn't even realize where his words were coming from, but he tried to gain strength from them, if only for enough time to climb into the boat and leave Mitchell behind.

Mitchell blinked once, looking like the entire world had imploded before his eyes. "I'll miss your Shakespeare," he said with a slight tremble in his voice. "Well then, do what you're told and keep your head down. I'll do everything I can to bring you back here with us."

"Thank you, sir." Andrew shrugged, smiling weakly. He reached into his pocket and extracted a string of prayer beads, all bunched into a ball. He pressed them into Mitchell's hand, telling him that it was something to remember him by.

Mitchell unballed the string, took off his hat, and slipped the beads over his head, letting them fall around his neck. As their cool smoothness pressed against his throat, he seemed embarrassed, as if he realized he should have brought something to give Andrew but had forgot.

Silence. A thousand luminous thoughts raced through Andrew's head, but he could not make himself voice a single one.

Mitchell also seemed to stall for time, no doubt fearful of his own ineptness, even more fearful of the approaching separation.

Andrew imagined himself leaning into Mitchell's solid mass, kissing him right on the mouth with all the tenderness and love he could muster. The thought made him wildly alive, breathless. The tips of his ears burned and his head spun. He couldn't restrain himself any longer. He leaned toward the officer, lips pursed.

Before he came too close, Mitchell held out his hand for Andrew to shake, stopping Andrew cold. Andrew grasped that hand, clung to it until the marines moved forward and clambered down the debarkation net two at a time.

Mitchell followed Andrew all the way to the net and stood on the quarterdeck to watch him slip aboard the whaleboat. The six oarsmen manned their stations on the thwarts. Ogden, acting as coxswain, stood at the tiller. Andrew was the last man into the boat. He sat next to Hudson, who was one of the oarsmen.

Once away, Ogden barked, "Let fall." The oars came down and were held a foot above the surface until Ogden said, "Give way together, boys." The oars dug into the water and the boat slid into the blackness. Working with brusque, overemphasized movements, the rowers strained to haul the boat across a mile and a half of water.

The marines sat with rigid backs. Black shoe polish covered their faces, their M1 rifles pointed skyward, and their ammunition belts hugged their waists. They all peered forward, trying to see through the inky night. Only Andrew stared at the ship. He knew that Mitchell stood on the bridge, binoculars pressed to his face, following their progress. He tried to imagine how the officer looked while straining to see him. He kept his eyes on the ship, gray superimposed on the night sky, until it merged with the blackness and he could no longer distinguish its outline.

Andrew wished more than anything that he would have brushed past that outstretched hand and kissed the officer on the mouth like he meant to, even with everyone watching. He'd had that one last opportunity to show Mitchell his love, to give him a gesture that he could carry to his grave, but he let fear snatch it from him. *Coward. I'm such a coward.*

THE roar of surf became progressively louder until the whaleboat came to that area beyond where the waves swelled up and toppled over as they raced to shore. Ogden signaled and the oars lifted out of the water and hung in midair. He studied the beach for a possible landing site.

Beaching the boat in huge surf was hazardous even in daylight, and Ogden had never attempted such a feat at night. If the boat should lean sideways to the wave even a smidgen, they would do a loop the loop and jettison the men from the boat like peas from a pod. If they capsized, every man would have hell swimming through the breakers— the marines especially, being weighed down by their weapons and packs.

Beads of sweat ran down Ogden's face. After two minutes of straining to see the layout, Ogden took hold of the tiller. The oarsmen, all facing the stern, saw a change come over Ogden. They collectively braced their legs and took a firm grip on their oars.

"We'll take her straight in from here, boys," Ogden ordered. He turned to see a wall of water speeding at them that was tall enough to block his view of the sea behind it. "Give way together and give it everything you've got."

Six backs bent and stretched toward the bow, away from the oncoming wave. The boat drove smartly forward. The boat's aft rose, going perpendicular as it crawled up the concave front of the monster. Ogden could reach out and touch the white ridge of foam at the top. The boat seemed to hang there, cresting the immaculate white foam. The crew rowed at a frenzied pace as they flew toward shore.

Water sprayed Ogden's face and the salty mist blinded him. Maneuvering on instinct alone, he deftly wielded the whaleboat through the waves. He blinked several times and his vision returned as another liquid monster was about to thunder down on them.

"Put your back to it… Christ! I'm out here with a bunch of fucking pussies."

The boat gained momentum, and by the time the next wave scooped down, they were far enough in front of it to keep from being swamped. The boat lifted above the raging foam, spinning like a spider being flushed down a toilet.

When the boat scraped sand, Ogden ordered, "Trail oars," in his normal voice. The six oarsmen hauled their blades into the boat and jumped over the side into waist-deep water. They seized the gunwales and heaved the boat high onto the beach. The marines leaped from the boat and spread out with rifles drawn to form a perimeter.

Unexpectedly, the night shattered with the sound of a rifle discharge; the noise echoed from above the cliff. Everyone froze. They waited, crouched while anticipating another shot, but only the waves pounding onto shore and the wind whistling up the cliff disturbed the silence.

Ogden signaled Hudson, and the big man passed the communications gear to waiting hands. The sound of two more rifle shots reverberated down the cliff. Hurlburt signaled his men to move out. They heaved the communications equipment to the base of the cliff, leaving Andrew and the other sailors to push the whaleboat into the surf.

Before they could move the boat, a red flash lit up the sky several miles east of the island.

Ogden hissed. "What the fuck?"

A roar grew louder and louder until an explosion ripped open the *Pilgrim*'s superstructure. More flashes lit the night sky. Funnels of water erupted all round the *Pilgrim*. The men on the beach collectively watched; each man held his breath. Another shell blasted into the *Pilgrim* and a huge fireball billowed above the ship.

The *Pilgrim* cut through the water, gaining speed. Her five-inch guns belched return fire.

Hurlburt raced to the sailors, shouting, "Get that boat out of the water and follow me. We've got to take cover. This will bring every Jap on the island down on us. Let's move it."

A fiery blast shredded apart the *Pilgrim*'s bridge and conning tower. Another shell sheared off a section of the bow and a tremendous explosion cleaved the forecastle apart. A massive fireball soared skyward. A heartbeat later, the *Pilgrim* nosedived into the churning sea. The sailors on the beach saw their ship going down with little hope for the hands aboard.

Andrew screamed, "We've got to help them."

He tried to push the whaleboat into the surf, but Hurlburt grabbed him by the shoulder and hurled him backward onto the sand. "We have to save ourselves before we're spotted."

A marine private ran up with his weapon at the ready. Again, Hurlburt ordered the crew to beach the boat and follow him inland. The sailors all glared at Ogden, who stood petrified, gazing out to sea where the *Pilgrim* was ablaze.

A panic seized Andrew. He leaped to his feet and tackled the private. In a desperate rage, he wrestled the Thompson submachine gun away from the marine and aimed the muzzle at Hurlburt's chest. His hands trembled. Beads of sweat erupted across his brow.

"Lieutenant, take your men and get the hell lost. We're saving what's left of our crew."

Hurlburt rested his hand on the Browning .45 holstered to his hip. "And if I don't?"

"I'll kill you and anybody who tries to stop us."

"You're a pacifist. You won't hurt anyone."

Andrew dropped the Thompson's muzzle and squeezed off a burst. The sand flew up inches from Hurlburt's boots. The sound rang in Andrew's ears as he pointed the muzzle at Hurlburt's chest again.

"Are you willing to bet your life on my convictions?" His voice was so flat, he was sure nobody would detect the absolute fear hiding beneath the words.

The color drained from Hurlburt's face, and his mouth twitched. He searched Andrew's eyes intently. What he found apparently convinced him that Andrew was serious, because he took his hand off his weapon and signaled his men to disperse.

"Waters," Hurlburt said, "if we both survive this, I'm going to see you court-martialed. You're looking at twenty to life." He raced after his squad. As soon as he reached the cliffs, he began to climb.

The sailors hauled the whaleboat into the surf and manned the oars. Andrew jumped in at the last moment and sat in the center of the boat, trembling.

Hudson patted him on the shoulder. "Guts! That took a ton of guts! You're a better man than the rest of us pussies put together! That's two I owe you."

Fighting down the acid-like bile at the back of his throat, Andrew glanced at the Thompson he still clutched with white knuckles and tossed the machinegun overboard.

Chapter Sixteen

April 28, 1942—0500 hours

ON THE *Pilgrim*'s bridge, all eyes were focused on the island, and no one noticed the red flashes eight miles to the east. Seaman Allard, perched in the crow's nest beside the communications antenna, spotted the tracers rocketing across the cloudy sky. He yelled into the talking-tube that connected the nest with the bridge.

"Here she comes!"

Mitchell leaned over the chart table, marking bearings along their course line. It took him a half second to register the lookout's warning. Hot needles stabbed up the back of his neck and along his shoulders. He dropped his pencil and raced forward, but before he could reach the wing hatch, he was hurled to the deck as a 250-pound, armor-piercing shell plummeted through the ship's superstructure, ripping apart bulkheads and decking as it passed directly through the officer's wardroom.

Clamor broke across the bridge. Bitton barked, "*Sound general quarters! Flank speed ahead! Emergency turn to starboard!*" He caught his breath and said in a normal voice, "Mr. Fisher, check the lookouts. Find out where the enemy is."

Mitchell realized that the crew now had three critical tasks: assess the damage, control the damage, and engage the enemy. Andrew and the others in the whaleboat flashed across his mind, but he knew the ship came first—they would need to fend for themselves. He pushed himself off the deck and staggered to the bulkhead. With shaky hands and a hideous ringing in his ear, he pulled the red GQ handle.

The battle-stations gong shrieked through the ship. Men on the bridge leaped to carry out the captain's orders. Towers of white water erupted around the *Pilgrim* while mordant black smoke billowed into the pilothouse, stinging Mitchell's eyes and making it impossible to see. On the starboard bridge wing, he pointed to an orange flash over the black plain. "There! Thirty degrees to starboard. Distance, I make at eight miles."

In a flash, the ship's propellers spun in a violent whir. As the ship built speed and came about, another shell blasted through the hull amidships, right at the waterline. The entire ship shuddered. Below deck, fuel oil and seawater flooded the forward engine room.

"Fisher," Bitton said, "as soon as our Goddamn faulty radar has a fix on them, commence firing! Mitchell, get damage control on those areas hit. I want to know exactly how we stand. Expedite all damage reports to the bridge."

Bitton grabbed Fisher. "Dammit, Monte, where are our guns? Get us in the fight, for God sake."

"Sir, radar shows five enemy ships eight miles to the southeast and closing at thirty knots."

Mitchell shook off his battle jitters, ignoring the thrum in his gut and the metal taste in his mouth. He grabbed the intercom phone and barked, "Now hear this. This is the Exec. Convey all damage reports to the bridge, on the double."

All the officers on the bridge pulled on life jackets and steel helmets.

"Captain," Mitchell said. "Our forward engine room is not responding and we are losing speed. Outrunning them is impossible. Maybe we can slip around the other side of the island and lose them."

"Good thinking, Nathan. Change course to get us around the back side."

The *Pilgrim*'s five-inch gun turrets discharged an ear-splitting salvo, followed by another. Red tracers flew in both directions as white-hot shell casings ejected over the forward deck. The *Pilgrim*'s guns bore down tenaciously, trading salvos in a bold and furious melee while the crippled ship tried to slip away through a field of erupting waterspouts.

Mitchell watched the red tracers crisscrossing the sky. His mind was numb and he struggled to think clearly. Despite all the extensive training and drills, he couldn't push down his feelings of panic. The eye-stinging smoke, the macabre light from muzzle flames, and the ringing in his ears all combined to create a feeling in his neck and shoulders as if molten lava were dripping down his spine.

Another shell slammed into the bow in front of the number-one gun, ripping an immense hole in the deck. The number-one gun went silent as orange flames vomited a hundred and fifty feet into the air. Red heat hit the bridge like an open furnace. Seconds later, blackened sailors poured from the forecastle, dazed and stumbling about the deck. Smoke boiled from the hole, which was ominously right over the powder magazine. Cocoa and Grady were part of the forward firefighting party. They helped drag a thick hose to the edge of the hole and sprayed seawater on the flames.

"Skipper," Mitchell yelled. "No damage control parties are reporting. The intercom must be dead. I'll have to lay below and have a look."

"Make it quick, Nathan. If they can't control the forward fire, flood the number-one magazine and jettison the ready ammo. It's our death sentence if that blows."

Mitchell ran along the main deck, past cursing men who wrestled with the water hoses. Another shell smashed into the deck amidships and he slammed to his knees. The shell ripped into the main boiler; live steam shrieked through the gaping hole, drowning out the screams from the scalded men in the lower compartments.

Mitchell stumbled to his feet and found Baker at the aft edge of the quarterdeck, barking orders to the firefighting party. He grabbed Baker and turned the chief to face him. The chief's face was streaked with soot and sweat, but there was no sign of panic in his eyes.

"Sir, the forward engine room is awash, but we've contained the flooding. There's a huge fire forward and I'm not sure we can bring it under control before the magazine goes, but we're giving it hell. And we lost a boiler, so all in all, I don't like our chances."

A scream echoed from amidships. "My leg, my leg!"

Mitchell patted Baker on the shoulder. "Flood the forward magazine and jettison the ready ammo. You need to somehow turn off the fuel valve to the boiler and have someone drag that man to sick bay."

Mitchell raced toward the bow, but an explosion forward rocked the ship and sent him staggering backward, tripping over a tangled mass of hoses. He hauled himself to his feet and pushed his way through a pandemonium of panicked sailors running aft. He heaved himself up the ladder to the bridge and searched through the black smoke. The dim form of the captain appeared, bent over and coughing into his handkerchief.

The captain straightened up and looked Mitchell in the eye. Bitton's eyeballs were rimmed in red while his face was blackened.

The helmsmen, radarman, signalman, and the lookouts all gathered around to hear the report. Their faces had each taken on the expression of stark terror.

"We've lost the forward engine room, a boiler, and the fire forward is still out of control."

Bitton stood silent for a moment. Before he could issue another order, an explosion launched a thirty-foot section of the forecastle skyward. It was the powder magazine. The deck jerked, and all the men on the bridge fell back as a wall of flames roared skyward.

Heat hit Mitchell in the face like a blowtorch's flame. Several members of the firefighting team, including Cocoa and Grady, were blown clean over the ship's railing. The *Pilgrim* and her crew paused, stunned like a bull struck between the eyes with a sledgehammer.

The forward sections took on seawater by the ton, causing the ship to list heavily to starboard. Mitchell felt a jolt of pure fear race from his heart to his bowels as he calculated how much longer they could keep her afloat: five minutes, probably less.

"We're licked," Bitton shouted as he tried to see through the smoke to the island. "At least we accomplished our mission. Pass the word to abandon ship. Get everybody in the water and take muster. I want to know who we've lost."

Before Mitchell could obey the order, all bridge electrical devices went dead. Emergency generators came alive to provide auxiliary power, but sparks flew and the lights sputtered before dying for good.

Mitchell couldn't believe how quickly the situation had deteriorated. Twelve minutes had passed since that first warning yell from the crow's nest, and now the ship was listing twenty degrees and was out of control. A dozen minutes from dead calm to catastrophe.

Mitchell ran onto the port wing and screamed at Baker to launch the remaining whaleboat, loosen the life rafts, and abandon ship. The orders flashed like lightning from one group to the next. The damage control and ordnance crews gave up the fight and turned on a dime into rescue units, hauling trapped men from flooding compartments and loading the wounded into the whaleboat and life rafts. It would take time to gather the wounded, Mitchell knew, time he was sure they didn't have.

Bitton yelled through the smoke to Mitchell. "Have Kelso send out a distress signal. It's imperative that he radio CincPac our position." He handed a key to the duty quartermaster. "Take all the logs and publications from my cabin safe and throw them overboard in weighted bags. Move it, man!"

The twenty-degree list slanted the deck so that it had an uphill climb to port. One engine room still operated, pushing the ship ahead at five knots. The weight of the incoming sea smashed through the auxiliary bulkheads, flooding one compartment after another. Men abandoned the wounded belowdecks and scrambled to save themselves.

Mitchell climbed the ladder to the radio shack and ordered Kelso to send a distress signal. Kelso wagged his head, explaining that he had no electrical power. There was nothing he could do.

By the time Mitchell and Kelso made their way to the main deck, the ship had lost nearly all forward speed, and thousands of gallons of fuel oil spewed from the ruptured hull, creating a poisonous blanket over the sea that spread behind the ship. The *Pilgrim* now listed thirty degrees, and a whirl of chaos unfolded as sailors raced down the sloping deck and into the sea's embrace.

Amidships, Baker and five sailors wrestled the whaleboat into the water while others freed the life rafts. The *Pilgrim* slowed to a crawl with her guns pointed out at queer angles. An incendiary shell hit the fantail, spewing fire all along the aft deck. Far up the slanting crow's nest, visible in the fire's orange light, the Stars and Stripes waved defiantly over the chaos below.

Mitchell smelled the nauseating stench of burning fuel oil, rubber, and human flesh. The ship shuddered beneath him as three explosions sounded in rapid secession throughout the interior. He sprinted to Baker's side and studied the situation. Most of the crew were mustering at abandon-ship stations or were already in the water, but he didn't see the captain anywhere.

"Chief, where's the skipper?"

"As far as I know, he never left the bridge, sir."

Mitchell dashed forward, taking the stairs three at a time. In the wheelhouse, Bitton was sprawled on the deck, unconscious. Firelight flickered across his blackened face. Mitchell grabbed Bitton by an arm and a leg, slinging the man over his shoulders in a fireman's carry. He climbed through the hatchway leading to the starboard bridge-wing. The ship now listed at thirty-five-degrees, and even with the weight of the captain on his shoulders, Mitchell easily stepped onto the edge of the railing and leaped over the side, clearing the deck and splashing into the sea.

He found himself in a dimension that had no bottom and no place to land, bobbing in a sphere of weightlessness. He struggled to maneuver the captain around and pulled the man through the water by the neck. He swam harder than he had ever done in his life, terrified that they would not get free of the vortex from the sinking vessel.

Another explosion sounded within the ship. At the same time, a shell smashed into the navigation-bridge. The stern reared high in the air, with one propeller still turning like a lazy windmill. With her proud bow under water, she slid into the blackness, letting out a high-pitched hiss as the main deck disappeared under the surface.

Mitchell turned in time to see the conning tower slide under. The enemy ships ceased firing. Then, only the agonizing screams from the wounded disturbed the silence as Mitchell wondered how many men were caught below deck.

In a flash his universe changed. A horrifying suction drew Mitchell and Bitton toward the ship—pulling, pulling, until they were wrenched under the surface.

Mitchell was no longer in the world of men and sky and sound, a place of light and darkness. There was only the black water and the suction that dragged him down. Mitchell kicked and clawed at the water, but Bitton's deadweight towed him deeper. The awesome speed of their descent spread goose bumps over Mitchell's scalp and the growing pressure felt like a vise crushing his skull.

My God, he thought, *I'm going to die.*

Forced to release Bitton, he slashed his way toward to the surface. His lungs burned. They felt as if they were bursting, but at last he blasted back into the world of sound and his lungs felt the sweet relief of new air rushing in. He shrieked, partly from fear and partly from the loss of Captain Bitton.

As his senses returned, he realized his surroundings. The sea was littered with floating crates of vegetables, shredded clothing, silent dead bodies, and screaming live ones, and everything was covered with foul black fuel oil.

There was no wind. Clouds darkened the sky. The men drifted, clinging to anything that floated. Nothing could be seen and there was nothing to feel but the chilly water, the fiery wounds, and the burn of fuel oil as it ate at their skin. The only sounds were grisly moans from the dying and the softer babble of prayers from the living.

Without the ship as a point of reference and little light to see by, the survivors drifted into an extreme state of disorientation, but slowly the clouds parted enough to allow a streak of moonlight to peek through. A ghostly light, partly obscured by smoke, spread across a sea of floating debris.

Mitchell drifted with his head back, gasping for air. He felt a jolt and realized that a shark had bumped him. He knew that sharks were capable of speeds of over forty miles per hour and would bump their prey several times to stun it before closing in for the kill—commonly known as bump and bite maneuvers—and where there was one, there were ten, or twenty, or hundreds. Death swam beside him, and he knew that he had hours, perhaps minutes, to live.

Sadness washed over him as he thought about Kate. He wished he had married her so his child would have his name, the child that he would never see. He thought of Andrew, and he felt a wave of thankfulness that Andrew had made it ashore. But sadness returned as he thought about his two regrets: that he would never see his child and would never see Andrew again.

He shook those thoughts from his head and reminded himself that he was not dead yet. He was an officer and others were depending on him. He tried to form a plan of action, realizing that he needed to gather the men into a group and move them across two miles of open water to the island. He yelled loud enough to be heard above the injured men's cries.

"This is the Exec. Swim toward the sound of my voice. Everyone, swim toward the sound of my voice."

The men paddled through poisonous fuel oil, thick as honey. It seeped into their eyes, mouths, and ears. They gagged on the putrid-tasting poison as it ate away their skin. Several men who were unable to swim out beyond the oil slick gave up and simply drifted in shock, breathing the toxic fumes and swallowing mouthfuls of the sludge.

Twelve sailors paddled toward Mitchell, and he swam through a field of oil to reach them. The oil burned his face and neck, making him realize that the crew must get free of the slick as quickly as possible. After reaching the men, he tried to see who they were, but their faces were all covered in oil and he didn't recognize a single one. He yelled again and the twelve added their voices, drawing the survivors to them.

Out of the darkness drifted the whaleboat that Chief Baker had launched. Baker and twenty sailors were aboard and another dozen sailors were in the water clinging to the sides.

"Lieutenant Mitchell," Baker shouted. "Is that you, sir?"

"Yes. Do you have any officers aboard?"

"Ensign Moyer is aboard, and Ensign Fisher is hanging over the side toward the bow. I'm sure as hell glad to hear your voice. Will you come aboard, sir?"

"No. If you have room, take the wounded aboard, and move away from the oil slick."

Mitchell huddled with the men in the water. More men joined the group. A few paddled up on life rafts, but most were bobbing on the choppy waves with only a kapok life vest to keep them afloat.

Mitchell felt more nudges and bumps under the water, and he was not sure if it was sharks or the men treading water around him. He saw a man twenty yards out dog-paddling for the group; the man suddenly screamed and was dragged backward at a tremendous speed before disappearing under the surface with a jolt. Mitchell held his breath, waiting, but the man did not resurface.

Someone yelled, "Shark!" and panic raced through the group. Men clinging to the sides attempted to climb into the boat and nearly swamped the craft. The men in the boat knocked them back into the water. Mitchell yelled for the men to say calm and to huddle in a tight group. They obeyed, overcoming their fear.

As Mitchell paddled to the bow to talk with Fisher, he heard several men pleading with God, promising to stop whoring and drinking and gambling, to become church-going men, if He would only allow them to live through the night.

Mitchell found Fisher clinging to the whaleboat's bow with a shocked expression on his face. "Monte, thank God you're okay. We need to get the men huddled into a tight bunch and make our way to shore. You take the port, I'll take the starboard."

Fisher said, "We're all going to die." He grinned and said it again, "We're going to die."

Mitchell lifted his hand out of the water and smacked the ensign's face. "Pull yourself together, man. We've got a hundred men here who need us to take charge."

Fisher went silent. A moment later, he rasped in a weak voice, "You can count on me."

Mitchell glanced up to see another swimmer fighting to join the group. He recognized Grady dragging an unconscious Cocoa through the oily water. Mitchell swam out twenty yards and helped pull Cocoa to the growing mass of survivors.

The men were tossed about the sloshing waves, and many were overcome with vomiting and diarrhea. They finally moved free of the oil slick, which helped to calm everyone.

Mitchell told Baker to keep the group moving toward the island. He scanned the water, hoping to see lights of an enemy ship that could rescue them, but he saw only blackness. *We must somehow make it to the island,* he thought, *before the sharks become more daring.*

A scream sounded back in the slick. Mitchell broke free of the group and swam toward the voice. Thirty yards out, he bumped headlong into a body. He turned the man around and saw that the sailor was dead. The face was charred beyond recognition and smeared with oil. The flesh was burned away from both hands, leaving the finger bones reaching above the water like claws. Mitchell vomited.

Recovering, he unstrapped the kapok vest and pulled the man from the vest, and the corpse sank.

Another scream a dozen yards away had Mitchell moving again. He found a man treading water; the sailor had no life vest and struggled to keep his head above water. Mitchell unstrapped his own vest and helped the sailor into it, giving him a shove in the direction of the whaleboat.

"Swim for the others. Move, man!" he croaked.

Mitchell remembered the kapok vest he'd taken off the corpse. He swam to the spot, but with no luck. Everything was steeped in oil and he couldn't see the vest. In the dark, he drifted on the black sea. Mitchell felt completely alone. Panic pierced his heart as he swam with all his strength for the whaleboat.

The boat was sixty yards away. Mitchell felt his body slowing with a deep and consuming fatigue. It took all the willpower he could muster to reach out, grab a handful of water, and pull himself forward. He realized that he might not be able to rejoin the group, and again, sadness smothered him as he thought about dying in this vast and lonely sea.

He felt something terribly strong grip his right leg and yank him from the world of air and sound, dragging him down. He felt it, eight hundred pounds of terror mauling him. Mitchell clawed at the water. He screamed, hearing the sound so clearly in his mind. The fish let go and circled.

What seemed only a moment later, he felt a hideous pressure clamp onto his thigh. Teeth gouged. His panic soared as he was wrenched deeper. It all happened in sickly slow motion. There was no time and no thought. It felt like he was being cleaved in two, severed. Mitchell surrendered to the horror. Locked together in this bizarre universe, he couldn't tell where he ended and the fish began. The fish let go and circled again.

Drifting in the blackness, life seeped from Mitchell, and he felt death's icy touch on the back of his neck.

As THE black whaleboat glided through the floating debris, Andrew perched in the center of the boat, searching. He spotted a waving arm through the gloom. He pointed and shouted at Ogden. The Chief yelled for Andrew to sit down as he pushed the tiller so the bow pointed at the waving arm.

Andrew ignored Ogden's order and prepared to jump overboard to save the man, but Hudson swung an arm and knocked Andrew onto the thwart.

"Stay put, rookie," Hudson shouted.

Andrew crouched in the boat. His frustration erupted from being unable to help the man in the water.

Ogden gave the order to ship oars and as the whaleboat slid past the man, he leaned far out from the stern and grabbed the man by the life jacket. With one powerful motion, the Chief hauled the man over the gunwale and into the boat. It was Skeeter Banks. His head was denuded of hair and his face and skull were covered with fuel oil. Only the whites of his eyes were not black.

Andrew clutched Banks's life jacket and screamed, "Mitchell! Where is Mitchell? Did he make it into the water?"

Banks's face was a mask of unrestrained horror; he'd stared at death eye to eye. His mouth moved. Andrew bowed his head so that his ear was right next to Banks's mouth. He listened with every fiber of his being.

A spasm of exquisite relief flashed through Andrew and he turned to Ogden and pointed off to port, yelling, "Mitchell made it off the ship. He's over there."

The oarsmen threw body and soul into each stroke as if it were their last act on earth. The boat glided forward while the rescuers began choking on the stench of fuel oil fouling the air. They saw the main body of survivors moving toward the island, but they kept their course across the field of debris, looking for Mitchell and anybody else left behind.

Andrew balanced himself in the middle of the whaleboat, scanning the water as precious minutes dripped by. His breath came fast and his heart pounded. He had the feeling that they had missed him, that somewhere in this oily hell the man he loved was dying. He saw a shadow moving. He peered closer. It was a hand clawing at the air above the water. Andrew yelled as he leaped over the gunwale. His legs kicked wildly as he dove and took Mitchell into his arms.

They broke the surface, and the boat was on them in a heartbeat. Strong hands hauled them aboard.

Mitchell gasped for breath, that sweet delirious taste of life. He had a hideous gash on his right thigh.

Andrew found a first aid box under a thwart, and inside were gauze bandages, syringes, and packets of morphine. He ripped the officer's pant from the injured leg, gave him a shot of painkiller, and wrapped the wound. By the time he was done, the boat had pulled alongside the large group of survivors and they began taking men aboard.

As much as Andrew would have loved to hunker in the boat and hold Mitchell, there were others who needed help. He nursed the injured until searchlights from the enemy cruiser *Aoba* stabbed through the night and surrounded them in a corona of brilliant yellow light.

Part II
Changi Prison

At first you get in a situation where you abhor it.
You can't stand it. It's terrible. But you can't get away from it.
So you stick with it. And then you get so that you tolerate it.
You tolerate it long enough, you embrace it.
It becomes your way of life.

—Lewis Haynes,
LCDR, Medical Corp,
USS *Indianapolis*

Chapter Seventeen

May 25, 1942—0800 hours

FORTRESS SINGAPORE, stronghold of the British forces controlling the trade routes between the Indian Ocean and the South China Sea, had a twenty-square-mile naval base that boasted docks large enough to supply their entire fleet. The British enjoyed a rather pleasant existence on their pristine emerald island, which sparkled like one of their crown jewels set within the waving blue Pacific. They believed that any attack on the island must be launched from warships, since no army could breach the dense four-hundred-mile Malayan rainforest to the north. Hence, their defenses relied on enormous guns pointed out to sea, which were useless against a ground assault.

The Japanese, however, did the impossible. Loaded with heavy artillery, they swept through the Malayan jungle like a tsunami, crushing all British forces in their path. On Feb. 8, 1942, Japanese artillery began shelling Singapore Island as Japanese troops crossed the narrow Johore Strait. The Japanese were greatly outnumbered by the island's defenders, and they were dangerously low on fuel and ammunition, so they attempted an all-or-nothing charge. Five days later, the allied forces surrendered in a stunning defeat. Fifty thousand British and Australian troops became prisoners of war, along with two thousand civilians, many of whom were women and children, and the Malays bowed to a new master.

The majority of POWs were shipped north to labor camps on the Thai-Burma railroad. The rest were marched twenty-seven kilometers from the heart of the city to a prison built on the Changi Peninsula, which forms the extreme eastern tip of Singapore Island.

Built before the war, Changi Prison was designed to hold two thousand prisoners, but the Japanese crammed fifteen thousand POWs within its walls. Women and children were housed at a separate, makeshift camp five kilometers from the prison.

The complex was built in onion-like layers. At the center was a sunbaked courtyard, surrounded by a dozen multistory cell blocks, which were surrounded by towering walls. The south wall had a gigantic gate that, like all the cell doors, always stood wide open so prisoners could move freely in and out. Outside the gate, a road circled the four walls. On both sides of this road were rows of thatched roof sheds the prisoners called "go-downs." Each shed was a hundred feet long and held forty beds.

There were four rows of concrete go-downs (twenty to a row) that housed the senior officers, majors and above. The other sheds were made from coconut fronds nailed to wood frames, which housed the junior officers and the overflow of enlisted men from the cell blocks.

A hundred yards of cleared land lay between the go-downs and a snarled web of barbed wire that encircled the entire prison. Beyond the wire were guardhouses, where Indian, Japanese, and Korean guards were housed. A watchtower with machine gun posts and searchlights stood at each corner of the prison, but there was little need for these towers because there was no place to escape to.

The *Pilgrim*'s survivors made the forced march from the military docks to the Changi Prison. Reduced to a ragged and filthy bunch, their bodies and uniforms were streaked with fuel oil, vomit, mud, and feces. They dragged along in a mechanical manner, the strong helping the weak, the weak helping the weaker.

Along the city streets, natives stood at the roadside, boldly offering bananas, boiled eggs, and cups of water, but the Japanese escort kept them back with their bayonets, which glistened brightly from the barrels of their .25 caliber rifles. These offerings were heartwarming, considering the brutal treatment that their captors inflicted, but especially so for Andrew because when he looked into the faces of the sympathetic locals, he noticed that many of the eyes staring back were Chinese.

A five-hour march brought them to the crest of a hill where the sixty-five ragged Americans caught their first glimpse of Changi. From a distance, the walls rising above a belt of green jungle looked enchanting, as if they belonged to a sultan's palace surrounded by an oasis. But as they marched closer, Changi took on a more sinister appearance, transforming into a sunbaked scab on the jungle, the color of dried bones.

Andrew didn't see the walls. Having lost all vital energy, he suffered from heat, thirst, and crushing weariness. All his attention zeroed in on moving his legs while supporting his handle of a makeshift litter that carried an unconscious Lt. Mitchell.

He held his knees stiff so that they wouldn't buckle under the litter's weight. If he stumbled, he risked taking a bayonet in the gut, as had three others. Bullets were a precious commodity, so the Japanese soldiers had become adroit with their bayonets. They drove the blade into the gut and scrambled the bowels by twisting the rifle with a flourish, leaving the victim screaming while dying a prolonged and agonizing death.

Moyer, Stokes, and Hudson manned the other litter handles, and they carried the same fear. Brutish guards kicked, clubbed, and stabbed the men who faltered. Eighty-eight men were pulled from the water, but after two weeks on Guadalcanal and another week crammed shoulder to shoulder aboard a foul-smelling cargo vessel, the number had dwindled by a quarter.

Andrew's temple itched like crazy under a bloody bandage wrapped around his head. He yearned to reach up and scratch under the bandage, but he was too afraid to let go of the litter handle.

Hour after hour they struggled through scorching heat, until they passed under a tower festooned with the Rising Sun. They marched through an opening in the barbed wire, up the path that led beyond the rows of go-downs, through the wall gate, and into a courtyard surrounded by cell blocks.

Andrew lowered Mitchell and crumpled to the ground. He had not had a drink of water in two days. His mouth felt cottony; his tongue hung thickly over his cracked lips. But rather than wish for death, which had become his habit, he focused on Mitchell.

He fought back his weariness and crawled to Mitchell's right thigh. Mitchell's pant leg had been ripped away, showing his bare leg and shoe. The sole of his shoe was hanging on by only a few threads. The leg was swollen and had a sickly gray color. Andrew inspected the rag pressed against the wound. It was filthy, but Andrew had nothing to replace it with. Pulling the dressing away, he scrutinized the angry-red, putrid-smelling wound.

They must have drugs here, he thought.

Another litter was laid beside him—the one holding Cocoa. Grady, who had helped to carry Cocoa's litter, collapsed beside Andrew. He leaned against Andrew and croaked, "We made it, Andy. Praise God, we made it."

Like Mitchell, Cocoa's lower leg had been badly chewed by sharks before the rescue, and it was festered and swollen to three times its normal size. Cocoa babbled incoherently. Sweat poured from his body.

Andrew had done his best to keep the wounds clean and dressed, but in the tropics it was impossible to keep infection away without antibiotics. Andrew closed his eyes, feeling the intense heat rippling off the pavement.

There were two seasons in this part of the globe: oppressively hot and monsoon wet (which was also oppressively hot). No winter and no spring, no hibernation and no renewal, there was only the monotonous heat with an occasional downpour.

The courtyard baked Andrew's mind, and in his delirium he began to relive portions of their torturous journey. Two weeks on Guadalcanal, slogging about a mucky hellhole with rats, leeches, blowflies, mosquitoes, maggot-infested piles of feces, and every strain of intestinal parasite, all surrounded by a bamboo fence. Andrew could still smell the pungent and indescribable stench.

On the first day Andrew had approached a guard, bowed, and used his best Japanese to beg for medical supplies to help the wounded. The guard's response was a rifle butt to Andrew's gut, dropping him like a stone. The guard had pointed his bayonet at Andrew's neck and screamed, "Yankee scum, next time you die!" Andrew crawled to his knees and bowed again, putting his face to the dirt.

Others were also targets of gratuitous brutality. The guards' fanatic hatred of the white race influenced their every action. They would steal anything that caught their eye: rings, watches, pocketknives, lighters. Smitty had his teeth bashed out by a soldier who noticed his gold fillings. On four separate occasions, the officer in charge became angry when a prisoner failed to understand his orders, given in Japanese. Three of those times the officer drew his revolver and shot the pleading prisoner in the head. The fourth man was knocked to the ground with a rifle butt to the face. The officer placed the tip of his bayonet on the man's neck and plunged it to the hilt.

Finally, they were led onto a tramp steamer and loaded into a cargo hold with floor-to-ceiling shelves three feet high and ten feet deep. They were wedged into the shelves, sitting cross-legged and hunched over, knee-to-knee and five deep. The temperature from the collective body heat quickly grew infernal in the ill-ventilated hold. Breathing became nearly impossible, and several men passed out.

Mitchell had a dangerous fever and his cadaverously pale body trembled, so once again Andrew begged for drugs and bandages. This time he was shoved aside by three guards holding bamboo canes and received a blow to the side of his head. As he crashed to the deck, one guard drew his revolver and pointed it at the other prisoners stuffed into the shelves so that they would not interfere.

"Please, Master, don't beat me," Andrew mumbled.

Rough hands, unbelievably strong, grabbed his shoulder and pulled from behind, jerking him to his knees and whirling him around to face a guard. Andrew's lips were pressed to the man's crotch. He saw the brown buttons of the man's fly, the weave of the uniform. It smelled of soap and sweat. Andrew's eyes followed the line of the uniform up to the man's face. The guard, stocky and powerful, slid his tongue across his lower lip. Andrew heard it, the sound of the man's moist tongue wetting his lip. Above the open mouth were eyes blazing like a tiger's.

A shiver ran up Andrew's spine. The guard's hand cupped Andrew's jaw, applying enough pressure to hold it in position, while his other hand unbuttoned his fly. The odor of sweaty flesh hit Andrew's nose. Another guard knelt behind him, leaned his head next to Andrew's, cheek to cheek. Hands fumbled at Andrew's belt. He caught the stench of whiskey on the man's breath while his pants and underwear were yanked down, bunching about his knees. The man's breathing was heavy and echoed in Andrew's head. Everything became a blur as Andrew was squeezed in the vise of these two men, one holding him from behind, the other towering over him.

Andrew understood the snarl of Japanese. "This is what we do to Asians who are white inside!" Andrew heard the man behind him spit three times into his palm. An electric charge ran from Andrew's heart to his testicles. He struggled to free himself, but there was no escape.

The ache in his head became searing waves of pain. The compartment went deathly still. Andrew looked to the side. Eyes were watching. All the *Pilgrim*'s survivors were stuffed into the floor-to-ceiling shelves, witnessing his shame.

The guard looming over Andrew let his pants fall about his thighs and pressed his cock against Andrew's lips. A slap across Andrew's face dropped his mouth open, forming a red circle. The guard cupped a hand behind Andrew's head and wrenched it forward.

As Andrew's face mashed into the man's sweaty pubic hairs, he felt a searing pain rip into his bum. He screamed a muffled cry. The compartment spun about him. He gagged again and again. He couldn't get enough air. He focused all his attention on gulping air between thrusts as the guards worked him over, roughly and clumsily.

Occasionally, details of what was occurring filtered through his numb consciousness: the taste of slick flesh, the stink of whiskey, the bristly pubic hair, the labored breathing, the animal-like grunts, the stench of vomit from the other prisoners.

An eternity seemed to pass before the man standing over him squeezed the sides of Andrew's head and pumped his hips like a jackhammer. All at once, Andrew was choking on sperm. Even while gagging, Andrew could feel the eighty pairs of horrified eyes helplessly staring.

The guard behind him savagely groaned in his ear and he knew it would soon be over. But he also knew that it would never be over. He would suffer this humiliation every minute of his life. Andrew whimpered as both men pulled free of him and he was finally able to breathe.

They shoved him to the deck and beat him with bamboo canes: five blows across the back, slamming him harder and harder; two severe blows to the head. He heard his skull crack, twice. His mind drowned in a sea of flames.

They hauled him across the deck and rolled him into the lowest shelf, where he lay perfectly still with eyes unblinking. In that tropical heat, Andrew felt cold. He wanted to move, to pull his pants up over his nakedness, but he couldn't. Rifts had opened in various parts of his body, in his mouth, his bum, his skull. He felt the hot, sticky, stagnant air within the ship's compartment course through these ruptures, touching something deep inside. At the same time, he felt his life force hemorrhaging out these same holes.

Mitchell's face hovered above him, looking helpless in a comical sort of way. There was something ridiculous about the situation. Grady slid closer, eyes as wide as saucers, and he turned and vomited.

Andrew wanted to tell them that it was okay, that the pain was seeping away, leaving only the frigid cold, but he couldn't speak. Mitchell curled an arm under Andrew's head and across his shoulders, but Andrew couldn't feel his touch.

"Christ, he's dead."

Andrew recognized Cocoa's voice but couldn't see him.

The hold-cover was lowered into place. Andrew was consumed by claustrophobic darkness. He became convinced he *was* dead. A moment later, he felt a cool breeze whisper across his cheek and under his wings, lifting… lifting…. The world below stood still as he glided high above the ship. He did not know if he was flying through time, or suspended, hovering in a still universe of blue sky and brilliant sunshine. He only knew that delicious feeling of freedom.

Ever so slowly, his feathered body fused with the sky and he became the wind. After a timeless span, things turned confusing. Harsh voices, burning light, and an incredible soul-consuming pain all rushed back to him, pulling him down.

The men in the darkness around him had become crazed with fear. They shrieked obscenities and lashed out at each other in claustrophobic hysteria until the guards opened the hatch cover once again, letting light and air pour into the compartment.

Andrew opened his eyes, blinked. The first thing that came into focus was Mitchell's face, which still held that comical expression. "You'll be okay," a voice said. He felt himself being pressed in a tight hug and he heard words hastily whispered. "I love you," or "God love you." He wasn't sure which, but regardless, he was startled to his core.

During the seven-day voyage, to escape the pain, humiliation, and stench Andrew often wished for death, for that freedom of flight, to never return to his body again. Every day, three or four men were given up to the sea, and he prayed he would be next.

Once, while waiting on deck for the daily rice ration, a prisoner stumbled to the rail and jumped over. Nobody knew who it was. Guards and prisoners all stared as the man drowned in the ship's wash. In the hold, Andrew emptied his mind and willed himself to have the same courage as the man who jumped.

Chapter Eighteen

May 25, 1942—1500 hours

IN THE Changi courtyard, the prisoners baked for an hour before the prison commandant sauntered in front of them and stepped onto a wooden box. He was a powerful man, about forty years old. He stood slightly under six feet tall and wore an immaculate, straw-colored uniform. A samurai sword clung to his side, tucked under his thick belt, and his black boots gleamed in the sunlight. In the center of his red-striped visor-cap sat the emblem of his regiment, which shined like gold from years of polishing. The cap covered a head of short iron gray hair, and his face and arms were burnt a masculine red-brown. He surveyed the ragged survivors while holding a swagger stick in one hand, slapping it against the palm of his other hand. Behind him spread a black shadow that seemed to move of its own accord.

He pointed the stick at the *Pilgrim*'s crew and, using a belligerent, baritone voice, announced in perfect English, "You are the first Americans to become prisoners of this camp. The Imperial Army has conquered the English, the Australians, and the Dutch. Now we are defeating the Americans. The prisoners of this camp are not prisoners of war, but rather, captives. A real soldier fights to the death and would not disgrace himself by being taken alive. You are no better than dogs, only concerned with saving your miserable skins. Thus, you will be treated like dogs. Obey the rules and you will avoid punishment. Break the rules and we will show no mercy. Escape is futile. There is no place on this island to hide. That is all."

Commandant Tottori's supercilious voice broke over the prisoners like a sea surge. Andrew felt a jolt in his testicles, as if the force in the man's voice were crushing his most tender flesh. He knew that resistance to this man's authority was unthinkable. In fact, even the officers and soldiers under Tottori's command leapt with surprising fervor at his most trivial orders.

As Tottori stepped from the makeshift podium and stomped from the courtyard, a short, pugnacious-looking captain took his place on the box. Using an interpreter, the captain explained the camp rules.

As the officer's truculent voice droned on, Andrew scanned the prisoners gathered on the courtyard's borders, the ones leaning against the cell block walls. They stared at the newcomers as if they were inspecting themselves in a mirror, seemingly afraid of what they found.

Andrew focused on one middle-aged prisoner wearing loose-fitting shorts soiled with tropic mold, wooden clogs, and a green Tank Corps beret. Round, protruding eyes dominated his face, and his body, wasted by malnutrition and amoebic dysentery, was nothing more than parchment-like brown skin stretched over sinew and bone, like the tortured steel framework of a building from which everything else had been sandblasted away. But those eyes, those colorless eyes, were so dull they didn't reflect any light. The other prisoners all carried that same emaciated look. The only differences between them were age, height, and color of hair.

Andrew tried to focus on the interpreter's words, but the heat allied with his exhaustion to make his head spin, and he couldn't reach through his dizziness to understand.

He leaned forward and rested his forehead on Mitchell's chest. The rhythm of the officer's heartbeat vibrated through his skull.

Mitchell's body rose. British prisoners lifted the litters and carried the wounded to the camp hospital. The man wearing the green beret led the Americans who could walk out of the courtyard.

Andrew and Grady struggled to their feet and followed a ragged line of the *Pilgrim*'s crew outside the high walls and down the outer road that cut through the go-downs. The crew turned off the main road and headed down a path to the ninth hut in a row of ten: Hut Twenty-nine. They filed into the hut and Andrew collapsed on the floorboards inside the entrance. Out of the scorching sun, his head cleared and his thoughts returned.

The man in the beret lingered inside the doorway, watching the crew file in. Ensign Fisher was the last one through the door, and the man addressed him with a nasal British accent.

"My name is Lieutenant Fowler. Welcome to Changi. This is Hut Twenty-nine and the American enlisted men will be housed here. I'm afraid that we weren't expecting you, so it will take us a day or so to make room for your officers. Until then, you'll have to sleep here."

"Ensign Monte Fisher." Fisher held out his hand, but Fowler only peered down at the gesture until Fisher pulled his hand to his side. "It won't be necessary to find other accommodations. There are only three officers. We can bunk with the enlisted men."

"Rather bad form for officers to fraternize with the ranks. Next thing you know they'll be calling you by your Christian name. You Yanks are notoriously undisciplined. Respect for the chain of command is essential. Now that America has been dragged, kicking and screaming, into the war, I suppose you'll have to sort that all out." He paused for a moment, and added with a smirk, "Along with growing some spine."

Fisher's face reddened and his eyes smoldered, but he held his tongue.

Fowler glanced down at Andrew and his nose wrinkled, as if detecting a foul stench. "Curious—are you Yanks enlisting Wogs?"

Andrew glanced up at the smirking officer and said, with a weary voice, "I'm an American."

"When you address an officer you will use the term, 'sir.'"

"If you're an officer, then you are pathetically out of uniform. And as I said, I'm an American. I'm not under British authority and don't have to kowtow to you or your bloody rules."

Fowler's face flushed. "Pity. If you are an American, that would make you yellow on the inside as well as the outside."

Ogden stepped forward from the circle of onlookers and grabbed Fowler by the throat, slamming him up against the flimsy wall. "Watch your mouth, you skinny fuck!"

Andrew held up his hand to stop Ogden, who let go of the lieutenant and retreated a step.

Andrew struggled to his feet to face Fowler. "I've always heard that a British officer is the consummate gentleman, but a gentleman would never humiliate himself by insulting another man to his face. So it seems that only the British upper class are gentlemen, and not the commoners."

Fowler's eyes narrowed and his jaw clenched. He hissed, "You'll pay dearly for that remark. I can promise you that, you yellow bastard!" He turned on Ogden. "And you assaulted an officer. That's a criminal offense."

"Lieutenant Fowler." A tall, gray-haired man wearing a shabby uniform and clogs, carrying a wooden cigar box under his arm, appeared in the doorway. He twisted one end of his handlebar mustache with his fingertips. "We can give our American allies a warmer welcome than that, don't you think? After all, we're all on the same side, eh?" The man's eyebrows lifted.

"Colonel Henman, I-I was…." Fowler stammered. "Yes, you are right of course. Frightfully sorry." He moved to the doorway and turned to Fisher, still visibly struggling to regain his composure. "You will catch on to the routine soon enough, old boy. Nothing changes from one day to the next. On each bunk you will find a water bottle, a tin mug, a spoon, and two billycans—one for rice and one for soup. You will need those to eat. Anything else you need, like tobacco and soap, can be purchased from Little Sister Wu. She's the Chinese woman who runs the camp store. Of course you'll need something of value to trade. Showers are at the end of the row and the latrines are up the hill from the west wall. Every day, a few men from each hut must work. Details gather wood for the cooking fires, bury the dead, and repair the airstrip. Be careful to tuck your mosquito netting in thoroughly—one tiny opening and those tenacious buggers will drain you dry in a single night."

Fowler paused, as if considering whether he had covered all the bases, and added, "Oh yes. If you're caught outside the wire, they'll kill you. And if you're caught breaking any camp rules, they'll send you north to the work gangs building the Burma railway. If you think this is hell, think again. Here they only starve you to death. There they also work you to death and beat you to death. Life expectancy on a work gang is three weeks." Fowler's voice shivered at the mere mention of the railway gangs.

Fowler turned to leave, but Fisher said, "Hold on, Lieutenant. I believe you owe Seaman Waters an apology."

"I quite agree," Colonel Henman added. "Come now, Fowler. Let's have it."

Fowler opened his mouth, but paused. His lips trembled as he wiped the sweat from his forehead. His expression went hard as he twisted his head toward Andrew, saying in a softer voice, "You have my apology, Seaman Waters." He glanced at Henman, who dismissed him with a flash of his eyes and a nod. Fowler whirled about and disappeared through the doorway.

Henman shook his head as he watched Fowler stride away, and asked to speak with the senior American officer.

Moyer stepped forward. "Hello, sir. I'm Chaplain Moyer, I mean, Ensign Moyer."

"A chaplain? Oh, capital! You have no idea how badly we require religious guidance. Seems our English clergy fell sick and passed on during the first months. They say the meek shall inherit the earth, but not in this camp, I'm afraid. I am sure you are not Church of England, but no matter. I would love to work with you to organize services for our boys, and of course the brave souls in the hospital need you so desperately. In this camp of perpetual starvation and sickness, the men who keep to their faith in those moments of deep anguish are the ones who survive. But so many boys give up too easily. It is as if they will themselves to die in order to end the suffering. Surrendering the spirit is an infectious disease, and it is spreading all too quickly here. Can I count on you, sir?"

Moyer's eyes shone. "Of course," he stammered. "It will be a privilege." His bewildered expression metamorphosed into an aura of joy.

"Smashing. Oh, I am forgetting my manners. I'm Colonel Thomas Henman." He extended his hand and Moyer clasped it firmly.

"This is Ensign Fisher, Monte Fisher."

"So pleased."

Henman stared at Andrew. "Young man, you're either frightfully clever or you know a thing or two about Englishmen. Your comment about not being upper class was the most injurious insult you can give a man like Fowler. Either way, I'd say you've made an enemy during your first hour in camp. I certainly hope you are not planning to make a habit of this sort of behavior, eh?"

"No, sir."

"Interesting that you call me 'sir' but refused Lieutenant Fowler the same courtesy."

"Sir, you earned my respect." The effort to speak used up Andrew's remaining strength. His voice trailed off until it was overpowered by the drone of flies.

"Well put, young man. Here, let me help you to bed." The colonel helped Andrew to lie on the bunk nearest the door. He pulled the cap off his own water bottle and held Andrew's head up to drink. Andrew swallowed a few mouthfuls before Henman laid his head on the pillow to rest.

"Sir," Andrew rasped. "When can I see Lieutenant Mitchell?"

"You must be referring to the officer they carried to the hospital. Do not worry about him, young man. Our medical staff are giving him the best possible care. I am sure he will be allowed visitors in the next day or two. You concentrate on getting yourself stronger."

"Yes, sir. Thank you."

"Now," Henman said, facing the officers. "I popped in to pump you for news about the latest battle developments. Perhaps we could take a walk and you can fill me in."

Fisher nodded. "Can't tell you much, and what I know isn't encouraging, but I'll be happy to."

"Jolly good. Any information helps." Henman lifted the box from under his arm and handed it to Moyer. "We took up a tobacco collection. Java tobacco is rather harsh, but one acquires a taste for it."

Moyer opened the lid. It was full of raw tobacco, rice papers, and matches. "Holy cow." Moyer smiled. "Thanks a million. I'll pass this around."

"A word to the wise," Henman said, his face falling into a pained expression. "Beware of the Indian guards. They are savagely cruel. They will beat you to death if you give them the least provocation." He wagged his head as his eyes turned a watery blur. "We trained them, brought them here, and worked beside them. When the Japs came, they turned on us. I swear I thought they loved us." His voice tailed off to nothing. A moment later, he said, "You officers must remove any symbol of rank. They stripped us of that, turned us into one chaotic mass with no visible chain of command. No sense to it, really, except to deprive us of our dignity. Damned inexcusable.

"One other bit of advice," Henman added. "Here we live by camp rules and by our wits. It is not much of a living, but most of the men manage somehow. The men who do not make it are the ones who lick the boots of the guards to get handouts, the ones who rely on doctors to pull them through, and the squealers who rat on their chums to save their own skins. Keep that in mind and you will all do fine." Henman took Fisher by the arm and led him through the doorway. "Cheerio." Henman saluted Moyer as he and Fisher strolled up the path between the go-downs.

The hut stood on three-foot-high stilts to avoid the creatures that crawl or slither, and to raise the hut above floodwaters during the monsoons. The door and windows were simple openings in the rough walls and provided no deterrent for flying insects: flies during the day and mosquitoes at night. Indeed, the drone from swarms of flies was loud. The thatched roof had low overhangs to keep out the sweltering sun, but the mildewed layers of thatching gave off a claustrophobic odor, like rotting flesh. Electric wires crawled through the rafters like centipedes, with naked bulbs hanging down every fifth bunk. There were two rows of bunk beds, and mosquito netting covered each one. Forty for sixty-five men, but twenty men were in the hospital, so for the time being only a few men would need to sleep in shifts.

Andrew's head cleared while he lay on the lumpy, kapok-stuffed mattress, and he sipped more water from his own bottle. Grady flopped down beside him and they pressed together, like babies instinctively nuzzling into the comfort of their mother.

Two hours passed before Andrew pulled himself to a sitting position and thought about cleaning up at the showers. Several crewmen had already showered and washed their clothes. Andrew longed to be clean. The only thing better would be something to eat, but dinner was hours away. He yanked Grady to his feet and they helped each other down the line of huts to the showers. They had no soap, but they scrubbed their bodies free of as much grime as possible, and they soaked and rinsed their clothes in a wooden washtub.

Walking back to his hut, Andrew lay down again and fell into a dreamless sleep. At sundown, Moyer jostled him awake and handed him a billycan full of rice and another full of fish broth.

Andrew savored his meal, and after eating, he felt fit enough to play Jah-Jai. He withdrew the flute from beneath his shirt, amazed that the instrument had survived the three-week journey intact. He folded his legs into a lotus position, brought Jah-Jai to his lips. He spread his fingers over the holes and ran through a series of notes. Sound rippled through the hut. He found it difficult to force air through his parched throat, but Mozart had a slightly rejuvenating effect and the notes grew stronger. But even so, he played the piece slowly, mournfully.

Men chose bunks, inspected the netting, and peered out windows. Some hobbled off to the showers while others rolled cigarettes and blew smoke toward the swarms of flies. Others simply paced about while getting accustomed to their new surroundings. They shuffled through the room as if dancing a slow waltz to Andrew's melancholy tune.

Moyer ambled to the far end of the hut and asked the men to gather around and kneel while he led them in prayer.

Stokes said, "Sir, will we make it? I mean, will I ever see my girl again?"

Moyer half smiled. "With God's help we made it this far, and I'm sure if He wills it, we'll all be going home soon. Of course we may need His undivided attention for that to happen, but let us pray for that, shall we?"

"But sir," Stokes said, "I've got to get word to my girl. You see, she's waiting for me to come back so we can get married. If she don't hear from me, she'll think I'm dead. I gotta let her know so she don't fall for some other guy. Can you help me, Mr. Moyer?"

"All we can do is pray and hope the Lord listens."

The men dropped to the floorboards as Moyer began. Only Andrew did not join in. He kept playing his tune to accompany the prayer. Moyer's voice grew stronger and seemed to fill the room with the Holy Spirit, just as Andrew filled it with Mozart. Some men prayed out loud, others knelt, trembling. Surprisingly, Hudson's voice was among the most passionate.

Mozart failed to overpower Andrew. Confusing emotions erupted deep inside him. He scrutinized his feelings as he played the doleful melody, probing beneath the humiliation of rape, the pain of beatings, the grip of starvation, and his concern about Mitchell's well-being, until comprehending that, at his core, he felt utterly grateful. For him the war was over—no more fighting, no killing, no waiting to be killed, and hopefully no more rape. In this camp, he could simply live one moment to the next, follow the rules, and wait for the day he would return home. Overwhelming relief washed through him like a cold stream. The prison was his genesis, he realized, a new beginning. He blew harder and the tempo quickened, filling the hut with spirited music.

CHAPTER NINETEEN

May 26, 1942—0600 hours

A CLOUDBURST drenched the camp as the sun rose above the green belt of jungle. Raindrops pelted Andrew's skin as he performed his tai chi outside Hut Twenty-nine. The downpour enhanced his enjoyment. The retreating darkness, cool air, and bracing rain all coalesced to create a healing energy that descended from his crown to his soles. He felt dizzy, drunk on the rain's freshness. His dancelike meditation abated into stillness, and he settled into a lotus position on the shady side of Hut Twenty-nine.

The relative coolness helped to keep his mind empty, but three weeks of eating nothing more than rice drew his attention to his vacuous belly.

The rain retreated, the clouds dissipated, the temperature soared. The air carried a sea-salt tang mixed with the delicate sweetness of jungle frangipani. Morning light spread red-orange hues across the camp, causing hundreds of puddles to reflect the colored light, making them resemble pools of shimmering blood.

A few minutes after sunup, the Indian block-leaders charged through camp yelling curses, rousing the men from sleep, many of whom had slept two to a bunk on bug-infested straw pallets. The prisoners stood in ranks for ninety minutes while every man was counted and recounted and the numbers tallied. Those who passed in the night were laid along the south wall and counted as well.

While standing in ranks, Andrew heard the faint ringing of bells from beyond the wall of rainforest. He was reminded of the great eight-hundred-catty iron bell at the Bai Hur Sze Temple, calling the monks to morning prayers. He recalled his last day there, the day he'd had an audience with Master Jung-Wei under a bodhi tree. The monk had told Andrew about a young acolyte who had attended his monastery many years earlier. The acolyte had tried diligently to learn his lessons and he studied the sutras every day, but he had difficulty understanding even the simplest concepts. Monks were notoriously harsh on slow acolytes, and this boy received numerous beatings. Still, he failed to learn. He became a joke. Every monk assumed he was unteachable. They ignored his tiresome questions and often gave him a sound smack to quiet him.

One autumn morning, the monks filed into the prayer hall and occupied every available cushion. Latecomers knelt on the hardwood floor. At one end of the hall sat the altar, and behind that stood a golden statue of the Lord Buddha. The altar was carved from sandalwood in the shape of a lotus flower, and on it sat the venerable monk who ruled the monastery. They said he had the ability to see directly into each man's heart and know that man's most private fears.

A smile adorned the abbot's face that morning. He wore a voluminous cassock, and held a string of jade beads in one hand and a bell in the other. The acolyte sat with his legs folded while he waited for the abbot's exposition of the dharma, delighting in the pure autumn breeze that drifted through the open doors to mingle with the sonorous voices of chanting monks.

Soon the volume of chanting grew soft, to a whisper, and ripened into silence as the abbot struck a single note on his bell. The tone soared to the hall's rafters and undulated through the cavernous room.

The abbot leaned forward. "Physical phenomena are illusions created by the duality of the human mind. Enlightenment cannot be understood by the intellect, nor can it be verbally transmitted. Only by abandoning the dualistic mind altogether can one achieve Enlightenment. To do this, you must envision your mind as a mirror that reflects what lies before you in the realm of physical manifestations. You must strive constantly to clean this mirror of the debris from self-absorption, and allow no dust or lint to attach itself to the surface. When the mirror becomes pure, free of any self-important particles, it will vanish altogether and you will enter the Buddha's realm. What I transmit to you is the Dharma transmitted by the Buddha. Are there any questions?"

Master Jung-Wei had explained that only a handful of monks had completely understood the exposition. Many grasped none of it, but nobody had the courage to admit his confusion. Silence blanketed the hall to a man, until this young acolyte crawled off his pillow and knelt with palms pressed together, saying, "Holiness, I do not understand."

The abbot's penetrating eyes opened wide. "State your question."

The boy stammered, "Holiness, the scriptures claim that there is no such mirror, that it is an illusion—there is nothing that a particle of dust can attach itself to. So how does one clean something that does not exist?"

After a minute's silence, the abbot signaled to his senior disciple, one he had personally tonsured. The disciple rushed to help the old one stand, guiding him off the altar and down the line of monks to face the acolyte.

The boy readied himself for a blow to the head, but the abbot crumpled to the floorboards. He knelt in front of the acolyte and bowed until his palms and forehead touched the floor.

Master Jung-Wei had gazed into Andrew's eyes, to the soft light shining within. "I told you that story to show you true courage. Courage is not a man firing a rifle on a battlefield. True courage comes when you see in your heart the moral path before you, and you know you are defeated before you begin, everything and everyone seems against you, but you are compelled to proceed anyway, and you strive to stay the course no matter what. You rarely succeed, but every so often someone sees into your heart and bows at your feet. That acolyte was not afraid of seeming a fool or taking a beating. He placed his love for truth above all else, and he eventually became the abbot of the monastery. He was the bravest man I ever knew."

A RUSH of harsh voices snapped Andrew out of his reminiscence. The Indian guards made their way through the ranks with scowling faces, wielding plaited leather whips. At the least provocation they lashed out at a prisoner's face or the side of his neck, and all the men around them jumped away en masse. The guards screamed to get them back into ranks and the count would start over. After the count was taken, the Indian guards marched away, and the men scrambled to form an impatient chow line.

Andrew hurried for a place in line while Grady ran to Hut Twenty-nine to retrieve their mess-cans, mugs, and spoons. It was an agonizing wait, made longer by the hunger gripping Andrew's belly.

They stood for thirty minutes before six men hurried to the front of the line, carrying twelve five-gallon cans that were once used to hold fuel. The men ladled out one cup of rice gruel and one cup of tea to each man in line. Andrew counted how many men stood between him and the food, worrying that there would be nothing left by the time he got there.

"Doggone," Grady groaned. "Tomorrow we gots to get here faster. This waitin' kills me."

Forty minutes crawled by before they neared the mush pots. Andrew paid close attention to how large a portion each man in front of him received. As he held up his own mess-cans, he ensured that he and Grady received the same measure of gruel and tea.

They raced to the shady side of Hut Twenty-nine and sat next to Hudson and Stokes, who were sitting on the ground with their backs against the hut wall. They set their mess-cans in the dirt so they could eat with one hand while fanning flies away with the other.

Andrew squatted on his haunches, native-style, while he ate.

"How do you keep your balance, sittin' like that?" Grady asked.

"You should try it. It's comfortable and it keeps your butt from getting dirty."

"No way. You look like a monkey sitting on a branch."

The tasteless food brought no complaints. Grady used his spoon to pick a few weevils out of his mush, but Andrew didn't bother. Bugs were protein and he needed all he could get. The food lifted his mood. It felt splendid to have something in his belly to temporarily stop the gnawing pains. He relished the taste of weak tea, and the rice gruel brought back childhood memories of summers at the monastery.

Andrew noticed that Hudson had altered the way he ate. Aboard ship, he would devour mountains of fried potatoes, slabs of roast beef, bowls of stew, stacks of bread with tasty butter, and wash it all down with mugs of coffee that were thick with cream and sweet with sugar. He would eat so fast that he never tasted any of it, wolfing it down until he was ready to burst. But after a month of near starvation, he had learned to nibble small amounts of rice at a time, munching it into a paste to extract every iota of flavor, rolling it on his tongue and sucking it into the sides of his cheek, holding it there for a moment before swallowing. To make it last. *Yes,* Andrew thought, *rice tastes like ambrosia if you take your time and tease your belly.*

Hudson leaned toward Andrew. "Rookie, I've been talking to some of the limeys. They say a man can't make it on his own, can't live on the four ounces of rice a day they dole out. You've got to form units and pull together to scavenge more food. You need at least three men, one to forage for anything edible, one to guard and cook what you've already scrounged, and one spare for when somebody gets sick. If nobody's sick, then two forage."

"Makes sense, but what's there to scavenge?"

"There are ways to make money to buy things like eggs and coconuts and bananas. What you can't buy, you filch."

"Steal?"

Hudson shook his head. "It's a simple redistribution of wealth is all. Don't look at me like that. This is dog eat dog. How about it, rookie, you, me, and Stokes?"

"And Grady?"

"Sure, but he's got to pull his weight."

Grady chuckled. "I gots lots of filchin' experience."

"Alright," Hudson said. "The four musketeers. All for one and… however the hell that goes. We start scouting the camp right after breakfast. Stokes, you're our supply officer."

Stokes sat staring at the dirt with a sorrowful expression.

Andrew nudged Hudson. "What's with him?"

"Aw, he's got the blues thinking his girl will run off with the next sailor that comes along. I told you bums that women were no good."

"Hud," Stokes growled. "I hear another word against my girl and someone's gonna pay."

"Hold your milk, boy. I didn't mean any disrespect. Pull yourself together and tell us what supplies we need."

Stokes finished his last smidgen of gruel and rolled his eyes upward. "Any kind of food, an electric hotplate, a pot, skillet, knife, soap, razor and blades, hair brush, tobacco and papers, and anything we can sell or barter: watches, rings, lighters, clothes."

"And toothbrushes," Andrew said.

"We're starving to death and you're worried about your teeth?" Hudson sneered.

"Hud, the Chinese invented toothbrushes. We know the importance of keeping our mouths clean. Trust me, if you want to walk out of here with teeth, use a toothbrush. You don't even need to brush them all, only the ones you want to keep."

Hudson snorted. "Okay, put 'em on the list."

Grady shook his head. "That's a ton of filchin'."

Hudson nodded. "That's why you can't survive alone. But if the limeys can form units, so can we."

"Okay, one for all," Andrew said. "Hand me your mess-cans. I'll clean up."

Hudson's can, which had a few drops of gruel in the bottom, was crawling with flies so thick it looked like a living can of black bean soup. Andrew gathered the cans to wash them in the showers, realizing how important it was to keep everything perfectly clean.

Stokes pulled a wooden match from his breast pocket and a rolled cigarette from behind his ear. He lit it, inhaled, and passed it to Hudson. Hudson took a drag and looked at Grady. He paused to stare at those pink lips before passing the cigarette to him.

"My God, that's harsh," Hudson said. "Wonder if there are any cigars in this swamp?"

Fisher marched over to address the crew who were sitting beside the hut. "I need four volunteers for work parties—two for the airstrip and two for wood detail. This afternoon I'll work up a schedule to divide the work evenly, but for now I need anybody who can carry a shovel or swing an axe."

Hudson jabbed Stokes in the ribs. "Maybe work will take your mind off your girl and you can scout what there is to scavenge outside the camp."

"Count me in, sir." Stokes lifted himself to his feet.

Fisher looked pleasantly surprised. "Okay, who else?" There was a long silence. "Kelso, Smitty, and Nash, fall in."

While Andrew carried the mess-cans to the showers, Hudson and Grady passed the cigarette between them until it was so short that it scorched their fingers. Grady pinched off the end and placed the smidgen of unburned tobacco in his shirt pocket.

"I'll find us a tobacco box today," Grady said.

WALKING back from the showers, Andrew ran into Moyer, who was returning from the camp hospital. Moyer looked tired, but his eyes carried a soft glow.

"Morning, sir. You look happy," Andrew said.

"I suppose I am. Last night I helped some boys at the hospital. They're so desperate for comfort. You should see their faces when I lead them in prayer."

"Did you see Lieutenant Mitchell?"

"He's in bad shape, and they had to amputate Cocoa's leg below the knee. Gangrene. Nasty stuff. They don't have any anesthetic, so poor old Cocoa went through some kind of hell. I held his hand through the operation, and I can tell you he's the bravest man I've ever met."

"Can I visit them?"

Moyer nodded. "I need to catch a few winks, but after lunch I'll take you there."

"Thank you, sir. I'll wake you for lunch."

THE latrines were simply boreholes in the earth, twelve feet deep, three feet wide. Each hole had a wooden cover with a removable lid. From the prison's west wall, thirty rows marched up the hillside, twenty-five holes to a row, which were spaced five feet apart. With no screens between the holes, everyone did their business in full view of everyone else.

Scanning the orderly field of hole-covers and the forty or so men squatting, Andrew noticed that all the men faced the same direction, downhill toward the prison wall, as if they were all seated in a cinema watching a movie being shown on the bone-white wall.

Andrew used a front-row hole. He didn't feel comfortable relieving himself with everyone behind him watching, but that seemed a better option than watching others in front of him doing their business.

Andrew removed his combat boots, marine fatigue pants, and underwear, and squatted native-style with one foot on each side of the hole. He cleared his mind while his bodily functions took over, listening to the whispering breeze as it caressed his face, groans from nearby men, and, from below the wooden cover, the faint clicking of cockroaches. Hundreds, perhaps thousands, of them running over each other to get to his droppings. He smiled, knowing that they kept the holes from filling up.

When he finished, he lifted his water bottle, poured water into his cupped left hand, and used that to clean any traces of feces from his bum. There was no toilet paper in camp, but using water with the left hand was something that he had done many times growing up in

Asia. In Indochina, people used the right hand for eating and the left hand for washing.

He climbed into his clothes and ambled to Hut Twenty-nine to wait for the afternoon, when he would see Cocoa and Mitchell.

ANDREW, Grady, and Hudson ate their lunch inside the hut. The room felt like a sauna, but outside there was no shade and the sun was relentless. Lunch was a billycan of rice, a billycan of fish soup, and a mug of weak tea. The soup had no chunks of fish, although it did taste fishy. No doubt the fillets fed the guards and the rest of the fish—head, guts, fins—was dumped into a vat of water to make broth. Still, it added a minuscule amount of nutrition to the rice.

Grady snapped his fingers. "I forgot." He pulled a blue toothbrush from his pocket and handed it to Andrew. It was well used but still had a few months of life left.

"Where did you get it?"

"Found it."

Andrew shot him a sideways look.

"Give it back if you don't want it, but don't go askin' how I got it."

Andrew leaned toward his bunk and slid the brush under his pillow.

Stokes glided through the door, carrying his lunch. His shirt bulged in front, making him look eight months pregnant. He placed his mess-cans on the floorboards and winked. "Today's our lucky day," he said as he unbuttoned his shirt and extracted a coconut. "The wood detail is hard-ass work, but look what I found."

"Mary and Joseph, that's fantastic," Hudson said. He took the coconut and swished it back and forth next to his ear. "There's milk sloshing inside, but how do we open it?"

Stokes grinned as he pulled up the pant on his left leg. Tied to his calf with a strip of bamboo cord was a parang machete.

"Holy moly!" Hudson shouted.

"The Jappos don't count the tools. It was easy to tie it under my pants. I was afraid they would search me coming in, but I decided to chance it."

While Stokes polished off his lunch, Grady used water from his bottle to clean four billycans. Andrew took the coconut in his left hand

and the machete in his right. With three swift strokes, he severed the crown. He measured equal portions of milk into each billycan, raised the parang again, and split the coconut into perfect halves.

The sound of the shell slicing open had a riveting quality, like the scream of a newborn baby. It captured the attention of every man in Hut Twenty-nine.

"Hey Hud, where the fuck did you get that?"

"You got to be light on your feet and smart as a whip to get these kind of extras. That leaves you bums out," Hudson said with a chuckle.

With his spoon, Andrew scraped the tender meat from inside the fruit, letting it fall into the cans holding the milk, an equal measure in each.

"Say," Stokes said, "you're pretty handy with that blade."

"I've done this a thousand times."

Andrew was sorry he had already finished his lunch, because the coconut meat would have added a rich flavor to the steamed rice. As it was, milk over meat was a sweet, protein-rich dessert. Andrew couldn't help smiling as he passed a billycan to each man.

They all dug in.

Andrew felt the protein surge though his system. He finished his dessert, tipped the cup over his mouth, trickled the last drops onto his tongue, and licked the inside of the billycan.

The four men leaned against Andrew's bunk, smiling. Sweat poured over them as Andrew idly scratched at bed bug bites while wondering where to hide the parang so no one would steal it.

"That hit the spot!" Stokes said. "Now if we only had a butt."

Grady extracted a half-smoked cigarette and a match from his shirt pocket. He scratched the match on the floorboards and lit the butt, inhaled, and passed it to Stokes.

Chaplain Moyer ambled up and invited Andrew to accompany him to the hospital. Andrew climbed to his feet.

"Think I'll tag along," Hudson said with a wink. "No telling what we can dig up there."

Chapter Twenty

May 26, 1942—1300 hours

THE hospital was situated on the first two floors of a concrete blockhouse inside the walls. Andrew and Hudson trailed Moyer across a blistering courtyard and ducked inside the door.

The rectangular ward had prison cells lining both long walls. Each cell was six feet wide, ten feet long, and twelve feet high. The bars had been removed so that they were open to the center aisle. An iron bed with a kapok mattress sat in each cell. Every bed was occupied. The familiar hospital smells of cleaning fluids and drugs were overpowered by the stench of vomit, rotting flesh, and the musty odor of death.

Moyer led Andrew and Hudson to a cell marked Bed 24. On top of a bare mattress and wearing only his skivvies, Cocoa lay propped up by four pillows, brushing flies away with languid sweeps of his arm. His haggard face showed dark circles under his protruding eyes, deep lines engraved his forehead, and a blood-soaked rag covered the stump below his left knee.

"Cocoa," Moyer said, using a lighthearted tone. "Look who I brought." He patted Andrew on the shoulder and smiled at Cocoa. "Say, I nearly forgot." He pulled a cigar from his shirt pocket. "Met a British colonel who had an extra, so we cut cards for it."

Cocoa's eyes bulged, his mouth lifting into a grin. "Bless you, Chaplain. You're a saint. And the fact that you won it at cards will make it taste even sweeter. Keep this up, and I'll turn religious."

"That would be miraculous. Pardon me if I don't stand around with bated breath, but I want to check with the doc about your leg." Moyer strolled down the line of cells.

Andrew took hold of Cocoa's hand. "How are you feeling?"

"Andy, they didn't even put me to sleep, for God sakes. They strapped me to a table and hacked away like I was a Goddamned Thanksgiving turkey. What the hell am I supposed to do now? What the hell am I good for? They cut away my life."

Andrew squeezed his hand.

Hudson said, "I guess this means you won't be kicking my ass anymore."

Cocoa flinched, snorted. "You got that right. My ass-kicking days are done."

Hudson stepped closer. The two men clasped hands.

"That was a beautiful fight," Cocoa chuckled. "I'm damn glad it was Mitchell who took that right hook and not me. I don't have much left, but I'll always have that."

"Once you're on your feet, I mean foot, we'll have some grand times again. An old salt like you won't let this slow you down. You'll strap on a peg leg and strut around like Blackbeard himself."

"All I want is to crawl under a palm tree in Papeete with a case of beer and a bottle of sippin' whiskey, and I'll watch the world wag on." Cocoa paused. "The funny thing is, even though my leg is burning, I can still feel my toes on the foot that ain't there. It's the damnedest thing." He held up the cigar. "Say, if you've got a match, let's fire this up."

Hudson's face lifted. "You bet." He took the cigar, snapped it into two pieces, and handed the larger half to Cocoa. He struck a match on the bedpost and they lit up.

Cocoa groaned, blowing a smoke ring at the swarm of flies.

"Man oh man, that's grand." Hudson said. "I guess our padre is good for something after all."

"Don't you say anything against Moyer or I'll jump up and whip you again. He held my hand through the operation. Don't know what I would have done without him."

"Never thought I'd hear you talk like that," Andrew said.

"Me neither… but life has a way of surprising you."

Two men carried a stretcher down the aisle, followed by a young man with long blond hair who wore a full-length sarong around his slim waist and a white, sleeveless medical smock cut low at the neckline. In that atmosphere of suffering and death, the young man looked perennially fresh and carried a gentle dignity. His sarong was made of pure silk, threadbare to the point of being nearly transparent, and it had the sepia color that silk takes on with age.

They sauntered to the bed across the aisle from Cocoa and began loading a corpse onto the stretcher. Before they could remove the body, a doctor strolled up, dressed in a butcher's apron speckled with blood.

He stood erect with grave formality, frowning at the young orderly's wavy hair, shaved armpits, and milky skin. "Clifford," he said, "collect the bedpans from twelve and twenty-three." A shade of venom permeated his voice. "And for God sakes, Clifford, you're a man, act like one."

"Y-y-y-yes, Doctor," Clifford said tartly with a swish of his head.

Andrew peered across the aisle, seeing a severely effeminate Clifford Baldrich looking as graceful as a stalk of bamboo gently swaying in the breeze. His face was unmarked and still carried a boy's equine beauty.

Clifford removed a clean handkerchief from a small purse hanging on his shoulder. He patted the perspiration from his forehead. "S-s-s-so many dead, and for what? I simply can't understand." He pulled a mirror and a powder-puff from his purse, made a few passes at his face, and redefined his lips with lipstick.

"Wow," Hudson said, his eyes following Andrew's gaze. "Ain't she a livin' doll?"

Andrew swallowed, fighting the bile coming up his throat. "She's a he."

"Sure she is, but she's still prettier than most the real women I've seen."

The blond glanced across the aisle and his eyes flew open. He took a hesitant step forward. "A-A-A-Andy? M-m-my God, Baby, is it really you?"

"Jesus, rookie. You know her?"

Clifford shrieked and ran to Andrew, throwing his arms around Andrew's neck. "O-o-o-h my sweetheart, what are you doing here? And what's happened to your head? My poor baby!"

"My ship sank and the Japanese Navy brought me here. How did you get here?"

"P-p-p-poppa and I were traveling to England, but we only got this far. Poppa thought the Japs would never take Singapore, but that sad mistake cost the dear man his life, poor thing."

"I'm sorry, Clifford, really."

Clifford nodded.

"What's happened to you? You're so...." Andrew couldn't finish. He flushed until he felt his face glow with heat. Clifford wore natural-colored powder to camouflage his freckles. The faint scent of eau de cologne hung in the air. *Where the hell did he get makeup in a place where you can scarcely find food?* Andrew wondered. His head throbbed with confusion.

"S-s-s-so girlish? I've changed, Andy. O-o-o-once I came here, I blossomed into a woman. I don't know how it happened, but it did. The men seem to like me this way. I suppose I was always like this inside, but being here let it come out, like a butterfly from a cocoon."

Andrew wanted to grab hold of his friend and shake this new Clifford until the old one reappeared. Fear ascended his spine, but he was not quite sure why.

"My name's Joe Hudson, but you can call me Hud." Hudson stared at the low cut of Clifford's white smock, obviously fascinated with the silky pale skin that showed a whisper of cleavage.

Clifford glanced at Hudson and smiled with his eyes, causing Hudson to blush. Clifford daintily took his hand. "P-p-pleased to meet you. I'm Clifford. A-a-any friend of Andy's is a friend of mine."

He turned to Andrew and scrutinized the brown-yellowish bruises covering Andrew's face and the soiled bandage wrapped around his head. "P-poor baby. Come with me. I'll clean your wound and change that filthy rag." Clifford glanced at Hudson. His eyelashes fluttered and his voice dropped. "I'll bring him back in a few minutes, Mr. Hud."

"Just Hud, kitten. I'll be waiting right here." Hudson winked.

Clifford led Andrew to a crude operating room and sat him on the table. He removed the bandage and examined Andrew's wound while making a clucking sound with his tongue. "B-b-b-baby, I need to clean this with alcohol. It's going to sting."

"I'm not your baby." Andrew felt his anger rising, and the fact of it confused him. Clifford had always been different from other boys, gentle and sensitive, so it was no surprise that he was a homosexual. Andrew's memory flashed on his own feelings for Mitchell, and Grady in the *Pilgrim*'s head—how exciting those kisses had felt. He didn't blame Clifford for wanting that, but how could he have become so effeminate? And how could anyone find his behavior appealing? Andrew's stomach heaved when Clifford came near.

"Cliff, how could you change so much? It's only been two years."

"I-I-I-It happened all at once, in a single night. A man gave me this sarong and I tried it on for fun. It was so pretty, so colorful. No one in camp had anything like it. So I tried it on and looked at myself in a mirror. Right then, my thin, awkward, inadequate shape turned into something else. I blossomed into something lovely and deliberate. I realized I was seeing a new person with new hopes and desires, and with new possibilities. I liked what I saw, it fit perfectly. So I kept this sarong. I'm never without it."

Andrew couldn't respond, realizing that the fear in his gut stemmed from an inkling that the same thing could happen to him.

Clifford soaked a piece of cloth with alcohol.

"I-I-I-I'm sorry about Mr. Cocoa. He begged us not to amputate. Said he'd rather die than be a cripple. It's tragic that life never gives us what we want."

"He'll be okay. Life is not about getting what you want or even what you need. It's about accepting what is, and experiencing that to the fullest. It takes courage to tackle life's trials, and Cocoa's got courage in spades. Sure, he'll be fine."

Clifford leaned his head to one side. "A-A-A-Andy, you sound like Master Jung-Wei. I mean your tone of voice and everything. That's amazing."

Andrew realized that Clifford spoke with a grain of truth. That was something his master would have said. Andrew heard Master Jung-Wei saying, "When you see something you admire in others, try to emulate that. When you find fault with others, examine your own heart."

Clifford dabbed his head wound and the pain became excruciating. Andrew focused all his attention on the pain. It consumed his being, driving his Master's voice away.

"B-b-but actually, he won't be okay. H-h-h-he has the same problem as everyone else, not enough protein, which means he can't fight off the infection. You need to be concerned about it too, even with this small wound. Some of the men are going blind from lack of protein and vitamins. It's killing everybody—dengue fever, dysentery, malaria, typhus, typhoid, gangrene, and beriberi. All treatable pathogens if we had modern medicines and a reasonable diet. If they only gave us drugs and meat, or eggs, or let us grow our own vegetables, these poor boys could recover."

"*Balachong* is pure protein. If I had a five-gallon can and a net, I could make some."

Balachong was a native delicacy throughout Malaysia. Villagers along the coast used fine nets to scoop up the tiny *gerago* shrimp that hover in the surf and along the reefs. They would bury a mass of the stuff in a seaweed-lined hole for two months, allowing it to decay and ferment into a gooey paste. They fried the paste and molded it into cubes. One thin sliver of cooked *balachong* would flavor an entire bowl of rice, and provided more protein than an ounce of sirloin.

Clifford glided to the medicine closet, returning with a bottle of iodine. He smeared the red liquid over Andrew's wound.

"S-s-s-sure, *balachong* is protein, but the ocean is two miles away. Even if you get under the wire and make it to the sea, you couldn't catch enough to make a spoonful."

"It doesn't have to be shrimp. There's a source of protein right here in camp, and they're breeding like rats."

Clifford stood silent, puzzled. A look of sheer disgust flashed across his face. "Y-y-y-you don't mean…. N-n-n-no! It's revolting. No one will eat it."

"I would eat it to save my eyesight, wouldn't you? Maybe we can keep people from knowing where it came from. We'd have to clean them thoroughly before we bury them, but it would solve the protein problem."

Clifford visibly fought off the urge to vomit. Recovering, he said, "I-I-I-I'll get as many cans as you need and we can make a net with one of my nylon stockings. But we must do it under cover of night." Clifford wrapped Andrew's wound with a clean bandage. "W-w-we'll make up a story about someone going under the wire to buy it in the village. The hospital could use a dozen cubes each week, but the whole camp needs it. Can you make enough for fifteen thousand men?"

"That's too big an operation to keep secret. Let me study it. Meantime, get me a couple of cans, your nylon stocking, and a pole. We'll start by making enough for the hospital."

"O-o-o-okay, I'll bring it to your hut after sundown."

"Great. Now, I really came here to see Lieutenant Mitchell. Where can I find him?"

Clifford caressed Andrew's face. "O-o-oh, baby, is he your friend?"

Andrew shuddered at the touch, his abhorrence becoming stronger.

"He's more than a friend. Much more."

Andrew followed Clifford up concrete steps to the second floor. Clifford explained as they climbed. "H-h-h-he has the same problem as Mr. Cocoa: gangrene. The doctors plan to operate tonight, but the wound is on his thigh, so they need to take off the whole leg. With a wound that large, we have no chance of controlling the infection, not without drugs. It will be a miracle if he pulls through. Even if he does, there won't be enough stump left to attach a wooden leg."

"If they treat the gangrene, could they save his leg?"

"Y-y-y-yes, if it hasn't spread. But we don't have the antitoxins. The Japs have them, but they don't just hand them over. Everything has a price, and drugs have the highest price of all."

"What does that mean?"

"T-t-there may be a way to get the antitoxins from Commandant Tottori. But even so, there's a long list of British officers who need it as badly as your lieutenant. There's no way Tottori will give you enough for everyone."

"If we get the antitoxin, can you fix him up before the doctors operate? I mean, cure him without them knowing we have the drugs?"

"I-I-I can do the procedure. At least I've seen it done. But how do we keep them from operating?"

They reached the top of the stairs and Mitchell's bed, Bed 201, was the first one on the left.

Mitchell lay unconscious. He seemed much smaller against the mattress, as if he was shriveling away. His breathing was shallow and rapid, and his body jerked about as if he was dreaming. He let out a moan, flailing at the air with his arms. He jerked up to a sitting position.

Clifford's voice soothed, "I-I-I-I'm here. It's okay, baby, you're safe."

Mitchell's eyes opened as Clifford cradled him. Sitting on the bed in the dimly lit cell, Clifford rocked him like a child. "A-a-a-a dream, baby, it's only a dream."

Mitchell wrapped his arms around Clifford's waist and squeezed hard, burying his face into Clifford's neck. His body shook uncontrollably as pain pinched his face. Clifford laid him on the pillow. Mitchell's eyes focused on Andrew, hovering on the other side of the bed.

"My God, how did you get here?"

Shocking. He had aged ten years overnight. He had the same short growth of fawn-colored beard, but his eyes and forehead had aged. They had taken on a drooping disposition. The eyes were larger and had the dull glow caused by intense pain. Deep lines scored his forehead, and his grayish skin seemed leathery.

Andrew decided that Mitchell had become even more attractive with that ravaged face, like a stirring Verdi opera: sad, and yet tragically beautiful.

"Ensign Moyer brought me. How's your leg?" He stroked Mitchell's hair.

"It has my full attention." He stopped suddenly, squinted. "I'm about to throw up."

Clifford grabbed a bucket from beneath the bed and supported Mitchell's head in his arm while Mitchell vomited. "P-p-p-poor man. Andy, hand me that water bottle on the nightstand."

Andrew uncorked the bottle and passed it to Clifford, who held the bottle to Mitchell's lips. Mitchell swished water around his mouth and spat into the bucket. Clifford leaned him onto the pillow. After taking a clean handkerchief from his purse, Clifford wet it and dabbed it across Mitchell's forehead.

"Y-y-you're doing fine, Lieutenant. The doctors will fix you up tonight. We're going to take that pain away very soon."

Mitchell struggled to get enough air. He seemed on the verge of hyperventilating.

Clifford wiped the sweat from Mitchell's face, being careful to clean the drops of vomit at the edges of the officer's mouth. He hummed a lullaby while his misty eyes shone down on Mitchell in a way that Andrew would never forget.

Andrew felt the smoldering heat of shame, shame that he had been disgusted by this gentle, compassionate friend.

"H-h-he'll sleep now. He's so weak from fighting the infection, poor baby."

Andrew leaned over to kiss Mitchell on the forehead. As he did, Clifford stroked Andrew's head. Again, Clifford's eyes smiled, lighting up his face. Andrew bent further over Mitchell to kiss Clifford on the cheek.

"O-o-oh, you're still my lover-boy. I was afraid you despised me."

They kissed again. This time lips lovingly caressed lips. Clifford looped his arm around Andrew and led him down the stairs.

"What do I have to do to get the antitoxin from Tottori?"

"S-s-s-sell your mind, body, and soul. He'll take it all, but it's the only way."

"Okay." There was no hesitation. "We'll need enough to stop Cocoa's infection too. How fast can you arrange it?"

"A-A-A-Andy, Tottori was the man who gave me this sarong, the one who made me what I am. Do you understand?"

Andrew swallowed. "How soon?"

"P-p-p-perhaps tonight. But how will we keep the doctors from operating?"

"That's your job. Listen, you set me up with Tottori and stall the doctors long enough to save Mitchell's leg, and I'll find a way to produce enough *balachong* to drown this damned camp. Deal?"

"I-I-I-I'll do my best, Andy. Anything for you."

Clifford led Andrew along the line of beds toward the front door. As they passed a bed, Clifford glanced over at the man and sighed. He shuffled to the man's side and checked his pulse, pulling the blanket over the man's head.

A pack of Kooas and a tin of matches sat on the nightstand. Clifford took them both to Andrew and held them out.

"Y-y-y-you know anyone who smokes?"

"Sure," Andrew said, taking the pack. He counted five cigarettes inside.

When they came to Cocoa's bed, Andrew said, "Come on, Hud. We've got work to do."

"Work, what kind of work?"

"We're going to mass-produce food!"

Chapter Twenty-One

May 15, 1942—1600 hours

"COCKROACHES!" Hudson shrieked. "I don't give a flyin' fuck what the wogs eat, no white man is gonna chow down on cockroaches."

Hudson, Stokes, and Grady sat on the ground with their backs against Hut Twenty-nine. Andrew squatted alongside them. "Keep your voice down," he said. "Nobody needs to know what it is." He lifted the pack of Kooas from his pocket along with the tin of matches. A hush fell over the men as Andrew passed the treasures to Stokes, their unit supply officer. Stokes examined the pack's contents and removed two cigarettes. He slid one behind his ear and the other between his lips.

Andrew said, "There's more where that came from, if you play along."

"Well, how do we make this stuff?" Stokes asked as he struck a match, lit the Kooa, and passed it to Grady.

"We scoop cockroaches out of the boreholes with a net."

"Sweet Jesus, I'm going to be sick," Hudson gasped.

"We clean them in a tub of water, mash them into five-gallon cans, bury the cans under the hut, and let it simmer for two months. The roaches decompose into an inch or so of thick paste with a smell that will blow your head off."

"I sure as hell believe that," Hudson snorted.

Andrew glared at Hudson, shaking his head. "We cook the paste in a frying pan and mold it into two-inch cubes. A tiny sliver in your rice is like eating an egg. It's pure protein."

"Don't it go bad rottin' in the ground?" Grady asked as he exhaled, passing the cigarette to Hudson.

"If flies get at it, you can get dysentery. But aged and fried properly, it's completely safe."

"If it smells so bad," Stokes said, "how are we going to keep it secret? Won't it smell up the whole hut when we cook it?"

"Good point. Let me think about that."

"It won't work." Hudson's tone was adamant.

"Two five-gallon cans per week," Andrew said. "Half of one can goes to the hospital, free of charge. That leaves three dozen cubes that we sell for a reasonable profit to the rest of the camp. With that money, we'll buy food, tobacco, and whatever else we need."

"Sell?" Hudson's eyebrows lifted high on his forehead. "Now you're talking sense. How much can we get per cube?"

"Maybe as much as ten dollars. Remember, a cube will feed three men for two weeks."

Hudson rubbed his chin as his eyes drifted skyward. "We'll need a middleman so if anyone sees us collecting bugs, it won't cause suspicion. A limey, or better yet, an Aussie. Someone everybody trusts. And the whole crew must be part of the production. There's no way to keep this secret inside the hut. That means splitting the profits."

"That's okay," Grady said. "That means splittin' the work, too. We'll get them to gather the critters." He pointed a thumb at the others hanging around the hut.

Hudson slapped Grady on the shoulder. "You bet, partner. We'll be management."

"Okay, we're agreed," Andrew said. "Grady, you're our digger. Use the machete to dig two holes under the hut tonight, about three feet deep, and mark the holes with dates so we know when to dig them up. When Clifford delivers the cans and net, I'll organize the gathering party. We'll need to clean them before we bury them. Stokes, can you manage the washing?"

"Count on me, Andy. I'll get Cord, Nash, and Banks to help."

"Hud, you organize security. Let the others in on the plan and have them standing guard when we clean the bugs. We don't want anyone walking in when we're up to our elbows in critters. And make sure no one breathes a word to anybody."

Hudson said that if anybody spilled the beans, he'd personally stuff them down a borehole. His tone was deadly serious because this operation meant survival for the entire crew, or what was left of it. Andrew added that they had to be careful even talking among themselves, and since they needed to do this under cover of darkness, and considering the nature of the job, they'd call it Operation Nightcrawler.

The unit shared a collective groan, but their excitement couldn't be masked. It was not so much the thought of making money, but rather the idea of pulling the wool over British eyes that sizzled every fiber of their beings.

Hudson lifted a deck of playing cards from his shirt pocket. "Let's get a few of the boys into a poker game. Once we get them gathered around, we'll break the news. Who knows, we might even fleece some of those future profits off them suckers before they earn them."

Andrew's eyes hardened. "Where did you get those cards?"

"Same damn place you got those Kooas. You don't think I was standing around that hospital with my head up my ass, do you? Besides, never ask where things come from. Consider it manna from heaven and let it go at that, even if you are a damned heathen." Hudson chuckled.

Andrew took his place in the chow line behind Grady. The sun turned orange as it dipped into the haze above the treetops, infusing the sky with peach-colored light. Andrew gazed at the top of the rainforest, which seemed to nibble at the lower edge of the sun. He stared at the huge disc, unblinking, and it appeared to revolve as it sank.

Clifford's face suddenly blocked Andrew's view. He told Andrew that Tottori had agreed to see them, and if Andrew wanted the serum, they had better hurry.

Andrew handed his mess-cans to Grady and followed Clifford out of the compound. Two guards led them beyond the guards' barracks to the commandant's hut, which was his office and living quarters. They climbed four plank steps and came to attention under a covered veranda.

Commandant Hikaru Tottori sat on a straight-back chair, having his head shaved by a Japanese corporal. Andrew noted that the corporal was extremely adept and meticulous, making slow, graceful sweeps with the razor. The commandant's eyes were closed. He appeared cool and relaxed in the shade as the corporal hovered above him. Ever so slowly, the corporal scraped away the officer's stubby hair to reveal the raw, animated contour of his naked head. The process seemed to take an eternity for that shiny, newborn head to emerge, looking fresh as a sunrise.

Without opening his eyes, Tottori barked, "Prisoners, at ease."

Andrew relaxed into a comfortable stance as the corporal wrapped a hot towel around the officer's head. Tottori remained motionless, but Andrew had the distinct impression that Tottori scrutinized him through the slits between his eyelids, as if studying a caged animal without seeming to notice at all.

Two minutes crawled by before the corporal unwrapped the hot towel and replaced it with a cool one. As the cloth touched Tottori's head, the officer moaned as if he were eating something delicious. The corporal began to massage Tottori's shoulders.

Andrew noticed a tortoise resting on the veranda next to a stone lantern. Its rugged, grayish brown shell was about the size of a hog's head and it had a cord tied around its leathery neck. The other end of the cord was attached to the lantern. Its wrinkled face had a sharp beak and two solid black eyes that stared intently at Andrew. Its face expressed a vast contentment, as if it were enjoying the tranquility of evening's cooler temperature.

The commandant stood, unwrapped the cloth, wiped his hands with it, and tossed it to the corporal, who bowed low. He dumped the towels into a pan next to the chair and made his departure while Tottori examined the prisoners.

"Well, prisoner Baldrich, what have you brought me?" He spoke with impeccable, American-accented English, and his penetrating voice was like hearing a rainstorm form words. He scrutinized Andrew with an unflinching stare.

Andrew was accustomed to being stared at. He'd been an oddity all his life. But Tottori's expression was so oddly reflective that Andrew felt Tottori was somehow studying himself as well. Andrew saw something quite different reveal itself in the commandant's eyes—raw desire. Andrew felt the heat of it burn his flesh.

Andrew grew confused and curious. He was not pretty like Clifford, so it could not be a question of beauty. Andrew wondered what qualities he possessed that could kindle desire in another man. Could it be his youth, a thin connection to vitality at a time when life could be cut short? Perhaps Tottori saw something of what he once was, and he wanted to devour that. Andrew said nothing. In the silence, he wondered if it was his move; was he expected to say something?

Clifford bowed; Andrew followed suit. They bent at the waist, dipping to the same level as Tottori's leather belt.

"Lower," Tottori commanded.

They bowed to the tops of Tottori's black boots.

"Lower."

Andrew sank to his knees and laid his forehead on the floorboards in front of Tottori's boots. Clifford followed his example.

This war revealed a new face to Andrew—the commandant's boots. Aboard the *Pilgrim*, war had a vague, shadowy, hidden face. The horror of that war was real, but impersonal. Andrew could only imagine the stricken faces of sailors passing into death's womb, could only guess at the anguish that wives, children, and parents felt when the telegram came. But that war had been replaced by this officer with shiny boots who had only to lift his foot to crush Andrew's skull. This new war was about domination—a strong, confident, conqueror holding Andrew within his power.

Andrew smelled the pungent aroma of shoe polish mixed with the sour stench of his own sweat. He felt those eyes, bright with lust, boring into him. And that voice, magical in its power, echoed in the pit of his stomach, fearsome and yet electrifying in the way the terse commands vibrated through his being. He was reminded of the men who had raped him. This new face of war was an intensely personal violation, a defilement of his being.

"Excellent." A tone of satisfaction shaded Tottori's voice. "You will dine with me, but first you will bathe. Clifford, escort him to the tub and give him a robe to wear after he cleans himself."

The prisoners rose. With downcast eyes, they shuffled along the veranda to a room with a large wooden tub filled with rainwater. Andrew stripped out of his fatigues and sat on a three-legged stool. His body trembled, still affected by the encounter with Tottori.

Clifford removed Andrew's head bandage, then used a bamboo dipper to pour cool rainwater over Andrew's head.

Andrew groaned. For the moment, he forgot about Tottori. He took a bar of English soap, Yardley's, and lathered his chest. The soap smelled like lavender. It overwhelmed him that, in this place and after all he had endured, he could remember what lavender smelled like. He meticulously scoured his body from crown to toenails.

Clifford filled a bucket with water and washed Andrew's fatigues with soap and a scrub brush. Once Andrew and his clothes were clean, Clifford rinsed them both with rainwater.

Andrew slipped into the tub. The cool sensation felt erotic.

Clifford carried Andrew's clothes out to the veranda and hung them on the railing to dry. Returning, he stripped off his white smock, silk sarong, and cream-colored panties. Naked except for a thin silver necklace, he soaped down and rinsed before joining Andrew in the tub.

Andrew couldn't believe the alabaster whiteness of Clifford's body. The silver chain around his neck highlighted his pure skin tones.

There was no embarrassment about being naked together. They had bathed together many times while growing up. The war, the camp, the hunger all faded as the refreshing water reminded Andrew of his joyful youth. They splashed each other and kissed while pressing together. Not sexually—rather, kisses from boys who had discovered that they still loved each other in a way that they could never love anyone else. They were two halves of the same being: yin and yang.

Clifford reached over the edge of the tub, grabbed a nail file, and gave Andrew a manicure. He filed each nail. When it was time to dry and dress, he covered his slim hips with his silk sarong, but did not put on his sleeveless smock. He pulled a sarong of mandarin red cotton from a shelf and wrapped it around Andrew's waist.

Clifford stepped back to inspect him, tilting his head to the left while admiring Andrew's black hair, sculpted chest, and mandarin red hips. He draped his silver chain around Andrew's neck and nodded his approval.

Andrew watched with fascination as Clifford opened his purse and removed a bottle of Crème Tokalon, which he applied to his cheeks. Over that he patted skin-colored powder—Houbigant. He reapplied his lipstick and dabbed a drop of eau de cologne behind each ear. His face done, he took the Houbigant puff and patted around Andrew's head wound, hiding it as best he could. They didn't bother to put the bandage back on.

"T-t-t-there, now everything is perfect. Let's go."

Tottori knelt before a Shinto shrine in the corner. He wore a sober gray kimono made from fine Chinese silk that was tied at the waist by a black cord. Andrew and Clifford waited at the door of Tottori's living quarters for ten minutes while Tottori remained perfectly still. Finally, he rose to greet them. They bowed into the room. Tottori bowed too, but not nearly so low. He waved them in and smiled broadly.

Andrew scanned the spacious room. The well-used furnishings looked as if they had been hastily thrown together. Light filtered through the open shutters, highlighting the sheen of dark, polished wood. The room had a traditional Japanese *tokonoma* alcove—the focal point in any Japanese house, where a classic scroll hangs or a flower arrangement sits, enhanced by the play of light and shadows. A wooden chest of drawers occupied the alcove, and on the chest lay several polished stones surrounding a simple flower arrangement: birds of paradise in a natural salt-glazed ceramic vase. In one corner rested a Shinto shrine—a stone statue sat beside a red porcelain bowl full of sand, which had smoking incense sticks poking out like porcupine quills. The spicy scent of the incense mixed with the aroma of broth simmering in a nearby kitchen, giving the room a rich fragrance.

Tottori addressed Andrew. "I didn't choose the furnishings."

Andrew dropped his gaze, saying nothing. He paid careful attention to externals—the dim light filtering through the shuttered windows, the density of silence engulfing the room broken only by a porcelain wind chime catching the evening breeze, Tottori's stiffness as he waited for a response, and the fact that Clifford's hands were trembling. He wondered why Clifford was fearful.

His focus moved inward. He felt no hate, no repugnance, and no longer any dread of Tottori, only a tinge of fear that Tottori would fail to deliver the serum.

"I don't know your name."

"Seaman First Class Andrew Waters, *Kakka-dono*." Andrew used the formal Japanese term for "Your Excellency, sir."

"Seaman? Your uniform suggests that you are a marine. What job did you perform aboard ship that required you to dress in fatigues?"

"I was the officer's mess cook, *Kakka-dono*."

They waited through a long silence before Tottori said, "In addressing officers up to a colonel's rank, it is proper to use the title 'dono,' but since my rank is that of colonel, you should address me as 'Your Excellency, Tottori.' But for tonight, let us forget about rank and formalities. Please call me Hikaru."

Andrew nodded. It was extraordinary how, by simply offering his first name, Tottori had transformed the entire situation into an intimate affair. With a single word, he had created a personal relationship between them. Was that by design? Andrew saw a smile in Tottori's eyes and realized the answer was assuredly yes. It was a small yet important victory for Tottori.

"Will you join me in a whiskey?" Tottori asked.

Clifford shuffled to a low chest against the wall and opened the lid. He removed a bottle of Haig & Haig Scotch Whiskey and three crystal glasses, placing them on a silver tray.

"Thank you, but I don't drink spirits."

Tottori nodded. "The French believe that strong liquor before dinner dulls the palate, but I will have some now. It is a habit that I picked up while studying in America. During my four years at Amherst, I acquired several such habits."

No doubt that's where you perfected your English, Andrew thought. *My compliments.*

Tottori stalked to a low table surrounded by thick pillows. Andrew followed and sat at the same time as Tottori, facing the commandant. Clifford glided up, carrying the drink tray. He stood at the edge of the table, waiting.

Andrew realized that he had not been invited to sit. Panic. He didn't know if he should jump up and apologize, or remain seated. He silently cursed his stupidity. Glancing at Tottori, he saw the officer perversely smiling at his obvious discomfort. Another small victory.

Tottori waved his hand in the direction of a pillow.

"Clifford, will you join us?"

Clifford lowered himself onto a pillow while placing the tray on the table. He poured one glass half-full of Scotch, and in another he trickled a few drops, enough to be social. The officer took the half-full glass and sipped. He lifted a pack of English cigarettes off the table and offered one to Andrew.

Andrew said he didn't smoke, no thank you. As he said it, he noticed a slight trembling in Tottori's outstretched hand.

Tottori removed a cigarette from the pack and lit it with a silver lighter, then blew smoke toward the ceiling. He took another sip of whiskey and didn't say another word for the time it took him to smoke the entire cigarette.

Andrew studied the officer while he smoked. His thin lips were colorless. They kissed the white paper, his cheeks compressed as he inhaled, and smoke lingered in front of the man's face.

Andrew glanced at Clifford, only to realize that his friend was trying to become invisible.

Andrew's discomfort grew razor-sharp in that silence. *This man is clever,* he thought, as his eyes brushed the table, searching for something to say. Something must be said, but Andrew understood that he couldn't be the one to initiate the conversation. He had that same agonizing feeling as he did on the twelve-to-four watches, waiting for Mitchell to start what they both desperately wanted. It felt like ten years had elapsed since standing watch with Mitchell. Thoughts of his love reminded him of the purpose of his mission—to get the serum—and he became anxious to negotiate an agreement.

Tottori crushed his cigarette butt in a clay bowl, audibly exhaling. He sipped his drink.

Andrew waited, embarrassed by the awkwardness of being ignored. He wondered if he would be dismissed or whether Tottori's interest grew within the silence. A drop of sweat slid down the edge of his face, dripping onto his chest. Another drop began the same journey. The silence continued long after Tottori finished his drink and Clifford poured him another.

It dawned on Andrew that this reticence was too deliberate. Something shrewd was being played out within this living silence—another Tottori victory in the making? Andrew quieted his mind and felt his emotions. This situation was not at all awkward, he realized. On the contrary, it deepened the intimacy that was already established. Without a single word, a bond was being molded, strengthened, and fired into something palpable. Realizing the ploy, Andrew felt a twinge of admiration for the man across the table. He found this superior intelligence seductive, and he smiled at the thought.

Tottori nodded as understanding blossomed cross Andrew's face.

The sunlight faded beyond the bamboo shutters, painting the sky lavender. A breeze jingled the porcelain wind chime as it drifted through the window, spreading warmth over everything. Andrew shifted his position and the floor creaked under him. As if that were a signal, Clifford rose and shuffled to the chest against the wall. He lit three oil lamps, placing one in the bedroom, one in Tottori's office, and the third on the dinner table before sitting once again.

Andrew wondered why Tottori bothered with this ploy. He held all the cards and he was shrewd enough to know it. He could demand anything, knowing Andrew must pay. Andrew was no longer innocent. He knew what it meant to be taken by force. With no misunderstanding and no need to be explicit, Andrew understood precisely what he was offering; he had only one thing to offer. He had no stratagem or intention to negotiate. His downcast eyes were not an indication of shyness, but rather, a sign of submission. He gazed into Tottori's eyes and saw that Tottori had accepted his offer. They shared an understanding. Without a word spoken, the die was cast.

Andrew discreetly glanced about the room. To his left was an open door, leading into an office with two straight-back chairs facing a massive, mahogany desk. Behind the desk hung a colorful poster of Mount Fuji, and under the picture were English words: *Visit Beautiful Japan.*

To his right, an open doorway led into a bedroom, dim and snug, with Japanese style quilts spread on the floor and a virgin white mosquito net draped from the ceiling, covering the quilts like a bride's veil. The polished floor planks reflected the lamplight. The walls were pale green, the same color as Mitchell's eyes. A chest rested snugly against the bedroom wall, and above it hung a sign in Japanese that read: *The Emperor's reign will last for a thousand and then eight thousand more generations, until pebbles become mighty rocks covered with moss.*

"That is taken from my national anthem, the '*Kimigayo*,'" Tottori said with obvious pride. "I keep it there because I love rocks. They are my hobby."

Clifford covered his mouth with one hand and giggled. Tottori threw him a questioning glance. Clifford explained, "T-t-t-the head monk of our school, Master Jung-Wei, gave Andrew the nickname Lingtse, which means spirit stone."

Tottori stared at Andrew with wide-open eyes while a beguiling smile dimpled his cheeks.

"You see the large stone on the chest?" Tottori said.

Andrew's gaze brushed the several polished stones lying on the chest.

"The large one is classified as yellow chert. It is essentially microcrystalline quartz. I found it here, in a cave by the ocean. It was formed when bedrock from the Paleozoic era rose above sea level. Notice the exquisite color. It is rare to find chert with that creamy yellow hue."

He rattled on for thirty minutes about several other prize rocks as if he were addressing a class of university students. Andrew understood that Tottori seldom talked so freely, and he obviously held a passion for rocks, but Andrew didn't follow the conversation. He dwelled on Mitchell's image without giving any thought to it.

Tottori finally noticed Andrew's disinterest and switched topics.

"How did you receive that cut on your head?"

Andrew lowered his gaze. "I was raped by two Japanese soldiers on the ship that brought me here."

Tottori became as utterly still as one of his stones. A minute passed before he said, "You have my sincere apology. War exposes the jackal in men." Tottori bowed until his forehead touched the table. He straightened up and explained that brutality was a way of life for a Japanese soldier. "He takes thrashings from his superiors as a routine reprimand, and he in turn beats those under him at the least provocation. He is taught that a soldier must fight to the death. Honor is everything to a Japanese soldier. That is why he has no pity for prisoners, who obviously have no honor. It is a pity," he added, "but it hardens them, and for Japan to be a world power, we must be as hard as tempered steel."

"I think war brings out a man's essence," Andrew replied. "For some it's a jackal, for others it's a tiger, for a few it's a crane. It depends upon the profundity of a man's compassion and the quality of his integrity."

Tottori stared at Andrew for a full minute before saying, "Quite so."

A shiver raced up Andrew's spine as he wondered how brutal Tottori would become when the jackal surfaced in him. Andrew couldn't help but ask, "What happens to the Japanese men who are captured?"

"If for any reason a soldier should be captured alive, his name is removed from his village register and his family will suffer his disgrace. They will never hold their heads up again. That is why we always save the last round for ourselves."

Two Malaysian servants entered the room, carrying trays of aromatic food. They knelt beside the table and placed lacquered bowls and bamboo platters in front of each man. There was hot miso soup, steamed shrimp atop rolls of rice, glistening red triangles of raw tuna beside pea green wasabi, shallow cups of soy sauce, grilled leeks immersed in vinegar, and of course, mounds of steamed rice with a hint of jasmine flavoring.

Andrew's stomach twisted into a painful knot. Never had he felt so famished or seen a meal that looked so appetizing. But a twinge of guilt made his heart shudder. He was not here to accept treats for himself, food that many prisoners would kill for. He came to exchange his body for drugs.

Clifford indulged in the luxury of declining to eat, swishing his head away from the meal. "N-n-n-o, thank you. I've had my dinner."

Andrew cleared his dry throat and mustered his willpower. "I've eaten, also."

Tottori's face shaded a blistering red. "You will both eat. That is an order." He nodded at Clifford. "You will eat as a show of good manners." Turning to Andrew, he said, "And you will eat because I require my whore to be supple, and that means having meat on your bones. You must gain weight."

There, Andrew thought, his gaze brushing the table again, *he has put a name to it. I'm his whore.* But something didn't jell. Andrew had been under the impression that tonight's fornication was all the payment required. If that was so, why was Tottori concerned about his weight?

Clifford sipped his soup while Andrew picked up his chopsticks, selected a beautiful sliver of tuna, and slid it into his mouth. He chewed, although the fish was so tender he didn't need to. He swallowed, ate another piece with a smidgen of fragrant rice. He felt strength flow into his limbs. Using his fingers to select one of the shrimp sushi, he then dipped it into the soy sauce, but before he placed it in his mouth, he asked, "Does that mean I must come here again, after tonight?"

Tottori grunted. "What you require is not trivial. We are talking of saving a man's life, are we not? This demands a substantial payment. I have the serum." He pointed to a satchel beside the front door. "In return, you are my whore for as long as I desire your services, be that a night, a month, or ten years."

Andrew's appetite vanished. He reined in his panic enough to slide the sushi into the red cavity of his mouth and chew. Sweat beaded on his upper lip. He had no choice, but somewhere inside a voice cried out for him to run, run as fast as he could.

The silence deepened. Andrew washed down the fish, rice, and leeks with steaming miso soup. The soup was rich, but he no longer tasted, heard, or felt anything except the panic in his heart, which slowly transformed into despair.

Tottori said, "Before you agree, please consider the consequences. I will oblige you to eat, bathe, and dress well. The other prisoners will notice, assuredly. They will presume you are my spy and that you do it for your own benefit. They will probably try to kill you. Do not make this decision lightly."

"There is no decision. As you have already pointed out, a man's life is at stake."

Silence.

Tottori bowed his head. "I admire you and envy him."

Andrew looked away, could not bear the thought of what he saw in those eyes.

"I am very happy," Tottori said, smiling. "Not because you agree to my terms, but because you and I are alike. We don't waste time with idle chitchat and we don't lie or hide our thoughts. We go to the heart of each issue and speak the raw truth or say nothing at all. I think that is a good basis for a relationship."

First I'm his whore, now he speaks of a relationship. Andrew ate the last of the vinegar-soaked leeks. His confusion grew into impatience because he sat stuffing himself with glorious food while the poison worked its way further up Mitchell's leg.

Clifford leaned close to Andrew. "This was normally the time I retired to the bedroom, but it seems I've been replaced. I'll take the treatment and prepare the patient. Come as soon as you can." He winked as he rose to his feet and turned to Tottori. "Be gentle with this one. He's worth loving."

Clifford bent to pick up the satchel on his way out.

The servants cleared away the dishes and brought plates topped with golden slices of mango over sticky rice. A rich aroma pervaded the room, tickling Andrew's nostrils.

"Coffee?" Andrew asked.

"A French roast. I hope you'll like it."

"Tea would have been wonderful, but the coffee smells exquisite."

"I have a weakness for French coffee. I spent the spring and summer of '38 in France. Have you been to Paris?"

Andrew shook his head as he chewed a slice of sweet mango.

"In April, cherry blossoms smother the city. There are cafes on the West Bank and nightclubs in the Latin Quarter. The grandeur of the Louvre, the opulence of the opera house, it's all so magnificent." He prattled on about Paris street life, the exquisite food and wine, well-dressed women walking under parasols, street artists, and, ooh-la-la, the all-night cabarets.

Andrew wondered about this mood change, why Tottori now filled the silence with what seemed to be an attempt to impress. Andrew understood that this chatter showed the commandant's discomfort. *He is not ready for us to be alone*, Andrew thought. *He's afraid of this intimacy.*

Tottori described the French countryside: villages, huge estates, castles, and gay picnics in green meadows peppered with wildflowers.

Andrew peered into what now seemed fragile and weary eyes, and he imagined a little boy pleading. It was as if the man were begging Andrew to take him away from this excruciating anticipation of death and allow him to experience life's passion again—the passion of holding something precious against your cheek. Tottori seemed so utterly vulnerable. *Is this another clever ploy*, Andrew wondered, *or could it be that he needs something more than a whore? Could he crave a companion, a confidant, a friend—someone to shelter him from the desperate loneliness of war? Perhaps he's right, perhaps we are alike.*

Tottori pushed his empty plate forward and stood. "You may go now. I believe Clifford needs you, but come here tomorrow before sunset, alone."

Andrew flinched at this sudden dismissal, as if he'd received a slap across his face. As he stood, his gaze locked onto Tottori's, penetrating, searching for something, but he had no idea what. His hands went to the knot below his exposed navel, untied the sarong, and let it slip off his hips. He stood before Tottori, naked, holding out the mandarin red cloth like a bullfighter's cape.

"This belongs to you."

Tottori blinked, unable to speak. Desire welled up in his eyes again.

Andrew felt his face flush as red as the sarong. He dropped the cloth and stepped into the empty space between Tottori's arms. The commandant smelled of English cigarettes, Yardley soap, and expensive aftershave—a pleasant, manly fragrance.

Hands roved over Andrew's body, caresses that lit his skin afire. Desire swelled within Andrew. Their cheeks hovered close together and brushed each other. This intimate proximity felt intensely sensual and utterly maddening.

Andrew kissed Tottori, a kiss so gentle that Andrew was reminded of kissing a baby. A heartbeat later, as easily as taking a breath of air, their mouths came together, hard. Tottori grabbed the back of Andrew's neck, locking his head in a vise, lifting him to his toes. Tottori's teeth brought blood. Andrew was only aware of those lips, but through the heat of their mingling passions, he felt the officer's pain, the sum of a lifetime of loneliness.

Tottori became as rigid as the yellow chert stone. Andrew leaned his forehead against the side of Tottori's neck, pressing chests and groins and thighs together, feeling the thump of his own heart and those rough hands caressing his nakedness. He embraced the man's pain.

"Hikaru, if you only want a body to use, I'll be that. I'll be whatever you need, and I'll return as much affection as you show me." *There,* Andrew thought, *I've used your name for the first time, and in so doing I've sealed the intimacy between us. This is my first victory, which eclipses all your earlier wins.* Andrew smiled.

Tottori groped for a response, letting Andrew know that the situation had teetered out of the commandant's control. He, who must always be in command, stood at a loss. His hands caressed Andrew's sumptuous amber softness, this sleek and imposing body, while staring into the depths of the youth's fragile eyes. He whispered, "If I love you, as Clifford suggested, will you love me in return?"

"Please, don't talk of love."

"Does that mean you can never love me?"

Andrew wondered if what he was feeling could already be love. It was not what he felt for Mitchell, but it felt equally as potent.

"I'm your whore."

They kissed. Deep, needful kisses. Seemingly in control again, Tottori lifted Andrew into his arms and carried him to the bedroom, leaving the red sarong strewn across the floor. He pulled the mosquito-netting aside and spread Andrew over the quilts like frosting over a wedding cake. As his lips explored the youth's porcelain smoothness, he became visibly enmeshed in powerful emotions. He pulled away.

Andrew patiently drew Tottori back again and, with trembling hands, fumbled at the knot holding Tottori's kimono. Tottori's hands moved to help, but Andrew whispered *no.* He wanted to do it himself.

A moment later the robe fell away. Andrew's body fused with Tottori. Flesh enfolded him, drawing him closer. Legs entwined. Tottori's body felt like sculpted stone, made inflexible by the assault of war. Years of fighting had battered and slashed and stiffened this flesh into an unyielding mass of scar tissue. Andrew felt afire against this granite dream. *Not yet,* he ordered himself. *Don't wake up yet.* He was convinced that this was too extraordinary to be substantial.

Andrew desperately wanted to bring gentleness into this body, to reel this man away from the ravages of war and restore the human quality to this injured flesh.

Tottori's lips murmured against Andrew's neck.

That smell, that manly smell, made Andrew tipsy. His breath quickened. He shivered. Tottori's lips moved over amber goose bumps until his tongue traced the outline of Andrew's nipples. Hands wandered, finding Andrew's stiff sex surrounded by downy softness. Tottori fulfilled Andrew's need with slow deliberateness, handling Andrew as if he were something incredibly delicate.

Andrew tried to respond in kind, tried to return this pleasure, but he lay paralyzed, overcome by electrifying sensations. Tottori built Andrew to the brink of climax and backed off, only to build him up again, teasing Andrew until he begged.

Andrew's head spun as lusty sensations shot along his body. This was his baptism, his flash of Enlightenment, the moment of total understanding about flesh. Andrew tumbled through the vast, miraculous reaches of space, falling toward an unknown destination. He was unafraid, however. He welcomed this exchange.

Instinctively, Andrew glided his hand down Tottori's chiseled torso and took hold of the man's hardness, guiding it to him. A spasm of intense pain made Andrew fall through space again. How long he tumbled he had no idea; enough time for the pain to withdraw. Bestial breathing echoed in his head, erupting from both their mouths. Desire welled up in Andrew that was more powerful than he was capable of controlling. Sweat-drenched, he clung to Tottori and felt the man's beating heart beneath the sensually sleek skin. He cried out and the room expanded to encompass the entire universe. Release. Pure, sweet, delirious release plunged him into an intoxicating liberation.

A collapsing of energy pressed them into a lingering embrace. Gratifying warmth spread throughout Andrew as his breathing returned to a tranquil rhythm. They lay tangled. Their separate breaths merged into a single stream.

Dim moonlight drifted between the window slats, dividing the light into bars across the floor. Nothing solid separated them from the guards or the prison. The camp sounds became loud. Voices brushed against the slats, as if the prisoners were standing on the terrace.

Tottori whispered, "Did I hurt you?"

"Not much."

"Then why look so sad?"

"It's nothing."

"Tell me."

"I was thinking of my losses. What I've given up and can't retrieve."

"Think about what you've gained. A man's life and a lover to care for you."

They fell silent. The camp din grew harsher, more penetrating.

Andrew couldn't look into Tottori's face. Sadness held him prisoner, replacing the man who, moments ago, had propelled him into ecstasy. His sorrow grew overwhelming.

Tottori seized a box at the edge of the quilts and extracted a ceramic jar, pipe, and lighter. He opened the jar and the odor of raw opium drifted up. The jar's contents looked like a dark and sticky loam. Andrew had seen men at home who smoked to the point where they could no longer eat. They melted away until death came striding by and, in a cloud of wonder, they followed.

Tottori filled the pipe, held a flame over the bowl, and inhaled. He didn't offer any to Andrew. The odor was sweet, like incense.

In this aftermath, Andrew fondled the notion of what it would feel like to cuddle Mitchell like this, and thinking of Mitchell brought back the purpose of the night's adventure. He pulled away from Tottori's embrace and peeked through the shutters.

"Yes, Lingtse, go to him. But come here at sunset tomorrow. I need you too."

They kissed, and Andrew understood that their passion had survived the sudden intrusion of his sadness, of Mitchell and the war. He felt a slight chest spasm, nearly imperceptibly. It was his heartbeat shifting into a new rhythm, a scarcely noticeable difference in cadence.

Chapter Twenty-Two

May 16, 1942—0100 hours

ANDREW strolled through the camp gates, kicking a stone as he went. He booted it three or four feet up the path, ambled to it, and kicked it again, repeating, repeating. His thoughts still lolled in Tottori's quilts. He knew he would never go hungry as long as Tottori was commandant, and he would have no problems from the guards; they would treat him with respect, at least to his face. Yet, he would always regret what he had gained and what he had lost. His losses seemed immense: the camaraderie of the *Pilgrim*'s crew, Mitchell's friendship, the joy of sharing a coconut with his unit. He was an outcast henceforth.

Other prisoners tramped about as if sleepwalking, moving fast or slow, forcing their way through the night, mangy as stray dogs. They were restless but without impatience, without happiness or sadness, without curiosity, moving from here to there, alone in a crowd where they were never and always by themselves.

Someone stepped onto Andrew's path to block his way. Andrew stopped and gazed into the shadowy face of Lieutenant Fowler.

"I saw you and that degenerate march to the commandant's quarters. Are you the new camp stoolie, or are you letting the head Jappo bugger your arse in exchange for food? You've been in camp only two days, and you've already sold your soul."

Andrew's mind struggled to engage this new obstacle. He saw the hate embedded in those colorless eyes. It was pointless to defend himself, he knew. This was the first salvo in a battle that would involve everyone. Regrets were equally useless. He had made his decision; there was no turning back. But all the same, his anger swelled, choking him. He was not fuming at Fowler, but at his situation, his lack of control within the chaos.

Fowler smirked. "You're the lice who cling to the conquerors' pubic hairs. Shameless. One thing about selling out: there is always a reckoning. You'll pay, and I'll see to it that you pay dearly."

Andrew understood that Fowler meant to destroy him, and it would be all too easy. His destruction would feed the hate that raged in Fowler's heart. Andrew also realized that his own destruction, his death, was the cleanest solution to this quagmire. Fowler's hatred could very well be his only ally.

Andrew's fury evaporated. He even grinned. "I've already paid, thank you very much." He stepped around Fowler and hurried toward the hospital.

ANDREW climbed the hospital stairs two at a time. Clifford waited by Mitchell's bed while Hudson and Stokes stood in the shadows.

Clifford took Andrew in his arms. "A-a-a-are you alright? Did he hurt you?"

"I'm fine. How's our patient?"

"H-h-h-his pulse is fast and his temperature is normal, which is bad. We'll start as soon as Grady brings some water. I asked your friends to help."

Hudson shuffled up and laid a hand on Andrew's shoulder. "Don't know how you managed to get this serum, but God love you both. I asked Nash to help, him being a pharmacist's mate, but he's scared shitless, so fuck him. We'll do it ourselves. I'll be in the stairwell and Stokes will be down the hall. We'll whistle if anybody comes near."

"Where's Grady?" Andrew asked.

"Keep your shirt on." Grady glided past them carrying an enameled basin full of steaming water. He sat it on the nightstand, and fanned his hands to cool his fingers. He lifted a candle from his pocket and lit it while Hudson and Stokes took their lookout positions.

Clifford opened the surgical haversack and, after draping a clean towel on the bed, placed the equipment on the towel. He told Andrew, "I-I-I-I've already performed an inventory. We have everything we need for the operation and follow-up treatments. O-o-one thing about Tottori, he doesn't skimp on a deal. There's enough for Mr. Cocoa too. I'll give him an injection when we've finished here."

Andrew removed the wool blanket from Mitchell's sweat-soaked body. The officer's chest was pocked with puncture wounds and a bandage hugged the right leg. Andrew hooked him under the arms and muscled the officer onto his back. He pressed Mitchell's head into the rough pillow. "We're here to fix your leg," he whispered.

"Cut my leg off?" Mitchell mumbled. "Oh God, no!"

"Sssssh. We have the antitoxin."

"H-h-he's delirious. Try to keep him quiet."

Clifford took a pair of surgical tongs and placed a syringe, forceps, and scalpel into the steaming water. He washed his hands with a new cake of soap, wiped his hands dry on the towel, and used the tongs to pull the syringe from the pan. Holding a vile of morphine up to the candlelight, he stuck the needle through the rubber stopper, drew a syringe full, thumbed the plunger back to the proper dose, and gave Mitchell an injection in the buttocks.

"T-t-t-this should dull the pain." Clifford handed Andrew a length of rubber hose. "P-p-put this between his teeth." Clifford waited until the hose was in place before unwinding the bandage around Mitchell's leg.

A putrid odor radiated from the wound as it emerged. The bandage against the leg had clotted to the wound, becoming meshed with the muscle tissue. His only option was to rip the wound bare, which he did quickly so as not to draw out the pain. Mitchell jerked an inch off the mattress. His screams were muffled as he bit the hose. Andrew fought to keep him on the bed.

"T-t-t-there, there, poor baby. The worst is over."

Mitchell lost consciousness. Clifford checked his pulse. "J-j-j-just as well." He turned to Grady. "H-h-hold the candle here, honey, so I can see." He studied the open wound, which was saturated with mucus. The flesh had large patches of greenish purple discoloring. "Ch-ch-ch-christ, have mercy. Baby, this is bad. Mu-mu-much worse than I thought."

The fear in Clifford's voice brought Andrew close enough to peer into his face, which was now devoid of color. "What's wrong?"

"W-w-we're too late."

Andrew inspected the wound and fought off the urge to vomit.

"Do your best, Cliff."

Clifford removed the scalpel from the hot water and meticulously carved away the putrid, rotting flesh, probing deep to insure he removed it all.

Andrew wiped the sweat from Clifford's forehead with the towel. Minutes ticked by. Andrew was amazed at how much flesh was sliced away. The procedure seemed to take hours. By the time Clifford glanced up again, the towel in Andrew's hands was damp and smeared with makeup.

Clifford dropped the knife into the water and painstakingly washed the wound. He sprinkled sulfa powder over the entire area before rebandaging the leg.

Andrew asked, "Cliff, are you Tottori's lover?"

"W-w-w-when I first came here, he couldn't keep his hands off me. My blond hair and white skin drove him crazy. But after I became a woman, he lost interest. You see, he's already got a wife. He doesn't want another."

"He's married? How can he be that way with me if he likes women?"

"H-h-h-he pledged to his wife that he would never take another woman. Believe me, he keeps his promises. He told me that a samurai gives his word and lives or dies according to his word. You understand? He's like Master Jung-Wei."

Clifford finished tying the bandage. "T-t-t-that leaves only two options: go without or do it with boys. He wouldn't dare corrupt a Japanese soldier, so that leaves the prisoners. I'm the only prisoner he's been with, but I knew he'd go for you because you have Asian beauty. He's a tender lover, which seems strange for someone so masculine."

Embarrassment prevented Andrew from speaking, but he remembered the softness of Tottori's lips and those sensual caresses. *Yes,* he thought, *very strange.*

"N-n-n-now pay attention because you may have to do this." Clifford filled the hypodermic with serum. He pointed the needle up and thumbed the plunger to release any air bubbles, took Mitchell's arm and found a vein. "I-I-I-It's got to be intravenous. Stick the needle into the vein and pull some blood into the syringe, see? That way you know you hit the vein. Then slowly push in the antitoxin."

He removed the needle, pressed a wad of cotton over the puncture hole.

"H-h-h-he needs an injection every six hours until the serum is all gone. That should take two days. We clean the wound, reapply sulfa, and change the bandage every day." He placed the instruments, bandages, and towels into the haversack. "H-h-h-he'll probably have a violent reaction, vomiting, fever, God knows what else. Stay with him until we can move him."

"Will he be okay?"

Clifford's face took on an aura of doubt. "W-w-w-we'll know in three days." Andrew's eyes grew large, so Clifford quickly added, "L-l-look, baby, we've done all we can. I made the first dose a heavy one. I think he'll make it, but I'm not sure. You stay with him until he wakes. I'll return before dawn to help move him."

Andrew hugged him. "I love you."

"I-I-I know, baby. I love you too."

AN HOUR before sunrise, Mitchell woke from a terrible nightmare. He leaned over the bed to vomit. Andrew held his head in one hand and a pail in the other. When Andrew handed him a water bottle, he swished his mouth and spat into the bucket.

"How do you feel?"

"Like the room is spinning and I'm going to be sick again. My leg?"

"We treated it with antitoxin. We're going to save it."

Mitchell lay on the pillow, visibly struggling to understand this new turn of events. Andrew explained about the treatment.

"But where did you get the serum?"

"In Asia, there's a black market for everything, even in this place. It's a way of life. You just have to know who to approach and what to bargain." Andrew folded a cloth and wiped the beads of sweat from Mitchell's forehead. Andrew told him that it was not over yet; Mitchell was still in danger. Now it was up to Mitchell to fight with all his will. Andrew adjusted the pillows so that Mitchell was propped up. He took an English cigarette from his pocket—one that he had pinched from Tottori—lit it, and placed it between the officer's lips.

"We need to move you out of here. If the doctors see you now, they'll know we have the serum and they'll take it. We'll hide you in Hut Twenty-nine. Clifford will tell them you died in the night and the corpse detail took you away. If you feel up to walking, we should go now."

Mitchell nodded.

Andrew helped him off the bed. Holding each other, they maneuvered down the stairs and out into the predawn. Clifford waited by the front door. They carried him along. It was a painfully slow journey, but they got him to the American hut before the sun rose over the treetops.

THREE days later, after sundown, Clifford dropped by the hut, carrying the satchel. He put a thermometer in Mitchell's mouth before removing the bandage. Hudson held a candle close to the leg while Clifford inspected the wound. The swelling was down and the green-purple coloring had disappeared. Clean scabs were beginning to form. He pulled the thermometer from Mitchell's mouth, read it, and smiled. He applied more sulfa powder, wrapped a clean bandage around the leg, and, using the last of the antitoxin, administered the final injection. He patted Mitchell on the shoulder. "W-w-w-well Lieutenant, Lady Luck adores you. You'll never dance the lead in Swan Lake, but I think we saved your leg."

"Thank you so much."

"Do-do-do-don't thank me. Thank Andy."

"Where is he?"

Clifford glanced to Hudson, who shook his head.

"H-h-he's off paying a debt."

Chapter Twenty-Three

July 15, 1942—0600 hours

SUNRISE in the tropics always happens quickly, yet by imperceptible degrees. Dawn's hush broke with trumpeting cocks at the seaside village. Pristine light bled through the slats in Tottori's bedroom windows, causing sanguine bands to spread across the mosquito netting and the pale green walls.

Even before Andrew opened his eyes, he felt his body threaded around Tottori. His arms locked him to Tottori's back, legs knotted together, and Andrew's erection roosted between Tottori's thighs. Andrew absorbed the warmth radiating from the man, luxuriating in the feel of smooth skin stretched over hard muscle. A sensation of safety enfolded him. He smiled sleepily before opening his eyes.

He listened to Tottori's rhythmic breathing, leaned closer to the officer's bare shoulder, and kissed the exposed skin. His fingertips glided down the man's flank and over the rise of hips. Tottori stirred. Andrew pulled away, not wanting to drag him from sleep.

Andrew's mind flashed on images of the previous night's lovemaking—exploring hands, tasting flesh, inflamed passion. He guided Tottori's hand to his face and kissed those fingers that had caressed him in the night.

Andrew slowly untangled himself, inching away until he was free to slide from under the mosquito netting. His right arm was numb from Tottori's pressing weight. He flexed both arms to restore the circulation, taking pleasure in his drowsy contentment.

He slipped into a kimono and stumbled into the washroom to douse his face with water. Back on the terrace, he signaled Do-Han, the native servant boy, to prepare breakfast.

Andrew strolled into the living room to find Jah-Jai leaning against the low chest of drawers. He lowered himself onto a pillow, folded his legs in his lap, took the flute, and played a melodious Chinese folk tune. The notes washed through the open windows, merging with the sounds of the prison stirring for roll call.

Morning's freshness intermingled with his music to bring a simple pleasure. He felt hungry after the night's lovemaking, and the sweet anticipation of a beautiful fried egg and pickled radishes over steamed rice added to his joy. After breakfast, he would return to the prison, but he didn't want to think about that hardship yet. He focused on the purity of his music and his growing hunger while keeping one ear cocked toward the bedroom, listening for the rustle of bedding.

Do-Han traipsed through the front door carrying a pot of coffee and two cups. He bowed and placed the pot on the table. "I bring food now?"

Andrew nodded, having heard Tottori moving about the bedroom.

A few minutes later Tottori appeared at the doorway in full uniform. "Celestial music and the smell of coffee, I must be in heaven."

Andrew lowered his flute. "Hungry?"

"Famished." Tottori sat beside Andrew, ran his fingers through Andrew's blue-black hair, and caressed the nape of his neck. "You were wonderful last night. We've been making love for two months and each night is like the first time."

"You were a tiger, but you look tired now. Did you sleep?"

Tottori frowned. "When I try to sleep, my mind churns over camp problems."

"Wish I could help."

"No one can help. We're low on troops, supplies are short, the prisoners are starving, and headquarters tells me to free up what few guards I have and use less food." Tottori shook his head. "Are they mad? The prisoners are skeletons as it is. And fewer troops? It takes people to maintain order. What do they expect?"

Do-Han scurried through the doorway carrying the breakfast tray. Tottori sat silent for as long as it took the boy to serve them and leave the room. Andrew dug into the mound of rice and egg while Tottori fumed.

"I've spent ten years learning logistics, artillery, battle strategy, and how to lead men in combat. I've fought on the frontlines in China. Now the generals dump this camp in my lap and tell me to make do with nothing."

Andrew savored the egg-yolk-soaked rice as he heard Tottori's frustration punctuate every syllable. For two months he had wondered how a man with Tottori's obvious compassion could sit by while thousands of men starved to death. Now he realized that the commandant would like to improve the situation, but didn't know how.

"I hate this job. I've not been trained to nursemaid fifteen thousand prisoners. I'm a warrior, a samurai. I should be on the battlefield, not getting fat and lazy on good food and a desk job." Tottori's voice rose to a shout even as he visibly struggled to calm himself.

"Thank you," Andrew said as he leaned toward Tottori and touched his hand.

"For what?"

"Who else do you tell these troubles to?"

Tottori pulled Andrew to him. They kissed. "If only you could help with more than kindness."

"The solutions are simple. You don't need my help."

"Simple?" Tottori's eyebrows lifted. "What is so damned simple?"

"Let the English officers have their rank. Make them responsible for everything inside the wire—roll calls, work details, food storage, cooking, and maintaining discipline. That will remove the Indian guards, who are too brutal anyway, and give the English something to do. The only thing you have to do is guard outside of the wire. You can do that with a skeleton crew, because there's no place to escape to. But you already know that."

"And if they refuse?"

"Are you kidding? As for food shortages, make them grow vegetables to supplement their rice rations and let them raise chickens for meat and eggs. Everybody wins."

Tottori picked up his rice bowl and chopsticks. "Wasn't it Shakespeare who referred to the general's wife as the general's general?" A grin spread under his nose before he shoveled rice into his mouth and chewed with gusto.

Andrew felt himself reddening. "I'm not your wife."

"But you are telling me how to run my camp. No, no, I am grateful, truly. And you are right. It is so simple I am ashamed I didn't think of it."

A knock sounded at the door, followed by the high voice of Tottori's secretary, Lance Corporal Kenji Misawa, announcing that the colonel had mail. Tottori commanded him to enter and the young man bolted through the door, coming to attention beside the table.

Kenji was medium height and slender, with droopy eyes that seemed to hide behind the wire-rimmed glasses of a ledger clerk. A whisper of peach fuzz above his full lips showed he was having little success at growing a mustache. Andrew stared into the youthful face as Kenji passed the stack of letters and a brown paper package to his senior officer. Once Kenji noticed Andrew's interest, he smiled, winked.

Tottori observed his secretary's reaction and scolded the corporal. Kenji went rigid. Sweat beaded on his panic-stricken face. Tottori dismissed him with orders to arrange a staff meeting in fifteen minutes and assemble the senior English staff in one hour. The corporal ran from the room.

Tottori chuckled as he opened a letter. "He approves of you. He disliked Clifford, but you are Asian, so he is happy for me, for you, and for him."

"Why him?"

"His life became much easier since you came."

"So there haven't been any others. Only Clifford and now me?"

Tottori let a note of doubt creep into his voice, "Are you so sure? Perhaps Kenji was my lover. Perhaps that's why he's happier now."

"Tell me, please. Is it true?" Andrew's voice had a mixture of pleading and pleasure. He could visualize them together—Kenji's quiet gentleness contrasting with Tottori's rough manliness. He found the image more than a little stimulating.

"Do you want it to be true?"

"Yes." Andrew laughed. His voice sparkled. "I hope there were several others, that I am only another of your many boys, indistinguishable."

"After Clifford's dramatic transformation, I decided to give up loving boys. But you're different. I can't change you. You, in fact, are changing me."

"How?"

"Let me read. This is from my wife."

Tottori had never mentioned the fact that he had a wife. Even though Clifford had told Andrew about her, Andrew went quiet with surprise.

A smile as wide as Tokyo spread across Tottori's face. He passed a photograph to Andrew, telling him that she had delivered a son and they were both fine. He leaned over and bear-hugged Andrew.

Andrew studied the picture as Tottori finished reading the letter. The pudgy boy's head had a thick wad of black hair and a scrunched-up face. Andrew grinned at his comical expression.

"She sends you her warmest wishes and said she is grateful that you keep me company."

Andrew dropped the picture on the table. He was so stunned he was unable to speak. Minutes later, he recovered. "You told her about me?"

"Did you think I was ashamed of you?"

"I suppose I did."

Tottori handed the brown paper package to Andrew. "Her gift to you."

Speechless again, Andrew fumbled with the string holding the paper together. He finally broke it and ripped away the paper. A sea blue silk sarong emerged, followed by strong leather sandals and a sturdy shoulder bag. Andrew's head went numb with shock.

"I told her your fatigues were too hot for this climate."

"Please tell her that I am honored, but this is too fine a gift."

"She reads English. Write her a letter and tell her yourself. I'll mail it for you."

It was an intriguing idea, but Andrew knew he would be too embarrassed.

"How I long to take you there, have you meet her, and show you Kyoto. It is the spiritual heart of my people. Kyoto holds our imperial past and our finest culture. You will love it."

Andrew wondered what Tottori would be like at home, with no camp and no soldiers snapping to attention at the sound of his voice. *This is how I desire him,* Andrew thought, *with all his trappings of power. Would he be as desirable if he were stripped of this war?*

"I'll take you there," Tottori said while he finished his rice. "But for now, get dressed and go to camp. I have meetings to attend to."

A SCATTERING of bleached clouds meandered across a cobalt sky. It was already hot. The sun hammered Andrew's back golden as he strolled past the guards and into the compound.

As he walked, he concentrated on the whisper of silk sensuously caressing his thighs. With Tottori, he allowed himself the luxury of self-indulgence, taking pleasure in the man's attention, but inside the wire, his thoughts turned away from himself. That territory of self-awareness was sucked clean, like marrow from a rib bone. In place of Andrew burned a drive to help others.

Dressed in his new sarong and carrying his shoulder bag, he thought of the treats he would give his unit. Before leaving, Do-Han had slipped him several rice balls stuffed with pickled plums, and two full packs of Kooa cigarettes.

Out of nowhere, a medium-sized stone smashed into Andrew's left shoulder, followed by English curses. He had been cursed and spit at daily, but this was the first physical attack. He ran out of throwing distance and kept running to where the go-downs began. A familiar tap, tap, tapping turned his head. Cocoa hobbled toward him. His wooden leg thumped out a sound like a metronome marking time.

Cocoa was a changed man. In addition to losing his leg, he had shed thirty-five pounds over the rest of his body. His large eyes dominated his bony face. His clothes hung on him like gunnysacks. A cord tied around his shrunken waist kept his baggy pants from falling, and loose folds of skin hung over the cord. It was not only Cocoa—every member of the crew now carried that same emaciated appearance, indistinguishable from the English and Australians. In this hellhole of starvation, only Andrew's face had firm, rounded flesh. Only he maintained a sturdy muscle mass and tight, supple skin.

Cocoa carried two mess-cans in each hand.

"Andy, you're just in time for breakfast. I got your rice gruel and tea ration for you. Man-oh-man, don't you look like a regular wog in that dress."

"Gee, thanks, Cocoa. Divvy up my chow with the unit."

Cocoa beamed. "God knows it must be rough as a corncob cooking for that stone-faced son of a bitch, but what a blessing that you get to eat your fill outside the wire and we get your rations."

Cooking for Tottori was the lie that Clifford spread to explain Andrew's leaving the camp every night and not returning until morning. The story was that Andrew left camp in time to cook Tottori's dinner, played music for him during the evening meal, slept on a cot in the kitchen in case the commandant woke and needed a midnight snack, and returned to camp after fixing Tottori's breakfast. Knowing Andrew's accomplishments in the galley, none of the Americans questioned the lie, but they were the only prisoners who believed it. Andrew had never confirmed or denied the story to anyone.

"Cocoa, I won't tolerate you calling Tottori names. He's an honorable man and he doesn't want to be here any more than we do."

"Sorry, Andy. I didn't mean to offend you. I mean, good God, I owe you my life."

Andrew was not sure if he referred to the serum or the fact that Andrew had brought Cocoa into the unit over loud protests from Hudson, Grady, and even Stokes. In Changi, no one could survive alone. The optimum number in a unit was three. In some cases units of four sprang up, but any more than four and the unit couldn't forage enough food. Andrew's unit already had four when Cocoa came out of the hospital, and no other unit would take him.

"You'd do the same for me. Say, you're getting around pretty good on that stump. Is the pain bad?"

"Only when I walk more than a dozen steps, but it sure beats layin' in bed. And thank God I can finally walk without those goddamned crutches. They was wearin' holes in my armpits. Yes sir, I'll never be a ship's cook again, but at least I'm mobile. Speaking of which, have you seen Lieutenant Mitchell?"

Andrew shook his head. He had not seen Mitchell in two weeks, since they had moved all three officers in with the Aussie brass. Mitchell had been bedridden with malaria; Andrew had smuggled him quinine pills, but he had had a rough time of it.

"Saw him walking about this mornin'," Cocoa said. "First time I've seen him on his feet since we got here. I guess that gangrene treatment really threw him for a loop."

"He has a strong will to live. That's the main thing that saved him."

"Don't you believe that, laddie. You're the only reason he's alive, and don't we all know it."

"Laddie? You're spending so much time with the Brits you're beginning to talk like 'em."

Cocoa chuckled, "Guess I am at that."

They made their way to Hut Twenty-nine. Hudson, Stokes, and Grady sat in a line against the hut's shady side, eating their rice gruel and tea.

Hudson let out a long wolf-whistle. "Hubba hubba. Look at those pretty new duds. Miss Clifford will die of envy when she sees that getup."

Cocoa handed Andrew's mess-can to Hudson and told him that everyone got a share. Andrew lifted a pack of Kooas from his shoulder bag, tossed it to Stokes, and doled out four rice balls.

"One more crack about my clothes and I'll stop stealing cigarettes for you bums."

Soft laughter floated up as Andrew helped Cocoa to a sitting position and squatted next to him.

"Say, rookie," Hudson said. "Any luck on getting some cigars?"

"Sorry, Hud. I'm still working on those."

Stokes seemed even glummer than usual. Every day that passed, he slumped deeper into depression. He was convinced that Chew-Gin had given him up for dead and started dating other sailors. The fact that they hadn't had time to marry meant that she was not family, so she wasn't notified that the ship had sunk. Andrew wished for the hundredth time that he could do something to cheer up his friend. Then he remembered something Tottori had said.

"Say, John, you think you can scrounge up some paper and an envelope?"

"Depends. What's it for?" His tone sounded suicidal.

"If you write a letter to Chew-Gin, I can get Tottori to mail it."

Stokes leaped to his feet, seized Andrew by the shoulders, yanked him up, and pushed him against the wall. "You mean it? You aren't fuckin' with me?"

"If Tottori won't mail it, I'll get Do-Han to do it."

Stokes hugged Andrew mightily, squeezing painfully hard, to the point that Andrew struggled to breathe. Stokes finally loosened his grip and Andrew sank to a squatting position next to Cocoa.

"I'll have it before you leave camp. I… I mean, I don't know how to—" Stokes turned his head away and covered his eyes with the crook of his elbow. A moment later he sat beside Andrew with a quiet grin.

Cocoa grabbed the nape of Andrew's neck and squeezed.

The men devoured their gruel to the sounds of spoons scraping metal. Stokes passed each man a cigarette and they all lit up. Andrew told them that Tottori was placing the British officers in charge of everything inside the wire, and prisoners could grow vegetables and raise chickens.

"Where we gonna get chickens?" Grady asked.

"Buy them from Little Sister Wu. We'll need wood and chicken-wire to build cages."

"That takes money we haven't got," Stokes stated flatly.

"We'll sell our *balachong*," Hudson said. "I've got an Aussie buyer all lined up. Too many people have seen us gathering roaches, but if we wholesale to this Aussie, no one will link him and us, so nobody's the wiser."

"S'matter with you?" Grady said. "An Aussie won't sell bugs to his own."

"This bum would sell to his mother for a twenty-percent cut."

"Sounds like the right kind of business partner," Cocoa said.

Hudson asked, "Is it time to make another midnight roach run?"

"Jesus, Hud, not after I've eaten," Cocoa groaned. "And why am I always the one who has to wash those damned things?"

"Why do ya think we let you in this unit? Sure as hell wasn't for your Hollywood good looks," Hudson snapped. "You gotta pull your weight, or what's left of it."

Grady removed a slip of paper from his hip pocket and studied the pencil markings. He announced that tomorrow they would gather a new batch, but today was two months since they'd buried the first batch.

"Jesus, no kidding?" Stokes said. "It's harvest day?"

Cocoa told them that he could rent a hotplate, spatula, and frying pan for a half dozen Kooas, but asked how they could keep it secret. Once they cooked that stuff, the smell would give them away. They needed a diversion, he added, something to mask the smell.

"Say," Grady said, "you know what waters my eyes? When those limeys drag their bedding out and burn away the bedbugs. We could carry out a few beds, start a fire under them, and burn our own bedbugs. Kill two birds with one stink."

"Good God, boys," Hudson said. "We got us a fucking Albert Einstein here."

Andrew didn't want to rent the cooking equipment, because they'd need it every week and the Brits might get suspicious. He suggested trading his old uniform and combat boots at Little Sister Wu's for what they need.

Cocoa scratched his head. "For good boots, sure. I could even get her to throw in more pots and some grub. Are you sure you want to give up your clothes?"

"I've got these new clothes now. See if you can get us some coffee beans and a grinder. We'll open up a coffee shop."

Cocoa's smile split his face in half. "Hot damn, boys, I'm in charge of the galley again!"

A chorus of groans erupted, followed by laughter. Grady snubbed out his cigarette, opened the unit's tobacco box, and dropped the pinch of unused tobacco into the box. "I'll go and dig up cans one and two. I'll leave the holes cause we're gonna bury two more cans tomorrow."

Hudson nodded. "Right. Stokes, you scrounge up some coconut husks. I'll pull KP and go contact our Aussie wholesaler. We'll meet here for lunch and cook the bugs after we eat."

"We better wait for an hour after we eat," Andrew said. "You can't believe what that smell is like."

"What are you going to do, rookie?" Hudson asked.

"Sit here and enjoy the morning. Don't worry, I'll be plenty busy come cooking time."

Chapter Twenty-Four

July 15, 1942—1000 hours

ANDREW hunkered in the shade with his back against the hut wall as he watched thin-blown clouds creep across the sky. His mind drifted in a sphere of emptiness as his chi expanded. His essence was about to take flight when he noticed something moving toward him. He felt it more than he saw it. When he narrowed his attention on it, Mitchell adjusted into sharp focus while everything else faded away.

The lieutenant limped down the line of go-downs, flanked by Moyer and Fisher. He wore a sweat-stained officer's hat and his soiled uniform hung loosely on his gaunt frame. Hunger and sickness had reduced him to leathery skin stretched taut over bones, leaving deep valleys at his temples and under his bony cheeks. His skin's curious, sallow glow was a result of taking the antimalarial drug, Atabrine, which Andrew had been able to get from Tottori. Dark rings surrounded those clear and discerning eyes, which were still the color of pale jade.

Mitchell smiled, his first smile since standing on the *Pilgrim*'s deck. His teeth seemed too big for his mouth, as if they belonged to some larger animal.

Andrew sucked in his breath. For him, Mitchell's face had become shatteringly beautiful.

The officers strolled up and stood before Andrew, studying his fleshy chest, sea blue sarong, and leather sandals.

"You've gone native," Fisher said. His smile seemed friendly, but his voice carried a disapproving undertone. "Fine cloth like that could only have come from one place."

Mitchell pressed his hand against Fisher's shoulder to stop him from exploring the obvious.

"Fatigues are too hot," Andrew said, fingering the cloth. "This is more comfortable."

Moyer nodded. "I'll have to keep my eye out for one of those."

"I don't have an extra sarong, but this came my way." Andrew lifted a black book from his shoulder bag and handed it to Moyer.

Moyer's eyes opened wide. "Praise God, a New Testament? Where on earth—" After a pause he said, "Bless you, Andy. God bless you. We're here to conduct the morning prayer. Will you join us?"

Andrew shook his head.

Moyer grasped Fisher's elbow, guiding him into the hut while Mitchell eased himself to the ground. He leaned against the hut and exhaled a deep breath.

Andrew's senses were keenly alive. He noticed everything—Mitchell's body so deliciously close, Moyer's voice murmuring through the hut, the prisoners who paraded by with exaggerated slowness, buzzing flies, and sweat sliding over his skin. This existence would last only as long as it took Moyer to utter his prayers. Then they would depart, leaving Andrew with an intense sense of loss. He wanted to fully experience the moment, every attribute of this coming together. It was the moment's mortality that made him so desperate to savor it.

They smiled at each other.

Mitchell seized Andrew's hand in his with a gentle pressure. He curved an arm over Andrew's shoulders and pulled him nearer, staring out at nothing with a look that showed poignant emotions churning within, either joy or sadness or both. The intensity of that stare terrified Andrew. He felt the officer's heart thumping.

Andrew let Mitchell have his silence while the officer visibly struggled with a puzzle, trying to fit the pieces together. Andrew made himself wait until enough pieces fell into place.

"I saw Cocoa this morning," Mitchell said. "I swear, every time I see that stump I go crazy thinking how close I came. I don't know how to thank you."

"You'd do the same for me."

"You nursed me, smuggled me drugs, and cleaned my diarrhea. I wish I could repay you."

"All that was easy. Easy as falling in love. I can't explain how, but caring for you has made me happier than I've ever been."

Mitchell edged closer. Their bodies pressed together until their faces brushed against each other. Andrew tried to pull away, but Mitchell's eyes held him there. They kissed. Andrew focused his entire being on those lips. He ceased to exist, becoming nothing more than the glorious feel of skin touching skin.

When they pulled apart, Mitchell wore a sad grin. Andrew tried to say that he loved Mitchell, but before he could, the officer covered Andrew's mouth with his fingertips. *He is right*, Andrew thought, *words will only diminish this passion.*

They passed through several minutes of living silence.

Inside Hut Twenty-nine, voices gathered into song. "Amazing grace, how sweet the sound, that saved a wretch like me...." Moyer's voice carried the others and gave each note its full measure.

Andrew pulled three rice balls, two eggs, and a pack of Kooas from his shoulder bag, passing them to Mitchell, who quickly hid them in his own bag. Contraband should only be shared with one's own unit, and supplying the officers' unit (Mitchell, Fisher, and Moyer) with food and smokes would have landed him in a world of hurt with his own unit. He remembered something else. He lifted a metal can from his bag and pressed it into Mitchell's hands.

"Talcum powder?" Mitchell asked.

"I miss that smell on you."

Mitchell took a cigarette from the pack and lit it. He waved the match out and dropped it in the dust as he exhaled.

"You seem so content," Mitchell said.

"Of course—the war is over for us. We follow the rules and we're okay."

"Don't you long for home?"

Andrew took Mitchell's hand in his. "This is my home."

Mitchell seemed puzzled, but he didn't linger on it.

"Don't you miss the outside world?"

"What's to miss?"

"Strolling down city streets, rare steak dinners in restaurants, taking your girl to the movies, baseball and beer on Saturdays, Sunday dinners with the family."

"I've never done any of those things. Most people need all that outside activity. I do most of my living inside, so it doesn't much matter what's going on around me. Guess I'm simple."

"There's a beautiful, exciting world out there. Remembering it is all that keeps me living from this moment to the next while we suffer through this hell."

"That outside world kept me silent when I needed to talk to you, drove me to nearly kill Lieutenant Hurlburt, beat me senseless and raped me while you watched. Here I can live, and love, and help people. Here I find moments of genuine happiness. Out there I'm a failure. Out there is my shame."

"Happiness? Do you mean cooking for Tottori? Do you enjoy being with him?"

"I'm happy right now, sitting with you."

"What's he like? What kind of man is he?"

The question hung between them. Andrew fumbled for a response, but his words caught in his throat, like a sparrow trapped in a cage. This blockage was not caused by shame. He no longer felt guilt about Tottori, and he didn't feel he betrayed one man for the other. They simply lived in different worlds. His feelings for both men were reconcilable. In fact, they were both necessary. Without Mitchell and Tottori, both worlds would collapse. But even secure in that knowledge, Andrew couldn't bring himself to speak about one to the other. He needed to keep those two worlds separate and distinct.

"Speaking of Tottori, I think I can get him to send a letter to Stokes's girl so that she knows he's alive. I can do the same for you. It shouldn't be difficult to get some paper and an envelope."

"Thank you, Andy. Sure."

"Can you have it ready by sundown?"

"I'll do what I can. Now tell me about Tottori."

Hudson walked around the corner of the hut with his arm slung around Clifford's slim waist. "Look who I found on my way back from the Aussie blockhouse," he said.

Clifford smiled at the sight of Andrew and Mitchell crouched together. When he noticed Andrew's new sarong, his eyes widened and his chin trembled.

Andrew wished that there was some way to give the cloth to Clifford without insulting Tottori, but that was not possible. Andrew and Mitchell rose to their feet. Andrew leaned into Clifford and hugged him, whispering, "Looks like you two are quite an item."

"W-w-w-well, he's not giving me expensive presents," Clifford said while fingering Andrew's sarong.

When they pulled apart, Mitchell took Clifford's hand and said, "I know I've thanked you a hundred times, but every time I see you I want to thank you again. The only bad part of being back on my feet is that I no longer have you caring for me."

Clifford blushed and leaned into Hudson.

"My Aussie friend will show up an hour after lunch," Hudson said. "So we're all set."

"What's going on?" Mitchell asked.

"Clifford," Andrew said, "can you take our lieutenant and find some paper and an envelope?"

"W-W-With pleasure. Co-co-co-come with me, Lieutenant."

AS LUNCH settled, Hudson cleared the hut and posted Banks, Cord, Allard, and Nash as lookouts. Stokes and Grady carried their iron-frame bunks out to the open area in front of the hut. With Ogden and Baker helping, they dismantled the posts on the top bunk, which fitted into slots in the lower bunk posts, and built a fire with dried coconut husks.

When they had enough coals, they spread the fire into a cigar shape, five feet long and as wide as a bunk. Keeping the flames low, they placed a bunk—support slats, kapok-stuffed mattress, and frame—over the coals. Quick as that, tiny bugs began falling into the flames, so many that smoke spewed up, smudging the afternoon air. The stench became noticeable. It drifted on the breeze and spread over every hut by the southern wall.

Stokes took a burning palm frond and passed it close under the mattress to burn out even the most tenacious bugs. When they had finished with one bunk, they lifted it off the fire and set the next one over the flames.

Meanwhile, Cocoa plugged a hotplate into a dangling light socket and heated a large skillet. Andrew and Hudson pried the lid off a *balachong* can, jumping back as the odor escaped. They had filled that five-gallon can to the brim with mashed cockroaches, each one as large as a man's thumb. After two months of decomposing, there was only four inches of black goop at the bottom of the can.

"Hell's bells. That smell would gag a maggot," Cocoa choked.

Andrew used a spatula to scoop up a generous portion of paste into the frying pan. Hudson quickly closed the lid. The paste emitted an explosive, rich, earthy stench, like a newly fertilized field after a spring rain, but powerful enough to water the eyes of everyone in the hut. The reek traveled through the walls and wafted over the southern end of the camp. Everyone within a ten-hut radius took notice.

Andrew mashed the paste flat in the pan and stepped away to wipe his eyes.

"That's the right thickness," Andrew told Cocoa. "Cook it gently under low heat and turn it every two or three minutes or it will spoil. It's got to be just right, not too dry and not too moist."

Hudson paced the floor several feet away. He growled, "Well, is it two minutes or three? For Christ sakes, rookie, we've got to be exact."

"Relax, Hud," Cocoa said. "You're squawking like an old hen. We know our way around a skillet."

A high-pitched whistle cut the air.

Hudson whispered, "Someone's coming. I'll handle it." He dashed to the doorway and saw Mitchell limping toward them. Hudson hurried to intercept him, taking him by the arm and leading him up the path away from Hut Twenty-nine.

"Sir, you don't want to go down there. We're burning bedbugs and it smells god-awful."

"No kidding. Never smelt anything so bad. I have a letter I want to give to Andy. Is he here?"

"Ain't seen him, sir, but you hand over that letter and I'll see that he gets it."

Mitchell was reluctant, but he passed Hudson the letter before limping toward his hut.

Hudson scurried into the hut in time to see Andrew turning the paste.

"How much longer?" Hudson asked.

"Three minutes, thereabouts."

A cloud of flies grew thick over the pan. The drone became loud. After three minutes, Cocoa lifted the pan off the hot plate and flopped the *balachong* onto a metal plate to cool. Andrew scraped a pinch off a corner with a spoon, mixing it with his lunch rice. Hudson and Cocoa watched as Andrew ate a spoonful of rice.

"Good God, I'm going to be sick," Cocoa said.

"Well, be sick outside, damn you," Hudson snapped. "How is it, rookie?"

Andrew swallowed and nodded his head. "Perfect."

"Let me," Hudson said. He grabbed the rice from Andrew, stuffed a spoonful into his mouth, and chewed thoughtfully. He swallowed.

"Not bad. I mean, it adds a ton of flavor, and you wouldn't think that fucking cockroaches could taste so good."

Cocoa grabbed the mess-can and shoveled rice into his mouth. His eyes looked to the ceiling as he chewed. "Needs sugar. If it had a smidgen of sweetness, we could double the price."

Hudson spit. "Jesus, what the fuck do you know? It's fucking perfect the way it is."

Hudson took another spoonful, followed by Andrew and Cocoa. Each man became a connoisseur as they thought of ways to improve the taste.

"You're right, Cocoa," Andrew said. "But where can we get sugar?"

"I got some from Little Sister Wu. You told me to get coffee beans and a grinder, but I like my coffee sweet, so I bought some. We'll cook the next batch with a pinch of sugar and see how it tastes."

"Great," Andrew said. "I'll mold this batch into cubes while you cook up another pan. Hud, better tell the boys to burn more beds. It'll take us a while to cook up both cans."

"I'm on it!" Hudson said as he hustled to the door with a smile on his face and dollar signs in his eyes.

They were cooking the fourth batch when a shrill whistle sent Hudson running to a window. He saw old Darby McGaven strolling down the path with his straw coolie hat cocked low and baritoning "Waltzing Matilda."

"It's our Aussie wholesaler," Hudson said. "He wants to see the operation." Hudson moved to the doorway and signaled the Aussie to step inside.

"Ruddy hell. What's that stink?"

Hudson smiled. "The smell of money. This stuff tastes better than it smells."

Old Darby glanced down at the frying pan and his eyes sparkled. "So that's what ya blokes've been up to. The whole camp's talkin' about yer gathering borehole bugs. We thought you ruddy bastards was all eatin' um like chips."

"This stuff is pure protein," Hudson said. "Once it's cooked, it tastes pretty good. Try some."

"No bloody way I'm eatin' that shit. I'll sell it, but I sure as hell won't eat it."

"Will prisoners pay good money for it?"

"Every man and his dog will want this, and they'll pay dearly. Course, I'll have to tell them some story about going under the wire. Can't let them know about you blokes."

Hudson showed him the entire operation, cans, cooking process, molded squares, and the weekly production schedule.

"Now that you've seen it all," Hudson said with a broad smile, "let's take a walk and talk about pricing." Hudson led Darby out of the hut with the two already deep in negotiations.

"Funny," Cocoa said to Andrew. "I think that's the first time he ever liked my cookin'."

They both burst out laughing.

Chapter Twenty-five

July 15, 1942—1700 hours

AN HOUR before sunset, Clifford and Andrew ambled along the road leading to the hospital. The sway of their silk sarongs enhanced the graceful quality of their motion. They talked about the day's events, and Clifford carried a cigar box full of *balachong* cubes under his arm.

"Stop right there." Fowler's nasal voice pierced the hot air. He and Sargent Cox marched up, their backs stiff, their manner formal. "Swishing around in skirts like pansies," Fowler sneered. "Balls are wasted on the both of you."

"Is there some point to your stopping us?" Andrew asked.

"There are new camp orders. The British officers are now in command of all activities inside the wire." Fowler smirked. "I'm the new Provost Marshal and Sargent Cox is my deputy. It is our responsibility to build a proper stockade and punish wrongdoers. I intend to see the both of you rotting behind bars for consorting with the enemy. You're living well now while the rest of us starve, but I'll make you nancy boys crawl for what you've done. You'll pay for all that fine food and special treatment. I'm watching your every move, and one day soon I'll have the evidence I need to put you away."

Andrew began to move around Fowler.

"Hold on," Fowler said. "What's in that box?"

"B-b-b-*balachong*, for the hospital." Clifford slid the box from under his arm and opened the lid to show a dozen cubes of dark gray paste.

"Where did you get it?" A rich aroma wafted up, which made Fowler swallow hard.

"F-f-f-from Darby McGaven. He has connections outside the wire that smuggle him a steady supply. He donated this to the hospital. Not that it's any of your bloody business." Clifford's tone broadcasted his contempt as strongly as Fowler's eyes revealed his envy.

"Everything you degenerates do is my business," Fowler snapped. Sweat streamed down his face. That much *balachong* was a windfall that would tide any man over for six months. Fowler's lips quivered as he added, "You're lying. Darby McGaven is a skinflint who doesn't donate anything to anybody."

"I suggest you take that up with him," Andrew said.

"I want an honest answer and I want it now." Fowler bit his lower lip. "Are you letting him bugger your ass for food, like you do Tottori?"

"Envy is a vile emotion," Andrew said. "It strips away all one's dignity. I feel sorry for you."

"Filthy whores," Fowler hissed and spat on Andrew's face.

Andrew wiped the spittle off his cheek as he leaned toward Fowler while cocking his fist. He stopped himself. Without another word he stalked away in the direction of the front gate.

Clifford eyed Fowler. "Y-y-you better tread carefully, Lieutenant, because all he has to do is whisper your name in Tottori's ear. You'll be swinging a pick on a Burma railroad gang the next day."

Clifford sashayed around Fowler and glided on toward the hospital.

Chapter Twenty-Six

July 15, 1942—1900 hours

IN THE tub room, Andrew washed away the camp grunge. Afterward, he sat up to his neck in cool rainwater while he waited for Tottori.

The commandant entered the room as if he couldn't wait to clean the war stench from his skin. He stripped off his uniform and sat on the three-legged stool. Andrew climbed out of the tub and poured a dipper of water over the officer's head. He took a bar of Yardley soap and scrubbed the hollow of Tottori's chest. They shared a smile as Andrew washed under the socket of Tottori's left under arm, up over the shoulder blades, into the right socket, and down the man's torso to the crotch.

Tottori was already hard when Andrew soaped his genitals. Andrew scoured down both legs and even cleaned the crevices between the commandant's toes. He scrubbed Tottori's back, finishing with the scalp, pouring dippers of water over the muscular body to rinse away the soap before they lowered themselves up to their chins in delicious rainwater.

They performed the ritual without speaking, as if they needed to wash away the war before addressing one another.

Andrew playfully splashed his lover. "Hard day?"

Tottori, his eyes closed, grunted.

"How did the British react when you gave them responsibility inside the wire?"

"They pissed on themselves like excited puppies. They saw it as a sign of weakness and began making demands, so I smacked Major Taylor across the face and screamed for ten minutes. That put them in their place."

"The camp was buzzing like Chinese New Year back home. Those dreary men were so jazzed. It's wonderful to see a spark of life in their eyes."

Tottori grunted again.

"They made my enemy the Provost Marshal. He said he'll lock me up for being your whore."

"Stay here. There's no point in going back."

Tempting as that sounded, it would make Andrew a deserter and a traitor. Andrew wondered if Tottori had covert motives. *Could he be jealous of Mitchell?*

As if reading Andrew's thoughts, Tottori told him that it wouldn't matter once Japan won the war. Andrew would simply stay in Asia where he belonged and travel to Kyoto with him. "I guarantee that you will be treated well."

Warmth spread throughout Andrew's body. This was another veiled message that Tottori loved him, and his gratitude grew immense.

"Suppose Japan doesn't win?"

"Our national honor will not accept defeat."

"I need a favor."

"If you start making demands, I will have to smack you and scream for ten minutes to put you in your place."

Andrew sat, silent, no longer certain if he should ask.

"Well, what is it?" Tottori chuckled.

"I have two letters that I'd like you to mail. They're both from prisoners who need to send word home."

"From the officer you are in love with?" Bitterness singed his voice.

Andrew went silent, refusing to discuss Mitchell.

"Mailing letters to the States is dangerous, but I can manage. Leave them on my desk."

Andrew wrapped his arms around the man's neck. They kissed. Tottori opened his eyes and they kissed again. His hardness pressed against Andrew's belly.

"Let's make love," Andrew whispered.

"Patience. Anticipation enhances the spice."

"Let's stay in the tub all night. We'll make love, have dinner, and fall asleep right here."

They kissed again. "Out you go," Tottori said. "We are already prunish, and I am hungry." Tottori hauled himself out of the tub, seizing a towel.

Andrew stared at his rugged nakedness while the echoes of Tottori's rejection mixed with Fowler's threats rang in his ears. He felt a complete and frightening meaninglessness to the reality of his life. This murky existence of living in two disconnected worlds, both of which were driven senseless by the absurdity of war, pricked his skin like a millions tiny needles. He tried to cry out but he could not utter a sound, could not even take a breath. His anxiety passed—at least he was able to breathe again—but the fear of being utterly irrelevant lingered. With more reflection, he was comforted by the notion that he was not alone. Everyone in the camp, on both sides of the wire, was equally as insignificant. He remembered something his master had once told him— significance is buried within the insignificant, so appreciate everything.

By the time they had dried each other and pulled on kimonos, Do-Han had set the table and green tea awaited them. Andrew's anxieties calmed to the point where he could pour tea for Tottori while pretending to enjoy the officer's conversation.

"If you insist on returning," Tottori said, "you must fight this Provost Marshal like a samurai. A samurai's state of mind is called *Mushin*. It means: the still center. It is the ability to stay utterly calm, read your opponent, and attempt to redirect his aggression. *Mushin* is to remain unbiased, have no emotional attachments, to stay open and flexible like the willow in a strong wind. If you control your mind in this way, you will control yourself and your enemy too."

The fragrance of ramen soup drifted through the open doorway seconds before Do-Han sailed into the room carrying two steaming bowls. Tottori fell silent as Do-Han served them, bowed, and exited.

Andrew welcomed a break in the conversation. He felt uncomfortable talking about the prison. To change the topic, he asked, "I'm curious why you joined the army. With your education and knowledge of other countries, you could have been a diplomat or international businessman. Why the military?"

"I am samurai, like my father and his father and his, as far back as three hundred years. Samurai means: to serve. I serve my country, my people, my ancestors."

Andrew picked up his chopsticks and spoon, lifted a bunch of noodles from the bowl, and slurped them down as Tottori explained that his family had been military leaders since feudal Japan. He talked about his father, so gallant and stirring in his uniform, and the pride his family enjoyed. Andrew used his chopsticks to pick up a bright red triangle of raw fish, beautifully arranged on a bamboo tray.

"When I joined," Tottori continued, "we had taken Mongolia. These new territories were hailed as our path to prosperity. There was a military buildup to protect against a Russian invasion and to fight the communist uprising in China. We thought we would fight a ragtag army for six months and return home victorious. We were sure our families and townspeople would hail us as heroes. You should have seen the send-off at the docks when we boarded the transport ships. Thousands of people cheered. A brass band played the '*Kimigayo*,' our national anthem. We felt the eyes of the nation on us, and we let ourselves be carried way with their euphoria."

Tottori fell silent, as if remembering the crowd's uproar. "We were fools, of course. We didn't know that you can't fight a little war. Once you put your toe in the water, you sink to your ears. But it was such a magnificent feeling at the beginning. But things went sour in China, and Roosevelt created the trade embargo to strangle us into submission. By then we had a dream of creating a unified Asia, and Japan had paid dearly for that dream. We couldn't stop after paying such an enormous price. We were sucked into a war we never wanted or intended, step by bloody step."

Tottori ate slowly and deliberately while his mind seemed to play with images of past glory.

"We have many faults. We're violent, arrogant, overconfident, childishly loyal, and our pride, yes, our pride is perhaps our worst fault. But when we succeed, when all East Asia is united under one rule, it will be our golden age, the start of a glorious era when Asia will command its own destiny, and Japan will be at the heart of it."

Tottori described his early years in the China campaign, leading troops into battle, the strong resistance of the Chinese, and the ever-present fear that Russia would attack from the north. He explained how, as the war dragged on, he slowly lost heart until, by the time he came to Changi, he hated every aspect of war and his role in it. "But then," he said, "war brought you to me. The very thing I hate most has brought me supreme joy."

"This place you call *Mushin*," Andrew said, "the still center, is where I go in meditation. But you say you can be in this space to fight battles?"

Tottori stared at Andrew.

A knock at the front door was followed by the familiar voice of Lance Corporal Kenji Misawa, announcing he had an urgent dispatch. Tottori ordered him to enter and the secretary bolted into the room, marched to the table, and stood at attention while Tottori read the dispatch.

From behind wire-rimmed glasses, Kenji's eyes glanced down at Andrew.

Andrew saw his interest. He ran his tongue over his upper lip and winked, a long, slow whiplash of his eyelid.

Kenji stood as stiff as a pine tree and blushed from collar to cap. A grin appeared at the corners of his mouth.

Tottori dismissed his secretary and watched him go. "Perhaps you think it's funny to tease my staff, but I don't want my troops gossiping that I'm sharing my bed with a floozy."

"Floozy?" Andrew roared with laughter.

Tottori insisted that it was not funny, but Andrew couldn't stop laughing.

"A floozy, that's what you've made me. Ha-ha."

"Can't you see that boy is smitten? It's offensive to lead him on."

Andrew's laughter faded, but his enjoyment swelled. "Now that we've affirmed I have a reputation for promiscuity, I'm certain that you will never fall in love with me. A man with your integrity could never truly love a tramp. I guess I'll wander through life a ruined man, always searching for love and never finding it. How tragic. Or if Kenji is smitten, when you tire of me and find another, you'll give me to him. Perhaps he'll love me."

"What about you—do you love me?"

Andrew looked down and leaned into Tottori's body. He felt the same heat coursing through Tottori as he felt within himself. "I'm sorry. I was carried away. We shouldn't talk of love."

AFTER dinner, while Do-Han whisked away the dishes, Andrew played Jah-Jai. Tottori unsheathed his samurai sword and picked up a sharpening stone. He sat cross-legged, meticulously running the stone along the blade. It gleamed in the room's serene lamplight. Its bluish steel was as pristine as a mountain stream. He occasionally held the sword in front of his eye to study the edge.

"This sword has been in my family for three hundred years. Our soul is fused into this steel."

"Tonight is only the second time since we met that you have mentioned your past. I was beginning to think that you were nothing more than this instant, with no personal history at all."

Tottori grunted. "Some men choose to dwell on the past in hopes of understanding what will unfold in their future. Not me. Like all men, I have a past that shapes my future, but I choose to focus on this moment and be surprised at what develops. For now, I regard my life as only these moments I spend with you."

He used a white cloth to wipe away a blemish and continued to sharpen. As he worked, Andrew watched the play of light on the mirrorlike blade. When it was razor-sharp, Tottori wiped it once again with the cloth and returned it to its scabbard. He repeated the process with the shorter, companion sword. Samurai swords always come in pairs, one long blade and one short.

That was their nightly routine: Andrew came before sunset, they bathed together and ate a sumptuous meal, and Andrew played Jah-Jai while Tottori did paperwork, wrote letters, sharpened his sword, or polished his stones. Later, Tottori spent an hour kneeling in prayer before his Shinto shrine while Andrew played. They did this until they could no longer hold in their mounting desire and retired to the bedroom. Tottori had to make love each night, hours of sensual kisses and caresses.

Andrew suspected that Tottori made love to chase away his fears. The commandant harbored much fear—an insatiable fear that created an equally insatiable lust.

Chapter Twenty-Seven

December 24, 1944—1000 hours

EACH day the number of POWs diminished. The prisoners conducted their morning ritual of checking their comrades who were unable to rise from their bunks. A man who could stand with help had five days to live; if he sat up but couldn't stand, he had three days; if he couldn't rise at all, he'd be gone by the next sunrise.

Andrew worked the burial detail, hauling the bodies onto carts for the long march out the gates, digging new graves beside the old ones, listening to the soulful words of Chaplain Moyer. He buried them all the same, captains and corporals, foot soldiers and orderlies, undistinguishable and anonymous. Mass graves were the final humiliation. Emaciated limbs became confused and tangled, fleshless faces pressed cheek to cheek, bodies huddled together as if seeking warmth, and the black dirt would absorb their souls, transforming their lost youth into fertile earth. That became the crude face of war. Not the stratagem of politics manipulated by leaders of nations or the chess game of generals played miles from the battlefields; war is the tragic and anonymous deaths of human beings whose seeds are lost forever.

The astonishment of being a survivor pressed on Andrew. Beriberi, dysentery, malaria, starvation, and suicide had swallowed a weighty toll over two and a half years. With each burial detail, Andrew's sense of guilt deepened. Guilt was by far his most cumbrous burden. The miraculous events that had shepherded him under Tottori's care were all that had kept him alive to bury the less fortunate. While handling the bodies, he felt utterly grateful for his good fortune and, at the same time, outraged.

The bodies had begun to whisper to him as he stacked them in the pits. Hideous, mournful, accusing rasps called to him. Even when he piled on the dirt—covering those gaping mouths, staring eyes, frozen facial expressions—the sound still filtered through, drumming in his ears. He threw himself into the digging and soon his exhaustion numbed his mind. It was the only way to silence the dead.

After a brief service, Andrew shuffled to Hut Twenty-nine to wait. Prison was waiting—for sunrise when you could not sleep, for chow when your stomach ached, for the hot part of the day to pass, for your hands to stop trembling from the horror of handling the dead, for a bath to wash away death's stench, for Tottori's sensuous caresses.

Andrew never thought beyond the next goal he waited for. The passing years had become an orderless jumble. The notion of time no longer existed. His only measure of time's passing was the accumulation of whispering corpses in the black dirt.

The sky opened up with a late-morning shower. Water dripped from thatch roofs and gathered in storm ditches. Dust turned to slippery goop, but that didn't stop Andrew from rushing to his bunk. He dropped his shoulder bag and removed his sarong before dashing out the doorway to have his nakedness enveloped by the rain's fleeting coolness. His body welcomed the stinging drops as he performed the fastidious movements of tai chi.

The reek of death seeped away. His mind soared beyond the voices in his head, lifting, lifting, until he floated above the clouds as his earthbound body achieved one elegant position after another.

By the time the sun had brushed away the clouds, painting the sky blue, his mood had turned serene. The voices retreated. Returning to his bunk, he took up Jah-Jai and played a soulful tune.

Only a few men were in the hut. John Allard was giving Kelso a haircut. Nash and Banks sat at a wooden table playing acey-deucy. Cord and Smitty played the food game. It had become a popular pastime where prisoners tried to out-torture one another.

Cord closed his eyes and his voice carried a note of rapture. "Pastrami and Swiss cheese on toasted rye bread, with plenty of mustard and an icy beer to wash it down."

Smitty groaned. "Mama's ravioli with three kinds of cheese and a bottle of Chianti." He smacked his lips while Cord twisted in agony.

"Cold, sliced peaches with gobs of whipped cream on top."

Kelso shouted down the hut. "Shut the fuck up until after lunch, for God sakes."

Hudson lay on his bunk. The woeful voice of Jah-Jai woke him and he sat up, grinning. His eyes sparkled with a mischievous quality as he trotted over to Andrew, extracting a length of pale yellow, embroidered silk from his shoulder bag. Hudson wore his pathetically patched pants, which were cut short, halfway to his knees. Andrew could count each rib bone through the pelt of hair that covered Hudson's upper body, but the glow in Hudson's eyes made him look like a pauper who had found a magic carpet.

Hudson unfolded the fabric. "Will Miss Clifford like this?"

Andrew lowered his flute, fingered the material. "He'll love it, Hud. Where did you get it? Little Sister Wu doesn't have anything this fine."

"I went under the wire with ol' Darby McGaven. He goes under all the time. I traded at the village for this and some food. I got a sack of dried shrimp, roasted pork, a bottle of native hooch, and five cigars."

"You'll get shot out there."

"Naw, ol' Darby has an understanding with the guards." He slid his thumb back and forth over two fingers.

"You took that chance to get Clifford a sarong? That's crazy."

"Miss Clifford is the only thing that means a damn to me. I'll do anything for her."

"Him."

"Whatever. It doesn't matter. I love her… him. Tell you the truth, that fuckin' Romeo, Ensign Fisher, has been buzzin' around her like a moth to a flame. I thought if I gave her something pretty, she'd pay more attention to me."

"Presents won't make him love you. Have you told him how you feel?"

"Tell a man I love him? Naw, I couldn't do that."

"Well if you do love him… her, then tell her. Knowing how you feel will make the difference."

"Thanks, rookie. I knew you'd understand, but do me a favor. Don't mention this to anyone."

"You think they don't know?"

"Doesn't matter what they know or don't know. I don't want them talking about us."

"Mum's the word." Andrew chuckled as his mood lifted. "You're certainly not the same wild man who chased women through alleys. Hard to believe a man could change so much."

Hudson nodded. "Two and a half years in hell makes a powerful impression on a man. I've even found religion. No, I mean it. Ol' Chaplain Moyer and I are like this." He held up his hand and crossed two fingers.

"I'm happy for you, Hud. Really I am."

"There's only one thing. I'm embarrassed to give this to Miss Clifford. I mean, what if I give it to her and she doesn't feel the same way for me?"

"Could be awkward. Say, tomorrow is Christmas. You could give it as a Christmas present. In fact, we could organize a holiday party with that pork and the hooch. We could give gifts to some of the others too. That would make it more natural."

"That's a great idea. We'll go all out and have a Christmas feast. We'll do it tomorrow around dinnertime. Let's walk over to Little Sister Wu's and see what we can get for the others. We'll need string and wrapping paper too. And we can pick up some bottles of rice wine, fruit, eggs, beans, and whatever else she has."

"Speaking of the others," Andrew said, "where is everybody?"

Hudson explained that Stokes and Cocoa were working in the vegetable fields, Ogden and Baker were on wood detail, and Grady was in the chicken coop. But he also had war news.

"That's why Darby keeps going to the village," Hudson said. "They have a hidden radio. The English are winning in Burma. The Americans are in the Philippines and are fighting in Luzon. And they're bombing Iwo Jima. In Europe, the allies have liberated Antwerp and Patton is kicking the hell out of the Jerries in someplace called the Saar Valley, but of course this time of year the snows are slowing down all progress. At home, FDR won a fourth term and Army beat Navy for the first time in five years, 23-7."

"What does all that mean for us?"

"It means that we're killing Japs by the thousands. Our troops are only a few hundred miles away. This war could be over in a few months. We'll be going home."

"Oh, no!"

"Oh, yes!" Hudson danced around in a circle.

"Hud, you can't go blabbing this news. If the Japs find out they have a radio in the village, they'll kill them all."

"You're right. Like you said, mum's the word."

"Speaking of Grady, that reminds me." Andrew pulled his billycan from his worn shoulder bag. The can was filled with scraps of leaves and worms that he had gathered while on burial detail. He ambled down the hut to the trapdoor in the floor and knocked. Legions of flies swarmed up from the plank floorboards. A minute later the trapdoor lifted and Grady's head appeared through the three-foot-square opening.

Grady had been watching the hut's prize Bantam cock, Samson, mount one of the hens. After Samson had finished, the hen ruffled her feathers to shake off the dust and ran about clucking and scratching while Samson strutted about, looking for his next conquest. There were thirty hens altogether. That ensured that each man in the American hut received two eggs per week. The flock had been purchased one by one with money made from secretly producing *balachong*. Now Grady had Delilah nesting five fertile eggs while Bathsheba nested another five. The goal was to expand the flock until each man got one egg every other day and the hut could stew one hen per week. Tending and guarding the flock was Grady's full-time job. He spent most of his day under the hut with them. They were his children, and he took great pride in them, as if he had nested each one himself.

The camp owned several chicken runs, which were maintained by the English officers. Altogether, the camp owned over five hundred and forty scraggy hens and two dozen cocks. They produced enough eggs to insure that each man in camp received one egg every two weeks. Some units were rich enough to have their own small flock, and their pens were in the same open area as the camp pens, along the north wall. The vitamins supplied from these eggs, the sweet potatoes and tapioca roots grown by the prisoners, and the protein from the *balachong* had eliminated blindness from beriberi and slowed the death rate by 70 percent.

Only the Americans chose to keep their chickens within the three-foot crawlspace under their hut. They simply ran chicken wire around the outside support posts. That was Cocoa's idea, to disguise all their activity under the hut while burying and unburying the cans of *balachong*. It also kept the rest of the camp from counting how many hens the Americans had. The birds added a barnyard odor to the hut, but Grady kept the coop spotless, and that kept the smell within tolerable limits.

"I brought your babies some grub," Andrew said.

"You know, Grady," Hudson said, "you're spending so much time down there, you're beginning to molt. You'll be sitting your black ass on a nest and hatchin' chicks before long."

"If that's what it takes, then you can bet your sweet Aunt Sara's titties that that's what I'll do." Grady took the billycan and disappeared under the floorboards.

Andrew closed the trapdoor and Hudson suggested that they visit the camp store after lunch to stock up for the party. On the way to Andrew's bunk, Hudson told him about his plan to increase the production of *balachong*. A year ago they had upped production from two cans a week to four. But the prisoners were desperate for more, so Hudson figured they could easily sell six cans per week. Maybe eight.

"Hud, there's no way to double production and still keep it secret."

"You should see what we can buy in the village: a whole pig, new clothes, fresh fish. We could eat like kings."

"Too dangerous. We need to get Little Sister Wu to stock more stuff."

"That swindler triples the price on everything."

No one in the American hut noticed the first whistle from three huts away, but everybody heard the second, more urgent whistle that came from the next hut over.

Andrew and Hudson halted in their tracks as Fowler and Cox climbed the steps and blocked the doorway. Fowler wore a rattan coolie hat, wooden clogs, and a rag draped over his hips. An armband on his left arm flaunted his rank insignia. His eyes looked like open wounds but were keenly alert.

Cox wore half a burlap sack knotted at the waist like a kilt. He was bone-thin and his complexion had a greenish hue. His face was scrunched up, no doubt from a painful spasm in his bowels that broadcasted another bout of dysentery was looming.

"Stand at attention when an officer enters," Fowler said, loud enough to be heard by everyone.

All the Americans paused for a moment before standing loosely at attention, enough of a pause to be insulting. Fowler, likewise, held the men at attention for a half minute longer than necessary in order to return the insult.

"Stand at ease," Fowler finally said. "Nobody leaves this hut until we have completed a thorough inspection."

Mitchell and Colonel Henman followed Fowler into the hut. Henman wore a patched uniform shirt, shorts, and clogs and carried a bamboo swagger stick. His handlebar mustache had grown long and extended several inches from each side of his face.

Mitchell said, "Alright men. I want everyone to fully cooperate with Lieutenant Fowler."

Andrew stole an appraising look at Mitchell. Their eyes met and Andrew smiled. Mitchell was Changi-thin, but a steady stream of food from Tottori's kitchen had managed to put a dozen pounds of restored muscle on his frame. His face had filled out and his warm, bronze coloring made him look as young and handsome as that first day Andrew had laid eyes on him. Mitchell carried a look of health, albeit no fat on him. He stood like a pillar of strength in comparison to his British counterparts, who showed no muscle at all. The contrast was startling.

Fowler sauntered the length of the hut and halted in front of Hudson and Andrew. He momentarily glanced at Henman, as if to reinforce his authority. "We've kept an eye on you. You've spent hoards of money on chickens, food, and tobacco. We also believe that you are in possession of a great deal of money, thousands. The only way you could possibly get that kind of money is by trading contraband with the guards or selling information to the enemy. Both, as you well know, are illegal."

Hudson's head leaned to one side. "What information would we be sellin'? All we know is today's weather and how bad the food is. How much do you think them Japs would pay for that strategic information?"

"Keep that up and I'll put you in the stockade for insubordination."

Hudson scoffed. "There's no law against trading with other prisoners, accepting gifts, or winning at gambling. We've done nothing illegal and you can't prove we did."

"I want to know exactly what you have and how you got it. Mind you, if you say you won it gambling, I'm going to investigate to see if that person corroborates your story."

Cocoa hobbled through the doorway with a smile on his face and a coconut in his shoulder bag. He stopped cold, as if trying to decide whether or not he should sneak back out. He moved forward; his wooden leg and crutch creaked wood on wood against the floorboards.

Lately, Cocoa had begun to use both his hollow wooden leg and a crutch because the pain in his stump was increasing by the day. The doctors planned to re-stump the leg to somewhere above the knee, but after two and a half years, he swore the memory of the first amputation was still fresh in his mind and he'd die before going through that again. This time, however, would be different: Andrew had promised to get him anesthetics. Losing the knee would make him less mobile, but at least he'd be able to tolerate the operation.

Mitchell watched Cocoa limp to his bunk, staring at that wooden stump grating against the floorboards. He visibly shivered before glancing at Andrew with a tender look that radiated pure gratitude.

Cocoa propped his crutch against the wall, pulled his shoulder bag strap over his head, and took out the coconut. "Today's a lucky day, boys. Look what rolled my way."

Fowler eyed the coconut as sweat beaded on his forehead. He turned to Hudson.

"How many chickens are under the floor?"

"Not my department. If you want to jump down there and crawl around in all that chicken shit counting them, be my guest. But whether there's ten or a million proves nothing. Chickens can be hatched from eggs as easily as bought with contraband."

"Whose department is it?"

"That would be Grady Washington." Hudson stomped on the floor three times. Seconds later the trapdoor lifted and Grady's head appeared.

Fowler stared at Grady. "Well, sailor, how many chickens are under this hut?"

Grady winked at Hudson. "I don't rightly knowd," he drawled. "I gots no head for figures. Evah time I starts countin' I lose track 'n has to starts again. Guess I ain't nevah made it all th' way through."

"Well count them. I want an accurate total before I leave here."

Hudson motioned to Cocoa for a cigarette. Cocoa popped the lid on the unit's tobacco box, which was a quarter full of loose straw-yellow tobacco. It also held slips of rattan grass that they use for rolling paper, a crumpled pack of Kooas, and a Ronson lighter. After pulling out the pack of Kooas, he offered one to Hudson and took one for himself. He flicked the Ronson into flame for Hudson and lit his own cigarette. Hudson inhaled and blew smoke in Fowler's face.

"You want one?" Hudson asked Fowler.

Fowler had not had a tailor-made cigarette in over two years. He glanced down at the pack while the odor from Hudson's cigarette lingered on the air. The shine in his eyes revealed that he would give his eyeteeth to have that pack, but pride is a mysterious thing. He swallowed the lump in his throat and said with a voice scorched with bitterness, "No, thank you."

"Pity." Hudson offered the pack to Mitchell and Henman, who both took one. Cocoa flicked the Ronson and held the flame under the ends of their cigarettes.

Fowler grabbed the Ronson and handed it to Cox. "Put that on the list," he said. "Cox will list everything we find. We intend to keep a running inventory of American items so we can gauge any increase in wealth as time passes."

Hudson drew a final drag on his cigarette before tossing the half-inch-long butt on the floor. Both Fowler and Cox stared down at the burning butt. Fowler closed his eyes and turned away, but Cox knelt and picked up the butt, snipped off the burning end with his fingers. Smiling happily, he opened his tobacco tin, pulled away the half inch of paper, and mixed the tobacco into his stash of dried tealeaves.

Cocoa also dropped his butt. As Cox reached for it, Cocoa stomped on the butt with his wooden stump and ground it into the floorboard. The smile on his face grew wide and joyful.

Fowler ordered everybody to empty their pockets and shoulder bags onto their bunks while Cox searched the premises, listing everything as he went.

Stokes and Cord, followed by Ogden and Baker, waltzed through the doorway carrying four billycans each. In addition to their own lunch, they also brought Hudson's, Andrew's, Grady's, and Cocoa's— one can of steamed rice and one can of watery fish soup per man.

"Chowtime," Stokes said before realizing what was going on.

Hudson glanced at Mitchell. "Sir, okay if we eat lunch before the rice cools?"

"Go ahead, Hudson. Eat by your bunks."

Hudson nodded at Cocoa with a wink. "How's about fryin' up some eggs?"

"Sure thing." Cocoa's smile was angelic.

Stokes sauntered to the unit footlocker, unlocked it, and opened the lid. Fowler and Cox were quickly there to inspect the contents. In addition to pots, pans, a hotplate, and a coffee grinder, there were five eggs laying in a pearl-white bowl, three sacks of coffee beans, a dozen bananas, four cans of sardines, six cans of condensed milk, two pounds of roasted pork meat wrapped in leaves, a sack of dried shrimp, and a bottle of hooch. There were also containers of cooking oil, salt, pepper, sugar, and seven packs of Kooas.

Neither Fowler nor Cox could conceal their amazement. Cox ran his tongue over his dry lip. Fowler was too dazed to ask where it all came from.

"We've been lucky at gambling," Hudson offered, patting Cox on the shoulder.

Stokes pulled the hotplate and frying pan from the box while Cocoa took the oil, eggs, salt, and pepper.

Fowler found his voice before Stokes could relock the box. "Just a minute. I want a closer look at that." He knelt and rummaged through the entire box, obviously looking for money, but he found nothing more than the food and cigarettes. He told Cox to make sure everything in the box went on the list.

Stokes took the pan and hotplate to the electric outlet, plugged in the hotplate, and set the pan on top. While the pan heated, Cocoa readied the oil and eggs. Normally for the midday meal, they combined all the unit's rice together, mixed in two raw eggs, and redistributed equal portions to each man. Today, however, they silently agreed to splurge.

Cocoa suggested frying up some pork meat as well, but Andrew vigorously shook his head no. He knew that would be going too far over the top.

Fowler and Cox examined every shelf, food box, mattress, and pillow. Bunk by bunk they made their way through the hut.

Cocoa broke an eggshell on the side of the pan and dropped the contents neatly into the hot oil. A sputtering sound filled the entire hut. Everybody froze. All eyes involuntarily focused on the frying pan. The sunrise-yellow yolk surrounded by a circle of clear jelly began to set. Cocoa repeated the operation until five eggs covered the bottom of the pan. The sizzle, an arduous, torturing sound, consumed every mind.

Cocoa used a spatula to work the eggs around the pan so they didn't stick. The unit stood at a respectful distance, drinking their soup and watching the amazing vision of frying eggs.

Hudson turned to Mitchell. "Sorry, we don't have enough to offer you some."

Mitchell's voice cracked, "We couldn't accept anyway. We're here on official business."

"Perhaps you'll join us for a cup of coffee after we eat?"

"Thank you, no," Henman said, but everybody knew he would kill for a cup of real coffee.

The marvelous fragrance of frying eggs is one of life's simple pleasures—that is, unless you're starving. Then it's bamboo-shoots-under-fingernails torture. Henman couldn't hide the strain any longer. He took Mitchell by the arm and suggested they step outside for a moment. He had something to say to Mitchell in private. Mitchell seemed only too happy to follow him outside.

Fowler leaned out the nearest window, taking breaths of outside air. Sweat streamed down his face. Every pop of grease echoed like a kettledrum. Andrew heard Fowler's stomach growl from twenty feet away.

Cocoa flipped the eggs over one by one, adding a pinch of salt and pepper to each. "The secret to fried eggs is spicing them while the little buggers are still cookin'." He smacked his lips together.

He visibly poured all his concentration into making each egg a work of art. "Jesus H., this smells so damn good. It's going to taste like heaven. Stokes, line up those rice cans." Cocoa pulled the frying pan off the hotplate. One by one he slipped the spatula under an egg, glided it over a billycan, and laid the egg neatly over the rice. He tilted the pan over the top of the mess-cans to let a thin stream of oil trickle over each egg until the pan was dry.

A hush haunted the still air.

"Chowtime, boys." Cocoa's voice cut the silence like a gong.

Each man in the unit picked up his rice and egg and brought it under his nose to savor the aroma. Andrew broke his yoke to let the golden nectar saturate his rice. He took a bite of egg and moaned.

Cox said, "Sir, I think I've found something."

Fowler raced over, nearly screaming, "Whose bunk is this?"

"That would be mine," Hudson said through a mouthful of egg. He strutted right up to Fowler and ate another spoonful of egg, chewing loudly.

As Cox uncovered the silk sarong and five cigars, Hudson looked as if a lightning bolt had zapped his testicles. He had forgotten about the silk. His mouth dropped open as the blood drained from his face. He stammered an unintelligible word and went silent.

Fowler's chest expanded. "Hudson, you are under arrest." Fowler's words were magisterial and final. "This proves that you're trading with guards. You couldn't possibly have gotten either of these items inside the camp." Fowler told Cox to ask Henman and Mitchell to step inside.

"I've got you now, you arrogant bastard," Fowler hissed only loud enough for Hudson and Andrew to hear. Hudson took another mouthful of rice and egg, trying desperately to act unruffled, but he couldn't hide the sweat beading on his forehead.

Andrew knew he had had it. Even if he told the truth about going under the wire, that was illegal too, and it would also implicate Darby McGaven. Going under the wire or trading with the guards, he was screwed either way.

Fowler glowed by the time Henman and Mitchell ambled up to study the contraband spread out on Hudson's mattress.

"Sir," Fowler said, "we were unable to find their money stash, but we did find this. There is no way Hudson could have gotten this from other prisoners or from Little Sister Wu. It had to have come from trading with the guards." A note of mirth colored his voice.

"Well, Hudson," Mitchell said. "What have you got to say for yourself?"

"Sir, I... I... I mean, sir—"

"Those belong to me, sir." Andrew set his half-eaten rice on his bunk and stepped forward. A dull ache rose to the top of his head, but he ignored it. "Tomorrow is Christmas. I got those as presents. Hudson was hiding them for me until I could wrap them. The silk is for Clifford Baldrich, the cigars are for Cocoa."

Hudson's body went limp. The relief in his face was evident to everyone.

"But where did you get them?"

"They were a gift from Commandant Tottori, sir. Lieutenant Fowler, you're perfectly welcome to corroborate my story with the commandant."

"You're lying!" Fowler's voice rose to borderline hysterical.

Andrew stared at Fowler with flinty eyes. "Prove it."

Mitchell said, "I can vouch for this man," He laid a hand on Andrew's shoulder. "He's not capable of lying. I'd stake my life on it."

Mitchell's solemn voice echoed in the pit of Andrew's stomach. He felt shame coloring his face in scarlet streaks. The dull ache in his head grew sharp. He glanced down at the floor, seeing the dark gap between the floorboards, and he wished with all his might that he could crawl right through there and keep on going.

Colonel Henman nodded his head, "All right, Fowler, seems we've done all we can do here. Let's leave these men to their lunch."

Fowler's face colored a scalded red. He gasped for breath. "You Yanks are scum. You have no discipline, no integrity, and no dignity. You gather wealth at any cost and flaunt it with grotesque arrogance. I hate you! I hate you all!"

"Now just a Goddamned minute," Mitchell said, his voice becoming brusque. "I've put up with this invasion of my crew's privacy and even your calling Waters a liar, but I won't stand for your insults any longer. I want you to leave, now, and don't come here again unless you have hard evidence. Now move out!"

"I quite agree," Henman said. "Fowler, there's no need for that kind of rubbish, 'ey what?"

Cocoa stepped closer to Fowler. "Let me see if I understand you correctly. An Englishman is calling Americans arrogant?"

Laughter burst from the men standing around their bunks.

Fowler stepped closer to Cocoa, but Colonel Henman grasped his arm and turned him toward the doorway. "That will do, Lieutenant. There seems to be nothing out of place here and no stash of money to be found. I suggest you rely on better sources of information in the future."

Once Fowler and Cox were twenty feet down the path, Henman frowned at Andrew. "We know about your making the *balachong*. The senior staff have known for some time."

Silence hung in the air until Hudson said, "Then you know how we're getting our money."

"Of course."

"Well, tell Fowler and get him off our backs."

"You've put us in a rather difficult position," Henman said. "You see, what you chaps are doing is smashing. Thanks to you, the death rate has dropped from fifty a day to five. We even had three zero-death days last month. That was unheard of before you came. And you've virtually wiped out blindness from beriberi. You supply the camp with a steady source of protein at a fair price, and we are extremely grateful. The difficulty is that if the men find out they've been eating cockroaches for the past few years, they'll undoubtedly rip you to shreds, and we won't be able to stop them. We don't trust Fowler to keep such an important secret. One little slip, and the camp forfeits the *balachong*, and you could very well forfeit your lives. Obviously we can't allow that. Please understand that the whole camp hates you as venomously as Fowler does. Not because you're Americans, but because you're living and eating so much better than they are, Darby McGaven excluded, of course. There's simply no way to hide it. That hate would explode like a powder keg if word got out."

Mitchell said, "We're doing our best to keep Fowler on a short chain, but we can't go so far that he becomes suspicious. This whole operation could backfire."

Stokes said, "So we keep producing *balachong* and hope he doesn't find out?"

"Actually, the reason that I mentioned it is that I'm hoping to persuade you chaps to increase production. I mean, you're doing a jolly good job, but it's not enough for ten thousand men."

Hudson told them that they had just been discussing how to double output without being noticed.

"If there is a way," Henman said, "I can assure you the senior staff will be delighted." That said, he and Mitchell walked the length of the hut. "Cheerio!" he said as he strolled out the doorway.

Hudson put his arm over Andrew's shoulder. "You saved my life, rookie."

Andrew grabbed Hudson's arm and flung it away. "If you hadn't been so bloody stupid I wouldn't have had to lie. Do you know what you've done to me? You bastard!"

Andrew raced out the doorway.

Grady patted Hudson on the shoulder. "Don't you fret, ol' Hud. Soon as he's had a chance to think a bit, he'll be jim-dandy. He's always peevish after he pulls burial duty."

Hudson shook his head. "Naw, rookie's been flying off the handle at everything lately. All that good food must be fuckin' with his head— too much protein or something. It's like he's slowly going loony. I sure as hell wish there was something we could do to help him."

Cocoa winked at Hudson. "Loony or not, he sure saved your ass."

"The colonel's right," Stokes said. "The Brits will kill us if they find out."

Hudson, Grady, and Stokes gathered around Cocoa, who sat on his bunk. Cocoa's face went hard as stone. "Well, boys, if the senior staff know about us, that means we have a little white mouse in the hut. It's the only way they could have found out about the *balachong* and the stash of money. We've been too careful otherwise."

White mouse was slang for an informer. They all turned to glare around the hut, trying to guess who it could be.

"It don't make sense," Grady said. "Who'd do such a low-down deed?"

"We need to be more careful 'bout what we say and what we show," Hudson said.

Cocoa smiled. "At least they didn't find our money stash. We kept that hiding place secret."

Stokes chuckled. "Knock on wood." He leaned down and rapped his knuckles on Cocoa's hollow wooden leg. They all laughed.

Chapter Twenty-Eight

December 24, 1944—1400 hours

ANDREW'S life had become a perfectly balanced pendulum swinging between days in the prison and nights with Tottori. News of the war's progress and the looming end of the hostilities had formed boundaries around the time those two worlds could ultimately survive, but Andrew forced himself to focus only on the moment.

He left camp early, couldn't wait to distance himself from the lie. As he hurried through camp, his mind rambled through a dense fog. He imagined himself strolling down a busy Saigon street. He could smell the charcoal cooking fires, hear the wind-song melody of people speaking the language of South China. Master Jung-Wei's soothing voice vibrated through his being.

"You are troubled, Lingtse." The old man's voice was as serene as ever.

Startled, Andrew turned, but there was nobody within a hundred yards of him.

"Lingtse," the voice returned, "it is not our abilities or even our deeds that determine who we are. It is our choices. Have you not chosen in every case to protect someone?"

"Yes, master, at the cost of my integrity."

"Is your integrity more important than those you love?"

"I've lost the person you taught me to be." Andrew had promised his master before leaving Saigon that he would follow the old man's teachings. Now, he tallied his broken promises. One: tricking the marine, which had cost the man his life. Two: coming close to killing Hurlburt on the beach. Three: becoming Tottori's whore. Four: lying to Fowler moments ago. Five: lying to Mitchell about his relationship with Tottori. Actually, he had lied to everyone about that, but did that mean a broken promise for each prisoner? He felt himself fall like a stone into a void.

"All you can be is what you are at this moment. Experience that and work with it. That's all anyone can do. Everything else is a dream of the ego."

He turned again to see nothing there, but there seemed to be a faint orange glimmer wavering in the afternoon air.

Andrew hurried out the camp gates. The voice had been so real that he questioned his sanity. This was not the first time Andrew had experienced hallucinations. But the fact that it was someone other than the dead he had buried made him worry that perhaps a sickness was gradually consuming his mind.

Climbing the steps to Tottori's hut, he stumbled over the tortoise that was tied to the stone lantern. He hurried into the living room and cut a direct path into Tottori's arms.

The surprised commandant stroked the nape of Andrew's neck. "I'm glad you've come early. You can join me while I explore for rocks."

Andrew wanted to tell him about the hallucination, that he was losing his grip on reality, but now that he was in Tottori's protective aura, he felt new clarity surging through him. He decided to say nothing and hope that the voices of the dead would leave him in peace.

An hour later they crawled alongside a streambed under a cloud-swollen sky. Tottori inched from one stone outcrop to another with his hammer tucked in his belt and a magnifying glass in hand. Andrew wandered behind him, carrying a canvas bag to hold the specimens.

It was the first time since coming to Changi that Andrew had been outside the camp compound. His heart throbbed as he took in the jungle sounds and earthy fragrances. Light poured over everything, creating a spectrum of colors. The stream was fed by artesian wells and the pure water splashed in brisk freshets. The forest teemed with lush, tantalizing life squirming with energy. Hairy palm-trunks reached for the sky, fleshy green plants as tall as a man seemed to burst with vivacious flowers, and flamboyant colored birds with grotesque beaks squawked while traversing the canopy. Within this jungle, he witnessed the moment-by-moment intermingling of life, creation, and annihilation, in all its dizzying exhibition of transformation.

When his rapture overwhelmed him, Andrew turned his attention on Tottori, who seemed oblivious to the wonder happening around them. He watched Tottori select a stone, scrape away dirt, and inspect it under his magnifying glass. Tottori took great pride in his small but impressive stone collection, with specimens ranging in size from a hen's egg to a hog's head. He piled pebbles around his office and placed larger specimens in front of his shrine. He also kept some in bowls of clear water to expose their glossy brilliance.

Tottori meticulously cleaned, polished and labeled each new specimen. Some rocks he split into segments using a cheap diamond stone saw, smoothed them with fine sandpaper, and polished them to a radiant luster. His collection was equally divided into three categories—igneous, sedimentary, and metamorphic. His true passion, however, was the mineral crystals such as quartz and amphibole.

"Why do you find these rocks so fascinating?"

Tottori held out a small green stone in his left hand. "This pebble reveals the history of the world. Some stones are formed from magma deep within the earth's crust. Many are created from living organisms. Coal is simply fossilized wood. Chert is created from sea creatures' skeletons compressed by the weight of the sea over eons of time. The earth will eventually turn the calcium in our bones into minerals, and our histories will also be reflected in stone. When I look within these silent, lovely rocks, I see my past and my future."

He went on to explain the important role of erosion—how water, ice, wind, and time reshaped living organic matter into these beautiful storybooks of history. Andrew only half listened. They had worked their way close to the sea and the scent of salt water saturated the air.

They crawled through twisting vines and over fallen tree trunks for another half mile. An eternity passed before Andrew stumbled through a thick stand of vegetation and saw the coastline. Blue-green water stretched to infinity. Vast. Incomprehensible. The space within him expanded.

He had forgotten that a world other than the prison existed. He wished that he had brought Jah-Jai so he could play music with the surf pounding the sand for an underlying beat. Tottori walked up behind him and enfolded him in powerful arms.

"I should have brought you here sooner," Tottori whispered. They merged while watching the sun wander toward the horizon.

Distant laughter violated their solemn stillness. Far up the beach, a dozen stout huts squatted on stilts under the palm trees, a few yards beyond the yellow sand. Several brightly painted dugout canoes languished on the beach with their sails neatly furled. Fishing nets draped from long poles. A horde of naked children began a game of keep-away in the surf.

"Come," Tottori said. "Let us pay our respects to the village elders."

They wandered down the beach until they stood before the largest hut. Three elderly men and a toothless old woman hunkered on the veranda, smoking pipes with long, slender stems. Forty feet down the beach a pig carcass roasted on a spit over glowing coals. The aroma of roasting meat wafted on the air.

Andrew followed Tottori up a rickety ladder and onto the veranda. They squatted on their haunches, emulating the Malays. Several natives emerged from the hut and gathered around. The mood turned lighthearted.

"*Tabe*, Wang San," Tottori said.

"Welcome, Tottori," said the oldest-looking man. He wore a maroon sarong, and a single piece of coral jewelry hung from his neck on a leather cord. He smiled, showing the few betel-nut-stained teeth he had left.

"How are you?" Tottori asked.

"Me good," replied the old one, groping for the proper English words.

Tottori pointed to Andrew. "*Ichi-ban* boy." Tottori took Andrew's hand, brought it to his lips, and kissed it.

Comprehension lit up their faces. The old man caressed Andrew's cheek, appraising his beauty. He nodded and winked to tell the officer that he approved of such a fine mistress.

A wave of satisfaction flowed through Andrew from being with these people and each one understanding his role.

"You cat?"

Tottori nodded, and food arrived minutes later: thick slices of roasted pork dripping in fat, grilled eel, baked sweet potatoes, millionaire's cabbage, fried bananas, fresh papayas, and a pitcher of coconut milk. *A feast for such a village*, Andrew thought. *They must be prospering from selling their nightly fish catch to the Japanese.*

Everyone ate, the women more shyly than the men. Andrew ate with his hands, licking the pork fat from his fingers. He ate more slowly than the others, savoring each bite, while he wondered how to tell the elders that their radio had put them in danger.

The old man turned to his wife and, speaking in Malay, said, "The food is not to the young master's taste. What else might we prepare for him?"

Andrew knew enough Malay to understand the old man's meaning and he replied in Malay, "On the contrary, Grandfather. This feast is beyond delicious as the stars are beyond the clouds. But something troubles me."

"What could be disturbing on such a night?"

Andrew could tell that Tottori didn't understand Malay, so he decided to gamble.

"Thou keeps a little snake, which interests the Englishmen greatly."

"Many things interest the English."

"This snake hisses news from far away."

The man's eyes widened perceptibly.

"This snake has poison fangs," Andrew continued. "A wise man would shoo it away. The English are like old women and love to gossip about such creatures."

"Thou, my grandson, are both wise and kind." The old one bowed to his guest while the others traded fearful glances.

"What did you tell him?" Tottori asked, obviously aware of the sudden mood change.

"I thanked him for his hospitality."

Tottori studied him with a curious smile.

Andrew quickly finished his meal so as not to seem impolite.

"Would thou have more?" the old man said.

"No, thank thee," Andrew replied, knowing that to overeat would be rude.

Women whisked the plates away and brought coffee. The men filled their pipes and lit them with a burning brand brought from the cooking fire. After they finished their coffee, Tottori stood and bowed. Andrew followed his example.

"We thank you for your hospitality," Tottori said. Andrew translated.

The old man waved a hand. "I'll not forget thy kindness. Go with Allah, my grandson."

The evening sky blushed a pure shade of lavender. The stars had not yet appeared, but the villagers gathered at the boats to prepare the nets. A few minutes later, they hauled the boats into the surf and glided across the water, leaving a green trail of phosphorescent light. The same light inflamed the surf and made the night seem magical.

Tottori led Andrew a hundred yards up the beach. They undressed as the moon peeped over the horizon. Holding hands, they dashed into the water, diving into an oncoming wave of green light. They swam underwater until they found a cold pocket in the warm surf. Breaking the surface, they floated lazily in the shallows.

The sea caressed Andrew's nakedness. It felt like a thousand silky fingers roving over his skin. For a second he was back at the Bai Hur Sze Temple enjoying a midnight swim with Clifford. Andrew playfully splashed a handful of water at Tottori. The air shattered with brilliant phosphorescent light. They tumbled in luminescence; were covered with it; radiated it. Seduced by such splendor—this delirious freedom, a full stomach, swimming naked with Tottori—Andrew trembled, humbled by sheer awe.

As Tottori hugged Andrew, the surf swirled around his loins and mixed with the heat from Tottori's body, igniting Andrew's insides. They kissed, a sensuous pressing of lips that seemed to last an eon. Tottori carried Andrew to the beach and laid him on the sand. Waves lapped at their legs. He smothered Andrew with his body. His mouth consumed Andrew like an act of communion. Andrew's hunger surged as Tottori's lovemaking became imperious and turned into an act of taking possession.

Andrew welcomed the aggression, surrendering to Tottori's brutality. He merged with the sand under him and the stone-hard body covering him while luminescent water swirled over their legs. It all coalesced into a sensation of ferocious love. This was the first time they had made love outside the confines of their bedroom. The weight of the entire universe pressed from all sides, crushing them together with such agonizing ecstasy that nothing but their hunger for each other survived.

Later, as the tide rushed out, they lay with limbs interlocked. Andrew's flesh was bruised. He looked into Tottori's eyes, and for the first time, there was no trace of fear. The terror in Tottori's mind had finally been incinerated.

Chapter Twenty-Nine

December 25, 1944—1000 hours

PREPARATIONS for the Christmas celebration began before dawn. Cocoa planned the menu and sent every man out to borrow, steal, and buy an extra hot plate, two stew pots, coconuts, bananas, papayas, and spices. Every egg in the camp was bought up at exorbitant prices. Grady killed three plump hens and plucked feathers all morning.

The feast had the entire crew dizzy with anticipation. Men who hadn't smiled in years were unable to contain their excitement.

Andrew fabricated a present for Mitchell. He had Do-Han scrambling to scrounge the materials: paper, string, cloth, thin bamboo sticks, and glue. Andrew also wrapped Clifford's silk sarong with the same colorful paper. At eleven hundred hours, he hustled to Hut Twenty-nine to help prepare the feast.

Cocoa set two stew pots on hotplates. He half filled one with water and added four pounds of *katchang idju* beans along with heaping spoonfuls of salt, pepper, and sugar. He planned to let the beans simmer for an hour before adding the two pounds of pork. As Cocoa unwrapped the banana-leaf sheath and brought out the roasted pork, a hush fell over the hut. Even the drone of flies seemed to fade into silence.

"Somebody pinch me," Ogden mumbled. "I've got to be dreamin'."

Cocoa cut the meat into half-inch cubes and, his face beaming, covered it with the banana leaves and set it close to the stew pot. "That's right, boys. This will be the best damn celebration this camp has ever seen. Today we eat like men."

In the other stew pot, Andrew brought the water to a boil and dumped in three cut-up chickens, innards and all. He added the grated meat from six green papayas, milk from four coconuts, salt, and pepper, and brought it to a boil. The air filled with a delightful fragrance. He covered it and took it off the heat. After an hour it would be ready to add the rice. That done, it was time to wait.

The Americans were on the second lunch schedule that day, so they hustled out of the hut at 1300 hours to stand in line for their rations of watery fish soup and steamed rice. To a man, they downed their soup to keep their stomach juices at bay but saved the rice for the feast to come. They ran to the hut like schoolboys playing a game.

The other prisoners took notice. Mouthwatering aromas drifted over the entire eastern end of the camp. It grabbed control of their minds and twisted their stomachs into knots.

"Bloody hell," said a stocky British corporal to his chums. "What's that brilliant smell?"

"Goddamned Jappos are cooking something bloody marvelous to drive us batty."

"It's meat! The Jappos are cooking meat."

"No mate, it's coming from inside the camp. It's got to be the Yanks. The Jappos don't eat meat, only fish heads and shit like that."

"Five long hours to dinner and those scum bastards are cooking meat. May they rot in hell."

"Dead on target, mate. Those bloody swine don't have the right to be living so high and mighty while we're starving. Why don't our officers bring them down a peg or two?"

At Hut Twenty-nine, the preparations were all but done when Stokes led Mitchell, Fisher, and Moyer up the hut steps. The men gathered loosely around the stew pots. Some tried to take their mind off the food by playing bridge, but nobody's mind was on the game, and nobody bothered to play the torturous food game while real food was cooking.

"Sweet Jesus, what's that glorious aroma," Mitchell exclaimed as he stepped into the hut. "You're going to cause a riot if you don't tone that down."

"We've got the perfect way to tone it down, sir," Hudson said with a gleeful smirk. "In about fifteen minutes we're going to suck up every last drop of this feast and get drunk as skunks on rice wine."

The officers all trooped over to the stew pots and inspected the mounds of food: a huge basket of eggs serenely awaiting the frying pan, shrimps soaking in a bowl of rainwater, and pork-and-bean stew bubbling on the hotplate. There was also a spicy green papaya salad with sardines, chicken and rice soup, and bananas and coconut meat for dessert.

Clifford sauntered up the steps to Hut Twenty-nine. As he stood in the doorway, Hudson rushed over to take his hand.

"Thank you for coming. You're my guest of honor."

Clifford leaned into Hudson and kissed his cheek. "H-h-how could I possibly pass up such a gracious invitation?"

Hudson led Clifford to where Andrew was stirring the soup. Andrew took him into his arms for a tender hug. Their cheeks pressed together so intimately that the men around them blushed with befuddled embarrassment.

"What's this celebration about?" Fisher asked in an overly loud voice, as if to break the sudden awkward silence.

"Good God, I'm surrounded by heathens," Moyer said, with a merry chuckle that made everyone laugh. "It's Christmas!"

"Wow, I had no idea," Fisher said. "I didn't even know it was December."

Skeeter Banks stepped forward. "Give us a prayer, Mr. Moyer."

Moyer beamed. "You betcha. Let's all bow our heads."

The men huddled around Moyer, silently staring at the floorboards. Moyer said a prayer of thanks in a solemn voice that reverberated through every heart. He told how the disciples who loved Jesus gathered around him at the Last Supper and showered him with tender love. The men gazed up to the rafters, spellbound, as if they could see their Savior floating there.

As Moyer's voice swelled with feeling, Hudson held Clifford's hand and occasionally said, "Amen."

Andrew took the lid off the chicken soup as he listened to the timbre of Moyer's voice. A cloud of fragrant steam drifted up, drowning the hut with richness. Little pools of fat globules floated on the simmering liquid. Andrew tossed in a handful of turmeric and *huan* and stirred the fat into the broth. He poured ten mess-cans of steamed rice into the broth, covered it, and took it off the heat. *Give it ten minutes*, he thought, placing a frying pan on the hotplate.

As Moyer spoke of Jesus, Andrew envisioned the Savior's body spread against the rough wooden cross, those sculpted arms, smooth chest, blood trickling down his face like tears. Andrew felt sweat sliding down his own face and wiped it away.

Like Andrew, all the men were drenched in sweat. It ran down their faces and chests and arms, dripping onto the floorboards. No one noticed the sweat, the heat, or the flies droning overhead. They were only aware of Moyer's reverberating voice and the magnificent fragrance of cooking meat. Occasionally they glanced at the stew pots to assure themselves this was no dream. A few carried a tinge of fear that they had died and this incredible smell was actually heaven. Either way, they knew that soon, very soon, they would eat meat.

Andrew lifted the lid off the pork stew, dipped a spoon into the bubbling liquid, and tasted. He added a pinch more turmeric, a dash of salt, and re-covered the pot.

Moyer's quavering voice told how, during the Last Supper, Jesus showed divine love for all of his disciples, even the ones who would betray and deny him, and how he symbolically shared his body and his blood with each man equally. Moyer's voice surged in volume as he ended the prayer. The room went quiet for half a minute. The men finished by singing two hymns: "The Old Rugged Cross" and "Just as I Am." With each hymn Grady's voice rose above the others. He added a jazzy intonation to the songs, like gospel singers in the Southern churches.

As soon as the second hymn ended, Andrew broke eggs over the frying pan while Cocoa chopped shrimps. The men grabbed tin plates, billycans, and spoons, and lined up, inching their way down the chow line. Grady dished up papaya salad with sardines. Andrew scrambled eggs with chopped shrimp. Stokes ladled chicken and rice soup into each billycan. Hudson laid down a bed of rice on each plate and spread pork-and-bean stew over it.

It was more food than anyone had seen in one place since leaving the *Pilgrim*. Each man downed two or three quick mouthfuls to alleviate the pain in his gut and chewed slowly to relish each additional bite. This was not simply a meal; it became an emotional feast. They made love with their mouths to every spoonful.

The officers were served last, and Andrew divided what little was left with his unit. Before he served himself, he glanced around the room. Most of the others were still eating. Some had finished and were licking their plates. He saw all the sweating, smiling faces, and he felt a glow of brotherhood in his heart, that feeling between men who were up against something horrible, and had nothing but each other.

As he scanned the faces, his vision fell on Mitchell's vivid green eyes staring at him. The glow in Andrew's heart blossomed into something scorching, something painfully exquisite. He hurried to fill his plate and sit next to Mitchell.

The eggs were fluffy without being dry. The pork stew was thick and meaty; the beans had absorbed the savory tang of the pork and the juice oozed onto the bed of rice. The chicken soup was equally delicious, with chunks of meat and yellow globules of fat blanketing the surface.

Silence descended on the hut, as if the universe were holding its breath, waiting for a verdict.

Mitchell took a voluptuous bite of pork stew and moaned. "Superb!"

"I've died and gone to heaven," Fisher said.

Contented laughter and satisfied belches peppered the hut as the men ate.

"Ensign Moyer," Mitchell said, "that was a beautiful prayer. You certainly have developed a feeling for God's word. It's remarkable how you've ripened under this hardship."

Andrew added. "You are certainly no longer that man who talked about the Phenomenon of Darkness."

Moyer nodded. "I spent my life looking for God in the faces of people who didn't really care, and I never saw a trace of what I was searching for. But I came here and saw God shining in every pair of eyes. When I'm with these boys, holding their hands and praying for them to live another day, it's as if I'm not here at all. It's like I've died and all I feel is warmth flowing into them, as if the hand of God were reaching through me." Moyer chuckled and wagged his head. "It's all I've ever wanted. I had to come here to find it. This is the true house of God, not those clean, antiseptic, white-shingled churches at home."

Andrew said, "It was always inside you. You had to step aside, to die, as you called it, to experience God. My favorite line in the *Shoyo Roku* said, 'On the withered tree, a flower blooms.'"

Moyer nodded. "The Bible said, 'Lest ye die, ye shall not be born again.'"

"Seems we're not so different after all. I'm happy that you've found what you wanted."

Moyer laughed, "Guess I'm the only one in this whole damned camp who's glad to be here."

Clifford stammered, "A-A-A-Andy is happy. He has everything he wants." He nudged closer to Hudson. "I-I-I'm happy too."

Andrew and Clifford traded smiles.

Cocoa hobbled to the cooking pots and placed the big frying pan on a hotplate. "Ho ho ho! I hope you bums saved room for dessert, fried bananas and coconut meat."

The men lined up as Cocoa browned the bananas. Andrew split coconuts with the machete and Grady scooped out the flesh, pouring the sweet nectar over the meat.

This time joyful banter passed between the men as they waited their turn. After everyone was served, Andrew gathered helpings for himself and Mitchell and sat beside the officer again.

Mitchell took Andrew's hand. "I had a dream about you last night. I dreamed that you were a bird caught in a net. I set you free and you flew away."

The knowledge that Mitchell dreamed about him threw Andrew into a tizzy. He leaned into Mitchell and kissed his lips, cheek, and neck. They kissed lovingly, with everybody watching; in all the excitement, they'd forgotten their circumstances.

Andrew murmured that he had begun loving Mitchell that first day, when the officer had confiscated his Yeats.

For a moment, Mitchell could not speak. He whispered that he'd thought Andrew was going to quote a scene from *Romeo and Juliet,* and that he was always amazed at how Andrew could remember such long passages.

"I can only quote *Henry V.*"

"Why is that?"

"At my master's monastery, while Clifford and I were in the garden reading, he had *Henry V* and I had the Confucian Canon. The other boys burned all our other books in the cooking fires. We were stuck there all summer with only those two books. I must have read them fifty times. We read them aloud to each other until we hardly needed the books at all."

Hudson cleared his throat, motioning his head toward the rear of the hut. Andrew kissed Mitchell once more and jumped to his feet. He followed Hudson and Stokes to the back corner. Grady stood and sang "Jingle Bells." Others around him joined in and soon the hut shook with everybody's joyous voice.

As the men sang, Hudson, Stokes, and Andrew marched down the aisle, each wearing a gold-colored paper crown and each bearing a gift.

Stokes handed Cocoa five cigars tied together with a red ribbon. Cocoa bowed his head, shaking it from side to side, and said that he was embarrassed that he didn't have something to give in return.

"Are you kidding?" Stokes said. "You've cooked us the finest meal we've ever eaten."

Cocoa nodded.

Hudson handed a package wrapped in yellow paper to Clifford, who sat dumbfounded.

"For you, Kitten. Hope you like it."

Clifford ripped open the paper and found the embroidered silk sarong.

"Oh, Hud!" Clifford leaped into Hudson's arms and hugged him. Strangely enough, it was Hudson and not Clifford with tears running down his cheeks.

Andrew gave Mitchell a paper kite with a long cloth tail and a ball of string. The paper was bright yellow, golden, with red letters painted on the front. Mitchell read the words aloud: "I soar on the wind when a man creates tension by holding the string."

Mitchell smiled with his eyes. Andrew knelt beside him and their lips brushed lovingly.

An embarrassed silence formed around them until Andrew said, "The Chinese invented kites."

"I'll drink to that!" Hudson shouted. "Where are those bottles of hooch?"

Hudson passed three bottles of rice wine to the crew, saving the stronger island hooch for his unit and the officers. He poured his cup three fingers full and passed the bottle to Fisher. As the bottle made its way around the group, Grady ran to Andrew's bunk and brought back Andrew's flute.

Cocoa passed a cigar to each officer, which Mitchell declined. Cocoa also gave one to Hudson and one to Stokes, keeping one for himself. Hudson took out his lighter, and they all lit up and blew huge plumes of smoke toward the rafters.

Andrew began to play a spirited Mozart tune, but Grady crooned, "Come on Andy, play 'Swinging Shepherd Blues.'"

Andrew nodded and the flute took on the jazzier tune. As he played, Grady sang in his clear, strong voice. "In a mountain pass there is a patch of grass where the swinging shepherd plays his tune...." Grady felt the music, and snapping fingers and tapping toes accompanied him. "His sheep never stray, dancing all day till they see the pale and yellow moon…."

Stokes swallowed some hooch and his face scrunched up like a prune. He jumped to his feet, swayed his hips seductively, and danced around the hut. Kelso struck a feminine pose and batted his eyelashes. Wolf whistles erupted as Stokes took Kelso in his arms. The music swung them around the room.

Hudson, who was already tipsy, bowed in front of Clifford. "May I have this dance, kitten?"

Clifford was giddy with laughter. He stood and was swallowed by Hudson's arms. They spun around the room. Others joined them.

"Wail on, shepherd, let it echo through the hills…." As Andrew played, he felt Mitchell's arm slide across his shoulder and gently pull him closer. Andrew smelled talcum powder mixed with the spicy aroma of hooch.

Andrew and Grady performed five more tunes before stopping. The men groaned when Andrew quit. The party was in full swing and everyone, for the first time, had forgotten where they were. The food had miraculously put the sap of life into their bodies and they wanted to laugh, to dance, to feel like men again. Their laughter sparkled like a rare diamond.

The joy, the moment, Andrew would carry in his memory to his last hour. He gave in and played more tunes, wanting to prolong the gift. Grady's voice brought soulful enchantment to the music. They played through the afternoon.

When Andrew finally stopped, exhausted but happy, Mitchell whispered that a breeze was blowing. His words were slightly slurred. Andrew could tell from the glow in his eyes that he'd had enough hooch to be flying himself.

They scooped up the kite and dashed out of the hut, making their way to the clearing between the go-downs and the wire. They attached the string and Andrew held the kite downwind as Mitchell let out thirty feet of string. The tight paper crackled against the wind. All at once, it flew upward.

Mitchell unreeled his ball of string as the kite climbed over the go-downs and even higher than the prison walls. The golden bird swooped this way and that while dancing high over the prison. In unison, the prisoners pointed skyward, tracking the kite with their eyes and fingers. The sun's rays reflected off the paper, causing the kite to radiate a golden light, like a lesser sun dodging around the clouds.

Mitchell's smile shined brighter than the sun itself. He let out a howl. "This is fantastic! It's as if I were soaring up there with it. I wish you had one too."

"I don't need a kite to fly. I'm a crane."

"What the hell does that mean? No, don't tell me. I don't care. I've never been as happy as I am right now." A startled look flashed across Mitchell's face. "I'm such a fool."

"What are you talking about?" Andrew said.

"I really am as happy as I've ever been. All I've thought about for years is getting out of this hellhole so I could be happy again, and what-da-ya-know, it was under my nose the whole time."

"When you look at something differently," Andrew said, "it changes what you're looking at."

They hugged each other. As they did, Mitchell accidentally dropped the ball of string and the kite tumbled to earth. As it hit the ground, an English prisoner rushed over and stomped on it, destroying the paper and wooden frame. He disappeared into the crowd that had gathered. The other British prisoners erupted in a malignant cheer.

Andrew and Mitchell ran over to the kite and stared down at the broken carcass. Andrew could still make out some of the words written in red paint: "man creates tension."

"Andrew, I'm so sorry."

"It doesn't matter. What you felt while you were flying it is what matters. Hold on to that."

"Stop right there, you two." Lieutenant Fowler's nasal voice pierced the hot air.

Mitchell stepped between Fowler and Andrew. "What is it this time, Lieutenant?"

Fowler barked, "Andrew Waters, I arrest you for collaboration with the enemy. I will escort you to the stockade, where you will await court-martial proceedings. I told you that some day I'd have enough evidence to hang you, and I've finally got it."

Mitchell flared. "I've had a bellyful of your picking on Andy. What the hell's this about?"

"Eyewitnesses saw Seaman Waters willingly having sex with Commandant Tottori on the beach last night. Took it right up the bum like the whores of Babylon. Filthy trollop!"

Mitchell whirled around to face Andrew. "That can't be. Tell him it's not true."

Wounded by the look in Mitchell's eyes, Andrew felt like someone was yanking his guts out a yard at a time. Bile forced its way to the back of his mouth; he had to swallow it down.

He dropped his head and stared at the ground.

CHAPTER THIRTY

December 27, 1944—1600 hours

THE MP hut crouched on the south side of the camp between the go-downs and the front gate. The sweltering room was divided in half by bamboo bars. It was so hot that even the flies hovered close to the floor, where it was marginally cooler.

On one side of the bars, Fowler slumped over a makeshift desk, staring out the open doorway. While he squinted against the refracted glare of the sun hammering the hard-packed earth, a spasm built in his bowels. He held perfectly still, hoping it would pass. *It doesn't feel like dysentery,* he thought, somewhat relieved. *It must be a touch of dengue.* He glanced toward the borehole toilets. He felt it turning into a bout of diarrhea, and he knew he needed to run for it, but before he could lift himself, it climaxed with only a small amount of bloody mucus oozing out of him.

Thank God, he thought, for the grass pad he wore in his underpants. He needed to change the pad for the second time that day, but that was more hygienic than soiling his only pair of pants. *Why haven't they brought lunch yet?* he wondered, hoping that food would calm his stomach. Waiting was agony.

Fowler glanced at Andrew for the millionth time and his mood turned even more sour. Although pleased to have nabbed the little traitor, he was not feeling the ecstasy that he had imagined. What didn't sit right was that Andrew didn't seem angry, sad, fearful, or anything else that a normal man would feel considering his predicament. He sat with a serene façade, as if his mind were soaring in the clouds.

Fowler watched Hudson and Clifford shuffle arm in arm toward the MP hut until they stood in the doorway. Hudson held a billycan of rice crowned with a fried egg. Clifford carried a mug of fresh coffee. The coffee's fragrance caused another spasm to jolt Fowler's bowels, and staring at that egg made his stomach growl like a wounded lion.

Fowler told them to leave the food on his desk and he would feed the prisoner.

"Nothin' doing," Hudson spat. "I'll hand it to him myself and watch him eat it, just so you can't steal it."

"That kind of impertinence should earn you a horsewhipping, and it would if you were in a proper army. A healthy dose of discipline is what you all need."

"I'm here to feed the prisoner, not to listen to your pompous bullshit. Are you going to let us by or do I have to get Lieutenant Mitchell?"

Fowler stared at that beautiful fried egg, still hot from the skillet, and nodded.

ANDREW spent a second day behind bamboo bars, sitting serenely on the floor while trying not to think of what he had done to himself only last night, but he could not quiet those thoughts. As evening's darkness had turned into pitch-black, before the moon rose, the voices from the graves grew loud, forceful. He saw the corpses rotting in the earth, oozing like poison into the cells of his brain. His head spun and his depression grew more unbearable by the minute. He pressed his hands to his ears, but that did nothing to silence the accusations from those festering carcasses. The hisses combined with the vision of Mitchell's outrage so clearly that he had wanted only to free himself of these ghastly circumstances. The idea of atonement swept into his thoughts, and he found himself willing to do anything, pay any penance, if it would wash away his shame and stop the maddening voices. Anything!

Desperate, he untied his sarong and twisted it into a rope. He fashioned a noose at one end, climbed onto the only chair in his cell, and secured one end of the rope to a rafter. He had no tears in his eyes when, without giving himself time to change his mind, he pulled the noose around his neck and stepped into space, kicking the chair aside so that he couldn't turn back.

The noose tightened. A harsh pain pulsed through his spine. Knowing he was about to die, he felt a rush of exquisite relief wash through him. His bowels and bladder loosened. His head spun from lack of oxygen. It felt gratifying to finally be in a position that he was powerless to change.

He let go of life and a veil of inky blackness covered everything. He had stepped off the path of striving, given up the suffering and strife and vanity the world had to offer, and stepped into the void. Nothingness. He felt himself merging with the blackness.

But while losing consciousness, the sarong ripped under his weight and he dropped to the floor before he could fathom what had happened. Crawling to his knees, he vomited. When his gut was empty, he fell over and lay in his own vomit.

He lay dead still through the night. In the dark hours before dawn, he gave up caring, content to let life have its way with him until death finally soothed his pain.

Now, with eyes closed and legs crossed, he sat wondering about what he had witnessed from his barred window at dawn's first light—a black Mercedes Benz drove up to Tottori's office and a Japanese officer emerged. Tottori waited on the terrace to salute the man before they disappeared into Tottori's office. Could Tottori's request for transfer have come through?

Hudson and Clifford moved to the bars and passed the mess-cans through an opening, but Andrew wouldn't take it. He said he was not hungry, but he did take the coffee, sipped the strong, bitter drink.

Clifford's face was scrubbed clean of makeup. Only the sheen of sweat covered it. He looked like a fourteen-year-old boy again, as fresh and pure as rainwater.

Andrew grasped his hands through the bars. "You're beautiful."

They leaned toward each other and kissed.

"Y-y-y-you look dreadful, my darling."

"How's Nathan?"

"Taking it hard, rookie," Hudson said. "I've never seen him like this. Can't tell what kind of bug is up his ass. He'll preside over your court-martial tomorrow, seeing as how he's the senior American officer, but I wouldn't expect any favors."

Andrew sipped more coffee. "I talked to Ensign Moyer this morning. He's defending me. He's how they found out. How they know everything."

"How's that?" Hudson said.

"You saw me on the beach, Hud, you and Darby McGaven. You told Moyer what you saw in confession. You've been telling him everything all along, about the *balachong*, the money stash, the radio at the village. He repeated it all to Fisher, never realizing that Fisher was feeding that information to the English brass."

"Mother of God," Hudson whispered. He choked, unable to breathe, then stammered, "That can't be. Priests are supposed to keep that shit to themselves. That was between me and God, for Christ sakes." Hudson dropped his head, looking defeated. "Fuck! I finally get religious and look how I screw things up. I'll kill that stupid bastard."

Hudson went silent, grinding his teeth together as if he were crunching on Moyer's bones.

"It's done," Andrew said. "I knew the risk I was taking when I started this."

"No, it's me," Hudson said. "Why is it always me who louses things up?" He shook his head as if still not quite believing. "They'll never get me to say a word against you, I can promise you that. Moyer won't talk either. Hell, he's your lawyer for Christ sake."

"They've got Darby. He's all they need."

Clifford said, "B-b-b-baby, tell them the truth. Tell them why you did it. Once they know it was to save Nathan's life, all will be forgiven. They'll give you a medal."

"I don't want Mitchell to know. Did you see the horror on his face? I don't want him knowing that it was for him. It would crush him. You understand?"

"Hold on a goddamned minute," Hudson snapped. "You're being ridiculous. You could get twenty years. You've got to spill your guts. It's the only way."

"I tried to kill myself last night because I couldn't stand facing him again, couldn't stand seeing what was in those accusing eyes. If this comes out, next time I won't fail. Besides, Nathan won't find me guilty. He can't. Believe me, he won't punish me."

"What makes you so sure?" Hudson said.

"Because he loves me, body and soul. He couldn't do anything to hurt me."

Hudson wagged his head. "He told you that? He said that he loves you?"

"Well, no. He never actually said it."

Clifford opened his purse, removed a compact mirror and a tube of lipstick, and began to reshape his lips.

"I want you both to promise me you won't say a word about the serum to anybody."

"D-d-d-darling, it sounds to me like you're using this trial to see if he still loves you. You're betting twenty years in prison that he loves you enough to find you innocent. And you want us to let you take such a reckless risk? That's a decision I simply can't make looking like a boy."

Hudson gnashed his teeth. "Don't be a fool," he snarled. "This isn't three days' bread and water."

"If he doesn't love me, the prison sentence doesn't matter. Promise me."

Guided by the mirror, Clifford finished his lips and applied Crème Tokalon and Houbigant powder to his cheeks, penciled the rims of his eyes, spread a hint of pale blue powder on the lids, and dabbed eau de cologne behind each ear. Once he was made up, he moaned a mournful sigh.

Hudson and Clifford nodded their heads in agreement, and left Andrew to his coffee. They staggered away from the stockade, holding each other like drowning men clinging to a life raft. Andrew sipped as he watched them go, trying to forget everything else and simply focus on the flavor of his drink.

Ensign Moyer wandered up the path from the go-downs, heading for the stockade. He walked through the front door and told Fowler he needed private time with his client. Fowler smirked as he left the hut.

Moyer dragged a chair close to the bars, sat, and told Andrew that, all things considered, it didn't look too bad. "They haven't got much of a case. The whole thing is screwed up."

Andrew studied his fingernails while his mouth hung slightly open. "Screwed up?"

"Well, for one thing, a court-martial board has to be made up of American officers. There are only three of us in camp, so Mitchell will preside, I'm the defense attorney, and Fisher will prosecute. We'll have British advisors, but the Americans must do it. The second screwy thing is that we don't have a Courts and Boards. That's a manual of US military regulations and laws. It also explains penalties and procedures and such. We're flying in the dark here because none of us has any experience with military law."

"Why don't they wait until we return home to have a proper court-martial?"

"If they do that, there'd be no case at all. You see, they only have one witness and he's an Aussie. No telling what will happen to him once we're freed. So the British are pressing to do it here and now while there's a slim chance of success. They want to make an example of you."

"So what do we do?"

"That depends. If you plead guilty, the whole court-martial is simply a formality. We can bargain. Mitchell has feelings for you, anybody can see that, so I'm certain he'll go easy on you. He might even let you off scot-free no matter what happens."

"I'm not guilty of treason. I did what I had to do. It was not for personal gain."

"Sounds to me like there was no criminal intent," Moyer said, staring at Andrew skeptically. "I'm no lawyer, but if we can prove what you say, then we're home free. Tell me exactly what you did and why and for whom."

"I can't."

"Don't be a lamebrain. How can I defend you if I don't know the truth?"

"If the story comes out, it will hurt someone. I can't let that happen."

"Tell me. Then we'll see if there's a way out of this without hurting anybody."

"I'm sorry, sir, but I can't tell you. You're a blabbermouth. It's because you couldn't keep your mouth shut that I'm in this fix."

Moyer's face flushed. He stared at his feet. "You're absolutely right, Andy. I'm a stupid windbag who loves to gossip. I'll carry this shame to my grave, but I swear by God that whatever you tell me I won't breathe to another soul unless you say it's okay, may God strike me dead."

Andrew felt his face take on a peculiar inner smile, radiating from within his golden, speckled eyes. He told his story, starting with his first day on the *Pilgrim*—Mitchell's kindness, Andrew's longing for the officer's companionship, getting caught having sex with Grady, the midnight watch conversations, coming to camp and making the deal with Tottori, his relationship with Tottori, falling in love with both men, his fear of hurting Mitchell if the truth was revealed, and his desperate need to know if Mitchell still loved him.

Moyer listened with his head bowed and his eyes bashfully down, as if trying to hide his shock.

At last Andrew ran out of words and sat staring out the doorway. He watched men shuffle by on the path. Purple clouds shrouded the sky and the first drops of an afternoon shower began to fall.

Moyer lifted his head with an effort. His eyes were dry, but he was choked up to the point that it took a minute before he could speak. "We'll plead not guilty and hope for the best. Their entire case rests on the testimony of one witness. It's your word against his. Even if they believe him, all they can prove is that you had sex one time with Tottori."

Andrew was humbled with gratitude.

"There's Hudson, but he won't testify," Moyer said. "Like I said, Mitchell has feelings for you, so you should do okay. Then again, he's a by-the-book man, so you might get twenty years. I must advise you to tell the court what you've told me. Nathan will be hurt, no doubt, but he's a man and he'll get over it. If you wait until after the verdict, it'll be too late."

Chapter Thirty-One

December 28, 1944—1000 hours

LATE-MORNING sunshine pounded on the desk that crouched in the middle of the central courtyard. Mitchell sat in a straight-back chair, leaning over the desk. Directly behind him hung an American flag on a ten-foot pole. The stars on the dingy blue patch were the color of old teeth, and the red and white stripes had faded to nearly the same color. A single sheaf of brittle, yellow paper with black ink writing on it lay on the desk.

Mitchell tried to read the charges, but the glare made it difficult to see. Sweat beaded across his forehead and a nauseous headache flared behind his eyes. It felt like a malignant diamond in the core of his brain, and each movement of his head made the diamond's multifaceted cut spray splintered pain-rays through his head.

He was angry that he had agreed to conduct the hearing in the courtyard for all to see. *Everyone would be more comfortable out of the sun and fuck these jackals licking their chops.*

His anger rose as he read, thinking that the inquiry had been botched. The charge of treason, which Fisher had presented the court, was ridiculous. The fact of the case, the only thing they could prove, was that Andrew and Tottori had sex one time on a beach two miles from camp. That was a serious charge, but it was not treason. He didn't believe anyone could prove treason, or even aiding and abetting the enemy, but Mitchell was not sure. His discomfort, along with his nauseous headache, grew immense. The only thing he was implicitly sure of was that Andrew's actions, whatever they might have been, were taken with honorable motives.

Andrew and Moyer sat at a rickety table facing Mitchell and slightly to Mitchell's right. Fisher and Fowler sat at a similar table to Mitchell's left.

Moyer whispered to Andrew, "Where the hell did they scrounge up that flag?"

Andrew tried to smile but his spirits failed him.

Mitchell read the charges aloud:

"In that Seaman First Class Andrew Waters, beginning on or about May 27, 1942 until now, did willfully, and without proper authority, engage in sexual relations with Commandant Tottori on a daily basis. Such a relationship assumes an intimacy that goes beyond the bedroom to include the passing of military information. This is an act of treason, being that the United States of America is in a state of war with the government of Japan."

Fisher and Fowler had meticulously gone over their case with Mitchell. He knew they expected no difficulty in proving the charges. It was common knowledge that Andrew spent every night outside the wire, that he was well fed, and that he received extravagant gifts from the commandant. They had one eyewitness, Darby Gaven, who would testify that he saw them having sex. There was also Hudson, who was an eyewitness but would take some pressuring to get him to corroborate Gaven's story. Mitchell was confident that Hudson would crumble under pressure.

All they could prove was an intimate relationship, but they intended to prove that there was treason as well, military secrets passed over the pillow after heated sex. After all, why else would the masculine commandant pursue a boy? But Mitchell knew that Andrew didn't know any military secrets. How could he, locked up in a prison for years?

Mitchell glanced up from the sheet of yellow paper, brooding, sallow, his blinding headache etched plainly across his face. He watched Fowler slide his tongue over his lower lip like a hungry wolf. Pride rayed out of Fowler's face and he could not keep the smirk from his lips. He had waited years for this day. Fowler scanned the thousands of spectators packed into the courtyard and watching from the barracks' windows. His smirk widened into a smile.

Mitchell's right hand shielded his eyes from the glare as he scowled at Moyer. "Defense counsel, how do you plead?"

Moyer stood. "Not guilty, sir."

A commotion arose from the onlookers. It started by the prison walls and soon the spectators were scurrying to make a path through the crowd. Commandant Tottori marched up the path and into the courtyard followed by four armed guards, their bayonets gleaming in the sunlight. He marched right between the defendant's and the prosecution's tables and stopped in front of Mitchell.

"Lieutenant Mitchell," Tottori said, "I would very much like to examine an example of American military justice. I hope you don't mind if I merely observe?"

Andrew glared at Clifford.

Shocked by the intrusion and unsure of what to do, Mitchell paused long enough for the realization to dawn on him that Fowler's witness would be mad to testify about what he saw outside the wire with Tottori listening. Tottori would ship him to the railway work gangs or simply have him shot.

A great, exquisite relief overpowered Mitchell. He nodded. "Very well, Commandant. You may attend these proceedings."

"I object!" Fowler's voice was loud and incensed.

"Overruled, counselor. Call your first witness."

Fowler stood and said with a shaky voice, "May it please the court, the prosecution demands that we move these proceedings to a hut and conduct this court-martial in private."

"Negative, councilor. Proceed with your first witness."

Fowler clenched his fists. "May we approach the bench?"

Mitchell nodded.

Moyer, Fisher, and Fowler gathered at Mitchell's desk. Fowler hissed, "You know damned well Gaven won't testify with Tottori here. I insist we move to a hut and not allow Tottori to attend these proceedings."

Mitchell's headache still raged, but he managed a grin at the sight of Fowler's anger. "Let me remind you, Lieutenant, that you are merely an advisor to the judge advocate. You have no authority to insist on anything. I should also point out that it was you and the other British officers who demanded that this hearing be conducted here so that everyone could observe. These proceedings are in progress; we will finish it here and now. You will either call your witness or I will dismiss the charges."

Moyer nearly ran to the defense table. Mitchell heard him as he leaned toward Andrew and said, "We've won. Praise God, we've won. They won't put their witness on the stand, so they have no case."

Fisher and Fowler slumped to their table and discussed their options in hurried whispers.

Mitchell watched Tottori glance at Andrew. Andrew refused to look at him. In Mitchell's presence, Tottori ceased to be Andrew's lover. Tottori became a void, an unmentionable indignity.

Mitchell was mildly surprised that Andrew treated Tottori as if he were an embarrassment. *Had Andrew always treated him like that, or perhaps it was having Tottori and me face to face that's embarrassing.*

Mitchell said, "Judge Advocate, this court is waiting."

Fisher rose. "Your Honor, we call Andrew Waters to the witness stand."

Moyer laid his hand on Andrew's arm. "You have to take the stand, but you don't have to tell them a damn thing. Just tell them nothing happened and we're home free."

Andrew stood and took the chair beside Mitchell's desk.

Fisher listed the evidence they had in a loud, clear voice—the nightly visits outside the wire, the fact that he was well fed, and that Tottori had lavished extravagant gifts on him. He asked Andrew to describe his relationship with Tottori, asking pointedly if they were lovers.

The question hovered in the humid air for all to see and hear, like the rape aboard the Japanese ship—there to confess or deny. Andrew refused to talk about his relationship, claiming that it was none of the court's concern.

Fisher said, "Fraternizing with the enemy is everybody's concern. We must know the truth!"

"Truth is inside you. I'm sorry, but you must find it yourself. I can't help you."

"If you don't tell the court the nature of your relationship, then, based on your special treatment, we have no choice but to assume you are guilty of conspiring with the enemy. That in itself is treason."

An eternity of silence passed before Mitchell said, "Andy, if it's not true, then there is nothing to be afraid or ashamed of. Please, tell us now." Mitchell's voice climbed high at the end, like a cry for help. His heart wrenched, realizing that the uncertainty was worse than knowing.

Andrew must have come to the same realization, because he dropped his gaze and told what the court wanted to hear: that Tottori and he had been lovers since his first days in camp.

Fowler lowered his eyes, but he was unable to contain his joy. It radiated from his face.

Moyer bowed his head in defeat until it touched the table in front of him.

"Was it for the food?" Fisher asked in a much harsher voice.

"My reasons are my own. Do what you must, I will say no more."

"Then you leave me no choice," Mitchell said. "I have no other option than to find you—"

"Wait." Tottori's voice cut the air. "I know precisely why he did it. It wasn't for food or anything for himself."

"Hikaru, no!" Andrew pleaded.

"Andrew Waters, be silent." The blood drained from Mitchell's face. "Commandant Tottori, will you please tell the court what you know."

"I object!" Fowler was on his feet, stabbing a finger at the commandant. "He can't be a witness."

"Overruled."

Tottori said, "Andrew agreed to become my lover in exchange for the serum that killed the gangrene in your leg, Lieutenant Mitchell. Saving your life was the price I paid to have Andrew. Saving you was the only reason he agreed to become my consort."

Mitchell sat as if heart-shot, mouth open, eyes screwed shut, blood draining from his face, fists clenched. His mind tumbled through blackness. A buzzing in his head kept any coherent thoughts from forming. A heavy silence around the courtyard grew tense. Through the misty numbness in his head, he managed to form a question. His voice was weak, scarcely audible. "Is sex the only thing you took, or was there more to this bargain?"

"Our deal was that he would be my consort for as long as I required, nothing more. Andrew shared my meals and my bed. He never passed information and he never asked for special treatment, although I was willing to give it."

"What treatment did you offer?"

"I tried repeatedly to persuade Andrew to leave the camp for good. To stay with me, not as a prisoner but as my lover. He refused me flatly."

"Why would he refuse such a generous offer?"

"Because he is a member of the American military and he has a duty to it and to you, his commanding officer. If he had left the camp for good, he'd be marked a deserter. If he were a civilian, things would be different, but he knows his duty and he intends to fulfill that duty."

The mist in Mitchell's mind lifted. He saw the situation in a clear, cold light. *Yes,* he thought, *if Andy were a civilian, then Tottori would protect him. But Andrew is a member of the USN and has acknowledged his guilt of the charge of consorting with the enemy.* He couldn't take Tottori's word that no information exchanged hands, and Andrew was unwilling to defend himself. What to do? He knew in his heart that Tottori had told the truth. He wanted more than anything to issue a not guilty verdict, but if he let Andrew off, free to wander the camp, he'd surely be killed by the British prisoners, who saw him as a traitor. What to do?

Mitchell glanced at Fisher and nodded.

"Seaman Waters," Fisher said, "is what the Commandant told the court correct? Did you become his lover in order to save your commanding officer's life?"

"I've already told the court that I will say no more."

"Then the prosecution rests."

"Ensign Moyer," Mitchell said.

"No cross-examination, sir." Moyer didn't even bother to lift his head.

"Judge Advocate, your closing argument."

Fisher and Fowler put their heads together and traded low whispers, which became harsh, angry-sounding grunts. They shook their heads with heated hissing, until Fowler slammed his fist on the table.

Fisher dropped his head and rose. "The accused stands convicted by his own admission. His motives, if we are to believe the Commandant, are irrelevant under the law. The court has no choice but to find the defendant guilty and punish him with the maximum penalty of military justice."

Moyer stood. "Andrew Waters is a hero. He has gone above and beyond his duty in order to save the life of his commanding officer. We cannot punish this kind of selfless act. We must find the defendant innocent of these charges and hope to God that he can forgive us." Moyer held Mitchell's gaze with his piercing eyes. "You of all people must realize what a sacrifice this young sailor has made, and who has benefited."

Mitchell lowered his head before saying, "Andrew Waters, do you have anything to add before I pass judgment?"

Andrew lifted his head high and said in a strong voice, "'Let me speak proudly: tell the constable, we are but warriors for the working day, our gayness and our gilt are all besmirched with rainy marching in the painful field.'"

The Shakespeare quote punctured Mitchell's heart as all the conversations on the *Pilgrim*'s bridge rushed back to him. The prayer beads that Andrew had given him on the *Pilgrim*'s quarterdeck still hung around his neck, and now those beads seemed to burn his flesh. Mitchell lowered his head and scribbled notes on the yellow paper, the whole time wondering what the hell he could do to preserve Navy regulations but release Andrew.

Mitchell scrutinized Tottori, who stood stone-faced and scowling. The answer, the only possible solution to this madness, blossomed in his mind.

He lifted his head and stared first at Tottori, whom he now realized had held the answer all along, then at Andrew, who sat with downcast eyes. He cleared his dry throat. "The defendant will rise and face the bench." When Andrew turned, their eyes met. Mitchell continued with a steady voice. "This court finds the defendant guilty of the charge of consorting with the enemy."

A crushing hush blanketed the entire assembly, like an athlete holding his breath at the top of a high dive right before the plunge. Only Fowler smiled. Andrew stared, his eyes growing moist. He showed no anger or disappointment, only sorrow, as if he was sorry that Mitchell must endure this humiliation.

"In light of these findings," Mitchell said, "this court sentences the defendant to a bad-conduct discharge from the United States Navy. As of this moment, Andrew Waters, you are a civilian. You are entitled to all benefits and back pay up until today, but as of now you will no longer receive any salary from the United States government. Your duty to the American military, and to me, your commanding officer, is finished. That is all. These proceedings are concluded."

Moyer barked a joyous laugh as he jumped to his feet, rushed to Andrew, and crushed him in a bear hug.

Tottori nodded at Mitchell. An understanding passed between them, along with a full measure of respect.

Fowler leaped to his feet, screaming, "You've let him off scot-free, given him exactly what he wants!"

"These proceedings are closed." Mitchell's voice was calm, with a hint of satisfaction at the edges. He snatched his sheet of paper and rose to his feet.

"He's a traitor. I caught him red-handed. I have witnesses. He deserves to be hung."

"Lieutenant Fowler, I said these proceedings are over. You're dismissed."

Fowler's temper snapped. "They're not over, you sniveling little twit! I won't let them be over until that queer bastard gets his due. He's been eating like a king all these years we've been starving to death, and by God he must be punished!"

Colonel Henman stepped from the crowd of stunned onlookers. "Hold your tongue, Fowler. No need for this dribble. This matter is closed."

"The hell it is. I have witnesses. The dirty bugger's guilty and I want him rotting in my stockade, begging for mercy. He'll crawl on his belly for scraps before I'm through with him."

"Fowler!" The colonel's voice cut the air like a razor. "Get hold of yourself. You're an officer in the Royal Army—act like one! Stand at attention. I said attention!"

Fowler's body went as rigid as a block of granite.

"In light of your behavior, I am relieving you of your post as Provost Marshal until I can discuss this matter with the senior staff. And if I were you, I would keep my mouth shut and hold the dignity of your rank high. That is all. You are dismissed."

"Just a moment," Tottori said as he pointed a finger at Fowler. "You would make my lover crawl on his belly for your entertainment?" He turned to his corporal and uttered a crisp sentence in Japanese.

The four guards jumped to surround Fowler and grabbed him by both arms.

"Lieutenant," Tottori said to Fowler, "you'll be taken to the transit stockade and shipped north to the railway gangs."

Fowler's thin lips drooped. His stony eyes looked dazed.

As the four guards carried Fowler away, Tottori stepped toward Mitchell. "I'm convinced that people in love are seldom happy for long. Love is the root of desire, and desire eventually brings unhappiness. It's ironic that the person you most love is the person who can cause you the most torment, because one always ends up attempting to possess him, which is an impossible undertaking. Possession is such a vile concept. No wonder it causes such pain. I will take him now, and perhaps when my time is up, you will be there to take him again."

Tottori bowed low, and turned to walk away. He stopped. "By the way, Lieutenant. Had you issued a verdict that would have harmed Andrew in any way, you would have joined that sniveling twit at the work camps." He turned again and wrapped his arm across Andrew's shoulder. "Let's go home."

With Tottori supporting Andrew, they marched out of the courtyard. Ten thousand pairs of eyes watched them go without a single blink. As they made their way through the huge open gate, Hudson sang in a loud, joyous voice, "For he's a golly good fellow, for he's a golly good fellow." Clifford and Stokes joined in. Several others took up the tune. By the time Tottori had led him out of the high prison gate, hundreds of American, British, and Australian were singing, "fellow, and so say all of us!"

As the lovers climbed the steps to Tottori's quarters, Andrew noticed that the tortoise Tottori kept tied to the stone lantern was missing. One end of the cord was still tied to the lantern, but the end had been cut or bitten off. Andrew searched the length of the terrace and spotted the rocklike shell at the far end, resting in the cool afternoon shade.

Tottori made a beeline to the bedroom and returned with his opium pipe. He sat at the dining table across from Andrew and held a flame to the bowl. It was the first time he had smoked during the day. He usually waited until after making love. He took another hit and passed the pipe to Andrew.

"Smoke," he said. "It helps." His fingertips caressed Andrew's cheek. "You're so beautiful it is agonizing."

Andrew took Tottori's hand and said, before inhaling the drug, "Thank you, although I would rather he had never found out."

"Every night I consume you, your flesh, your spirit, and I relish every mouthful. But this love has turned into torture because it must end soon. There is no prolonging this joy."

"I don't understand," Andrew said.

"I release you from your debt. You gave me much more than that serum was worth."

"Hikaru, what's happened? Tell me what's wrong."

"My superior has disclosed a report from Admiral Shimada, an analysis of massive air and shipping losses. American forces will soon be poised to launch an assault on Japan itself. Japan will assuredly lose this war. There is talk of negotiating a peace offensive and settling for any conditions that would let Japan retain her honor. All is lost."

"Hikaru, I'm so sorry. What will happen if the Americans invade your homeland?"

A visible, terrifying apparition revealed itself behind Tottori's dull eyes. Andrew sensed that every moment now was a countdown to some future mourning. The realization of this approaching sorrow would overshadow any attempt at normalcy.

"I will make arrangements to smuggle you across the border before that happens. You can make your way to Saigon. As for me, I've requested another transfer to a fighting unit. I've been turned down, but I'm not giving up. I implored my superior for a transfer. He must understand, my honor must be allowed the fitting end of defending the homeland."

"What will happen to the prisoners?"

Darkness veiled Tottori's face. "It's useless to speak of it."

Andrew moved into that hollow space between Tottori's arms, embracing the man's immense and appalling pain while the opium carried his mind across the universe and into a new dimension.

Chapter Thirty-Two

May 28, 1945—1000 hours

AS THE scorching days passed, a new pattern emerged. The hours spent together seemed grueling; every minute was an ordeal. Andrew and Tottori drifted on an ocean of sorrow that stretched into infinity, but at the same time had a rapidly approaching end. Only the opium could dull the pain. They both spent the long days in a drug-induced fog.

Silence pervaded Tottori's quarters. Andrew often asked him why he remained so silent. Tottori always answered with a taciturn stare that said: all is lost, what's the point of talking? Tottori's entire being exuded this maddening silence.

Andrew occasionally lifted himself above the opium-induced mist to initiate a conversation about routine topics, but every subject twisted its way into the minefield of their onrushing end. Andrew had the bizarre feeling that he was living with a dead man, that the life force within Tottori's body was merely a sad hoax.

As the days bled on, Tottori was plagued by migraines. He lay limp on his bed, ghostly white, motionless, with a wet cloth over his eyes. During these attacks, Andrew realized that Tottori was mortal, that the possibility of losing him was real.

Tottori no longer made love. Desire, like every other emotional response, had been sucked away by the opium. He had no potency. Sometimes, he tried to behave as before, taking baths, eating a scrumptious dinner, carrying Andrew to the bed. But once there, he simply hugged Andrew and gave an apologetic smile. The sorrow in his eyes was all too visible. *His pain*, Andrew thought, *he's in love with it. He makes love to it instead of to me.*

At night under snow-white mosquito netting, Andrew embraced the officer, but Tottori was unable to respond. As the fibers of blackness wove a shroud around them, Tottori sucked his life out of the opium pipe. He clung to the pipe as desperately as Andrew clung to him.

Chapter Thirty-Three

August 12, 1945—1600 hours

THREE weeks of continuous torrent, gushing drains, mud, and the echo of rain battering the roof. Andrew had grown sick of the sound of it, and of the constantly damp sheets, blankets, and clothing.

He sat on Tottori's veranda with his body folded into the lotus position. His chi expanded until he felt boundless. His essence soared up on wings above the gray cloud cover. Wind brushed his face and the sun's golden glare penetrated his eyes. The clarity of the light was stunning. The mass of clouds below him swirled like a boiling soup, but up there the day was warm and buttery.

In that wondrous flight, the world washed away unnoticed until, through the whisper of wind, he heard the faint shouts of angry men. He resisted the urge to descend, but curiosity won him over. Sitting on the terrace, he opened his eyes.

Shouts erupted from Japanese guards herding a new batch of prisoners up the muddy path that led into the prison. They passed a dozen yards away from Tottori's hut. Through the rain, Andrew saw that the prisoners were American marines. About forty of them sloshed by before something caught his eye, something familiar. It took him several seconds to realize that what he saw was Lieutenant Hurlburt, the marine he had threatened to kill on Guadalcanal.

Andrew smiled, thankful that the officer was still alive. He picked up the opium pipe at his side, but realized that the contents were completely charred. He needed to refill the bowl, but his stash was inside the hut. The thought of standing seemed too great an effort. He picked up Jah-Jai and brought it to his lips. Notes of a Chinese folk tune rippled through the damp air.

The rain turned into a fine drizzle at dusk. The camp sounds weaved together with the darkening night sky to form an intense gray mask. Clifford trudged down the muddy path to Tottori's headquarters. Andrew met him on the terrace and they embraced. He had come for a bath and dinner.

They wasted no time pulling off their sarongs and soaping each other down. A quick rinse and they slipped into the tub. They embraced again before Andrew asked about Mitchell.

"H-h-h-he's fine, happy, really. The whole camp is celebrating. Those new prisoners brought wonderful news. The war will soon be over. We won in Europe, the Americans and Russians are in Berlin. Hitler is dead. The Americans have taken Okinawa. That's only three hundred miles from the Japanese mainland."

"If it ends the war, then it can't be bad," Andrew said, but a note of doubt seeped into his voice.

"B-b-but there's a problem. Maybe you can help. You see, a marine officer has vital information about the invasion of Japan. He must get to the island rebels so he can radio that information to the Allied Forces. You've been to the village."

"This officer wouldn't happen to be Lieutenant Hurlburt?"

"Ca-ca-ca-captain Hurlburt. How did you know?"

"Unlucky guess. What about old Darby? He knows the village elders."

"H-h-he died two weeks ago."

"Who died?" Tottori stood at the doorway.

"Nobody you know," Andrew said. He smiled. "Join us. It feels great."

Tottori shook his head and walked to his office.

"How about Hud? He's been to the village."

"H-h-h-he said he never met the villagers. He hid in the jungle while Darby did the negotiating. T-t-t-there's something else. The guards are taking work details into the jungle to dig pits. The rumor is that they're for mass graves and they'll kill us all if America attacks the Japanese mainland."

Andrew was not convinced. Rumormongering was a favorite pastime in the camp. Rumors were the only thing that spread faster than disease. It often seemed as though half the prisoners were pathological liars and the other half were willing to believe anything. It was all a harmless game to pass the time, and Andrew had learned to believe nothing until it was proven.

"Hikaru wouldn't do that."

"Ho-ho-hope you're right."

After their bath they joined Tottori for dinner—bowls of noodle soup accompanied by golden bits of tempura. The tempura was superb, with eel, squid, octopus, and shrimp.

Tottori ate in silence while Andrew and Clifford made attempts at small talk. Clifford supplied scraps of gossip about the Americans. Tottori became woozy on Suntory, a strong Japanese liquor. He could no longer procure the bottles of Haig & Haig Scotch Whiskey that he preferred, but the Suntory anesthetized his pain equally as well, and when he needed something stronger, there was always the opium pipe.

After dinner Tottori knelt before his Shinto shrine, focusing all of his energy into willing a transfer to a fighting unit. Andrew knew the officer would sit there like a stone for hours.

Andrew whispered in Clifford's ear that they should go visit Mitchell. They slogged into the prison. It was the first time Andrew had been inside the wire since the court-martial. He was thankful for night's cloak to hide him.

He waited at Hut Twenty-nine while Clifford went to find Mitchell and Hurlburt. While waiting, Hudson told him how profitable the bug business had become since they'd stepped up production, which was great considering that there were now forty-five new mouths to feed. They talked about the work parties digging enormous pits, which could only be for mass graves.

"That Captain Hurlburt said we're kicking holy shit out of the Japs," Hudson said. "We'll invade their mainland any day now. Soon as that happens, they'll butcher us. Might even happen before then. They'll kill us all so they can move these troops to defend the homeland."

Andrew swallowed. "Tottori is incapable of murder."

"What's a few thousand prisoners to the Jappo big shots? The idea of our troops landing on their beaches will drive them mad. They're capable of anything."

"You're wrong."

"They'll machine-gun us in those pits," Stokes said. "I'll never see Chew-Gin again."

"The only thing to do is live until that happens," Andrew said.

"Here, here," Moyer said, climbing the steps to stand inside the doorway. Mitchell and Hurlburt followed him. Fisher, now an outcast among the Americans, was not with them.

Mitchell smiled as his eyes found Andrew's face. They both lit up, a faint luminous glow in the dim that surrounded them. They stared at one another until Mitchell said, "Good to see you. What's this about you wanting to help us?"

Andrew nodded. "You have information that must get to the allies. I don't know the guerrillas, but I have met the village elders. At one time they had a radio. I can take you to them and act as an interpreter."

Hurlburt scoffed, "You're the commandant's whore. I wouldn't trust a traitor like you as far as I could throw you."

"If you've got a better option, then take it. I'm offering my help as a way to thank Nathan."

"Nathan, not Lieutenant Mitchell?" Hurlburt said.

"I'm a civilian now. I'll call him any damned thing I want, and whatever I do call him is none of your business. If you're too good for my help, fine. I'll leave you in peace and best of luck."

"You're both acting like schoolboys," Mitchell said. "He's right, Captain. He's our best chance."

"A traitor is no chance."

Andrew said, "Suppose I take you both, Nathan and you. Surely you understand that I wouldn't do anything to harm him. So I'll lead you both to the guerrillas and you both get away."

"You're trying to save his skin from the mass graves?"

"What do you care as long as you get your information to the allies? Besides, there won't be any mass graves."

"I'd like to show you something," Hurlburt said, "so you understand how critical it is for the allies to get this information." He looked at Mitchell, who nodded.

Hurlburt carefully removed a folded slip of paper from the cuff of his shirtsleeve and handed it to Andrew. "In August of last year, the Jap War Ministry issued a directive to all POW camp commandants. That's what the allies need to know before they invade the Japanese homeland."

Andrew unfolded the paper and, holding it toward the nearest naked bulb, read:

When the battle situation becomes urgent, the POWs will be concentrated and confined in their location and kept under heavy guard until preparations for the final disposition will be made.

Although the basic aim is to act under superior orders, individual disposition may be made in certain circumstances. Whether they are destroyed individually or in groups, and whether it is accomplished by means of mass bombing, poisonous smoke, poisons, drowning, or decapitation, dispose of them as the situation dictates. It is the aim to not allow the escape of a single one, to annihilate them all, and not to leave any traces.

A tense silence hung in the air as Hurlburt took the note and replaced it in his sleeve. "You, me, and Mitchell are the only ones who have seen that. No one else needs to know yet. Okay? How soon can we move out?"

Indecision spread over Mitchell's face, but he nodded at Andrew.

Andrew was stunned. He managed to say, "I'm ready now. I know the roving guard's schedule and the way to the village. Get whatever you need and let's go."

Moyer shook Mitchell's hand, telling him to take care. He hugged Andrew. "Thank you."

Andrew only had time to nod before Hudson's arms crushed him in a bear hug. Andrew hugged Stokes and Grady. They all smiled, but they were unconvincing smiles. Clifford leaned close and gave Andrew a kiss, told him to be careful. Cocoa said, "After the war, you and me are gonna cook up a meal these bums will never forget." At the mention of after the war, they all went awkwardly silent.

"Let's move out," Hurlburt said.

They blackened their faces and limbs with mud as they moved through the camp, keeping to the shadows. They crept under the wire behind the boreholes and slipped into the jungle easily enough. After years of no escapes, the guards were lax. Within the cover of the trees, they looked at the camp, which seemed as peaceful as ever. Men strolled about; some squatted over boreholes. Guards paced like zombies outside the wire. Andrew peered through the window of a go-down only two hundred yards away. British officers chatted, yawned, and enjoyed each other's company before going to bed.

They crawled a few yards deeper into the protection of the foliage and stopped again. Andrew fought a whirlwind of fear. He struggled to suppress the mad urge to dash into the safety of the camp. He stared at Mitchell to try to bolster the strength in his heart.

Mitchell whispered nervously, "Which way?"

Andrew signaled to stay put and keep quiet.

In the jungle the mosquitoes were ferocious, and Andrew had to summon all his willpower not to slap at them when he felt them bite.

Soon they heard the crunch of vegetation, and they froze as two outer perimeter guards passed a dozen feet in front of them. The guards stopped to exchange a few words. One pulled a pack of cigarettes from his pocket. They leaned their rifles against a tree and both lit up. They exchanged more words.

Andrew and the officers stayed as still as mannequins. Andrew's breath raced and he felt light-headed. He imagined that the guards could hear his teeth chattering.

Suddenly the guards stopped talking and grabbed their rifles. Andrew was certain that they'd been spotted, and wondered who would be the first to die. But the guards ambled away, continuing their rounds. Andrew waited another minute before he signaled to move out.

Still blanched with fear, the men stumbled in serpentine fashion away from the camp. They then crawled through the jungle at a painfully slow pace. Bats chased insects over their heads, and unseen birds called out with coarse voices. The gurgling sound of running water led Andrew to the creek, where he and Tottori had explored for rocks, and it guided them to the sea.

An hour passed before the jungle opened onto the beach. They stared out at the vast Pacific plane. Andrew looked to the spot where he and Tottori had made love. A smile creased his lips before he moved on. They crawled through the jungle foliage up from the beach until they saw the village.

"Behind us," Hurlburt hissed.

The faint sound of footsteps drifted through the underbrush. It was impossible for Andrew to hear over the roaring surf, but the captain's trained ears picked it up.

"A native," Hurlburt whispered. "He's barefoot."

A moment later, a Malay youth tramped by, close enough for them to hear his breathing. He meandered to the village, where he climbed the ladder of the nearest hut and disappeared through the doorway.

They crouched behind some coconut palms to survey the village. There were a dozen or so structures on stilts, each with a ladder leading to a veranda attached to a palm thatch hut. Now that the drizzle had stopped, the Malays were socializing on their verandas. A dog barked, pigs grunted. The sound of broken laughter sprouted here and there. On the beach, close to the phosphorescent surf, the fishing boats sat with furled sails and fishing nets hung on racks waiting for the night's work. The place had a simple, peaceful ambience, as if war had never touched it.

"Seems okay," Mitchell said.

Andrew nudged Hurlburt and pointed to the headman's hut, where he and Tottori had shared a meal. "That's the elder's hut. Those men on the veranda are the headsmen."

Hurlburt nodded, squatting down to wait.

Andrew moved out, keeping to the shadows. He climbed the ladder to the elder's hut and stepped onto the veranda. Three elderly men squatted in a circle, smoking pipes with long slender stems. Andrew hunkered on his haunches beside them. They all fell silent, staring at him as if he had dropped out of the sky.

"*Tabe*, Wang San," Andrew said. He smiled serenely, as if his being there was a common thing.

"Welcome, Tottori's *ichi-ban* boy," said the oldest-looking man. He wore a sarong and a single piece of jewelry around his neck. He smiled, showing his few betel-nut-stained teeth.

"How art Thou?" Andrew asked.

"Me good," the old one replied, groping for the proper English words. "Thou eat?"

Andrew knew that a refusal would be insulting, but he was too nervous to be hungry. He told them he had already eaten, but asked for coffee.

Wang San signaled to someone inside the hut. Soon a pretty young girl brought them all coffee.

Andrew knew they must finish their coffee before he mentioned his objective. It would offend them if he rushed right into business. Andrew drank the strong liquid slowly, so as not to seem impolite. His mind groped for a way to ask the elders about contacting the guerrillas who, rumor had it, operated on the island.

The elders resumed their conversation. Andrew understood enough Malay to follow along as they discussed the possibility of a good night's catch. He finished his coffee. "Grandfather. This coffee is more than a sultan could hope for. I have no way to thank thee for thy hospitality."

Wang San said, "Thou are welcome. Does thou wish more?"

"I wish only for one thing, Grandfather."

The old man flashed a wicked grin, obviously thinking that Andrew was talking about sex.

They all snorted.

Andrew smiled and shook his head. "Thou knows of a bird, which flies over the sea and sings to the American armies?"

The old man's smile faded. "There may be such a bird in the jungle."

"My friend must find such a bird to carry a message as quick as the wind."

Wang San's eyes widened perceptibly. "This will help end the war?"

The Malays went silent, no doubt wondering whether or not to trust Tottori's boy. Andrew listened to the village sounds. Dogs continued to bark and pigs grunted. Behind him, in the hut, women's voices chattered in soft tones. Singing rang from a nearby hut. Men on the beach prepared the nets.

"If Allah wills it so," Andrew replied.

"Thou, my grandson, were kind to us once. Perhaps there is a way." The old one bowed to his guest while the others traded fearful glances. The men filled their pipes, but Andrew pulled a pack of Kooas from his shoulder bag. The elders smiled as Andrew passed out the tailor-made cigarettes. They lit up with a burning brand brought from a cooking fire and finished their coffee in silence.

"Is this man in the prison?"

"No Grandfather. He and a friend wait beyond those trees," Andrew said, pointing.

Wang San drew on his cigarette and called out a name. Moments later, a middle-aged man climbed the ladder and stepped onto the veranda. Wang San told Andrew that this man would lead them to the guerrillas, but they must not return. They must join the rebels against the Japanese.

Andrew bowed. "I thank thee," he said, using his best Malay. "Thou are brave indeed."

"I do a foolish thing. I place the safety of my village in thy hands."

"Fear not, Grandfather. I will guard this secret with my life."

The old man waved a hand. "Go with Allah, my grandson."

"We are all in his hands, may his name be praised."

The evening sky turned dark even though the clouds had scattered and the stars bit through the firmament. Andrew led the guide to the officers and explained that the man would lead them to the rebel camp, and that they must join the rebels or somehow make their way to the allies. They must never return to the prison or the village.

"But you're coming with us," Mitchell said.

Andrew shook his head. "If I don't return, he'll send troops to scour the jungle. You can trust this man."

"We're square," Hurlburt said. He held out his hand. Andrew gave it a firm shake. He turned to Mitchell and signaled to move out.

"Be right with you."

Hurlburt and the guide moved twenty yards toward the beach and waited.

Mitchell took Andrew in his arms.

Andrew whispered, "Everything I've done was for you."

Mitchell held him tighter. "After the war, I'll find you. We'll start fresh. Stay alive until then." They gazed into each other's eyes, but it was too dark to see anything.

Mitchell turned and hurried to where Hurlburt waited. They disappeared into the jungle, leaving Andrew alone in the night.

ANDREW made his way to the prison. The eastern sky grew pale as he made his way up the steps to the veranda and tiptoed into Tottori's bedroom. The room was lit with a nearly depleted candle. Even in the dim light, Andrew saw that Tottori was not in the bed, as he expected. There was a slight noise in the shadows behind him. He turned. Tottori moved and Andrew jumped in surprise. He tripped and stumbled to the floor. He crawled to the bed and lay on the cool linen, staring up at the commandant, not bothering to deny the accusation that was so clearly written on the commandant's face.

Without uttering a word, Tottori knelt beside Andrew. His finger caressed Andrew's cheek. He pulled Andrew's sarong from his hips. For the first time in months, Tottori was sexually aroused.

They kissed, hungry kisses, while at the same time Tottori maneuvered himself between Andrew's thighs. Andrew absorbed his passion with quiet gratitude. He had betrayed his lover and now submitted to the mixture of tenderness and excitement as Tottori unleashed his pent-up desire.

Tottori entered him with one deep thrust, uttering a tigerlike growl. Pain ripped through Andrew. He welcomed it. Wrapped himself around it. Waves of pain mixed with relief washed through him as Tottori's hips ground him deeper into the bedding. With Mitchell safely away and Tottori able to make love again, this pain seemed a pitiful price to pay for such treasures.

Tottori's passion incinerated every other thought and emotion in Andrew's consciousness until nothing existed beyond their lovemaking, ending with gentle kisses and soft caresses. For a few precious hours, as the morning light bled through the open shutters, the outside world was forgotten—no war, no prison, no betrayal, and no future. There was only sumptuous flesh, their binding love, and the dawn's carmine rays.

Chapter Thirty-Four

August 13, 1945—0800 hours

MORNING showers. Dawn's hush broke with cocks trumpeting the muted sunrise. As Andrew's consciousness rose from slumber, he heard the muffled patter of raindrops drumming the thatched roof. Blades of dull light bled through the window slats, turning the bedroom walls gray.

Even before Andrew opened his eyes, he felt Tottori holding him snugly under the linen sheets. Arms locked him to Tottori's chest. Lying perfectly still, Andrew absorbed the man's warmth.

"Are you hungry?" Tottori whispered.

"Famished."

Tottori ran his fingers through Andrew's blue-black hair and caressed the nape of his neck.

Andrew turned to him. "You look tired. Were you up all night?"

"Wide awake. Did you find the rebels? Were they able to radio the message?"

Andrew stared into Tottori's eyes. "You knew?"

"While you were gone, I ordered a muster and found that two American officers were missing. Just because you are not my camp spy doesn't mean that I don't have one. Tell me, did they find the rebels?"

"I think they will. You know what was in that message?"

Tottori said, "I can assume. Let's pray the Americans liberate the camps before they invade the mainland. Now, go to sleep. I want to hold you for a few more hours."

Andrew closed his eyes, overjoyed that his faith in his lover was not misplaced, and his breathing deepened as he gratefully drifted into slumber.

Coming awake to the harsh sound of tires skidding on gravel, Andrew reached for Tottori only to find he was alone. He sat up and listened to voices echoing from Tottori's office. Brisk, tense voices. Tottori barked orders.

The morning air washed through the open windows, merging with the sounds of the prison stirring for breakfast. Andrew felt hungry after the night's adventure, and the sweet anticipation of an egg over rice had his stomach growling.

Do-Han hurried through the door, carrying a cup of coffee and a rice bowl. He smiled a greeting as he bowed, placing the food on the floor. Andrew yawned happily. "Breakfast in bed?"

Do-Han said, "Colonel say, you eat now, pretty damn quick."

Andrew nodded, hearing Tottori's terse voice in the next room. He wondered what was up.

He downed his rice with coffee, lifted himself out of bed, pulled on his sarong, and strolled onto the terrace. Heavy drizzle grayed the landscape. To Andrew's surprise, Kenji stood under the roof overhang, wearing a native sarong and sandals, and he was not wearing his wire-rimmed glasses. It was the first time Andrew had seen the secretary out of uniform.

Andrew admired the man's attractive black eyes and his finely sculpted chest until Kenji blushed to the color of a ripe peach.

Tottori appeared at the door in full dress uniform. Andrew stared at the officer but didn't recognize him. Behind that familiar face was someone who was not Tottori, someone unfamiliar. His blank stare studied the prisoners inside the wire. Neither Kenji nor Do-Han seemed to notice the substitution, but it was too real for Andrew.

Scrutinizing this man, Andrew found him beautiful. *Yes,* Andrew thought, *this new Tottori is youthful and handsome. It's as if the cares of a lifetime have lifted off his shoulders and his spirit soars across the sky.* Andrew cried out, a faint helpless cry. This change could only mean one of two things—either Tottori had received his transfer or the war was over.

"Lingtse, come to my office."

Andrew followed Tottori.

Lying on the desk were two swords in their scabbards and a leather-bound book. Tottori touched the book. "In high-ranking Japanese families, the patriarch keeps an ongoing diary. This book holds the lives of my father, his father and his, as far back as three hundred years. My family is samurai. A samurai's entire history is documented in his family diary and his soul is captured within the steel of his swords." Tottori's right hand moved to grasp the longer of the two swords. "You, being an outsider, can never understand the utmost importance of these cherished things to a Japanese family. It is more important than our lives."

Andrew nodded.

"The Americans have a bomb that can obliterate an entire city in an instant. They've dropped two of these bombs on Japan. Two hundred thousand civilians were incinerated." Tottori halted to take a deep breath. "Now Russia has also declared war on Japan." His eyes gazed at his sword. "Japan will surrender within days. My superior has already surrendered Singapore to Lord Mountbatten. All is lost."

"Hikaru, I'm so sorry." He stopped, because his words sounded pitifully inadequate. There was nothing to say, no way to console such horror.

"Sorrow. Yes. The whole of Japan weeps. So many precious lives lost, an entire generation." He paused and took a ragged breath. "Lingtse. I require one more service from you. After that, our bargain is complete."

"I have no wish to be free of you."

"You will carry my diary, my swords, and these two scrolls to Kyoto and deliver them to my wife. Kenji and Do-Han will smuggle you out of Singapore. You and Kenji will travel through Malaysia, Siam, Indochina, and on to Japan. By the time you reach China, you should be able to enter my homeland."

"You must keep them with you."

"Please understand how important it is that you deliver these articles to my son. He must have them. Kenji has sworn to do everything possible to deliver you to Kyoto, but don't put all your trust in him. These swords are priceless. He may think to steal them. He could buy a sizable farm for what these would bring."

"You should be the one to hand them to your son."

"There is no telling what will happen when the English come. I will not have my swords hanging on some English officer's wall as a war trophy. That shame would dishonor my ancestors. Lingtse, you must do this. I'm begging you."

Tottori suddenly sounded weary and his voice was tinged with despair. He insisted that it was his moral obligation to insure his sword and diary be preserved for the generations to come. It was clear that he attached supreme importance to his lineage. "My son is the end of the branch. He must have my swords and diary."

Tottori had ancestors stretching back through centuries, and also the possibility of descendants stretching an equally long time into the future. Andrew had nothing. He knew little of his grandparents or aunts and uncles. He hardly knew his father. He had no history and was certain that he would never create any descendants. *Who will remember me?* he wondered.

As if reading his thoughts, Tottori said, "I have given a full accounting of our time together in this diary. You are now part of my family history. My descendants will read about you and tell their children about us for generations to come. They will tell poetic tales of how you inflamed my heart. You have become immortal."

Andrew bowed low. "I'll do what you ask on one condition."

"Anything."

"That you will do everything in your power to protect these prisoners. There will be no executions. You must promise me. If I hear about mass killings, I'll throw these into the sea."

"You think me capable of murder?"

"I think you will honor the orders of your emperor."

Tottori stood and, taking a black cloth shoulder bag, wrapped the swords and diary within the bag. "These prisoners will remain unharmed. You have my word. Come, there is no time to lose."

Kenji and Do-Han waited on the veranda. Dressed in native garb, they would blend in with the locals. They shouldered their bags and prepared to leave. Andrew had only enough time to snatch his flute.

Tottori took Andrew in his arms. They melded into one. Tottori whispered, "My happiest moments were spent in your arms. You, above all things, showed me true joy."

"I'll wait for you in Kyoto."

"Once you have delivered these, you are free to go home."

"My home is here," Andrew said, tapping Tottori's chest with one finger. "I look out of your heart's window and view the world through you."

"I will hold you in my mind until my last breath."

Kenji, Do-Han, and Andrew set out from the prison at a brisk pace. Kenji wanted to be well away by nightfall. They would slow their pace once the rainforest to the north had swallowed them. Do-Han would guide them as far as Siam and then return to Singapore.

They were a half mile away when a gunshot, loud and hideous, echoed from the prison. Andrew froze, thinking that Tottori had gone back on his word and was executing the prisoners. He turned toward the camp, waiting for the next shot and the next, but there was only silence. Even the birds fell silent.

Andrew glanced at Kenji, whose eyes were brimming with tears.

As comprehension set in, Andrew tried to voice something between a wail and a grisly scream, but no sound escaped his open mouth. His body howled a hideous wail, but the sound was caught in the gravitational pull of the sudden black hole in his heart. He stood, shrieking in utter silence.

He tried to run, but Kenji grabbed and held him. Struggling, Andrew fought like a tiger, but Kenji was strong. Andrew spent his strength and sobbed into Kenji's shoulder.

"No choice," Kenji whispered. "Too many honor."

Pain came from every direction, crushing Andrew under a suffocating weight. At first, he was not sure whether this was new pain or somehow combined with the pain of losing Mitchell, but then he thought there must be some mistake, a momentary error. This outrage couldn't be. Tottori was indestructible, immortal, a god. If Tottori was indeed dead, then everything was dead; life was merely a sad hoax.

Andrew thought he had known all the angles, thought he had figured it all out. He knew he would always have his man and that somehow they would be together. He'd forgotten about death, about the possibility of it.

The jungle closed in around Andrew like a great book snapping shut after the end of an engrossing story. His whole being shriveled to nothing. He felt as if he was moving swiftly from one moment to the next, but how could that be? He wanted to take the short sword from the cloth bag and plunge it into his heart, wanted the whole world to end. And why not—he was dead already, he could hear the voices from the black earth calling him. Death seemed natural, a natural chain reaction. His could be the last, the very last death of this war.

The unfathomable mystery, the single thing he couldn't quite grasp, was why he loved this man so deeply that the loss could only be consoled by his own death. How could he possibly need anyone so fiercely? Did it have something to do with the opium? Was his need for Tottori somehow mixed with his dependence on the drug? Or could his mind be so unstable after months of smoking the drug that life no longer mattered? Or could love alone drive a man to death? Whatever the cause, it didn't really matter. The end result would be the same.

The drizzle turned to rain. The wind died to nothing more than a breath. Birds shrieked. Their voices echoed through the soggy air. He knew he must deliver his package. *It was Tottori's last request,* he thought, *but afterward my turn will come. I'll end this agony. Yes, after Kyoto.*

Part III

Japan

Only the dead have seen the end of war.

—Plato

Chapter Thirty-Five

August 15, 1946—1000 hours

THE war ended with such a sudden and terrifying wretchedness that it catapulted the human race into a mixture of shock and abhorrence and relief. The horror unleashed on Hiroshima and Nagasaki did not kill as many people as did the conventional bombs that ravaged other cities. B-29 bombers leveled fifty-six square miles of Tokyo, along with Osaka, Kawasaki, Yokohama, and Kobe. The wooden buildings went up in firestorms. Of Tokyo's eight million residents, all but 200,000 were killed or forced to evacuate. The atomic bombs, however, defined a new era in warfare, a new profundity of how mankind could destroy itself.

The crane is the symbol of Japan's Emperor in much the same manner that the crown symbolizes the reigning monarch of England. On August 15, 1945, the voice of the Crane was broadcast over the airwaves for the first time: "Cultivate the ways of rectitude, foster nobility of spirit, and work with resolution so as ye may enhance the innate glory of the Imperial State and keep pace with the progress of the world."

In factories and shops and homes, people listened to the Imperial Rescript announcing the cessation of hostilities. Hundreds of thousands gathered at temples, shrines, the imperial palace in Tokyo, and the Kyoto palace. A mass showing of sorrow and shame. One of the mightiest nations in the history of the world knelt, weeping for their lost generations, but also from relief. The burden of war, death, and devastation had ended.

Seventeen days later, aboard the battleship *Missouri* in Tokyo harbor, General Douglas MacArthur told the world, "A great tragedy has ended. A great victory has been won. The skies no longer rain death, the seas bear only commerce, men everywhere walk upright in the sunlight. The entire world is quietly at peace. The holy mission has been completed."

The queer result of the war was that, even in crushing defeat, Japan accomplished its most cherished aim: Asia had freed itself of

Western domination. Great Britain had lost Burma and would soon lose India, an independence movement was launched in the Dutch East Indies, the French were driven from Indochina, and the communists took control of China. A self-governing Asia would rise from the ashes of war.

Chapter Thirty-Six

December 12, 1946—0800 hours

A BRILLIANT sun rose after an all-night snowstorm, bestrewing crimson light between the sagging tile rooftops and through the bare branches of the maples and the snow-covered cedars. The city awakened after a long night's slumber.

The park across the street from the Kobe Imperial Hotel was blanketed in snow.

Dressed in black quilted pajamas, thick overcoat, and a peasant's straw hat, Andrew squatted on a bare spot under a great pine, playing Jah-Jai, his flute. He sat a few yards from the main path that led through the park, and he not only played, he waited. He knew they would come, as they did every morning.

He had waited since even before the workmen swept the snow from the stone path. Now he heard the clacking of wooden *getas* on the walkway. He looked up to see a grandfather being led by an impatient flock of children, begging him to hurry. A few minutes later, an old woman in a potato-colored overcoat rushed by carrying a wooden bucket and a washrag, no doubt heading for the nearest public bath. He paused, watching her pass by, feeling an immense hunger in the depths of his belly. He played on.

His hunger was not for food, but for the opium he regularly smoked to slay the pain that stalked his waking hours, pain that had the power to reduce his vision to pinpoints of grayness and render him unable to move without causing shards of glass to slash inside his head.

The opium kept the hurt at bay, but it also robbed him of any appetite. Little by little over the past year, his body had melted away with each draw of the pipe, until he finally resembled the starving prisoners of Changi—leathery skin stretched over bone and cartilage, bulging eyes like those found only on nocturnal animals.

Over the sound of his flute, he heard faint voices calling, voices of those prisoners he had buried in the mud of Changi. And as the voices grew louder, he felt the ache in his head swell, crushing him, devouring what was left of him. It took over his mind and what was left of his gaunt body.

He laid Jah-Jai across his lap and pulled a pipe and a Ronson lighter from his coat pocket. He brought the pipe to his lips, lit the black loam, drew in a lungful of sweet relief, and another. The voices faded into delicious silence. Heat seeped into his wasted muscles. His hunger folded in on itself and was forgotten.

He placed the pipe in his pocket, picked up his flute, and played once again. As notes tumbled from the flute, he felt his body sinking slightly deeper into the soft damp earth.

Andrew spotted them strolling down the snow-dusted path, a child in his arms and a baby in hers. He wore his dark naval uniform. His white hat and gold buttons gleamed in the sunlight. She wore pleats and a thick wool sweater. The baby was bundled in a cocoon of powder blue blankets with its tiny face peeking out.

A gust of wind, or perhaps a squirrel, shook a branch on the tree they were passing under and a fine cloud of snow fell through the air around them, sparkling crimson-gold in the light and surrounding them in a halo of brilliance.

Andrew stopped playing, awed by the vision. He felt his heart fill with Divine presence (or could it be the opium?). *It's a sign*, he thought, and that gave him the courage to finally do what he had come there every morning for a month to do.

He brought Jah-Jai to his lips and played a melodic tune. He kept his head down as they passed and, as often happened, she stepped off the path and dropped some coins on the ground in front of him. He nodded but did not look up until they were ten yards down the path, heading toward the US Naval headquarters building.

Andrew looked up and played "Swinging Shepherd Blues." The notes sailed over the crisp air, filling that little corner of the park with a jazzy sound in the same way the sun filled it with light. Andrew watched intently as they took a few more steps before halting. She stared at Mitchell as he turned to stare at Andrew.

It was the first time since coming to Japan that Andrew had managed a good look at his face. Andrew had remembered the singular details of that face: the jade-green eyes, slightly weak chin, strong eyebrows, short fawn-colored hair, and the fresh glow of his skin. But Andrew was surprised to find that he had lost the vision of what the entire face looked like, since his memory always focused on only one detail or another. The face was restored to the same fullness as the first time Andrew had studied him on the beach at Viti Levu, with perhaps a slight downward turn at the ends of the eyes to suggest sadness.

Warmth flashed through Andrew as the two men stared at each other. Mitchell staggered backward a step, putting his hand on her shoulder to steady himself. His lips parted, his eyes opened wide and glistened in the sunlight.

Mitchell lowered the toddler to the ground and took a few hesitant steps toward Andrew. Then he ran. Andrew jumped up in time to be swept into Mitchell's arms. The force of Mitchell's embrace lifted him off his feet and he struggled to breathe with Mitchell crushing him. Andrew's skeletal body went limp. His head tingled from lack of oxygen. He surrendered to the strength and emotions surging through their joined bodies.

They sank to the ground until they were both on their knees, with Mitchell stroking Andrew's face.

"I thought you were dead. I returned to the camp when the English parachuted onto the island. Tottori was dead and you had disappeared. I thought he killed you. Dear God, the life went out of me."

"You told me to stay alive until after the war, that you'd find me and we could start new. It took some doing, but here I am."

"Look at you. You're skin and bones. What's happened?"

Andrew peered over Mitchell's shoulder. The woman held her baby and clutched the child to her side as she walked toward them.

"Honey, what's wrong?" she asked. "Who is this man?"

Mitchell's face dropped at the sound of her voice. "Andy, this is my wife, Kate. This our daughter, Helen, and the baby is little Andrew." He turned to gaze at his wife. "Kate, this is Andrew Waters, the sailor who saved my life, the man we named the baby after."

Awkward silence followed, accentuating the whisper of the breeze blowing through the branches above. Andrew eyed the boy, seeing Mitchell's green eyes and fawn-colored hair stamped onto the boy's features.

"I'm very grateful to you, Andy," she finally said, "and I'm delighted to meet you. We thought you were dead all this time. Isn't it a wonderful surprise that you made it through?"

"Yes, wonderful," Andrew said, looking at Mitchell.

"Honey, get off your knees. You're ruining your uniform."

Mitchell rose and, still holding Andrew tight, lifted Andrew to his feet as well.

"Kate, take the kids to the apartment. Andrew and I have some catching up to do."

"Of course. Perhaps we can all have dinner tonight? We can take Andrew to the officer's club and have a real American meal. That should put some meat on his bones."

Mitchell shook his head. "We'll see. I should be home at the usual time."

"Well, I hope to see you tonight, Andrew Waters." Still clinging to her baby, she led Helen down the path they had come.

Andrew gently pulled away from Mitchell's embrace and bent to retrieve Jah-Jai. Standing straight again, he watched a squirrel scamper across the white-powdered ground and dash up a tree. A bird screeched. The breeze stung Andrew's eyes. He felt he must say something. He concentrated, saying slowly, "Kate is a real knockout."

Mitchell laughed, no doubt from relief.

Andrew felt a panic welling up inside him. Mitchell's expression changed, becoming sober. *Does he feel it too?* Andrew wondered.

Mitchell draped his arm over Andrew's shoulders and squeezed. He stepped back and appraised Andrew's face.

"You've lost so much weight. Are you sick?"

"I'm feeling better by the minute."

"This is so bizarre. I've been thinking about you for so long now, and here you are. Listen, I have to check in at headquarters. But that shouldn't take long. Then we can grab a bite to eat and you can tell me what happened to you."

Andrew nodded as his panic faded.

MITCHELL'S office was housed in a converted three-story hotel, which surrounded a Zen garden that showcased a shallow pond fed by a stone fountain. The pond was alive with koi, a collage of orange, yellow, white, and black movement. Rising from the water, a vermilion-painted *torii* stood—an arch that normally towered over paths leading to temples and shrines. The hotel was originally built for wealthy tourists and businessmen, but now housed a department of the US occupying forces.

Andrew was at once uncomfortable. He followed Mitchell across a plush, deep blue carpet toward the front desk. The building had been transformed into something foreign, something American. It had an immaculate nonsmell. Healthy-looking, nondescript men in snappy uniforms rushed by with unemotional expressions. Everything was so competent, so deliberate. The lobby literally hummed with purposeful activity. Andrew felt like an alien, a mouse scurrying across the floor before someone could step on it.

Maneuvering beyond the MPs at the front desk was surprisingly easy. Mitchell leaned over the white marble countertop, said something quick and sharp to the MP, and pointed to Andrew. The MP didn't flinch. He responded with a crisp, reedy voice. Andrew looked for any hint of suspicion in the man's face, but found none. Even so, his ears burned. He felt inadequate and sordid in his quilted pajamas and straw hat. He longed to take another toke from his pipe, but was too fearful.

Mitchell guided Andrew to a sofa that faced the garden and told him to wait, saying he wouldn't be long. He hurried through the lobby and disappeared up a flight of steps.

Andrew stared at the torii, mesmerized by the elegantly minimalist structure: a blood-red arch rising from the mirrorlike pond. The movement of the koi caught his eye. *How appropriate to have a pond here,* he thought. A body of water, in both Chinese and Japanese cultures, symbolized centralized power. It showed who was in charge of Japan. Andrew saw the koi swirling beneath the surface, like the colorful Japanese people now trapped within the Americans' military might. Indeed, on the wall at the far end of the garden hung a cartoonishly large American flag, looking garish behind the cool slumber of the manicured garden.

Andrew saw an old man, a gardener, perched on a narrow gravel path beside the pond. He stooped over a bonsai tree with a pair of shears, meticulously clipping away each branch that had outlived its time. He shaped the tree, which could have been as old as three hundred years, into something breathtakingly beautiful.

Andrew sat transfixed by the gardener's assiduous movements. It was as if the man were doing tai chi, only dancing a duet with his tree instead of by himself.

Fifteen minutes crawled by before Mitchell returned. "Shall we grab a bite to eat here in the restaurant? They do a pretty good job with ham and eggs."

"Can we go somewhere less American?"

Andrew watched Mitchell's expression change, as if a loose gear had shifted in his mind and his old shipboard self began to operate, once again letting Andrew lead him outside the boundaries of normal.

He grinned, nodded.

They wandered to an out-of-the-way neighborhood, strolling down winding streets lined with shops. Above and behind the shops were elongated wood-framed houses. It was past breakfast time, but the smells of grilled fish and miso soup still clung to the air. They passed a teahouse, a vegetable stand, a noodle shop, a flower vendor, all opening their doors for another day's business. People wandered by, some dressed in drab business suits and some in somber kimonos. Mitchell towered above them all. Several boys whooshed by on bicycles, shouting encouragements to each other as they raced down the slippery street. A priest begged at the door of a teahouse, holding his wooden bowl out while the temple bells called for midmorning prayers. The melodic gabble of women gossiping echoed across the street as they swept away the night's snow from their doorsteps.

When they came upon a shrine, Andrew's face brightened. He took Mitchell's hand and led him under the giant torii and into a stone-floored courtyard. Andrew loved visiting temples on winter mornings when everything slumbered under the snowy blanket of the previous night's storm. They stitched tracks across the pristine white carpet and stood side by side before a Shinto shrine. Andrew grasped a thick rope that was attached to a bell hanging from the roof. He clanged the bell several times to wake the temple spirits. An offering box sat in front of the shrine. Andrew pulled three coins from his overcoat pocket and dropped them into the box. He took three slender sticks of incense from a covered stone box and lit them before placing them in a bowl of sand, which sat in front of a statue of some local deity. Andrew told Mitchell to make a wish and bow three times. They closed their eyes and bowed, again, and again.

Back on the street, Mitchell asked Andrew what he had wished for.

"Nothing. My wish is happening right now."

Two doors beyond the shrine stood a neighborhood sake shop. There were no customers that early in the day, but Mitchell said he wanted to sit and talk. The emptiness of the shop seemed inviting.

They ducked through the blue and white entryway curtains and a surprised, middle-aged lady sang out, "*Oideyasu!*" She wore a somber, gray, long-sleeved kimono with dangling obi sashes, and her long black hair was piled on top of her head. Her *zories* tapped out a soothing rhythm as she hurried over to them, stopping several feet away to bow. She dropped to her knees and waited to help them remove their wet shoes.

Andrew felt embarrassed to have a woman on her knees at his feet. Standing once again, she waved an open hand at a table by the window. Andrew took off his straw hat and overcoat. They moved to the table and slid into chairs facing each other.

The woman shuffled over. Her round face had a thin layer of white cornstarch, and red rouge colored her lips, similar to the make-believe geishas so common in establishments frequented by US military men. Andrew, however, found it hard to believe that any servicemen wandered this far off the main boulevards.

Mitchell ordered a beer. Andrew asked for tea.

"*Hai!*" The woman nodded, mumbling something that neither man understood.

Andrew focused on sounds coming from the street, the nervous movement of Mitchell's fingers, and the surge of feelings rushing through him. He noticed everything all at once. It was as if they were not reuniting lovers, but gladiators who had miraculously survived the arena. Each breath seemed special; each feeling was a blessing.

They sat in silence, not needing words, gazing at each other until the woman returned carrying a tray with a frosty glass and a steaming cup. She arranged the drinks on the table and shuffled away.

Andrew wanted an explanation of Kate, the story of how they had first met, how she became pregnant, and why Mitchell had married her. The story hovered between them. He needed to hear it, as a priest felt compelled to hear the confession of a sinner.

Before he could voice his question, Mitchell asked, "Say, do you know what happened to Hudson? He's listed as missing in action, but he was still alive when we were rescued. No one knew what happened to him."

"I saw Hud and Clifford in Saigon about six months ago. They disappeared as the troops took the camp and made their way to Indochina. Hud captains a ferry on the Mekong, between Saigon and Sadic. Clifford makes it sound like they're very happy, but I think they're having a tough time making it work. They are so different from each other. They do have moments of happiness, and Hud loves him dearly."

"What about the others?"

"I lost track of them."

They fell silent again. Mitchell sipped his beer. "Cocoa stayed in Singapore. He opened a noodle shop close to downtown. Can you imagine him cooking noodles for the locals?" They shared a soft chuckle. "And Stokes hitched the first ride he could swing for Tahiti. He and Chew-Gin are expecting their first child in February."

"Will he take her to the States?"

"She won't fit in back home. People would look down on her. No, he's planning to stay in Papeete. Grady reenlisted. They sent him to gunnery school. Last I heard, he was assigned to a minesweeper operating out of Manila."

"That's wonderful."

Mitchell loosened his tie and unbuttoned the top button of his shirt. Andrew saw the string of prayer beads pressed to the officer's neck, the beads he had given Mitchell their last night on the *Pilgrim*. A surge of warmth washed through him.

"You know," Mitchell said, "I never reported the court-martial incident. Your record is clean. It said you served your country honorably and went missing in action. That's what it said because that's what happened. You can go to the States without shame, and you have a considerable amount of back pay coming."

Andrew wagged his head. "I'm surprised that Ensign Fisher didn't spill the beans."

"Once he realized why you did it, he was the most sorry of all of us."

"What about Chaplain Moyer? What happened to him?"

"He bailed out of the service and returned to Singapore. Told me that he wanted to open a chapel somewhere in Southeast Asia where he could help the poor and spread God's love."

They sipped their drinks until Mitchell asked, "How did you escape? How did you get here?"

"I'm not sure. Once I left Changi, it became one long blur. Tottori arranged to have his assistant, Kenji, bring me here. He proved to be a resourceful guide. We spent time in Bangkok, Saigon, and Hong Kong, but the rest was all traveling, village to village, crossing mountains, rivers, and rice paddies. Each day was the same as the one before it and the one after it. I can't remember any of the details. It's as if I've no past. No past and no future. I've fallen out of time."

Andrew felt himself sweating and his hands trembled. Also, the voices in his head were becoming noticeable. He craved a hit on his pipe.

"Where are you staying now?"

"With Kenji's family. His parents and two sisters live here in Kobe. That's why we came here. I happened to see you on the street about a month ago. I decided to stay long enough to talk to you."

"You seem so strange. Are you okay? I mean, are you all right, mentally?"

Andrew's eyes widened a bit. "I go through periods where I'm not myself, when I'm taken over by something else, something… twisted. But Kenji gets me medicine for those times." That was the first time Andrew had admitted it out loud. He looked up and gave Mitchell a somewhat mocking, fabricated smile as his hand seized his pipe, needing some right then to quell the rumbling voices. He stopped himself. "When I first met you, I told you that I knew who I was, what I was, and that I was comfortable with that. But that person died in Changi. I don't know anything about myself. Right now I'm feeling a bit ephemeral. I'm dreaming that I'm drinking tea with the man I love, I've found everything I've been searching for, and it will all vanish in my next heartbeat."

Andrew knew that he felt much more than that. He felt a peculiar combination of vulnerability, betrayal, and destabilization. All these swirling emotions hummed between his temples, like blood boiling in his head. And behind the hum were the voices, calling. But he was not about to let Mitchell know all that. Hiding those feelings, he knew without understanding why, had something to do with self-preservation.

They fell silent until Andrew congratulated Mitchell on his promotion to captain and asked how long he planned to stay in Japan.

"A new A1Nav came over the Fox skeds last week, announcing a revised point system for discharges. If I decide to leave, I have another fourteen months, which I'll spend here working for Naval Intelligence. If I get out, I'll go to the ranch, but they're guaranteeing me my own command if I stay in, and that's sounding mighty attractive right now."

Andrew had a flash of understanding. If Mitchell returned to the ranch, he'd be strapped with Kate, the kids, and ranch work, day in and day out for the rest of his life. A naval career would allow him long absences from his wife. Andrew suspected he didn't love her. She would live on the ranch and raise their children, waiting for his brief visits.

Andrew felt genuinely sorry for Kate. He waited a moment before saying, "That would be terribly hard on your children. Don't you love them either?"

"I love them dearly, but don't you see? You and I belong together. I think I've known it all along."

Andrew studied a smudge of grease on the table while holding in the emotions that threatened to burst.

"I became mad when you went missing." Mitchell said. "I thought you had died and I wanted to die too. Life—I mean getting married and having kids—didn't matter once I had lost you. It was the easiest way to go on living. But now that you're here, we can't let anything separate us again. You must understand. Everyone must understand. We must never be separated again."

It was a good speech, and Andrew knew that Mitchell meant what he said, but his mind struggled under the growing pain of how he could possibly make it work. He shivered, knowing that he had every reason to be ecstatic, energized, grateful—hadn't he been given everything he'd been longing for? How far away were those days of loneliness and yearning now? Wasn't that what he needed to save himself, to gain the strength to give up the opium, to become strong again while cradled in the loving care of this man? He knew he needed to say yes, but the word dissolved on his tongue like a sugar cube.

He thought of Kate and the children, wanting desperately to dismiss them as a mistake, casualties of war. *And why not, he doesn't love them*, Andrew thought. *He loves me. He said so.* But Andrew realized that he was fabricating a dream too insubstantial to be real. He couldn't trust himself. His mind was weak and dizzy from starvation. This whole conversation could be his sick mind playing tricks. He must listen to his gut telling him that he could never brush aside Kate and the kids, that they would haunt him like the dead buried in Changi mud.

"You want me to follow you from port to port while Kate sits home washing diapers and waiting for your letters? How can that work? How long before guilt erodes what we feel for each other? How can I respect a man who would do that to his wife and children?"

Andrew scrutinized Mitchell's face as he silently struggled with the puzzle, moving pieces around in his head, trying to force his weakened mind to think clearly.

Three more customers walked through the entryway curtains. The woman cried out "*Oideyasu*," welcoming the new group.

"I'll find a way. Stay with me until I find a way to make this work. There must be a way."

"You think I'd take you away from your children? Have them grow up fatherless because of me? You don't know me at all."

Mitchell opened his mouth to object, but stopped.

It's an unsolvable problem, Andrew thought, *the sound of one hand clapping.*

"If we can't be together, what will you do? Will you go home, to Indochina?"

Andrew pressed the small of his back against his chair. "I once told you that you were my home. Now I have no home and no place to return to. All I have is Changi."

"Why are you here, in Kobe? I mean, why come here if it wasn't to be with me?"

Andrew stared at his glazed teacup. "I have Commandant Tottori's personal items that I promised to deliver to his wife. She lives in Kyoto. I was on my way there when I saw you on the street."

"And after that?"

Andrew glanced at the street. He felt that twisted shadow stalking him, overtaking him, and he shook his head to keep it at bay. He wanted to explain how he was drawn from the empty void of loneliness by Mitchell's love and had lived a wonderful dream for a few fleeting years, but now he must return to that void. He cleared his throat, but all he could say was, "There is no after that."

It seemed so easy to say now that the shadow had taken control; the voices calling from the earth sounded so soothing. He had no fear of what awaited. In fact, a cold calm settled inside his belly and he saw his only option with icy-clear vision. For one who has lost everything there was only one thing left. That final formality was more than a logical conclusion, it was a welcome relief.

Andrew took a long, heavy breath. "Once I've given Mrs. Tottori her husband's things, I'll have worked out all my karma. There is nothing after that. It was only the hope that we could be together that has kept me alive this long."

Andrew expected to find a sadness take hold of Mitchell's face, but there was something more complicated there, an expression revealing that he knew Andrew spoke the truth—an emptiness, the sudden loss of something nameless, yet profound.

"I never realized it," Andrew said, "but I've lived only for beauty. The kind of beauty that is beyond what is reflected in one's eyes. First Clifford, who has an angelic, simple innocence; and you, with your clean-cut, manly elegance; and Tottori, whose strength of character made his sexiness extraordinarily beautiful. Even Master Jung-Wei, with his old, failing body, had the most exquisite spirit of any man I've known. For me, now, there is no Clifford, no Mitchell, no Tottori, and no Master Jung-Wei. My existence is estranged from beauty. I have nothing I care about. Tottori took his life because he would not allow himself to live with the shame of defeat. Just so, I can't bear to live in a world devoid of the beauty I love."

"I won't let you."

"If you have any compassion for me, you won't try to stop me. The memories of you are now unbearable. There are times when I wish I could obliterate them, to forget these last five years and return to the pure mind I had before. But I know that to erase those memories would mean to forever lose the most wonderful experience of my life. I won't let them go, but it seems I must let go of you."

Mitchell looked bewildered and desperate. "This can't be good-bye. I'm not losing you again."

Andrew took Mitchell's right hand in his own. "I'm so sorry. I have no right to be this morbid with you. Having you so close and yet not being able to have you makes me crazy. Please, forget what I said. I'll go to Kyoto and, after that, I'll let destiny decide what happens."

"I'm coming with you. I'll take a week's leave."

"Stop—"

The pain in Andrew's head grew monstrous, the voices shouting. He brought both palms to his temples, trying to press the pain away, desperately craving the black loam in his pipe. The light coming through the windows shifted, quivering with a yellow color that pierced his retinas.

"You have special gifts. You'll make Kate a very happy woman, and hopefully your children will grow strong and happy as well. You've made your karma and you have your duty. Tottori taught me that nothing is more important than family. I have no family. I must go alone."

Before Mitchell could utter another word, Andrew moved around the table to cling to him. Their lips found each other and they kissed, hard, passionately. After a moment they relaxed, and Andrew smiled under the kiss. His cheek pressed against the officer's shoulder. "Raising your children. For the first time in my life, I feel envy. Envy of what she is able to give you. I love her for that, and envy her."

Andrew felt the cold draft sluicing over his feet and Mitchell's warmth covering his frail body. Tears came up slowly in his eyes, the way a spring fills with water. They broke free of his eyelashes and slid down his cheeks, falling warm on the back of his hand.

"Good-bye, without any bitterness or regrets. I love you."

Mitchell wrapped his arm over Andrew's shoulder, holding him tight.

Andrew broke away. He hurried to the doorway, slipped on his clogs, and grabbed his coat and hat. As he was about to dash through the streamers hanging over the door, Mitchell let out a sorrowful groan, begging him to come back.

Every eye in the sake shop turned to stare.

Andrew said, "'I did never know so full a voice issue from so empty a heart: but the saying is true: the empty vessel makes the greatest sound.'"

Mitchell managed a smile. "I've always loved hearing you quote Shakespeare."

"'And so, fare thee well: Thou never shalt hear Herald no more.'" In a blink, Andrew disappeared through the doorway. He hurried down the street, hugging his overcoat about him while clutching the pipe and lighter. He brought the stem to his mouth and sucked the life out of the charred loam in the bowl.

Nothing in his life had changed. He still carried the same loneliness as before, the same sense of failing to find happiness. The voices retreated, but he knew they would return by sundown. There was only one way, now, to rid himself of them. Love, he understood, was an emotion that could bring joy and sorrow, and apparently it also had the power to take a precious life.

Chapter Thirty-Seven

December 30, 1946—1900 hours

THE train from Kobe pulled into the Kyoto station at sunset. It had been a sad journey. The train had chugged from Kobe to Kyoto by way of Osaka and stopped at every small town along the way. The third-class carriage was old and shabby. The seats sagged like the belly of a swayback mule. Several windows were broken out, which allowed smoke and cinders from the coal-burning engine to pour into the freezing carriage, making Andrew's throat raw. An old tabby cat prowled the aisle for mice, and by the size of her, Andrew assumed she found plenty.

The passenger cars were crammed with families making their way to Kyoto for the *Hatsumode*—the New Year's pilgrimage to various shrines to pray for blessings. At each stop, the train had emptied as fast as a cyclone, and people stood in groups, talking and laughing. Sometimes families were met by relatives from the town, and a party-like atmosphere would flourish on the platform. Food vendors in every station sold grilled fish that were as long as an index finger and served over bowls of rice with pickled vegetables, pure white tofu, and plenty of sweet candies. Only Andrew went hungry.

From the train's window at the Kyoto station, Andrew saw a long valley protected by high snowcapped mountains on three sides. At the base of the mountains were orderly clusters of cherry trees and random patches of bamboo. Further up the slopes stood a thick evergreen forest, which was powdered with snow. There are over a thousand temples in and around Kyoto. Most of these treasured sanctuaries were nestled into the foothills.

A blue sky spread above the valley, as blue and vast as the ocean. A single cloud floated across the expanse like a lifeboat drifting aimlessly across a calm sea.

The Kamo River cut down the east side of the valley. Clear, icy water tumbled over granite boulders. The rushing water sounded melodic, as if the river were singing its way through the valley. West of the river lay the city; its bustling town center was surrounded by finely manicured parks, temples, and immaculate neighborhoods where the houses had rooftops made with blue tiles overlapping like fish scales. The houses stretched from the downtown markets to the base of the mountains.

Golden red light toppled off the mountainside, intensifying the blue rooftops and causing the city to sparkle. This vision of tranquil beauty became painful as Andrew realized that this was the last leg of his journey. Tomorrow he would leave Kenji for the first time in over a year and dash to the finish line, alone.

From the station platform, Kenji led Andrew east, over the Kamo River and away from the city. They wandered through the narrow streets of a suburb until they came to a traditional *ryokan* hotel. It lay in the shade of Mt. Kiyomizu, an arched mountain with a thick pine and bamboo forest that swayed in the wind like the mane of a lion.

At the front door, an old man knelt to help them remove their shoes and then hurried behind the desk to check them in. Half a dozen antique lacquered lamps lit the lobby, giving the room a warm glow and veiling the corners and alcoves in shadows. Kenji held up an envelope with a local address written on the front. The note inside requested an audience with Mrs. Tottori on the following day. He asked the clerk if he would send a boy to deliver the note.

The clerk graciously agreed, saying it would be delivered within the hour. He took the note and showed them to their room.

Andrew studied the furnishings. In one corner stood a folding screen that displayed a mountain scene painted in the Zen style. In the alcove hung a scroll with Japanese calligraphy on it. Andrew asked Kenji to translate.

Kenji read out loud:

"No gambling,

No prostitution,

No mah-jongg,

No noisy parties,

No credit!"

The sliding doors were thrust aside and a woman knelt in the doorway. Her lavender kimono covered three undergarments that showed at her neck, framing her ivory-colored face. She did not wear her hair on top of her head like geishas; it fell about her shoulders and flowed down her back in a ponytail. *Tabi* socks covered her feet and a sash was tied around her waist with a huge knot in the back. She bowed low and rattled off a burst of Japanese.

Andrew caught the words "bath" and "dinner," but the only thing that he understood was that her name was Fumiko.

She carried a bamboo tray into the room, and on it were steaming hand towels, a pot of green tea, and two cups. She set the tray on the low dining table and bowed again before leaving.

An iron stove warmed the room. Andrew and Kenji shucked their traveling clothes and pulled on the blue-and-white-checkered kimonos that they found hanging in the closet.

Andrew sat at the window overlooking the garden. He took two puffs of his pipe to beat down the voices in his head. A moment later he took Jah-Jai and played a meditative tune that Kenji's father had taught him.

Kenji sat at a low table, sipping tea and studying a book of English grammar by candlelight. Every so often he said a word or sentence out loud. "Ruvrey music."

Andrew corrected him, "Lovely. La. La. Lovely music."

"Ruvrey. Ra. Ra. Ruvery music."

Andrew smiled through his drugged haze, knowing that many Japanese had trouble with the English *L* and also understanding that he himself mangled the Japanese language equally as badly. "Okay, try saying beautiful instead of lovely."

"Andrew is beautifur!"

"No." Andrew corrected again, "Andrew's music is beautiful."

"Yes, music is beautiful too."

"You did it. You pronounced the *L* perfectly! Say it again."

"Andrew is beautiful, and his music is lovely." Kenji flashed a proud smile. "Now I sound rike American."

"Like an American. And yes, your English sounds perfect. I'm proud of you."

The sliding doors opened and Fumiko was on her knees, bowing.

Kenji glanced up from his book. "Time for bath. After, Fumiko will prepare dinner."

In the tub room, Kenji was first to strip off his kimono and sit on the stool beside the cypress-wood tub. Fumiko dipped a wooden bucket into the hot water and poured it over Kenji's head. With a bar of soap and a washrag, she scrubbed him from head to soles. Lather clung to his compact body like white frosting. A thorough rinse, and Kenji eased into the tub while Andrew sat on the stool and went through the same scrubbing. Fumiko was visibly shocked by Andrew's thinness. She washed him as gently as a mother with her newborn.

The tub was so hot it took minutes for Andrew to immerse himself. Once in up to his neck, he closed his eyes and drifted in the lovely heat. Over the past year, he and Kenji had bathed together many times, and most nights they had shared the same bed. Andrew felt a deep-seated comfort in those intimate situations.

Kenji's coarse hair was slicked down like an otter's pelt. Without his wire-rimmed glasses, his face took on new dimensions. Unveiled, his smooth face and huge black eyes made him look like a different person altogether.

Kenji tilted his head to one side. "Why so sad?"

"Bathing is the saddest time for me, because Hikaru and I had so much pleasure in the tub. In the cool water, he would hold me. I can't help thinking of him."

"When I soak with you is hoppiest time for me. I never have friend to share bath before. Come, I hold you so you be hoppy."

"Happy. Ha, Ha, Happy," Andrew corrected.

"Happy," Kenji said as he gently pulled Andrew into his arms.

Andrew didn't resist. He felt hard muscles under silky skin enfolding him. He closed his eyes and his mind reached back, feeling Tottori's embrace. He laid his head on Kenji's shoulder and sighed.

They stayed nailed together until the skin on their fingers pruned. They toweled and dressed and returned to the room, where Fumiko was preparing dinner. She knelt beside the low table with two place settings. On the floor, a charcoal hibachi sat next to a large tray of raw fish, eggplant, and mountain vegetables. Another tray held bowls of soup, noodles, and tofu.

A note lay next to one place setting. Kenji read it and told Andrew that it was from Mrs. Tottori. "She will send someone to meet you here at one o'clock tomorrow. He will take you to her."

Fumiko served them hot sake followed by bowls of miso soup. Andrew claimed he had no appetite, but Kenji scolded him, saying if he didn't eat, he would get no more opium.

They leisurely drank their soup while she cooked fish and vegetables over the hibachi. As she worked, she hummed a soothing song that no doubt had been passed from mother to daughter for a millennium. Both men studied her movements as she prepared each item in the time-honored methods of her culture. She was an artist. The strict economy of her every move seemed to emphasize restraint and simplicity.

Andrew and Kenji looked into each other's freshly scrubbed faces and Kenji tilted his head to one side. Their eyes returned to watching Fumiko's artistry. For dessert, she sliced a sweet bean cake, which had the delicate shape and color of a plum blossom. She poured them each a cup of green tea and left the room to wait behind the door.

Once they finished all their dinner and another flask of sake, Fumiko stacked all the dishes onto her tray and carried them from the room. She returned five minutes later to move the table against the wall, creating an open space in the center of the room. She pulled a soft futon quilt from the closet and laid it over the floor, then spread linen sheets and another lighter quilt over the futon. Finally, she placed two hard pillows at one end. All the bedding was as white as falling snow and had the same crisp scent.

Fumiko shuffled to the door, bowed low, and slid the door shut.

Kenji had not only drunk his share of the sake, he had polished off Andrew's share as well. His face glowed with boozy pleasure.

They hung their kimonos in the closet. Andrew blew out the candles, leaving the room drenched in the luminous moonlight drifting through the window. As they crawled between the sheets, Kenji drew Andrew nearer until they pressed together.

Andrew smelled the rich scent of sake. He didn't try to move away.

"Don't leave me tomorrow," Kenji mumbled. "I don't want to live without you."

Andrew lay in Kenji's embrace. It was the first time Kenji had ever said something so personal to him. He groped for a response, but realized from Kenji's deep breathing that Kenji had already drifted to sleep. Andrew lay awake, locked within Kenji's arms, craving one more puff from his pipe, until morning light drifted through the shutters and penetrated his eyelids.

AT ONE o'clock, a monk dressed in a dark gray kimono with white undergarments and a large straw hat came for Andrew. In the tiny hotel lobby, the monk bowed and introduced himself as Omi Tottori, Colonel Tottori's nephew.

Before leaving the hotel, Kenji caressed the back of Andrew's neck and leaned over to kiss Andrew's cheek. He said, "Meet me at Nanzen Temple after your visit. It's the same *Rinzai* sect as Omi, so he can take you there. I'll be waiting."

Andrew nodded but didn't look at Kenji. He reached into his shoulder bag, where he carried Tottori's swords and diary, and pulled out Jah-Jai. His fingers caressed the yellow grain weaving through the bamboo before he placed it in Kenji's hands.

"Keep this for me until I see you again."

Kenji's eyes widened. He shook his head and tried to pass it back, but Andrew insisted, telling Kenji that it was only until they met at Nanzen.

Andrew followed Omi along the Kamo River and through the narrow alleys of the Gion district. The last snow had melted, so the streets and sidewalks were dry, but it was bitterly cold. Andrew felt the chill bite through his overcoat.

Kyoto is the spiritual soul of Japan because of its numerous temples and shrines, which were all preserved because the Americans refused to bomb the city during the war. But as Andrew made his way along the busy shopping streets and through the neighborhoods, he realized that if these manicured temples were Japan's soul, then these wonderful shops and houses and people thriving in the city's center were the marrow of its bones.

The houses in the Gion district had high walls, tiny gardens, and bamboo blinds over the windows. The symmetry and simplicity of the latticework on doors and windows were beautifully picturesque. They passed shop after shop, wooden buildings with sagging beams and stone floors, which displayed the handmade wares that made these people unique, even in Japan: noodle shops, teahouses, tofu shops, broom makers, textile shops, flower vendors.

They stopped at a bakery and Andrew bought a half dozen glutinous rice cakes, *mochi*, which were a traditional New Year's food. They also stopped at another shop to buy pickled plums, *umeboshi*, which are used to make a traditional New Year's tea. Both, Omi assured Andrew, would make fine gifts for Mrs. Tottori.

While passing a knife shop, Andrew tugged at Omi's sleeve and pointed, indicating he wanted to have a look. They ducked through the wood-frame doorway and Andrew inspected the array of handmade knives. Some were very elaborate, with mother-of-pearl dragons inlaid on the handle. Some were simple kitchen knives honed razor-sharp.

Andrew selected a knife with a long, thin blade made for gutting fish. The image of a carp was carved into the wooden handle. He asked how much and Omi translated. Andrew pulled money from his shoulder bag and paid the asking price without attempting to haggle.

Omi led Andrew through a narrow gate that opened onto a compact garden. Andrew heard the voices calling from the Changi graves, felt the buzzing at his temples, but he would not take out his pipe, he thought, until after.

A path paved with square stones bent through the garden. They passed under the bare branches of plum trees and walked to the side of the house, where Omi pulled open a sliding door and bowed. Beyond the door was a large room with a traditional *tatami* mat floor, sparsely decorated with low-standing furniture.

In the center of the room, a young woman sat on a yellow cushion beside a table. Her perfect posture enhanced her elegance, and her face displayed an expression of consummate dignity. Folded around her body and framing her face was the most brilliant long-sleeve kimono that Andrew had ever seen. Embroidered onto the golden colored fabric was an exquisite maroon phoenix. A lavender sash completed the outfit.

No woman on the streets would dare to wear such a brilliant costume. Even a year after the war, they would have been rebuked for going against the tide of patriotic sobriety.

Light bounced off the golden material, shining into Andrew's eyes. He stood, bewildered, leaning heavily against the doorframe. He could not quite believe that this woman was substantial. She seemed too dreamlike, as if a master painter had created a silkscreen masterpiece to represent the tragic soul of all Japan.

Andrew was captivated by how her black hair fell over her shoulders. Her head turned and he saw a plum-colored stain splashed across half her face.

She studied him for a half second and bowed. She lifted her head and their eyes met again. Deep within her gaze blazed an absolute suffering.

Those shattered eyes brought Andrew face to face with the purity of his own grief. Crushed by her actuality, he wanted to flee from this woman who shrouded herself in immense sorrow. But he knew that running away would be futile. He turned his eyes away, unable to look into the depths of those pupils that mirrored his own anguish. He desperately needed his opium, but it was too late for that. He had to find the strength to see this through without it.

She said, "Please join me. I have prepared tea." She spoke Japanese, which Andrew didn't completely understand, but Omi acted as interpreter, telling Andrew in fairly good Mandarin what Mrs. Tottori had said.

If she was at all shocked by his skeletal thinness, it didn't show. It was as if she understood perfectly. She lifted her arm and pointed to a pillow across from her. Her long sleeve swayed beautifully as her arm made this graceful movement.

Andrew, still not convinced that she was indeed real, remained speechless. He did, however, remove his clogs and step into the room. He walked to the table and lowered himself onto the pillow, all the time staring at her enchanting features.

Omi removed his straw hat and shoes, and followed Andrew into the room, kneeling behind her.

She spoke again and Omi translated. "We are honored that you have traveled all this way to see us." She lifted a porcelain pot, filled a teacup, and set the pot on the table. She presented tea to Andrew according to etiquette, bowed, and poured herself a cup.

Andrew studied her movements while he listened intently to the rustling of her silk kimono as she moved.

"The honor is mine. Thank you for seeing me." Andrew had difficulty modulating his voice while trying to keep his emotions in check. What was so painful, he realized, was that they shared a common bond of inexplicable guilt. Guilt that they somehow had failed to keep their man alive, that there was something they could have done differently but didn't. Guilt became their union, the heartbreak that made them one.

They raised their cups and sipped. The tea tasted salty. Mrs. Tottori noticed his surprise and explained, "On New Year's, it is our custom to drink 'Great Happiness Tea,' which is made from green tea and pickled plums. The plums add a slightly salty flavor."

Omi proved indispensable, for he was truly a well-intentioned interpreter. He seemed to disappear and Andrew felt as though he and Mrs. Tottori understood each other perfectly.

A handful of seconds tiptoed by, each one separate and distinct, each one a burden. Time peeled away until it didn't exist at all. She picked up a plate of *mochi*.

He set down his cup to accept one. He took the bag of plums and *mochi* that he had purchased at the market and asked if she would accept his gift.

She took the bag and peeked inside, making a show of seeming overjoyed. She excused herself, took two of the cakes, and laid them as offerings at the house altar where the family's ancestral spirits were enshrined. She placed another two cakes on display in the *tokonoma*, the formal alcove, beside a hand-painted lacquer bowl. That done, she shuffled to her pillow and knelt.

"I must say, Mrs. Tottori," Andrew said, "You are younger than I had expected."

"Please to call me Ayoshi. There is no need for such formalities. We are brother and sister, brought together by the love of our husband."

"Ayoshi, you grant me too much honor. Hikaru was your husband. He loved you. I was merely a companion while he was away at war."

Ayoshi's shiny black hair came alive as she shook her head. She told Andrew that, long ago, when she was hardly more than a girl, her family had sent her to Oregon as a picture bride, only to be rejected by her intended husband because of her facial scar. The man sent her back to Japan in shame. Her family was so humiliated, and her chances of marriage so remote, that they were ready to sell her into prostitution. That's when Hikaru Tottori heard of her troubles and called on her family. He proposed that she marry him before he had ever seen her.

Andrew's eyes widened. He understood that she needed to tell her story, to say it aloud before putting it behind her forever. Warmth washed over him, gratefulness that he could perform this service of allowing her to release her immense guilt out loud. His eyes encouraged her to continue.

"He married me not for love but because he was too kind. He did not love women. I need husband, he need son. Love came after. I loved him for his kindness, for saving my life. He loved me for making a home and giving him a son. But the love in his heart, Andrew, was you. I knew he loved you before he knew. A wife understands. You gave him happiness that I could not. I am forever grateful."

Andrew sat stunned.

"My brother, I love you for what you gave our Hikaru."

For the first time since Tottori's death, Andrew could feel the pain retreating without the aid of his pipe. The voices hushed. A warm stillness massed inside his chest, which felt as dense as silt.

A toddler bounded into the room. A mass of jet-black hair crowned a face dominated by round, pink cheeks. He wore a blue kimono and white socks on his tiny feet, and he squealed as he ran into his mother's arms.

The mist of sorrow lifted from her face and a burst of joy radiated from her. She was transparently smitten, and he was comically and hopelessly enchanted with her. He reminded Andrew of a cartoon character, Mickey Mouse—small and yet animated to appear larger than life.

She hugged the boy to her slender body and turned to Andrew.

"This is our son, Andrew Tottori."

"Andrew?"

"Of course. Hikaru insisted. That's when I knew that you brought light to his soul. My only regret is that Hikaru never held his son. Would you like to hold him?"

Andrew nodded.

Ayoshi whispered in the boy's ear. Little Andy jumped up and leaped into Andrew's lap, grabbing Andrew by the neck and squeezing. Tears formed in Andrew's eyes and slid down his cheeks. Ayoshi wept as well. He felt immense joy intertwined with immeasurable sorrow, and he saw those same emotions mirrored in her face.

The boy leaned away and saw Andrew's tears. He pressed his chubby face to Andrew's cheek and licked the tears off. Andrew could not help laughing at the boy's unexpected antics. For a brief moment, he forgot how near he drew to the climax of his elected path, and his sorrow dissipated. He was left only with the joy of having this boy licking his face like a puppy.

Little Andy released his grasp and sat in Andrew's lap, smiling at his mother.

Andrew withdrew the swords from the shoulder bag that he had carried over a thousand miles. "These belonged to your father. He had me bring them here so you could have them."

The boy's eyes bulged as he took the short sword in his stubby fingers. He glanced at his mother to see if it was true, and she nodded while wiping the tears from her cheeks. She said something to the boy that Omi did not translate. The boy crawled off Andrew's lap and carried both swords to the *tokonoma*, laying them next to the cakes that Andrew had brought. He ran from the room with a squeal of delight.

A question hovered in her pupils. Knowing what she wanted, he said with an unsteady voice, "However much Hikaru loved me, I love him more. For his strength, his honor, his gentleness, his humor, and for the goodness I found in his heart."

She bowed. "Thank you. You make my sadness easier to endure."

"I have these for you." Andrew removed Tottori's diary and the two scrolls from his bag, and placed them on the table.

She picked up one of the scrolls and read the haiku poem written on it while Omi translated:

Content,
I feel like the calm sea,
After a storm.

A single tear was trapped within her eyelashes. A long moment of living silence hovered over the table before she picked up the second scroll and read silently. She lifted her head. "Hikaru's last wish was that you and I raise his son together. I am to teach him beauty and grace, and you are to teach him strength of character. Together we shall lead him down the path to manhood."

Andrew could still smell the scent of Andrew Tottori lingering about his neck, feel the warmth of the boy's hug. Something shifted inside his heart and he was about to agree, but he heard the voices returning, growing loud in his head. His vision darkened, becoming a thousand pinpoints of red and orange light, and the pain, that hideous pain swelled from the base of his neck to his crown, merging into one excruciating spike at the top of his forehead. He felt a cold chill run from his heart to his testicles. He shook his head while reaching for his pipe. He mumbled, "As much happiness as that would bring me, I cannot. I must complete the path I follow. I must leave you now."

"Then when you leave us, please to know that you are a cherished member of our family. You will always have a place in our hearts and a place to come home to." Ayoshi bowed low as Andrew rose to leave. When she raised her head, she was weeping again. This time her tears seem to be cleansing, washing away what had been a painful question for her. These grateful tears, more than words, thanked Andrew for his role in this drama.

For a tiny slice of a second, Andrew wanted to endure the pain so that he could stay and make a life with this woman and her child, but the twisted sickness tightened its grip. He momentarily felt paralyzed by it. He mustered his will and rushed out the door and through the garden.

On the street, standing on the frigid stone in stocking feet, Andrew sucked the life out of his pipe, once, twice, a third time until there was nothing left but ash. Omi walked up, carrying his clogs. He dropped to his knees to slip them onto Andrew's feet.

As the pain retreated, Andrew bowed to a wide-eyed Omi, thanked him for his services, and said good-bye.

Rising, Omi asked if Andrew would like him to lead him to the Nanzen temple where he was to meet Kenji. Andrew told him no. He had his own path to follow.

Omi bowed. He straightened, told Andrew that he was proud to have Andrew as an uncle, and bowed again. Andrew bowed as well before turning to leave. He walked only ten paces before Kenji stepped out of the protection of a doorway and the two faced each other.

"You're going the wrong way. The Nanzen temple is north."

"What are you doing here?"

"I was worried you might be lost, so I came to help you find your way. Come, let's join the *Hatsumode*. We'll make a pilgrimage to the five major temples and pray for blessings."

Chapter Thirty-Eight

December 31, 1946—1600 hours

KENJI led Andrew on a tour. They joined the stream of people, literally hundreds of thousands of pilgrims, moving from temple to temple, all anxious to begin a new year and move beyond the mist of sorrow. The streets were clogged. Each temple had a long waiting line. The air hummed with a particular sound, the voice of this city at the peak of its brightest celebration. It sang a soft, well-mannered melody that spoke of hope.

Andrew was carried along by this voice, which seemed to call directly to him.

As they made their way from one temple to another, Andrew noticed that many of the women lit up the crowd with gay kimonos that they had stored away during the war years. Against the mass of drab robes, they seemed like wildflowers spread across a spring meadow.

At each temple, Kenji lit incense and said a prayer. He guided Andrew through the grounds and explained why the gardens were laid out as they were, or why the shrines were positioned in a particular section of the garden. Andrew realized for the first time that Kenji carried a wealth of knowledge about his spiritual culture.

They strolled up the slope of Mt. Fudosan to watch the sunset. The mountain was covered with red pines and thickets of bamboo grass, all dusted with snow. When they came to a stump halfway up the slope, they stopped to enjoy the sky as it slowly turned from gold to vermilion to deep lavender. As the sky transformed, the snow covering the trees mirrored the change.

The cold air gave Andrew a chill, which meant that his opium high was fading. He also felt hungry, realizing that he had not eaten since last night. He pulled his pipe from his coat pocket while asking Kenji for more loam.

Kenji shook his head; there was no more. Kenji told him they would start the new year without it. They would face the pain together, and somehow work through it.

Andrew was not upset. He knew that soon, very soon, the voices would be silenced forever, the pain would stop cold. His karma was finished. Sweet relief was hours away. He tossed the pipe onto the frozen ground, feeling the hunger expand in his empty belly.

As if reading his mind, Kenji leaned into him and ruffled his hair. "Let's go to that noodle shop we passed. I'm starving."

THE streets were now aglow with paper lanterns and lit storefronts. They weaved through the crowds—men dressed in Western suits and traditional Japanese *haoir-hakama,* women in kimonos. The music of *taiko* drums, flutes, and the clip-clopping of wooden *getas* on pavement floated on the snow-scented air.

As they reached the noodle shop, a teenaged boy dashed out the door holding a tray of fresh noodles. He stacked it onto five other trays on the back of his bicycle and sped away down the street. Kenji nodded at the boy as if that guaranteed a good meal.

They luckily got a table without having to wait. It was warm in the shop, and the place was packed with customers, all slurping down bowls of noodles. Andrew ordered rice and pickled vegetables, but Kenji insisted that they both have the house specialty—a one-pot soba noodle dish called *hokoro*—and a flask of sake. The *hokoro* was prepared at the table. They watched the waiter set up a charcoal burner under a handcrafted Mongolian hot pot. He poured the broth into the hot pot and added a variety of mountain vegetables and two heaping mounds of soba noodles.

Kenji explained that noodles were always eaten on New Year's Eve because traditional belief was that the long noodles would grant them longevity. The broth smelled heavenly, but by the time the noodles were ready, Andrew's growing pain had overtaken his appetite. He ate only a few mouthfuls. He tried to figure a way to free himself from Kenji so that he could finish his journey and put an end to the pain.

After dinner they wandered down the valley toward the Chion-in Temple, which was where Kenji wanted to be at the stroke of midnight. They stopped at temples and shops along the way. Kenji seemed careful to not let Andrew out of his sight.

They ambled under the arch of the Chion-in Temple and strolled around the gardens. Food and trinket stalls crowded the temple yard. It was nearly midnight, and although the bright stars lit up the heavens, the garden remained steeped in shadows.

Andrew concentrated all his attention on following the gravel path that led through the garden. A crowd of worshipers huddled on the steps of the temple.

Kenji took Andrew's hand and led him to a corner where a stone bridge spanned a pond. On the far side of the bridge, a lantern gave off a yellow glow, and beside the lantern sat a stone bench. Kenji guided Andrew over the bridge, and turned toward the temple. From this corner of the garden, they could see the Great Bell and the path leading from the bell to the temple.

They sat on the bench and watched a procession of monks snake single file from the temple to the Great Bell. Four thick posts supported a blue tile roof. Under the shelter of the roof hung the Chion-in Temple bell, the largest in all of Japan—165,000 pounds and as large as a house. Shortly before midnight, dozens of young priests would strike the bell with the end of a stout cedar log horizontally suspended by ropes.

While watching the procession, an old lady, perhaps a priest's wife, crept up beside Andrew and placed a cup of green tea beside him. She placed another beside Kenji. When Andrew glanced down, it was as if the cups had magically appeared. They sipped their tea, and again Andrew tasted the saltiness of the traditional "Great Happiness Tea."

The moon rode higher, turning the sky a purplish white. Soon it would reach its zenith. On this clear night, even the rarely seen stars bit through the firmament. The temple grounds and the surrounding snow-covered cedars all gleamed a luminous white. The temple lamps had minimal effect.

The assemblage of priests took their positions around the bell. The onlookers grew silent, waiting for the first gong. An aged monk took hold of the rope attached to the log and hauled the log back with all his weight. He let it fly. The great bell tolled with an ear-shattering sound that reverberated throughout the valley, with a voice that was deep and aged and pure.

The reverberations soaked into Andrew like water on dry sand. In the stillness left by the bell, he glanced at the pond. It imperfectly reflected the bright sky. Through his pain and the whispering voices, he thought about Tottori in those last moments. How Tottori had lovingly held him and sent him away. He saw Tottori in the pond's reflection, kneeling before the Shinto shrine, saying a prayer for his wife and son, a prayer for Andrew as he took the gun from the leather holster. He pulled the hammer back, felt the cold steel touch his temple, heard the explosion. But did he feel his skull burst open? Was there ripping pain, or pleasure, or nothing at all? And what came next? He died in an instant, but Andrew was well aware that an instant can span an eternity. Andrew saw a fine trickle of blood running down Tottori's cheek and over his lips. His eyes were wide open, empty, staring into nothingness. Did he feel the rush of his essence spilling out into the void? Was there pleasure in the release from leaving all worldly cares behind?

"Can you feel it?" Kenji asked.

Andrew stared at him, not quite understanding.

"This close, you can feel the bell's pulsation inside your body. It vibrates every cell and brings your whole being into harmony with it."

"I feel it. It feels...." He paused. Shocking, he thought, but realized that was not right. Exhilarating? Not that either. He realized that the vibration hummed beneath his flesh. It seemed to drive away the pain, silence the voices. His whole being quivered. He had no words for what he felt, so he remained silent.

"Would you like to ring the bell?" Kenji asked.

Andrew nodded. "But I'm not a priest."

"Wait here." Kenji hurried across the bridge and bowed before a bald-headed monk. They exchanged words. The old one stared across the garden at Andrew and nodded. Kenji led the monk across the pond to meet Andrew.

The monk spoke to Andrew in Japanese and Kenji translated, "The bell of Chion-in bears the inscription *Kokka Anko*, meaning: Security and peace in the nation."

The old one gave Andrew a friendly smile. "You are welcome to partake in the New Year's celebration by helping to ring the bell, which must be rung 108 times. You see, we believe that during the year a man is likely to have committed 108 sins, so by ringing the bell as many times, all sins are expiated and a man can begin the New Year immaculate. On the last stroke of the bell, our New Year begins. Tradition requires that each man who rings the bell at midnight is obliged to drink one cup of sake for each stroke of the bell that he sounds, so take care in how many times you ring the bell."

Andrew bowed. As he did, he felt the knife inside his coat pocket poking his ribs and he realized that ringing the bell could very well be his last act before death took him. His hand slipped into his pocket and his index finger caressed the cool metal blade. He straightened up and looked at the old monk to say thank you.

The monk sucked in his breath as he peered into Andrew's eyes. "My son, you hold much pain in your heart. The heart is too fragile an instrument for such grief. Whatever brought about this pain, let it flow away from you like the tide. Give up a piece of it with each strike of the bell, and learn to give yourself to life as the sea gives itself to the beach, to give and take during the high tide and the low."

The monk led him to the bell and Andrew took hold of the rope. With Kenji's help, he pulled back the log and hammered the bell five times. Each strike sent a quivering through his being. As his body reeled, the old monk's words echoed in his head.

When he stepped away from the bell, handing the rope to Kenji, he felt disoriented. A monk guided him to a table, where he downed five cups of sake.

The strong wine opened Andrew's head. He felt woozy and a little sick. He staggered to the bench to watch the other men strike the bell. He felt his own heart beat wildly as the vibrations rumbled through him.

Is it really possible to end my life? he wondered. It seemed bizarre to be contemplating suicide when the entire country was celebrating the New Year, new beginnings, and rebirth after surviving so long and painful a war. Still, the idea of death seemed deeply comforting, even mournfully beautiful, like sailing over the infinite sea at sunset. He could leave his loss and his history behind. This longing for comfort consumed him.

Kenji sat beside Andrew. He had rung the bell seven times and his face was flushed from the sake. He told Andrew that, while Andrew visited Mrs. Tottori, he had gone to the Jingo-ji Temple and asked to become an acolyte. They had accepted him, and he would begin training tomorrow morning with the New Year. The Superior had also agreed to take Andrew. They could go into the service of the Buddha together. They could continue to live with each other.

"I didn't realize you were so devout. Do you really want to become a priest?"

"No choice. When Colonel Tottori sent me away with you, I become deserter. My family must live with this shame. Now, if the *Kempeitai* find me in Japan, they hang me. The monastery will give me new identity. They protect me. I can live safe life within the temple. You too. You come live with me."

Andrew could only stare at Kenji. The bell's vibrations kept drowning out the voices, but his world seemed to tumble out of control. His chapped lips trembled with unrealized words.

Kenji said, "In my language, samurai means: to serve. We will be Buddha's samurai. We will serve Buddha, the people, and each other. Please, Andy, it will be too lonely a life without you."

Realizing the sacrifice that Kenji had made and the shame he had willingly brought upon his family, Andrew saw the young soldier with the large eyes hiding behind wire-rimmed glasses in a new light. A transformation came over Kenji's face. Andrew saw a courageous beauty shining from behind those dark eyes.

Andrew realized what had gone unnoticed, what he had not thought to look for—devotion. This past year, Kenji's love had secretly flourished, unrequited. Kenji had experienced the solitude and suffering that came from secretly loving someone, and Andrew realized that Kenji had been a prisoner as surely as Andrew was inside Changi. Andrew knew too well what anguish he would cause when he took his life. *Am I capable of that?* he wondered.

The idea of living as a monk, sharing a life with this courageous soul, was a tantalizing idea. *And being this close to Ayoshi,* he thought, *I'll help her raise little Andrew, be an uncle to him.* But thinking of trying to live up to Tottori as a father figure caused a shadow of doubt to cross his mind, and doubt turned to despair.

Andrew looked into Kenji's eyes and said, "I wish it were that simple."

"Life is simple if you don't get tangled in the web of past and future. You can take pleasure in this moment, this simple, perfect moment."

"I'm not really needed. I mean, life will march on with or without my pitiful contribution. Tottori's son will grow up. You'll become a priest. Mitchell will raise his family. The Americans will go home. When you think about it, it has already happened. Life has already marched on and left me behind. I'm not needed."

"I need you." Kenji's irises attained an immense depth. Again the man's beauty revealed itself.

"You're kind," Andrew whispered. "Very kind, but I would only fail you as I've failed the others. That's it. I'm a failure. I've failed to give lasting happiness to any of the men I've loved."

Andrew wanted to stop, to talk about something else, anything else. But Kenji's fingers touched his jaw, gently turning his face until they looked eye to eye. He leaned closer until Andrew caught the pungent scent of sake on his breath. His arm wrapped around Andrew, pulling him closer in spite of Andrew's resistance. Their embrace was warm and oddly comforting.

"What demons do you fight? Do you know? I think you fight your own pride. Yes, pride. I think your pride will not accept that these men you love have abandoned you. You cannot defeat pride. It is indestructible. The more you fight it, the more you smother it with opium, the more powerful it becomes. To win this battle, you must ignore it. Lose your pride and feel your pain. It cannot survive without you feeding it."

The cold December night wrapped itself about Andrew and burned his cheeks while his heart oscillated with the tolling bell. He shivered, rubbing himself to stimulate his circulation.

"I will never abandon you," Kenji said, "in this lifetime or the lives to come. Never!"

The sky was perfectly clear. The moon was a sharply defined crescent, bathing the garden in silver light that seemed to dance among the shadows. Andrew tilted his head upward to stare at the sky, through the firmament, beyond the myriad of bright, familiar shapes, beyond even the dim specks from the most distant stars, into the darkest spot of the vast unknown. He found himself within that vastness looking back down to earth, seeing his tiny pinpoint of suffering acted out on this grand scale of enormity, and he realized that his agony, that he, was nothing more than a finger snap. He suddenly felt sheepish that he had made such a drama of it.

His mind returned to earth when he felt the arm around his waist pull tighter and heard Kenji's voice murmur in his ear.

"Stay with me until the spring. Live at the temple and become a monk with me. I'll show you the Spring Festival, the first blossoms of the plum trees, and the cherry blossoms. All Japanese go to the gardens to admire the trees."

Kenji took Jah-Jai from his shoulder bag and pressed it into Andrew's hands.

Andrew took the flute, looking down at the simple bamboo stick that had given him so much pleasure over the years.

Kenji touched Andrew's cheek again, turning Andrew's head until they were face to face. He kissed Andrew on the lips, a fragile kiss.

Kenji's lips felt alive, thrillingly human, loving. Andrew seemed to pour himself into the kiss, feeling giddy.

Kenji leaned his forehead against Andrew's, as if wearied, and the corners of his mouth rose. "Stay with me until April. I will show you how life buds in the spring. A monk's life is a hard one, but that is no matter. As for your pain, we will conquer it together."

The moon's liquid light seemed to intensify, pouring silver radiance on the temple, an early promise of hope for the coming year. Andrew glanced up, startled. The night sky with a crescent moon as its focal point was the most perfect sky imaginable. Kenji's firm breath on his cheek accentuated that perfection, the way a single flute carries a different melody above the string and brass harmony within a symphony, highlighting the submerged symmetry of the entire composition.

"Okay. I'll stay with you until spring."

Andrew felt a spark of intensity flare up within his being, and he desperately wanted the winter to stretch on forever.

Postscript

MITCHELL hired a taxi to take him and his family from the Kyoto train station to the famous *Kinkaku-ji*, The Golden Pavilion, northwest of the city. As they rode along the busy streets, Mitchell leaned his head out the open window to watch the shops and people stream by.

The city was littered with pink cherry blossoms and a sweet scent drenched the air. Mitchell felt glad that he decided to stay in Kyoto after the wedding, to enjoy the Spring Festival. It had been over a year since he and Kate had had a vacation together.

The taxi pulled up to the curb in front of the temple. They piled onto the sidewalk. Mitchell sparkled in his dress whites; Kate and the children also wore white.

"Hey, old buddy," Fisher said. "I wasn't sure you would come."

Mitchell saw Lieutenant Fisher rush toward them. Fisher looked the same as he had on the deck of the *Pilgrim*—strong, handsome—and his hat tilted back on his head, showing his forehead.

They shook hands. Two years had passed since they had last seen each other.

"I wouldn't have missed your wedding for the world. I had to see the woman who finally lassoed you. She must be very special."

"I think so," Fisher said, turning to Kate. He held out his hand. "You must be Kate."

Mitchell made the introductions and said, "I can't believe you stayed in the Navy. I thought you went home to run for Congress or some other important post."

"I gave up all hopes of public life when I decided to marry Uiko. Voters wouldn't take to her."

"I'll be damned. I sure had you figured wrong."

"How so?"

"I figured you wouldn't let anything stand in your way of becoming a bigwig politician."

"You had me pegged perfectly. What you didn't count on was how Changi would change me. I learned there that being a bigwig can let you help some people, but you end up destroying others. Guess I lost my taste for that kind of responsibility."

"With a Japanese wife, you won't have an easy time in the service either, but hopefully that will change."

"Say, what about you, why are you still in uniform?" Fisher asked.

"I get my discharge in two months. After that, I'm not sure what we'll do. We'll most likely return to the ranch, but I'll sure hate to leave Japan."

"Same here. Say, I've got to get back to the wedding party. We're about to start. Let's talk more at the reception banquet."

Fisher turned to leave, but he stopped and turned. "Thanks, Nathan. You don't know how much it means to me that you're here."

MITCHELL herded his family through the immaculate gardens toward the temple where the ceremony would take place. The Golden Pavilion consisted of several buildings—the Hall of the Sacred Fire, the Hall of the Lords, the Assembly Hall, Tenkyo Tower, and the monk's residential apartments. The main temple, the Golden Temple, was a three-storied tower named for the gold leaf covering it. The building's elegant lines showcased its pure Zen architecture. The temple was supported on pillars and extended over the Kyoko Pond, and its fine-grained wooden roof was crowned with a golden phoenix statue.

As the pond and temple came into view, both Mitchell and Kate stopped under a plum tree. Pink blossoms drifted down to land on their hair and shoulders as they stared open-mouthed at the sight before them.

The temple shimmered in the spring sunlight, and the building was reflected perfectly on the mirrorlike surface of the pond. The image reached across the water to touch Mitchell's soul. He focused on the brilliant golden statue of the phoenix. Its wings spread as if it were taking flight, and its golden-speckled eyes gazed at him. It seemed to bravely pull itself out of the ashes, and the bird's pose reminded Mitchell of Andrew performing tai chi. At the thought of Andrew, his hand unconsciously rose to his neck and fingered the string of beads he still wore, the prayer beads Andrew had given him on the deck of the *Pilgrim*.

"My God," he said.

"Do you think that's pure gold?" Kate asked.

"Sure looks like it, honey."

Drums began to beat. Over by a crowd of people, a procession of priests, followed by the wedding party, marched beside the pond on its way to the Golden Temple.

Mitchell hurried his family along. They joined the crowd of onlookers.

The first to pass were the dozen white-robed priests. They had white stockings covering their feet and their sandals were five-inch platforms. They wore very tall, clam-shaped hats that were coal black with a white cord looped around the top of the hat and tied under their chins to keep the hat in place. Behind the priests were two bridesmaids wearing beautiful white blouses draped over flowing pink dresses. Following the maids, and walking under a gigantic red umbrella, were the bride and groom. They both wore white. Her kimono was thick, quilted satin, making her look as though she were emerging from a magnificent cocoon. The bride's family followed. The men wore Western-style tuxedoes and the women wore colorful kimonos. The procession snaked through the garden to the Golden Temple, where the vows would be exchanged.

As the couple passed, Mitchell's eyes followed them until he noticed one priest in the crowd of onlookers who was staring at him. Mitchell was not at all surprised. Many Japanese stared at him. He had become accustomed to being an oddity in this land. He nodded at the priest, and turned to watch the procession make its way into the temple. He looked back at the priest a minute later with the nagging feeling that there was something faintly familiar about the man.

The priest stood with another priest, a woman, and a child. He whispered to the priest next to him, and they all strolled toward the front gate. It all came together in Mitchell's mind: that amber face, the graceful movement. Mitchell began to walk, then ran toward them. He grabbed the priest.

Andrew, his face fully restored to fleshy beauty, smiled.

Mitchell crushed him in a bear hug.

Kate and the children came running. "Honey, for God sake, what's wrong?"

"Nothing is wrong, sweetheart. You remember Andrew Waters?"

"Oh my," she said. "Honey, let go of him. People are staring."

Andrew introduced his adopted family: Kenji, Ayoshi, and little Andrew. Mitchell introduced his family, and everyone bowed several times, all the time smiling.

When little Andrew Tottori heard that Mitchell's toddler also was named Andy, he screamed, "Hey, we have the same name!"

The adults laughed, gazing down at the children as they giggled at each other.

Little Andrew Tottori took Helen Mitchell by the hand. They ran after the wedding procession, dashing along the stone path that led into the Golden Temple.

Kate and Ayoshi laughed at each other and hurried after their children.

Mitchell stared at Andrew's restored face. "You look wonderful. You must be happy now?"

Andrew nodded with a comforting muteness. He lifted his head and the sunlight made the golden specks in his weary eyes shine, the ends of his lips lifted into a smile. His laughter shimmered like a jewel on the morning air.

The soft timbre of Andrew's voice reassured Mitchell that they would continue to see each other in some capacity, and joy mixed with pride swelled in his chest until he felt intoxicated, woozy. He struggled to keep his breath steady. He turned to watch Kate and Ayoshi chase after their children as he said, "This is such a beautiful wedding. I'm sorry that Kate and I didn't have our wedding here in Japan. Are you coming to the reception banquet? If you are, then you must sit at our table. If not, no matter. Kate and I are staying in Kyoto for seven days. We can have lunch tomorrow, and perhaps dinner. Are you free tomorrow?"

When no response came, Mitchell turned to see that Andrew and Kenji had disappeared. He scanned the crowd but didn't see them anywhere. He waited for Andrew to reappear, but his hopes grew faint as the minutes passed. He swallowed, moistened his lips, lowered his head, and slowly turned toward the wedding procession. He took a firm, calming breath, and followed after his family.

THAT was the last time he saw or spoke to Andrew, and well into old age, Mitchell was never sure of the exact instant of Andrew's departure. On his deathbed, grasping a string of prayer beads, with Kate once again reading *Henry V* aloud to him, he realized that instant had never occurred.

ALAN CHIN enjoyed a twenty-year career working his way from computer programmer to Director of Software Engineering, but he lost interest in computer science when he began writing fiction. He walked away from corporate America in 1999 and never looked back. Since then he has traveled to over forty countries, scuba-dived the Great Barrier Reef, tracked black rhino in the Serengeti, and dined in most of the capitals of Europe. Oh yes, and he's published eight gay-themed novels and three screenplays.

In 2007, *QBliss* magazine awarded their Pride In Literature award to Alan for his debut novel. In 2010, Alan's novel, *The Lonely War*, swept the Rainbow Literary Awards, taking top honors in four categories: Best Fiction, Best Historical, Best Characters, and Best Setting.

Alan currently spends half of the year traveling the globe and the other half writing at his home in California.

You can visit Alan's website at http://alanchinauthor.com and his writer's blog at http://alanchinwriter.blogspot.com.

You can also e-mail Alan at Alanhchin@aol.com.

Also from DSP PUBLICATIONS

Willow Man

By John Inman

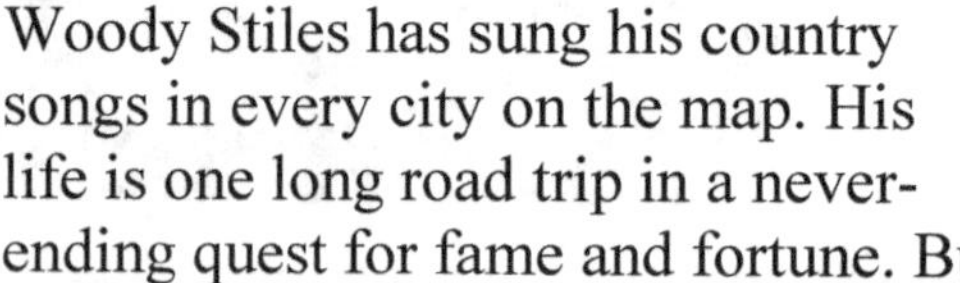

Woody Stiles has sung his country songs in every city on the map. His life is one long road trip in a never-ending quest for fame and fortune. But when his agent books him into a club in his hometown, a place he swore he would never set foot again, Woody comes face to face with a few old demons. One in particular.

With memories of his childhood bombarding him from every angle, Woody must accept the fact that his old enemy, Willow Man, was not just a figment of childish imagination.

With his friends at his side, now all grown up just like he is, Woody goes to battle with the killer that stole his childhood lover. Woody also learns Willow Man has been busy while he was away, destroying even more of Woody's past. And in the midst of all this drama, Woody is stunned to find himself falling in love—something he never thought he would do again.

As kids, Woody and his friends could not stop the killer who lived in the canyon where they played. As adults, they might just have a chance.

Or will they?

http://www.dsppublications.com

DSP PUBLICATIONS

visit us online.
WWW.DSPPUBLICATIONS.COM